MAKE IT TAKE IT

MAKE IT TAKE IT

RUS BRADBURD

FIRST EDITION
10 9 8 7 6 5 4 3 2 1

Library of Congress Cataloging-in-Publication Data

Bradburd, Rus, 1959-
Make it, take it / by Rus Bradburd.—1st ed.
p. cm.
ISBN 978-1-935955-43-6 (alk. paper); ISBN e-book 978-1-935955-44-3
1. Basketball coaches—United States—Fiction. 2. Basketball—Scouting—United States—Fiction. 3. Basketball players—United States—Recruiting—Fiction. 4. College sports—United States—Recruiting—Fiction. I. Title.

PS3602.R335M35 2013
813'.6—dc23

2012018405

Book, cover design and photo by Anne M. Giangiulio
Composited by Lee Byrd
(Mrs. Lee Byrd to you; aka *his lovely wife*)

Shout out to Keith Wilkinson
for posing as the frustrated coach who graces the cover of *Make It, Take It*

for **ROBERT BOSWELL**

THE KING OF SIAM

A flat tire on Jack Hood's car stalled them.

Steve Pytel could already feel the intense heat as the peaceful cool of the April desert morning burned away. Wasteland spread in every direction—creosote and cactus, a graveyard of dead mesquite trees. Occasionally a car would zip by.

"Join me over here," Hood said from the narrow shade of a telephone pole. "Yesterday I laughed at a Mexican lady hiding like this at a bus stop. Today it's not so funny."

The telephone pole's shadow did provide some relief. Pytel and Hood were nearly the same height but Hood was bigger. Thicker. They stood back-to-back, as if help might arrive from somewhere off on the horizon.

Jack Hood had recently moved to town as the new basketball coach at Southern Arizona State University and soon he'd be deciding Steve Pytel's future. Since Hood's arrival, several candidates had been close to accepting Pytel's job—the assistant position that he was clinging to—but one by one, he'd learned, they'd declined.

The college's administration had appointed Pytel to temporarily lead the transition to the new regime, but since then he'd hardly been alone with Hood. How could he keep his job if he couldn't even get face time with the new boss? Pytel tried to make it clear that he was anxious to remain on staff, had suggested lunch, coffee, whatever, knowing he might not get another paycheck after the first of May. It wasn't fair to be led on, yet he suspected that that was exactly what Hood was doing.

Pytel held hope for the first time that morning when Hood offered to show him his new house, five miles beyond the city limits, in the shiny silver Audi. Pytel saw this little trip as The Interview, a chance to shine. Although Hood hadn't used the word "interview."

Pytel had lived in the Southwest for years and knew the sun could push you out of bounds. He had developed strategies to deal with the heat—white shirts, short sleeves, all cotton, a freezer full of water bottles, and ice in his beer at night.

Pytel's wife Stephanie teased him about his routines. She was comfortable in town. A transplanted Californian, her skin held a deep tan, whereas he turned pink or blistered at the slightest exposure. She wasn't thrilled about the peculiar ethics of college basketball, or his desire to remain in the business now as an assistant coach. "You're slogging around knee-deep in this shit," she told him. "And for what?" Their salaries were not so different, and she claimed her own job teaching kids was noble. Stephanie wondered why he couldn't just get his high school teaching certificate. Why not get out today? Hadn't the door been left open when Pytel's previous boss was dumped after another average season?

If he got an offer from another university, he'd planned to ask her to try a new location, but she was now suggesting she would not tag along if he left town.

Of course he wanted to keep his wife, yet he wasn't ready to leave college ball. He was pushing, instead, in the other direction—he'd been an assistant coach far too long, and he deserved the chance to run his own college team. He could name coaches who'd gotten that shot who weren't nearly as qualified. If he could have convinced Stephanie to discuss it at length, he'd have admitted the appeal of the huge salary a head coach commanded.

Weeks earlier, before Hood was hired, Pytel had made some inquiries about the head job on his own behalf, tested the waters, but was told twice that the team was not doing well enough—universities did not promote assistants from losing teams. Most schools didn't keep them around at all. Pytel now believed that being attached to a winner remained as one of two prerequisites to his professional advancement.

The second was this: Pytel had learned, after his own informal survey, that the percentage of head coaches without children was miniscule, nearly as small as the number of single head coaches. He was now convinced that completing the trinity with Stephanie would increase his marketability. Having a baby, of course, would also keep her on board, or maybe even keep her at home temporarily.

He had been to the fertility clinic on the day Jack Hood was named to the position Pytel coveted. For two hours he waited to be called by a nurse, which gave him plenty of time to retrace his steps, figure how his career had broken down at this crossroads. A decade earlier, as an assistant at another college, he'd come close to being selected as head coach. Just thirty-two years old at the time, he'd been derailed by what he now understood was the kiss of death: the black players had publicly endorsed him. That wouldn't happen again—lately they seemed to speak a new language, one he no longer had the patience to learn.

This was Pytel's basketball resume: practicing his long-range shot religiously as a boy on the graveled driveway, a euphoric ritual. Next, a scholarship to a school called Morehead State. After graduation, it was weekend coaching clinics while he taught American history at a Detroit area high school. Then an entry-level job back at his alma mater, where he'd gotten too friendly with the black guys. Finally, the assistant coaching job at State. And this was the sum of his knowledge: a college program's success hinged simply on one thing—the prospects you could lasso for your team. Pytel's job was to hunt down good players and keep them eligible.

Now, in order to advance his career, he had to keep his job, help put a great team on the court, and start a family. How difficult could that be?

Stephanie had been through lengthy medical sessions and the tests had proven her capable, which only raised Pytel's level of anxiety. He'd gotten kneed in the nuts once in college, was black and blue for weeks, and he suspected he was sterile. The fertility clinic was an exercise in humiliation. Before he left, he instructed the nurse to call him with the results. If the news wasn't good, he could figure a new plan of attack. He'd been waiting ever since, waiting to learn if he was to blame.

"You think a person has to love his job," Pytel said to Stephanie when the regime change was announced, his job jeopardized.

"Your job is a soul-killer," she replied. "It's got you thinking like the older teachers I work with." In the faculty lunchroom, she said, her colleagues had the hundred-yard stare. They couldn't wait to get away from their students and thought Stephanie was weird because she ate with her class, trading sandwiches and knock-knock jokes.

Pytel said he used to love his work, although he hadn't for years. Like many coaches, he wished he could recapture a feeling about basketball that he couldn't articulate and hardly remembered. "But if I thought you were correct," he added, "I'd quit today." How could a game become a soul-killer, anyway? He liked basketball, liked kids, and that used to be enough. Pytel was going to ride this out, see if Jack Hood would retain him. Hood would not have been Pytel's first choice, but naturally nobody had asked him. He couldn't imagine he'd really have to choose between a wife and a job in college ball.

"You're sinking," she said. "This is your time to get out of an awful business. This should be a life raft, not a fresh start."

As they'd exited campus, Hood had asked Pytel his opinion of the new Audi. Local car dealers supplied the basketball and football coaches with freebies.

"It's the same model they issued to Jerry Conroy," Pytel said.

"That pink coach?" Hood sniffed. He was already deriding the man he'd replaced—Conroy had led the "Tough Enough to Wear Pink" campaign for breast cancer awareness. "No, it's not the same model," Hood added, patting the leather seat. He explained that this was the second Audi he had been given as the "courtesy car" perk. The first model didn't have leather seats and so it never left the show lot.

Hood drifted around the road, couldn't seem to stay between the lines, and the weaving pulled Pytel gently from side to side. Hood announced he had a story to tell.

"This was back East, as everyone around here calls it," he said. He'd been at a private university before State, where he'd earned an NCAA tournament bid, the only time in that school's history. His first year there he'd given a scholarship to a player named Willie Norfolk, a nice kid but a mediocre student. Hood said he'd been in Norfolk's home to recruit him, consoled his mother who cried while she detailed the hardship of raising a teenager in their crumbling North Philadelphia neighborhood. He was impressed with the lady—despite the Ritz crackers and grape Shasta sodas she'd welcomed him with. The mother was the key when recruiting black kids, but there was a corollary, Hood said. "An over-attachment to a strong-willed woman screws up a guy's head."

Hood learned after Norfolk enrolled that he'd made a mistake. "Norfolk couldn't play dead in a cowboy movie," he said. Like any coach, Hood grew to resent him and needed to take away Norfolk's scholarship, use it to attract a better player. A kid could quickly prove to be a bad investment, a mistake, and that left the coaches wishing he would get the message and go home, go anywhere. "You're nodding your head," Hood said, "so I know it's happened to you, too."

Pytel had, in fact, delivered the bad news of a withdrawn scholarship on two occasions. The first time he was overcome with guilt. The second time it felt good, taking a knucklehead down a notch.

"Like all our challenged students," Hood continued, "Willie Norfolk developed a close relationship with the lady in charge of tutoring the team—a real slut, but that's a story I'd need a few beers to tell. Anyway, by the time I realized we didn't want Norfolk around, he was already banging this lady, who actually had the same first name as the kid's mother. Leah. That's something that would keep most guys from bedding down an older woman."

That spring, Hood gave Norfolk's scholarship to another prospect, a much better player. Norfolk was not yet aware his full ride was gone though, and Hood needed him to drop out on his own accord: school policy handcuffed Hood, wouldn't allow him to revoke a scholarship, unless a player had been arrested. He met with Norfolk, told him he didn't fit into their plans, and although Hood cared about his future, he'd be better off at another college. Which was probably true. "If you try to fit a round peg in a square hole, you just fuck up the peg," he said. But Norfolk said he wanted to stay, even if he had to ride the bench.

Almost on cue, as Pytel and Hood reached the city limits sign, miles from any service station, the driver-side tire on the Audi blew. Hood jerked the car onto the gravel shoulder and cursed. He had no idea, he admitted, how the car's scissor jack worked.

Pytel could feel Hood's resentment as his story was put on hold—going from boss to supplicant. Pytel immediately recognized it as an opportunity to show his resourcefulness. He popped the passenger door open and got out. "Want to unlatch the trunk?" he said, arms draped over the car's roof, peering in. "I can change this thing, pronto."

"You'll do no such thing," Hood said. "It's not our problem." He found a business card in the visor. "Royal Motors," he snorted, and punched a number into his phone. "Put the owner on," he said. He would not leave a message. Hood explained their situation a minute later, but sputtered over the specifics. "My location?" he said as he got out of the car. "It all looks the same to me."

Pytel told him the name of the road, which Hood relayed before clapping the phone shut. That was when Hood noticed the shade of the telephone pole and invited Pytel to join him. Pytel decided to not ask Hood why they couldn't simply wait in the car with the air-conditioning blasting. Instead, he figured he'd get to the point, his point anyway, although Hood had not concluded his story about Willie Norfolk. "What kind of person are you looking to hire?" he asked.

"It's simple, really," Hood said. "We can't expect ghettoized players—overgrown children, really—to be loyal to anything. And a college's loyalty goes only as far as a legal contract. But human loyalty, man to man—" He paused, stepped out of the shadow to face Pytel. The sun glistened off his slicked-back silver hair and momentarily blinded Pytel. "Loyalty, that's all anyone in this business can cling to."

Hood scowled, taking in the desolation around them. "Where the hell is that tow truck? Five minutes, my ass."

Pytel pivoted and the two men faced the same direction. Without a word they inched sideways to remain in the long narrow shade.

"We've been stuck ten minutes," Hood said moments later. "Still no fucking help." He trudged back to the car, where he kicked the offending tire. "We're outta here."

Pytel followed, assuming Hood would lock it up and they'd call a taxi from the side of the road.

"You're driving," Hood said, and he lofted the keys to Pytel, who nearly flubbed the simple catch. "What a piece of shit this car turned out to be, huh?" Hood added. He slid into the passenger's side and jabbed the flashers on before Pytel understood what he was being asked to do: possibly damage a car that simply needed a flat tire fixed. For a moment, he wondered about a confrontation—he could say he would not drive, would not screw up somebody else's vehicle. He could toss the keys back. That would have ended the interview, he knew. Anyway, Hood looked so confident, relaxed. The car was, after all, his responsibility.

The low rumble of the flattened radial agitated the steering column immediately, and the tighter Pytel gripped, the more his arms shook. *What about the rims?* he almost said, but understood this must be some sort of test, that Hood wanted to see how he'd react to the reckless stunt. He shut up, kept his speed down. Two passing cars beeped while their passengers pointed out the crippled car's front tire.

"German engineering," Hood said. "It's an all-wheel drive. Now, back to my story about Willie Norfolk." He reclined his seat. "I didn't want to hurt him. But word came back that his eligibility hinged on a sociology paper due at the end of the semester. It was an evening class, one that half of our team enrolled in each year."

The professor was a stickler for attendance and punctuality, and his class was the only hurdle in an easy major. If Norfolk didn't screw up, he'd be fine, and he'd at least pull a "B." Hood knew what was going on—Leah the tutor was writing the paper. Norfolk only had to sit by her side and try to comprehend what the words meant in case anyone got wise and started to ask questions.

"You see my dilemma?" Hood asked. "I *wanted* Norfolk to fail. I was hoping a good kid would flunk out."

The grind of metal rim against the road began. When they ran over a small pothole, the jolt caused Pytel to bite the tip of his tongue. He struggled to keep the car straddled over the dotted line. The steel rim was digging a rut into the hot asphalt.

Hood shouted now over the grating noise. "We were in the last week of school, and our guys still played in pickup games. That Monday afternoon I had to interrupt them to tell a different player to get his sorry ass to the student health clinic before he infected any more coeds. On my way back up to the office, I saw Norfolk's backpack on a seat. I knew it was his because it had his self-proclaimed nickname, *The Duke*, in gothic letters. Can you believe that? Duke Norfolk? Duke, my ass. The imposter. Just below his nickname was his sociology paper in a clear-blue plastic binder. I remember the title. *Cultural Relativism and Values*."

Hood had hurried back to the office and called Leah the tutor, but just as he'd hoped, the call went instantly to her answering machine. Her office was closed for the day and there'd be no way for Norfolk to get another copy before class.

"I returned to the arena, to the power switches at the top row," Hood said. "With my hand on the light switch, I gauged the distance down to the backpack. Then I killed the lights."

Pytel imagined Hood creeping down the steps of the basketball arena in the dark, the players cursing.

"Willie Norfolk did not turn in his paper that evening," Hood said. "So he flunked the class. We had our scholarship back. And I'll tell you this, which might surprise you. He came to my office the next week to tell me he was going to fail, and we wept very real tears together. It was my duty to phone his mother, the other Leah, and let her know her son wasn't going to succeed. I was sorry about what I'd done in every respect." Hood powered down his window and spat. "Do you understand what I'm telling you, Pytel? I had to do the wrong thing for the right reason."

"Got it," said Pytel, although in that moment he wondered if he'd be liable for damage to a car he wasn't supposed to be driving. He forced himself to focus on Hood's story, which seemed to be mostly a device for Hood to show off how maniacal he was. Did he expect Pytel to agree, to say damn right? Admit to doing the same thing? Pytel had made complicated ethical decisions before, like any coach. But he'd never stolen a player's homework and damned his future. Yet he sympathized with Hood's choice—it only took a few non-players and soon enough you were losing games. That was precisely what doomed Jerry Conroy in the last few years—he'd gotten more concerned with philosophical issues than recruiting. Players who could not produce had to be weeded out, and that was why the real game being played was often the coaches against their players.

"The point," Hood said, "in case you haven't figured it out, is that I should have had an assistant coach who I trusted to take care of this. That's where the loyalty part comes in."

"Got it," Pytel said again. This time he really did get it. And this drive was indeed a test. Hood was asking him, in effect, to demonstrate his devotion to putting together a good team.

"Would you have done that for me?" Hood asked dreamily.

"Or, wait. Better yet. Would you have killed Norfolk's chances without me even asking?"

Pytel wasn't sure if he was expected to answer this time.

"You think about that," Hood said, and he pointed out his own driveway. "Jesus, watch out, be careful of our new cactus. By the way, my wife is at home. You'd better make sure you're able to deal with her, because you and I won't get along if you can't make peace with Vicky."

It's a McMansion, Pytel thought. That's what Stephanie used to call houses whose garages were the prominent feature, places desperate to convey class with their gaudy bluster. Pytel had initially been enamored of their own historic home, a place that didn't even have a garage, but it must have been cursed. The first of many problems was a busted irrigation system that left a slimy lake around the place. Stephanie had taken to stating their address as 2650 Misery instead of Missouri.

"This is my starter-castle," Jack Hood said, leading him inside. Stained glass, vaulted ceilings, marble hallways. At the arched doorway, Hood handed him a phone. "You talk to the car dealer. It's ringing. Tell them our new location."

Vista del Rey Road, Pytel knew that much.

"The *end* of Vista del Rey," Hood said, as if reading Pytel's mind. "You might say we're the only first-rate house with a second-rate car."

Pytel stood in the doorway, his back to Hood, and asked for the service department. The mangled Audi was in full view. The belts of the tire had spanked and dented the paint on the fender's panel. The tire, of course, was totally gone.

While on hold, Pytel could feel Hood move closer. "Put it on speaker phone," Hood said. "I want to hear this."

Pytel did, explaining their location to the service manager.

The man was irate. "What's with you?" he shouted. "My best guy is going up and down Mesa Street searching for an Audi. What did you do, call Triple A?"

"We drove it home," Pytel said. "Coach Hood had an important interview."

"Oooh, good one," Hood whispered, and Pytel instantly felt Hood's hand on his shoulder.

The manager said they'd redirect the tow truck.

Someone was clacking down the stairs. A woman's voice—and remarkably nuanced whistling. Pytel recognized the jazz standard, "Someday My Prince Will Come."

Vicky Hood brought smoked salmon sandwiches into the shade on the back patio, where a ceiling fan wobbled at high speed. Was she older than her husband or younger? Hard to determine because she kept her sunglasses on, indoors and out. She was thin but not athletic, her short blonde hair a dye job. They should go ahead and eat without her, she said. She was on a diet. When she returned with iced teas, Hood insisted she make him a Bloody Mary.

"For Chrissake," she said, sitting down. "It's Monday and it's not even noon."

"Come on," he grumbled. "Can't you do something around here besides spend my money?"

Vicky twisted to face Pytel. "Isn't he grand? Tell me about Steve Pytel. Are you married?"

Hood grabbed his wife's tumbler and took a sip.

"That's water, Jack," she said. "I can get you one, or you're welcome to share mine." Then to Pytel, she said, "It's hard to believe that a woman with all I have to offer is still in love with Jack Hood. Let's pretend he's not here."

Hood pushed back in disgust, the wrought iron chair grinding against the cement as the tire's rim had earlier. He called Vicky a bitch and went inside.

"Who are you again?" she said. "I mean, why are you here?"

Pytel told her of his role on the previous staff, and how he'd been in charge of the program's transition before Hood was hired. "I hope I can stay on with Coach Hood," he added. This had been true an hour earlier, although now he wasn't so certain. Stephanie would have plenty to say about his first assignment, driving five miles on a flat tire. He was, for the first time, aware there was now a chance he would be offered the job, but there wasn't yet a single thing he liked about Jack Hood.

"*Coach* Hood," she said. "Everyone says *coach* like he's a doctor or something. He's not, you know." She gulped at her drink as if it really were liquor. "You could be our son's age. If we had a son, I mean. You didn't answer my initial question."

"My wife teaches at Desert Crossing Elementary," he said. "She enjoys her job, and she won't leave." He was trying to communicate his wife's love of the town, but it came out more like a plea for sympathy, and Pytel wished he could answer again.

"So it's not just your career that concerns you," she said. "It's understandable then, why you'd be groveling. Listen, I like to make it clear to everyone Jack interviews, just so there won't be any surprises."

Pytel inched forward in his seat and studied her dark glasses.

She said, "He is the worst person I know. If it wasn't for the fact that he so dreadfully needs me, I'd have left him years ago. Years!" She laughed as if this was the funniest thing she'd ever heard.

"I'm sure you're joking," Pytel said.

"Jack told me that if he keeps you, you'd make a lot more than your previous salary. How about that? It makes him look common to have a staff with pathetic paychecks."

"That could make me happy," Pytel said, knowing a sizable increase was likely impossible. The lead story in the latest campus newspaper detailed a faculty senate resolution complaining about Hood's new salary.

"I'm going to change the subject, sweetie," she said, and she lifted her sunglasses. "Do you see these bruises under my eyes?"

Pytel could not make out any bruises in the shadows of the patio, and he said so. She stood, nearly toppled, and gained her balance on the solid chair. She let go slowly, as if experimenting. Pytel wondered if Hood's hunch was correct, that she had been drinking. As she stepped out of the darkness into the sunshine, she spun back to Pytel like a runway model. "Look," she said, and turned her head from side to side in the direct light, as if she were being slapped. There were indeed bruises just to the outside and below each eye, above her cheekbones. Pytel imagined the sound of Hood backhanding her. He felt sick.

She walked back to the table in a straight line, as if sobered up by the slaps, or the noonday sun, and she put her hand over Pytel's. He halfway expected her to begin weeping, but she smiled. "It's not what you think," she said. "That's twenty grand for plastic surgery by the same doctor who fixed up Ginger Spice, and it was worth every one of *Coach* Hood's dollars. He'll be making that each week now and I'll be a new woman by the end of the year, with all new parts. You go to a new job, you might as well be a new person, right? But we'll be stuck with the same Jack Hood." She sighed. "Eat, there's no telling when he'll be back."

The hum of the tow truck seemed to shake the patio's tile. With that deep sound came a rumbling of dread in Pytel's gut.

"Pytel," Hood called from inside, "your tow truck is here."

The living room held only the couch, a big-screen television, and an enormous portrait above the fake fireplace of Hood in a white suit. The new coach was sprawled out on the couch in the living room, his feet propped up, Bloody Mary in hand, reading an old sports section that Pytel recognized: one that announced Hood's own hiring. Ten years ago Hood had been one of the hottest head coaches in the country until his program crashed amid a transcript-fixing scandal. His next job in the East, and his eventual success, was his rebirth. The article quoted a Dean at that school as saying they were glad Hood was departing.

"Go down and deal with this guy," Hood said as he swung his feet to the floor and folded the paper neatly into his armpit. "I'm going to observe your people skills."

Pytel paused at the top of the steps for a moment before descending. The tow truck driver walked around the car, scratched his head and mumbled. He had on a red work shirt with "Royal Motors" embroidered above one pocket and a patch that read "Larry" above the other. He was squat, barely five feet tall, muscled like a rugby player—the kind of guy who might resent tall people—and his ears stuck out from under his matching red cap. On his left forearm was a tattoo of crossed swords. "You Jack Hood?" Larry asked.

"He's in the doorway up there," Pytel said, and offered his handshake as a consolation.

Hood was leaning in the door's arched frame, twenty yards behind Pytel. He didn't wave or speak. Halfway through one drink, he had a second one in his other hand, at the ready. Pytel was near enough to the house that Hood could see they were talking, but far enough that he probably couldn't hear everything.

"What the hell happened?" Larry asked. "This is a fifty-thousand dollar car. Do you know the cost of just one of these wheels?"

Pytel spoke softly. "We had an important meeting," he said, "we had to get here for a conference call. He couldn't wait any longer."

Larry lowered himself, chest down, to the place where the tire used to be.

"Did you bring a new tire?" Pytel said. It was a stupid question, but he couldn't think of anything else to say.

"Yeah, right, a new tire," Larry said. "You guys ruined the rim. There's been a helluva lot of damage." He push-upped himself to a kneeling position and looked to the house for some kind of explanation, but Hood was gone. "Not only is the rim ruined," he said, "and the axle bent, but the entire hub assembly has been destroyed. Not to mention the axle bearings, which are likely shot. This is going to cost you a fortune to fix."

Pytel knew he couldn't exactly apologize, so he launched into a sort of these-things-happen doublespeak.

Larry cut him off. "What's the matter with you people?" he said, dusting off his knees. "Why would you do something like this?"

Pytel thought the guy might want to fight, the way he was shaking his arms out. He realized instead that Larry was close to weeping, as if the car had been his own Christmas present. "Listen," Pytel said, "I know how you feel, but I'm not really responsible. Jack Hood is, the guy who was in the doorway a minute ago. Money doesn't mean anything to him, he can easily afford it." In that moment, Pytel understood that Hood would never pay for the damage. He'd expect the dealer to cover the cost. Hood came back in the doorway, just one Bloody Mary in hand, Vicky behind him. He raised his glass in a silent toast.

"You shouldn't worry about it," Pytel said, louder this time. "That's all I'm saying."

"That's not the point, the money," Larry said. "It's a senseless way to treat an automobile. It's criminal."

"Get that piece of junk off our property!" Vicky yelled. Hood shooed her back into the house. He reappeared alone.

"He's our new basketball coach," Pytel said. Vicky screamed something else from inside but it was muffled.

"I don't care if he's the King of Siam," Larry said. "What an asshole."

Larry returned to the car, and began hissing *what an asshole*, as if that might somehow patch and inflate the tire. He got back on all fours and shortened his chant to *asshole* as he crawled around, occasionally rising and dusting off his pants again before he resumed the angry mantra.

"Come on, stop saying that, okay?" Pytel said. "This isn't your car, and it's not coming out of your paycheck."

Larry ignored his request, shook his head as if trying to decide his next step.

Hook the Audi up and tow it away, Pytel thought. *Simple*. He finally suggested as much.

"I'm going to have to flatbed this vehicle," Larry said with an air of importance that irritated Pytel. "I've got to call in for a bigger truck and get all four wheels off the ground."

"We'll be here," Pytel said. And then quietly, "You're taking this too hard."

Larry started in again with the chant, and he slowly rocked his head in time to the word before he paused to eye Pytel. "You're no better than him," he said. "You could have stopped him. The flunky of an asshole."

Larry lumping him in the same dumpster as Jack Hood made Pytel sweat. This is what he got for being the peacemaker.

And all this for a man who probably *was* an asshole. Pytel would go home, tell his wife what happened, and admit he was out of a job. Maybe he could convince her to let him go on the job market. That meant talking her into leaving town. He couldn't see himself taking classes to get a teaching certificate. Vicky Hood had called it groveling, and she was right. And groveling for what? To hook on with a guy he couldn't stand.

The sun was behind the front porch now. Or Hood had stepped deeper into the shadows because Pytel could no longer see him clearly. It was getting hotter by the minute. Larry was on his feet now, still repeating that word. *Asshole.* He turned over his shoulder to say it again. When Pytel shoved him—with both hands on his back—he hadn't planned to knock him over. But Larry tried to pivot and his heel caught on the edge of the driveway. He stumbled to get his footing and spun, as one arm circled wildly for balance. He fell backward onto a clump of cacti.

Pytel immediately knew his own coaching career—at State, or anywhere else—was dead. That might have been a relief, but when this incident made the newspaper, he'd have to leave town in disgrace. Even a high school teaching job was out. They couldn't continue their house payments on one salary. His realization of what would transpire over the next month stunned him: he'd apply for coaching jobs that he couldn't get if this story got out. If he left town, Stephanie would remain, and she'd move into a townhouse alone. But where *would* he go, now that he was done with both Jack Hood and maybe even with college basketball?

He stepped gingerly over the jagged rocks to pull Larry up, but Hood appeared somehow and slid in front of him. It was only then Pytel understood that the tow truck man was impaled on a cactus and couldn't move.

"Let's celebrate," Vicky said as she closed the front door and locked it. "Who wants a drink?" she asked Pytel.

"Victoria, please shut up," Hood said.

They stood together at the edge of the picture window and

watched two grim-faced Hispanic men lug a massive chain and hook it to the rear axle of the Audi. The men had not beeped or bothered to ring the doorbell to get permission from anyone in the house. Larry had refused Hood's offer of an ambulance and was waiting in the second truck. The tow truck dragged the Audi onto the back of the new and larger truck. "I wanted a gold one anyway," Hood said.

Vicky handed Pytel a Bloody Mary. He took a slug and thanked her. The drink was more vodka than tomato juice. "I'm screwed now," he said to nobody in particular. "That guy will probably have me arrested or sue me," he added, and nodded at the window. He didn't expect an answer, and he didn't know whether to walk home or call a lawyer. Or toss the rest of his drink in Hood's face.

"We saw him try to punch you first," Vicky said. "Didn't we, Jack? And you ducked, right? That was clearly self-defense."

Pytel's cell phone rang and he was about to switch it off when he saw it was the fertility clinic. He excused himself and retreated to the back porch with the wobbly ceiling fan.

"Your sperm count is normal," the nurse said. Pytel thanked her. This was important news. "And they're good little swimmers," she continued. "It's like I told your wife. When you're ready, it'll happen."

"I'm ready," Pytel said, although it was none of her business. He and Stephanie could proceed, his embarrassment about the entire procedure now behind him. He started back towards the front of the house. Not that he was about to share this good news with Jack Hood.

"Well," the nurse said, "I mean when you're *both* ready."

Weeks later, though, going through the medicine cabinets, Pytel would find her birth control pills, check the prescription date, and remember the nurse's choice of words. Stephanie must have had doubts, told the nurse that she was not yet prepared to commit to a child with him.

"Finish your drink," Hood called.

Pytel returned to the picture window in time to witness the trucks drive off with the damaged Audi. Hood told his wife to fetch the keys for her sedan. "I can drive," he said. "I've got work to do at the office. Hurry up."

"You drive?" Vicky said. "Isn't that how you got into this mess?" She dangled the keys in front of him, but snatched them back when her husband reached. Hood grabbed her sunglasses off her face instead and tossed them across the empty tiled room. He said, "I was *not* driving that damaged vehicle." He pointed his drink at Pytel. "He was."

"I'm on my first vodka," she said, "and you're over the limit. Every limit." She reached for Pytel's arm and pulled him out the front door.

Vicky's sedan was in the massive garage; the backseat was jammed to the roof with moving boxes. She got behind the wheel. "You sit in the middle," she said to Pytel. "He *is* an asshole," she added in a whisper, as if she'd heard every word the tow truck man had said.

Remains of the tire, shards and strips, were strewn across the road like a trail of clues in a fucked-up fairy tale. A buzzard was pulling at one piece and didn't move even as the sedan whizzed by. Hood said how disappointed he was in the way the episode had turned out. "Pytel, you've got to learn to keep your cool," he said, "even if you never coach another day. I don't care what sort of names the tow truck driver was calling you. Your reaction was unacceptable. What kind of coach loses his head like that?"

Pytel nearly told him to fuck off.

"Restraint, that is what I'm talking about," Hood said, as if in response to Pytel's thoughts. "You've got to learn restraint." Hood had surprised Pytel with the tenderness he displayed in lifting Larry off the cactus.

"Just offer Mister Pytel the goddamn job right now," Vicky said, "or are you waiting for him to inflict more damage in your name?"

"Victoria, for the love of God, I'm trying to teach this man something about life. And throw that drink out the window."

"Make the offer," she shouted. "Double his salary."

Pytel couldn't stifle a sarcastic laugh.

Vicky pressed down the power window and tossed the entire tumbler out, but not before winding up, so most of her Bloody Mary splattered on Pytel's neck and chest, coloring the front of his shirt a weak red. Ice cubes from her drink began melting at his beltline.

"Oh, take that shirt off right now," she said. "We'll stop for a bottle of club soda to make sure it doesn't stain."

Hood grabbed his dripping forearm, as if Pytel might indeed disrobe. "Who's doing the damage now, my dearest?" he said.

"I apologize, Mister Pytel," she said. "Send me the cleaning bill, okay? But did you know that tomato juice is the only remedy to get the smell of a skunk off you? Think about that for a minute."

"Do you see what I mean?" Hood asked him. "Restraint. Keep your composure. Look at me. I will not shove her ass-first onto a cactus like you might, although it's certainly tempting. And I'm not telling her the precise place on her person that she should have shoved her tomato juice. Instead I take a deep breath and remind myself who's in control here. Why don't you do that with me now? Let's draw a slow deep breath together."

There was no harm in that, so Pytel did, in unison with Hood, exhaling at the same instant. He imagined himself blowing out his anger.

Hood no doubt thought Pytel had flunked his big test. Things would get awkward for Pytel when he got home. Stephanie would be thrilled he wasn't coaching, but that joy would evaporate if he told her he'd decided he still wasn't ready to walk away from the game. Maybe he'd wait a day to bring that up, see if the guy from Royal Motors had called the police. And exactly what would he do then for work?

"I want Mister Pytel on your staff," Vicky said.

Hood ignored her. "That's where we were stranded," Hood said, a new happiness in his voice. "That's where it all began." He pointed at the tracks, the sandy gravel of the shoulder where they had first veered off the road, what felt like weeks ago. The afternoon sun was even hotter, and the shadows of the telephone poles spread across the arid landscape. Hood asked his wife to pull over, but Vicky refused. "Jesus, Victoria," he said. "That was our stop."

"Are you kidding?" she asked. "I'm not going to leave you there like a couple of fools. You wouldn't be any better off than you were four hours ago. Just offer him the goddamned job before we get to school." Then to Pytel: "Your seatbelt isn't buckled. Buckle up."

Pytel obeyed, struggling to find the loose ends. His throat was parched, the price of drinking liquor in the desert. He felt cramped, wedged between Hood and his wife like an overgrown child, knees together. His feet, balanced on the hump, had gone dead, and the sensation, or lack of it, crept up his legs.

"Jesus, that sun is powerful," Hood said, dickering with the visor. "This was a productive day. I'm really impressed by your sense of loyalty, Pytel, although I don't agree with your crazy methods. You've got potential." He crossed his arms and appraised Pytel. "I guess the job is yours."

"Oh," said Pytel.

"Thank you," Vicky said.

"Whatever your salary was, count on getting twice that." Hood slapped him on the leg. "You'll have your house paid for in ten years," he said, somehow doing the math before Pytel could.

Pytel had practically walked away from the business minutes before. He'd tell his wife he was certain he could again some day. And he'd share the good news about his fertility.

"Congratulations," Vicky added. The car slowed, and Hood put his hand on Pytel's reassuringly, a fatherly gesture.

"We'll be good together," Hood said.

RIVERSIDE

Despite the July heat I raised the car windows, stretched both arms, and manufactured a casual yawn. Then I locked the door with my left elbow. I was delayed in Detroit, at a stoplight on a corner overrun with street people. The air-conditioning had crapped out ten miles from the airport, and now, mid-morning, damp ovals spread under my arms. Doubling back to the Avis counter to berate a clerk and trade cars was not an option. This was supposed to be a hit-and-run affair, and I wanted out of Detroit that evening.

The night before I had phoned a man named Tree Turner, and he told me about a young player. When Tree talked, I listened. He talked, as always, from Detroit. I had been listening in Las Vegas, where it hadn't rained in nine months. Tree's rec center was a magnet for good players, and he knew the kids better than their high school coaches. He had been a resource for years, worth more than any scouting newsletter. He found sponsors for the city's elite summer team, but he never traveled with them, hadn't left his hometown in years.

The player, Tree said, was Jamal Davis, who had not yet turned seventeen. Jamal wasn't playing in Las Vegas, but Tree said he might one day be better than any of his other kids I'd been scouting all day. I'd never heard of Jamal Davis because he'd been hurt most of his junior year. Hardly anyone knew of him. Tree used the words *wingspan* and *untapped* and *God-given*. Here was the interesting part: no other college coach would see him play all summer, since Jamal wasn't playing with Tree's team. Jamal had made a commitment to work as a counselor at the New Beginnings camp for kids. That got me excited. You don't hear words like *commitment* and *employed* when it comes to basketball recruits. I was already tossing clothes into my Nike bag when Tree said the kid was 6'5" but wore size eighteen shoes.

The summer "evaluation period" sucked—every assistant coach rode the bleachers for a month in Las Vegas, Orlando, or Chicago, sometimes for twelve hours at a stretch, and this would be a chance to duck out, at least temporarily. I booked a midnight flight to Detroit.

I was one of the few white coaches Tree would speak to, because I'd paid attention to him before he got to be important. And for some reason he liked my new boss at State, Jack Hood. Tree knew details that could give you an edge in recruiting his Detroit kids. "You can sign him," he might say, "but unless you bring his girlfriend you'll never see him." Or, "Talk to his father all you want, but he only listens to his grandma." Or, "He's a talent, and he'll be the star player in your state penitentiary."

Tree's gym was a model facility—new lockers, a redwood floor with a Detroit Pistons logo at center court, every light blazing. He achieved this by maintaining a wide circle of friends. He could tell you the names of the children of each member of the Park District Board, and he'd inquire after them regularly. When he appeared before the Board and listed his players now attending college on basketball scholarships, it was a formality—his audience was already convinced. But his fundraising didn't stop there. A sympathetic CEO who loved hoops provided his girls' team with uniforms. A big-time drug dealer sponsored the boys traveling teams.

Tree told me there would be little competition to challenge Jamal at this New Beginnings camp. It was a neighborhood program for children of all ages, games and crafts, all kinds of sports. That was fine. I could watch Jamal shoot around by himself at some point, which might be enough. I was already thinking ahead to signing him to a National Letter of Intent in November before anyone saw him play a game as a senior, locking him in so Michigan or Michigan State couldn't scoop him up in April.

Understand that in July, a coach can't speak to a prospect in person, only on the phone. But as soon as I got to the New Beginnings camp, I'd yank on my coaching gear with "STATE" emblazoned across the chest. I'd hang out at the camp for an hour or so to make sure that Jamal Davis saw my shirt. He would know that I'd come a long way. I might even meet friends of his or people with influence who I could talk to.

Jamal's mother had answered when I phoned from the airport that morning. Within three minutes I knew that she was clueless and wouldn't be a factor. When she said, "Whatever college he wants to go to is fine with me," I put a thick line through her name. She was one of those displaced Southern Baptist ladies who had moved to the big city to work in the auto plants as a teenager.

"You're going to be disappointed, Mr. Pentel," she said. "Jamal's working. At the New Beginnings camp. In fact—"

"It's Pytel," I reminded her gently. "*Coach* Pytel." She told me the New Beginnings Center was down the block from where they lived. She said something more about the camp, but it sounded like a religious pitch—I tuned her out, jotting the Center's address down and putting another line through her name.

The one old lady behind the desk inside the New Beginnings Center seemed impervious to the heat. I announced who I was, mentioning Southern Arizona State twice. I was there, I said, to observe their camp.

She looked at me over the top of her glasses. She wasn't

expecting a visitor. "The New Beginnings Center Camp isn't here," she said. "The camp *itself* is near Freeland."

"Freeland?" I asked, feeling for a pen.

She unfolded a huge Michigan map. Two or three hours to Freeland. Past Saginaw.

I didn't curse or let on that I was upset. This lady might come in contact with Jamal Davis; she could be a friend of the family or an aunt. Anyway, it wasn't her fault that my day had just gotten longer. I could still get there well before dark, and Jamal would be even more impressed that I'd gone through the trouble. And I'd be checked into the Marriott by midnight.

My thirst was giving me a headache, but I wasn't going to stop until I was out of Detroit. On the highway, I decided I could save valuable time by not stopping for a Gatorade or the piss break it would necessitate. I'd just hang on as best I could.

A couple hours later, I rolled past the hand-painted sign that announced the New Beginnings Camp. I parked next to an old yellow school bus and put on a fresh State shirt. A flock of kids was playing softball. On the other side of the field, a handful of kids shot baskets at a bent wooden backboard on a dirt court. One looked pretty tall. I walked toward him, but a graying black man with mutton-chop sideburns and long, ropey muscles intercepted me halfway there. He had a whistle around his neck, and a Bible next to his clipboard. He was 6'3".

"I'm Reverend Oliver," he said in a tone you'd use to get someone off your property. "What do you need?" The Reverend looked like he'd played a little ball in his day. He wore a moderate Afro and probably had since the seventies.

"I'm Steve Pytel, a college coach." I turned square to him so he could see the lettering on my shirt. "I understand that Jamal Davis is here working, and I've come up to see him."

"This isn't a basketball camp," he said. "He won't be playing any games here, he's one of our counselors."

Jamal was very important to us, I told him, and I'd been tracking his progress for the last two years. I couldn't actually talk to Jamal in person until September, I explained. Reverend Oliver didn't seem interested. In fact, he looked angry. I asked how long he'd known Jamal.

"I used to play ball with his father. His pop and I grew up together, and the young man needed someone to look up to."

I imagined the dinging of a Las Vegas slot machine—Jamal's father figure. We walked through centerfield of the softball game. Midway, Reverend Oliver stopped to face me. He was a serious guy, probably a ferocious rebounder and defender in his day—the kind of player who knocked you on your ass, but would gladly hoist you back on your feet. "Are you watching the flood?" he asked, raising an eyebrow.

"I'm sorry?" I said. I didn't quite hear him with the bells in my head still going off. Watching what flood?

"I said, *Are you washed in the blood?* Have you seen the light?"

"Well, yes. Of course."

He reached out to shake hands again. Then he pulled me in, my right hand still locked in his, and hugged me hard with the other. Our faces touched, and I felt the sandiness of his cheek.

We continued our stroll until we came to what was being used as a basketball court. Jamal Davis—it must have been him—was goofing with a handful of grade-schoolers. Each dribble brought up a puff of dirt; any missed shot shook the plywood backboard. They played one-on-one, took turns using typical playground rules—make it, take it. If you scored, you kept the ball, stayed on offense, and another defender came out and got his chance. These rules—a sort of cutthroat, rich-get-richer system—are used by city kids everywhere. Jamal held court, laughing—not at the boys, I could tell, but with them. Nobody could stop him from scoring, not that this was any kind of test, because he was at least a foot taller than anyone else.

After a few minutes, Jamal must have gotten bored because he put up a shot from ridiculously far. He missed, and the ball caromed long. The small defender, who was plenty fast, doubled back for the ball. Long rebounds often hit the ground, where being tall becomes a disadvantage. Jamal angled forward and they got to it at the same instant. Rather than grab the ball with two hands and power it away from the boy, Jamal stretched for it with just his left hand as it bounced. He snapped it into a between-the-legs dribble. Then, as the boy lunged for it one more time, Jamal spun back in a reverse pivot as he recovered his balance and went right into a jump shot—all in one fluid motion. The shot missed, but that didn't matter. It was a maneuver of breathtaking grace and agility, the kind I would have gladly replayed on a game film.

Across the field a trumpet sounded and the games ended. A swift river of black boys rushed by us, and I nearly reached for the Reverend's shoulder to keep from getting swept away. Some kids were arguing about the last inning of the baseball game but when they got close to Reverend Oliver they quieted. Jamal herded his little crew along, and as he got close he noticed me, then looked at Reverend Oliver, and back at me. He had a bounce to his step, as though at any instant he could rise up and slam a ball through a hoop. I clasped my hands behind my back to offer an unobstructed view of my shirt. He was closer to 6'6", with huge hands. Like the young campers, his face was smooth and innocent.

"Jamal, this gentleman is a college basketball scout," the Reverend said. "He's come a very long way to spend time with us."

I grinned and started to introduce myself but Reverend Oliver cut me off. "But he's not allowed to talk to you now." The younger kids continued to stream around, between, and behind us.

"That's right," I agreed. "I'm not allowed. NCAA rules."

Jamal smiled sweetly. He checked out my shirt again and walked off with the parade. The moment was worth a hundred recruiting letters. I could have departed that instant and the day would have been fruitful.

Reverend Oliver told me what a good kid Jamal was, and I agreed again. The kids had all disappeared inside a cinderblock building up the hill. "We have our quiet time now, with Bible study and prayer," he said. "It'll take a couple hours. But you're welcome to stay around and join us for dinner in the cafeteria at seven," he said, and pointed up the hill. "The evening service starts at eight and you'd be welcome at that as well."

I didn't want to drive all the way back to Detroit after my short bump with Jamal—I felt lucky and wanted to learn more about him. But I wasn't wild about the idea of a three-hour wait for cafeteria food. "I'll join you for the service at eight," I said, "if that's all right." I'd skip the meal and relax. Jamal would see me again at the service, where I was sure to stand out.

I could use the time to clear my voicemail, phone the office, and update our mailing list by adding the name Jamal Davis. I'd check in with Tree Turner, let him know I'd arrived. But back at the car I remembered that the air-conditioning was shot, and my cell phone insisted I was outside the customer service area. I tossed the phone back in the car and slammed the door.

Four hours. I wandered the campgrounds, keeping in the shade of the cottonwoods, alone with the humidity and the Michigan woods. Cheap cabin-type barracks where the children must have slept were clumped together. Not a soda machine or water fountain in sight. A cluster of picnic tables sat between the overgrown baseball diamond and the bent basketball goals where most of the grass had been worn away. I went to the exact spot where Jamal had done his astonishing move and tried it myself in slow motion. Even with an imaginary defender and ball it was impossible to do without losing my balance. I knew I wouldn't see Jamal play in a real game, but it didn't matter. That kind of nimble dexterity was exceptional, simply could not be taught. This kid looked like a player and I trusted my instinct.

At one edge of camp, near a shallow river, I found a massive rock in a shady spot. With nobody in sight, I took off my coaching shirt and rolled it into a pillow.

I had been an assistant coach for over ten years. Despite the regime change, I still had a job. Not the greatest job, but still, I enjoyed certain benefits, things that guys my age in other professions didn't have. Like the glamour that came with the big crowds and TV games. Of course, nobody came to see the assistant coach, but I could easily imagine the thrill of being the boss. That was where the big money was and every assistant aspired to that position. Free gear, too. I hadn't paid for shoes or athletic apparel in years. And I could golf for free, if I had the time or the interest. The courtesy car, there was that. I could get it washed for free whenever I wanted. I'd traveled to most of the fifty states. I'd never seen the Statue of Liberty or the Grand Canyon, it was mostly Holiday Inns and high school gymnasiums. But still, they were free trips. Also, any employee at my college could enroll in one free class every semester. I thought about that quite a bit and planned to take advantage of it soon, maybe even that September.

A friendly breeze kept the bugs off me. Exhausted from the early flight, I dozed off on the rock. The angling sun woke me a couple hours later. I was disoriented for a moment, I'd slept that hard. My shirt was too wrinkled to smooth out.

Most of the seats for the evening service were taken, although I arrived plenty early. Five rows of folding chairs were perfectly aligned, about twenty across. I took my place in line at the water fountain, but Reverend Oliver escorted me away, took me by the arm to a middle row. "You've decided to join us," he said. "That's good." A dozen youngsters stood or slid their legs sidesaddle so I could squeeze through. The cool steel of the chair felt good on my back. I was surrounded by black faces.

An organ flanked the pulpit, with an old man, barely alive, seated behind it. Reverend Oliver took his place next to him. The organist began a slow number, and the sound bounced off the cinderblock walls and settled over us. We were jammed in so tight that I touched arms with the boys on both sides of me, but they didn't seem to mind.

The choir walked to the front, arranged by height, decked out in purple robes, moving with a slow confidence, as though they were the team to beat at a tournament. They must have been counselors like Jamal Davis. They were humming along with the organ. Of course, Jamal was last. The music stopped.

Jamal noticed me—how could he not?—and smiled. I was glad I'd stuck around.

Reverend Oliver stepped forward to the pulpit. He was angry again.

Using that same "get off my property" voice from earlier in the day, he said you could fool yourself but not fool God. He talked about being *in* the world but not *of* the world. He said that all the riches of the world would be dust one day, and I could tell he meant it. "I've never seen a hearse with a U-Haul on the back," he said, and we all laughed. If he said something he really meant, he'd say it twice, but much louder.

He said that we all had to account for what we'd done in this world. I felt like the room was getting smaller; the boys squeezed against me, the temperature rose. I was surprised they could sit still. One boy stood while Reverend Oliver was speaking, and he yelled, "Tell us the truth!" and another rose behind him and called out, "That's what I'm talking about now!" Many of the boys around me started to holler too, in a way that would have landed them in the principal's office if they were at school. They all agreed with Reverend Oliver and pounded on the metal seats. Most of the kids were smiling, but he still looked angry. He made his point again about not fooling God. "Nobody in this room can deny that," he said. One at a time, he pointed at several different kids, ones who had probably been in trouble, and bellowed, "You can't deny it!" He pointed at me last. "You! You can't deny it either." I couldn't. I don't think he could have said anything that I would have denied.

He nodded to the old man behind the organ, who jump-started a rollicking number. The boys next to me started to move in time to the music, bumping into my shoulders, and I had to move with them and sway in long rhythmic shifts. The music got louder and the boys began to clap on the upbeat. We all rocked to the same cadence, the way I'd seen the fans at black high schools move as one. The row in front of us rocked in the opposite direction, as did the row behind us, and a lot of them had their eyes closed, their heads tilted back. I was the only one not clapping, and that felt odd, so I clapped too. Everyone glistened with sweat although I was still dry. Jamal Davis smiled, his eyes shut, his face drenched.

Reverend Oliver shouted over the music and our clapping, shouted about sacrifices. That made me think about some of the things I'd sacrificed because of coaching. My job wasn't grueling, like working construction, but it was time-consuming. My wife says we are awash in misunderstanding largely because I was a coach. She said that I "ascribed varying values to human beings depending on their height." But even if that were true, was it so unusual? Did stockbrokers pal around with guys who declared bankruptcy? Did real estate agents befriend the homeless? What stung worst was when she implied that I had no identity without my job. "If you peeled away the coaching," she asked, "what would be left?"

The choir started a call and response, and sang, "Are you going to be ready to go?" and we sang back a resounding, "God's gonna ease my troubling mind." That was how we answered every one of the choir's challenges; when they changed the call to, "Can you walk the straight and narrow?" we had the same answer. Next they asked, "Will you meet Him by the riverside?" A couple of kids jumped up and stood on their chairs. Soon everybody did, and I don't know why but I stood on my chair too, and rode on the wave of the organ and the clapping and singing, and the sound built up, and then the organ player stood as well, but continued to pump out the song, hunched over, doing a little two-step in place. We all kept clapping, swayed back and forth and back, when a strange lightheadedness seemed to lift me. Jamal Davis was now the only choir member with his eyes open, and he was weeping. Heat radiated from the front of the building, and I felt the warmth in my face and something broke in me and I finally began to perspire too.

The music continued, and I looked up at the sixty-watt lights on the ceiling, then to the synchronized spontaneity below. And I thought—there's a purity here, something real and authentic. Reverend Oliver smiled at last, with everyone in the room in agreement and entrained to the music. This was the first time he'd smiled since I arrived at the camp. He raised both fists in the air as though he'd sunk a game-winning shot. Every choir member was soaked, although I couldn't be sure what was sweat and what were tears. These kids had something in their lives, something simple and honest that I lacked. I didn't know whether I wanted exactly what it was they had. But I knew this: I didn't want what I had anymore.

I fell. My temple slammed against a steel chair. Everything went dark.

Hands on my chest woke me. Kids carried me out of the building, my face to the ceiling, and they held me above their heads as if to keep me dry. The music kept going, and the choir changed their part to something about the spirit hitting you, and the kids continued to answer back. Even the ones who carried me.

The boys set me down next to the river, flat on my back. The lights from the buildings up the hill kept us from total darkness. I must have slipped in and out of consciousness, because I remember being carried out but not the trip to the riverside. My whole body ached, but in a good way, like I'd played a rough pick-up game. One of the kids cupped his hands into the slow-moving water and tossed what he could salvage into my face. I rose up onto one elbow. The ground was warm and moist, and I could see shirts, but not faces.

Moments later came a crunch of footsteps and the kids scattered like sparrows. Reverend Oliver crouched next to me with a can of something that faintly shined in the thin light. I gulped until it was gone. A soda. Orange, I thought, or maybe root beer. It's funny, in the dark some of your senses become more acute and others you lose. He took the empty can and leaned over the river to fill it up. I would have drunk that down too, but he poured it slowly over my head.

I was lying on the ground in the dark next to a river, my head and shirt soaked, with a man I had only just met that day, yet I wasn't anxious to move. I wouldn't have been a bit surprised if Reverend Oliver asked me to stay the night, just to be safe.

When he stood up, I reached for his hand, expecting him to gather me up and carry me to a soft cot in one of the cabins. He didn't.

"That was quite a scene in there," I said finally. "Very powerful."

I could feel his eyes on me in the darkness. A cold dampness seeped through my khakis at the hip where most of my weight was. I began to talk, the way I do when I've had too much coffee, rambling on about growing up Catholic, although that didn't mean much to me, it was just a habit. I was still uncertain about exactly who was who in the Bible. Reverend Oliver was a powerful speaker and I told him so, and how the choir and the music really knocked me out, and I laughed at my own unintended pun. Then I told him how shallow my life felt at times. I had a lot of questions for him, although I wasn't sure where to begin. I wished then that Reverend Oliver could talk to my wife, even both of us together, and I began to tell him about my situation with her. He was squatting now, close enough to touch me.

"I haven't believed one thing about you to be true since the minute you got here," he said. His voice had a rough edge to it, like his cheek had earlier. But he stayed close to me, silent for half a minute. Then he walked back towards the camp. He must have stopped and turned back, because I heard him call out, "I want you out of here in five minutes."

My damp clothes clung to me on the way back to Detroit. I checked into the airport hotel at midnight. When the alarm went off I was already awake, feet propped up on the desk, watching the morning planes and the sheets of rain. My pants, with their muddy stains, hung from the corner of the bathroom door.

A *Detroit Free Press* sat under my door, and I folded it into my bag for airplane reading. But when I phoned Tree Turner, he insisted I come visit him before I left town. I never made the pilgrimage to Detroit without seeing him, he said. I re-booked my flight for mid-afternoon.

Tree was outside the rec center having a smoke, staying dry in the overhang of a doorway. He had the thick arms you'd expect from a guy with his name, and his hug nearly crushed me. He laughed, showing off his two gold teeth, and we slapped palms a few times. I presented him with a new coaching shirt, still in the wrapper, a dark green polo type just like the one I had on. The shirt was my yearly offering to Tree. "My man, Coach Pytel," he said.

Tree showed me their new locker room then chased a couple of kids away from his office door. "We got important business," he told them. I wanted to tell him about my experience at the New Beginnings camp, how I'd been hit with something that left me to wonder what the hell we were all doing, and how Reverend Oliver had made me leave. I wasn't exactly close to Tree, but we had helped each other for so long I figured I could talk to him.

Before I could find the words, a teenage girl in a yellow halter-top brought a stack of mail in. She sat down on his desk. Tree called her "Sugar" and told her this wasn't a good time. Sugar, or whatever her name was, pouted, but didn't move. He shuffled through some papers on his desk. She crossed her arms, hopped to her feet, and walked out.

"My intern," he said, winking at me. "How did it go with Jamal Davis?"

"The camp was a three-hour drive." I smiled, so it wouldn't sound like a complaint. "I thought it was right here in the city."

"Was it that far?" he said, flipping through his mail. "I've never been. Did Jamal see you?"

"Sure," I said, "but that Reverend Oliver didn't seem too cool about Jamal coming to State. He never warmed up to me. I mean, you said nobody was recruiting the kid, then this guy acts like I'm dealing rocks."

Tree leaned forward in his swivel chair and slapped down the pile of mail. "Fuck Reverend Oliver," he said, "and his self-righteous ass. I knew him in the old days, from way back. I know exactly who he used to be."

"He acted like he was pretty close to Jamal," I said. "I didn't make too good of an impression." I should have told Tree right then about the clarity I'd felt in the cinderblock building. About how shallow my job sometimes made me feel. Although I knew not to talk to Tree about my marriage.

"That phony fool," Tree said, "he won't have nothing to do with Jamal's decision. Acting like he's all important now and he's different just cause he's been to church. I could tell you about that motherfucker's past. I'm talking twenty-five years ago, shit that the nigger should have been locked up for." Tree stood, and it felt like he was mad at me, too. "People don't change that much, Pytel. I know who he used to be, so I know who he is." He patted my shoulder. "He ain't gonna have shit to do with Jamal once they get back from that fantasy camp in two weeks. I only agreed to let Jamal go there cause he's such a nice religious-type kid. I wanted to get him out of Detroit any old way. Even if it wasn't to Las Vegas."

"I guess I feel better about it then," I said.

Tree started in again. "You stay on Jamal. Send him shit. Be nice to his mom. I'm telling you, you can sign him in November if Jack Hood likes him." That did set my mind to rest a little bit.

Tree picked up his *Free Press* and waved it at me. "You read this?"

I hadn't, it was in the rental car. Turns out that Nate Wilkerson, who had been too good for us to even imagine recruiting two years ago, was in some trouble. At 6'10", he had led the state of Michigan in scoring and rebounding as a high school senior, and was named to *USA Today's* high school All-American team. Tree had told me then not to waste my time recruiting him: Wilkerson wanted to play in the Big Ten. But now, despite a great freshman season, he was looking to transfer.

"Why is he leaving school?" I asked. A player like this could revive us. And my career.

"He beat up his girlfriend."

"That's enough to get him put out of school?"

"Broke her nose," Tree said. "It's the third time he's had a problem. And the second girl. The other times didn't make it to the paper, so as far as you all are concerned it's the first time. His school just couldn't keep him." Tree opened up his palms to the ceiling, as if he was holding Nate Wilkerson out for me. All I had to do was take him.

"Tell me about him," I said, and clicked my pen.

"He ain't no *great* kid," Tree said. "He needs to get away. He's too close to trouble now. You guys are perfect cause you're a long way from his friends. A fresh start with you at State, a chance to blossom. Can you imagine how much pussy is running around at his school? Who could focus?"

I thought for a minute. This shouldn't change anything as far as signing Jamal Davis in November. But Nate Wilkerson could be our best player the day he arrived—big men were impossible to come by. He could lift us above the rest of our league in his sophomore year—he'd have to sit out one year as a transfer.

Tree tapped his desk.

That girlfriend stuff would blow over. I could connect Wilkerson with a school psychologist through Student Social Services. We'd cover our asses at the very least in case he got worse, but maybe we could even help Wilkerson to grow up. I could spend lots of time with him during his red-shirt year to help him mature.

"Make up your mind," Tree said.

THE ETYMOLOGY OF FAMILY

Two black men stood on the steps outside Cooley High School in Detroit. Tyrone Gage was a recruiter, an assistant coach for Southern Arizona State. His wallet bulged in his back pocket, although he kept his cash separate, in the front. It began to drizzle and Gage offered to give Jamal Davis a lift.

Jamal Davis, more a boy than a man—and State's top recruit—said Vanessa was sick that morning, had missed seeing the game that just concluded.

Who the hell is Vanessa? Gage wondered. This was the first time he'd heard her name, but Gage said he hoped Vanessa got to feeling better. She must have been Jamal's sweetheart. The two continued talking over the roof of the rental car even as the rain picked up.

Jamal finally noticed the car. "Wow," he said. "Is this yours?"

Gage told him this was a rental; his own ride was back home. That's what he liked about Jamal Davis, his innocence. That's what everyone liked about Jamal. He was a nice religious boy with big hands and feet, and lots of growth ahead. Gage unlocked the car.

"I got y'all's Christmas card," Jamal said when he'd settled in. "Thanks." Seated in the car the kid was Gage's height, but his knees angled way up. Jamal pointed him to the parking lot exit. "Your team's not doing so good, huh?"

"*Our* team, baby," Gage said. "We're just surviving." *Until you save us*, he nearly added. "Plus," Gage said, "Nate Wilkerson has transferred to State. You remember him, right?"

"He got in trouble over that girl. My mom don't like him. She says—"

"He's changed a lot. Tell your Mom that, and tell me when to turn again."

Jamal ran his hands over the digital climate control, twirling it down five and ten degrees, like a kid with a new toy. He brought the temperature back up, raising it five degrees, testing the air with his palm. Gage let him play with the controls without comment. Kids were funny.

Jamal took a deep breath and folded his hands. "I think I made a mistake by signing with State."

It was all Gage could do to keep from stomping on the brakes. "Come on," he said. "It's going to be perfect."

"Something's come up," Jamal said. "Something happened."

"What's wrong?" Gage asked in a tone he'd use with a child.

"You can't tell my mom."

"Man, please, like I'd discuss this with your Mom," Gage said, as though he and Jamal were friends. Traffic slowed, then stopped. Two ragged men argued on the sidewalk, waving their arms as if trying to fly.

Every last brother on State's team was mad at Tyrone Gage because he held the black players accountable for the team dropping four in a row. Somebody had to demand some goddamn accountability. He was now a thousand miles from home on a recruiting trip, a trip he thought of as an escape, a sprint from the burning building that their basketball season had become.

A trip to see Jamal Davis should have been uplifting. Yet Gage had sensed Jamal was in trouble a week ago when he sounded upset on the phone. "I better get up there," Gage told Jack Hood, "talk about his ACT score and make sure his transcript is in order." Like somebody should have done for Gage back when he was eighteen.

Gage had attended a state school in Wisconsin with dubious academic requirements, a school he opted for over the humiliation of junior college. By the time he was twenty, his knees had buckled, he'd lost his shooting touch, and his game fell apart. He wasn't even a very good small college player in the end.

Because he hadn't played at Duke or Indiana, he had to scrap to begin his coaching career, taking on full-time school security work—shaking down high school thugs for weed or cigarettes, checking IDs—jobs he damn sure didn't need a bachelor's degree for. After work he drove to Chicago State to get his indoctrination in coaching, and he stuck around for night classes to earn a diploma.

The Chicago State gig led to a coaching spot at a teacher's college in Chicago, a job he'd held for a decade. He got lucky there with a couple recruits who'd powered the team to a winning record; by chance, they happened to be the only team in Chicago that year with a winning record, a fact that became a headline in March of 2002 in the *Chicago Sun-Times*. A week later, Jack Hood began wooing Gage, offered him a raise and the title Recruiting Coordinator. Hood represented all the things Gage had missed as a player and now wished for as a coach: the big time. Publicity. Gage had gotten, as dumb as it sounded now, star-struck. He hadn't been patient enough to wait for a better offer, meaning a school on the rise.

"Gage, you married *up*"—he'd heard that comment four times at his own wedding. Celysha—it sounded like "delicious," that was his first line to her. She was lighter skinned, from the suburbs, and valedictorian of her mostly-white high school class. By age twenty-four she'd earned her master's degree. She had an expectation of success in her voice that, at first, soothed Gage. Plus, she didn't say *fuck* and *nigger* every third word, like the girls he'd grown up with around 63rd Street.

Celysha reminded him of his career path almost daily. Her success in advertising was part of his problem. No coaches had wives who were more successful than they were. She pushed Gage to push himself, move up, demand a raise, apply for better jobs.

Now, in Gage's second season at State, the program was unraveling. He was supposed to be the go-between to help player-coach relations, typical shit for the black assistant. Only black men could talk to black kids? The fact that he no longer *liked* the players compounded Gage's frustration. They didn't give a fuck about his old school work ethic, didn't want to hear about his upbringing in Englewood. They mocked him behind his back, he was almost certain, in the same way he and his boys would have talked shit about Celysha if she'd attended Englewood High School.

The team was struggling and the fastest relief was to take off, go recruiting, and avoid the gloom. Jamal Davis was their silver lining, an oxymoron in size eighteen sneakers—an untainted and gullible city kid.

Being in Detroit to avoid the team's collapse meant Gage would miss road games in Wyoming and Colorado. All that fun, hours of videotape. Any hope for this season was gone, but things would be better next year, with Jamal.

At Christmas, the word around the Midwest was that Gage and Steve Pytel were geniuses for signing Jamal. Now it was February and the talk had shifted—Jamal had been foolish to sign at State, a Detroit sportswriter had written; he could have done quite a bit better if he'd waited. No doubt Jamal had read that article.

Whatever was troubling the boy, Gage would inspire him with his own story: how he'd led the city of Chicago in scoring when he was Jamal's age. Nobody mentioned anymore that his high school team had hardly won a game; the city's leading scorer was still the city's leading scorer. A lot of the other dudes who had done that wound up as NBA stars. Gage never got tired of describing the hurdles he kicked over.

"Vanessa is pregnant," Jamal blurted. Then he leaned forward, head in hands, and sobbed.

The outburst came so suddenly and dramatically that for a hot second, Gage was certain that it was an act. Gage had to check himself from asking Jamal if he was sure it was his baby. Instead he said, "She's been tested?"

Jamal didn't answer, just bawled louder. Okay, she was definitely pregnant and Jamal was definitely the father. Gage had to distract him, get him back to thinking clearly. He said, "Look up. Don't I need to turn here?"

Jamal sniffled. "No, go straight."

"How old is your Vanessa?"

"She's eighteen. Older than me, but she's just a junior. Her mother goes to our church."

Gage needed time to stall, time to think. He had barely gotten to know Jamal during the kid's forty-eight-hour recruiting visit to campus in October, despite staying close by most of the weekend. Jamal was such a pleasant boy that Gage didn't want to leave him alone with the black players for fear they'd frighten him off. Instead he turned Jamal over to the three white players, who were more suited to Jamal's let's-rent-a-nice-movie personality. Sure enough, they did rent a movie: *My Giant.*

The streets they were driving could have just as easily been his Chicago as Jamal's Detroit—currency exchanges and liquor stores, take-out-only restaurants—but of course Gage didn't recognize any of it. "You can't just quit playing ball," Gage said. "What're you going to do, get a job at McDonald's and not play for us?"

"I don't know." Jamal was about to start crying again, then wiped his eyes, sat up, and took a deep breath. "I heard that I could ask you guys to release me out of my National Letter of Intent."

Appear calm, Gage thought. Be a friend. "Son, how's that gonna help?"

"Vanessa says I could go to a school that's closer to here and help raise my baby. I been praying about it."

"I don't think we're allowed to let you out of the scholarship. It's like a contract, it's binding." That wasn't exactly true, but he said it anyway.

"Or," Jamal said, "I could just go to a junior college nearby. At least until the baby's born."

"You don't want to do that—throw away your future?" Gage braked hard. A boy with a bicycle balanced on his shoulder had stepped right in front of them. It was a lemon-yellow Schwinn ten-speed, exactly like Gage had bought as an eighth grader. He'd shoveled snow all winter in the University of Chicago neighborhood, a thirty-minute trek on foot from Englewood. He rang the doorbells of the college faculty his entire Christmas break, yessirring everybody, pleading for the honor of shoveling their sidewalks. He'd bought the ten-speed the day the weather changed in April. The bike had been stolen after he'd owned it for just a month.

"We missed our turn," Jamal said. "Sorry. You gotta go back."

"Can't I just turn up here?"

"This one doesn't go through." Jamal seemed certain.

Gage cut into an alley to get turned around. "You got to think about what's important for your family now," he said.

"My mom won't even—"

"Your family means Vanessa now. Ain't that right? I've been down this road," Gage said. He knew he couldn't say what he thought: *Vanessa was the one with the problem, not Jamal.*

Jamal shifted in his seat, his back now to the passenger's door to face him. Gage had to be careful what he said here. Jamal might be too frail for a question like, "Are you sure you're the father?" Instead, Gage asked, "What's the best thing you can do, for you and the baby? Huh?"

"Get my degree?"

"Alright, that's a start," Gage said. "But the biggest thing is to make yourself marketable, be a provider for your family. How are you going to get that done?"

"Get my degree?"

"No, man," Gage said, "by *playing ball* for a living. And the place to do that is with us. Initially, I mean. Then you're off to the League or else to Europe."

"Can't I do all that close to home?" Jamal wiped his tears again with the heel of his hand.

Having a player interested in what he had to say for a change felt good. "If you go to junior college, you're just slowing down the process. If you go to some small college," Gage added, "you're fucked, excuse me. I mean your career is through. You won't get where you want to be sitting on some bus with a bunch of dudes eating Whoppers after playing in front of a hundred fans."

"I didn't say anything about a small college," Jamal reminded him.

Even after doubling back on the same street toward their missed turn, none of it looked familiar to Gage. The boy with the yellow bicycle had disappeared.

Jamal's tears stopped. This was one kid you couldn't joke with or tease, because he'd take you seriously and absorb every word.

"Actually, Vanessa wants me to stay around here," Jamal said.

So that was it. This stupid bitch wanted Jamal Davis to piss away his whole life, the entire opportunity. Gage would've given anything to get this kind of offer as a high school senior. It was hard to listen to a player—a boy, really—toss State's future away with a dumb-ass decision. No point in fooling myself, Gage thought—*my* future.

"I didn't say it was going to be easy," Gage said. "You'll have to be apart from her for a year. Then she can join us on campus. With the baby. You'd be on your own for just nine months, really."

Gage eased the car into a tow-away zone to talk Jamal through his imagined future: Vanessa would get a job right on campus, Jamal's sophomore season. The university had a free day care. They would live in married student housing, with a closed-in back yard where their son could play. He wanted a son, didn't he? When Vanessa was ready, she could even start classes, too. What did she want to major in?

"Entomology," Jamal said.

Gage froze, like a bad shooter with an open three-pointer. Then he pulled the car back into traffic too quickly. Someone honked at him from behind. "We've got a great program in that. Remind me, and I'll send you a catalog." More than likely, this

Vanessa would forget Jamal before the year was out. One cold winter day, Jamal would figure that shit out.

When Jamal spoke again, his voice lifted for the first time. "Hey. Coach Gage. Would you talk to Vanessa about that stuff?"

"Sure, man." He offered a pen from his coat pocket. "Just write down her number."

"I mean right now," Jamal said. "Just the three of us."

It was gratifying to have Jamal trust him, and Gage needed to keep their best recruit, but he damn sure wasn't going to get that intimate. Jamal's invitation made it sound like a Sunday picnic. Next Jamal would ask him to be in the delivery room for the birthing, then he'd ask Gage to be the godfather.

Gage asked, "Tonight?"

Jamal nodded. "Why not?"

"I guess so," Gage said. "I think you're right about not telling your mom just yet. I'd wait a bit on that." At least until he got out of town.

"Then we're headed the wrong way again," Jamal said. "We just passed Vanessa's street."

"You think Vanessa's mother is going to be home?" Gage asked. That's all he needed.

Vanessa lived in a twelve-unit building. Most of the names on the mailboxes were secured with tape. None of the hallway doors were locked, just like where Gage was raised. Jamal led him upstairs and let himself in with his own key. The jiggled lock woke Vanessa. She was on a couch, covered with a plaid blanket, the TV on low, and she woke up with a stern look. She was barefoot and wild-haired.

Jamal bent down to kiss her forehead. "Meet one of my coaches," he said. "This is Coach Gage."

"Coach from where?" Vanessa asked.

"From my college," Jamal said.

She wouldn't look at Gage. Not yet. She pushed the blanket back. Narrow hips, lean muscles in her arms. No earrings. A tomboy. She wasn't showing yet.

"You told him," she said.

"He wants to talk to us about everything," Jamal said. "He has some good ideas."

Gage took his cue and sat down. "I want what's best for the both of you."

She sat up and turned to Gage for the first time. He hadn't seen a girl whose hair was in a natural since he was in high school himself. "There's not no *both* of us now," she said. "There's three of us." Her voice was deeper than Jamal's and there was an edgy attack in it. She was trying to get in the first punch, put Gage on his heels.

"Well, the best thing for all three of you," Gage continued, "is for Jamal to be a success." He leaned forward and clasped his hands, trying to look respectable. "On the court and off. And his best chance of that—"

"His best chance of that," Vanessa said, "is not to be fucking some lil' old college girl with all her Tommy Hilfiger clothes on the floor." Jamal flinched a little when she cursed. She'd planned the pregnancy, Gage thought, used Jamal as her ticket to a better life. Was it too late to tell him he could do better than this alley cat?

"I don't think that's going to happen," Gage said. "But if he's here in Detroit working at Burger King, in the long run that doesn't help either of you."

"What's wrong with Burger King?" Vanessa said, kicking off the last of the blanket. "I work at Burger King."

"Nothing," Gage said, backpedaling fast. "That's not what I'm saying. Jamal and I talked about a one-year period, right, Jamal? Really only September to May. Then you and the baby come down and join us."

"Oh," she said, "so now there's four of us? So nice of you to join the family."

Jamal pitched in, giving Gage a moment to gather himself. "I can just concentrate on my grades for the first year," Jamal said. "And ball."

She turned to Jamal, and her tone sweetened for the first time. "That's what you were doing this year, baby." There was a hint of a smile and she seemed feminine, finally. "Now I have to wait eight more months."

Gage tiptoed back into the fray. He hated to tiptoe. "You have to think of the three of you as a team."

Vanessa stood up. She was built like a lightweight boxer. "You teaching him to run away from his problems. You not going to step on me." This was the second time she pointed right at Gage. "Why you making him choose between basketball and me?"

"Basketball and *us*," Jamal reminded her.

"The choice I'm saying would be the harder road for Jamal at first," Gage admitted. "I want him to see into the future, though, and not throw away his chance of playing major college ball."

Vanessa didn't answer for a long while. Thank God he had Jamal there as a buffer. He needed to get gone before Vanessa's mother arrived. The mother might be worse—pushy *and* religious—if she already knew about the baby.

Gage could feel it coming. Any minute now, Vanessa would say she wanted to come to State with Jamal when he did, and wanted a good-paying job in her major field. She was going to ask for a car too, something Jamal hadn't even done. Gage wasn't even sure what *etymology* was. Or whatever Jamal called it. She certainly didn't look anything like a pregnant woman. Could she have made this whole scheme up? When Vanessa returned to the couch, Gage stood and examined the family pictures on the TV, careful not to get fingerprints on the glass. She looked presentable when she got cleaned up. In one photo her dark brown skin was set off by a strapless yellow dress, what looked like ladybug earrings, a matching flower behind her ear.

"Jamal," she said sweetly, "did you bring me my Orange Crush?"

"You didn't ask for no Orange Crush."

Gage nearly volunteered to get it for her. Something told him not to.

"Yes I did, baby. It won't take you but five minutes to go to the corner."

Gage dug in his pocket for change, but Vanessa had a solid

dollar. Jamal kissed her cheek and asked Gage if he wanted a soda too. Gage didn't. She lay back down.

Gage stood at the window and waited to see Jamal below. "How long have you lived in this building?" Gage asked.

"I want to get me an abortion," she said. "You heard me," she added, before Gage could ask her to repeat it. "But Jamal can't find out. You know how he is. All devout."

"I'm not stopping you," Gage said. That was for real. Maybe he just needed to get out of her way.

"I need a ride to the clinic. Jamal don't have no car. Yet. And I'm not taking the bus when it's over."

"You want me to drive you to a clinic?" Gage said.

"And back. You have to wait there for me. We going tomorrow morning."

"What are you going to tell Jamal?"

"That he should go on, take his sweet ass to your university and play. That's what you want anyway, right?" she sneered.

"Sure. But what are you going to tell Jamal about the—"

She sounded it out, slowly, nodding in time to each syllable, as if Gage were stupid: "Miss—care—edge."

Gage woke the next morning in a mild panic: he hadn't played this Vanessa deal smart. It wasn't like she couldn't take a taxi, which he would have gladly paid for. Maybe she needed him to sign a waiver of consent or something because she wasn't twenty-one. He couldn't put his signature on any document that had her name on it. NCAA rules. In any case, she needed more than a driver.

Gage chauffeured Jamal to Cooley High and backtracked to get Vanessa. He parked a little ways down from her apartment complex to collect his thoughts. The morning paper said that State had won at Wyoming, a very rare road victory. Gage called Pytel to get the details, and they giggled like children. State had gotten hot from beyond the three-point stripe. Maybe Colorado State could be beaten as well. Gage didn't give Pytel any details, just told him Jamal was going to be fine.

Vanessa appeared just as Gage stepped out of the car. She'd been waiting, watching him while she smoked.

"You didn't think I could find your door?" Gage asked. Who waited outside in this cold?

"Lots of folks scared to come into our building alone," she said. "I was seeing if you were, too, without Jamal to protect you. Why you laughing like a fool so early in the morning? We got serious business to attend to." She had a backpack slung over her shoulder. She slammed the car door, directed him ahead, and coughed hard. "How many kids you got? What's your name again?" She held her cigarette palm-up, between her thumb and forefinger.

"Tyrone Gage. My wife and I have one girl."

She cracked her window, blew smoke out. "And? What else?"

"And," Gage said. "And I have a son from a previous relationship."

"What kind of relationship was it?" she said pleasantly, and indicated again with her cigarette.

"He's a junior in high school now."

"Ain't that sweet? Just like me. Who's his momma?"

"She lives in Chicago," Gage said. It had been years since Gage had been able to speak to the woman without her screaming at him through the phone. Celysha took the news of a previous child reasonably well; they'd hardly been dating a month when it came up, and now they only spoke of his son during Christmas week, birthdays, and arguments.

Vanessa said, "You all have shared custody, I'll bet. He stays with you every summer, and he's in Chicago the rest of the year. Get together every Thanksgiving, is that right?"

Gage cursed, then honked at a car ahead of him that turned without a signal.

"When was the last time you saw this son in Chicago?"

"Long time."

"I thought so," she said. "A long time. A long goddamned time." Her backpack was at her feet, her hands on her knees. She looked much younger than the night before, much more like a schoolgirl. Except for the cigarette. "Pull in here," she said.

"Another Orange Crush?"

"Not quite."

Gage wheeled into the First Independence Bank lot and let the engine run. She'd better be fast here. This wasn't the kind of field trip he wanted to spend the whole day on. But she didn't budge, just sat and looked dead ahead. Here we go, Gage thought.

"I need six hundred dollars."

"What you telling me for?" Gage finally said, his voice more tentative than he'd intended.

"Cause you need this procedure done worse than me. Jamal won't go to no school a thousand miles away and leave a baby here in Detroit, can't you see that?" she said. "If I have the baby, I have Jamal." Then, for emphasis, "You ain't the only motherfucker in the world with six hundred dollars, by the way."

She was a real box of chocolates. Alright, as long as we're speaking bluntly. "I had you pegged as a someone who was using Jamal to get ahead in life. Climb on his back."

She raised an eyebrow. "Just like you?"

"Why you cutting him loose, then?" Gage asked, and pulled at his collar. They always made the collars on these shirts so tight. "I don't get it. Next fall he'll be smiling for the team picture at State."

"Look, *coach*." She bit on the word. "I don't need nobody's help. I can get ahead on my own. Anyway, Stevie Wonder could see me and Jamal don't fit together. Jamal would've seen it too. Maybe in ten years, but one day. He's a precious boy but I can't be tied to nobody. You and Jamal aren't the only ones with plans either. I have to choose my career, which is not as no mother." She snorted. "I'll wait here. Leave me the keys for the radio."

"I can't get five hundred from a cash machine," Gage said. It flashed on him again that maybe she wasn't really pregnant at all.

"*Six* hundred. Not on no debit card you can't. You have to use your credit card. Try the machine and if it don't work, you go inside to a real live teller and sign for it."

"I'll get you two hundred."

She folded her arms across her chest. "Two hundred means

we going to K-Mart to pick out some baby clothes. They got nice kid stuff there. Pajamas with feets."

"Three hundred then," Gage hedged.

"I think it's a boy, I can feel it, so we should get mostly blue, huh? Hurry then, cause K-Mart opens at nine. We can be first in line." She turned to him with a phony smile.

The wind nearly blew Gage's car door shut on his leg. He shouldered it back open and went in the walk-up lobby, just inside the double doors. He didn't want to show his driver's license to anybody if he could help it. Three people were ahead of him. The woman at the cash machine had an infant under her arm and another child pulling her coat. She hissed desperately at the screen every so often, as if using voodoo, then started the process again. Gage dialed in Pytel's phone number on his cell, but the call went straight to voicemail.

In the car, Vanessa was having a conversation with herself, or that's how it looked. The reflection of the windshield made it difficult to see. Was she going through his daytimer or changing the radio station? He pulled his wallet out.

The woman at the front of the line turned around and announced, "Please excuse me," and began again, poking keys. Her older child broke free and ran to the door. She bolted from the machine, grabbed him by the hood, and pulled him back to the front of the line. The boy hollered in protest. Outside, Vanessa had her hands on top of her head. Was she still talking to herself or laughing? The lobby was hot. Gage took off his coat and waited his turn.

The reception area of the Planned Parenthood Center was pleasant enough. They could just as easily have been there for a sore throat. Gage whispered to Vanessa that he wasn't going to sign any papers. NCAA rules—he couldn't have his name on any documents. She took Gage by the arm and sat him down, kicking her backpack under a chair.

"Fool, don't nobody need your name on anything," she said, a little too loudly. Then she whispered, "I got me a fake ID. You must've just got off the farm. You a country nigger."

"Fine," Gage said. "Let's just get through this."

"Alls you need is to do what I say. You're doing fine sitting there looking stupid. You almost halfway done. Try your best not to lose your car keys."

Gage reached for some magazines. When she returned from the registration window, he offered her one. It was either the summer food issue or the world at war. She looked at the cover of the food magazine, back at his, and switched with him. He flipped through a section called "Poolside Drink De-Lites," then leaned his head back and closed his eyes. He needed to be back at the high school before 3:30 to make sure Jamal's core classes were in order, get the guidance counselor excited about Jamal being awarded a scholarship, and ask her to help register Jamal for another SAT exam. Gage opened his eyes when he felt Vanessa lean against his side. He thought she might be asleep, but she was reading—an article about Baghdad on the brink of collapse.

"Sondra James," a nurse announced, and Vanessa stood up. Gage grabbed for her before recalling the fake ID. The door locked behind Vanessa.

A woman crossed the waiting room to sit next to him. She wore a pink pillbox hat and matching outfit, Sunday clothes, and smelled of something. Candy maybe. Gage stood for a moment, adjusted his pants, and sat back down. She was plump and had the fuzz of a mustache barely visible against her black skin. For all Gage knew, the woman could have been Vanessa's mother. She looked like a kook.

"I tried to talk mine out of it until the last minute," she whispered to Gage. "Told her I'd help with the raising. My daughter's in there too," she said, nodding at the door. "Our children are beyond us now. It's in God's hands." She smiled.

"She's not my daughter," Gage said matter-of-factly.

"Oh. What is the nature of your relationship?"

How to explain Jamal Davis to this woman? And how his hopes—all of their hopes—were tied to Jamal? Let her think whatever, he didn't want to explain how great a player Vanessa's boyfriend might be in two years, so he spoke to the woman as if she were a sportswriter. "No comment," he said.

The woman gave him a surprised look and shuffled back to her seat.

Vanessa jarred him awake when she pulled her backpack from beneath his feet. He didn't know how much time had passed. She looked…smaller. Of course. Or paler, if that was possible.

"You ready?" she said, and walked away gingerly.

Gage followed, unlocked the passenger door, and took her elbow. She weakly karate-chopped his forearm, zipped open her backpack, took out a pillow, placed it squarely on the seat, and sat down. Gage closed her door.

He eyed her every few blocks. She seemed almost serene, hands on her thighs, singing faintly to herself. At a stoplight she took out the bank envelope and flipped it into his lap. "Your six hundred dollars," Vanessa said.

Gage let it sit, keeping both hands on the wheel. What was the catch?

"I paid last week during my exam. You got to pay first, fool. This isn't the dentist. I got me a credit card that matches the ID. Don't ask me how." She lifted her slim hips. "This pillow don't help me one bit, I don't know why I brought it."

"What did you need me for, then?" Gage said, and nodded down at the sealed envelope. He slowed the car to a crawl.

"What difference does it make?" She powered down her window and groaned. For a moment, Gage was certain she'd vomit. But she coughed, spat hard, turned to face him, and winced as she adjusted herself. "I told you, I needed a ride." She waved him back into traffic. "You was willing to do anything to get Jamal down there, and I wanted to know what he was worth to you. Now it's like you was paying me to have this procedure done, and I'm not about that."

She began to weep, but not like Jamal. Her tears were bitter. "This ain't me," she said and pointed to her wet cheek. "I'm saying shit that don't make sense because they got me full of painkillers and tranquilizers. Just drive. Don't believe nothing I say, I'm high on pills. You're driving like a damn old lady. Can't you see all those folks behind us?"

"So what are you going to do?" Gage asked. "When Jamal comes to State, I mean."

"I'm already enlisted in the Army."

"But you've got one more year of high school."

"I'm going through basic, going overseas, get my GED. Germany first, they say. I get my twenty years in, be studying business all the time, see? And maybe I'll go to college on the GI bill. Collect my Army pension and open my own store. A restaurant or something." Then, after a pause, "They not letting pregnant girls enlist."

Gage cut the engine outside Vanessa's. On the pavement in front of her building, three little boys were riding their bikes in a tight circle. They leaned into their turns and their own speed seemed to cause a sudden rush of wind. Trash swirled upward around them. Gage moved to get out of the car, but she backhand slapped his shoulder. "Leave me be," she said. She forearmed the door open, stood, and gathered up her pillow, stuffed it inside her pack, and kneed the door shut. Gage followed her in his rearview mirror, until she was at his side. Before Gage could roll it down, she planted a kiss on his window.

CUSTODIAN

Coaches like to point to the pertinent statistics: I retired three years ago, at the age of fifty-nine. For thirty years I coached college basketball, meaning a lot of seventy-hour weeks. The last four years were here at State where I still attend most of the games.

My wife says that she saw enough basketball to last her the rest of her natural days. Fair enough. I go alone and use a legal pad to note any bad habits I see us fall into. In the morning I construct my notes into a detailed scouting report with an explanation of strengths and weaknesses, as if I was an opposing coach and wanted to draw a bead on our boys. My replacement—a sorry excuse for a man named Jack Hood—asked me to do that my first year of retirement. It gave me as much pleasure as it had many years ago, when I was an assistant coach and just starting to figure things out. Thinking about your team is one of the joys in coaching, one of the few left for me, and I take pleasure in the mental exercise.

I mail a report of my observations to Steve Pytel, one of my former assistant coaches still on staff, although "thank you" cards are no longer sent in return. Yet, if I'm asked my opinion by a sportswriter, I'm never caught off-guard. Our newspaper still seeks me out for a quote from time to time, though rarely about our current team. More often it has to do with the death of a former coach at a rival school or some bit of history.

A new season has just begun. I've been astounded by the raw talent of a freshman named Jamal Davis and the improvement of a high-flyer named Leonard Redmond. The controversy over our accepting a thuggish boy named Nate Wilkerson has cooled. Despite this talented trio, it seems as if our team chemistry was concocted in a remedial high school science class. This season, Jack Hood is squirming because, if my sources are correct, his position is in peril. He hasn't been here at State long, although it certainly seems as though he has. I confess to a mild feeling of satisfaction watching him sweat.

We won a lot of games my first year here, and I made friends around town and gathered support. My teams never won a conference championship, but we did come in second place that initial season, earning an invitation to the NCAA tournament. That gave me some leeway with the fans, maintained the level of interest, and I was able to keep the local paper's sports editor on my side, at least for a while.

When the administration called me in without warning one sunny spring day, I was without a clue as to the occasion.

"What are your plans, Jerry?" my athletics director said the instant I sat down. I was too stunned to answer directly. The Chancellor was there as well, which I did not anticipate. I had to stop myself from saying, "You're my friend, Pete. Four basketball seasons is not enough time to make a change."

I recovered quickly, though, tabulated investments and retirement dollars, and had the foresight to make sure they'd let me keep my summer camp for one last June. "My plans for what?"

The Chancellor said I'd been a credit to the university, and he thought this would be a good time to retire. With the success we'd had my first year, I thought I might get longer to prove myself. I did not, and my retirement came earlier than I had planned. I had plenty of years at other colleges behind me, so I didn't force the issue and turn the situation into an ugly legal battle. This was to be billed as my "choice." I was humiliated with a brief re-assignment at State as a fundraiser for the very same Chancellor.

Few men get to choreograph their own funeral though, and I felt fortunate to help plan the farewell gala and press conference. I recommended good choices for speakers at this tribute—anyone but Jack Hood, who had already been named as my replacement. I even picked the menu.

My wife Kate wore a blue blazer to that luncheon, with the pin she'd bought our first year that read "Southern Arizona State" in 14-karat gold. She looked exactly like the woman I'd married years before, with her tiny nose and perfect posture. When we walked out of the banquet hall, I reminded her that she needed to follow me to the Buick dealer's lot. I had to return my sedan to the booster who had donated it. I remember a long pause after I said to Kate, "Don't be sad."

"This is the happiest I've been in years," she said.

I don't pay much attention to the University's monthly magazine, *The Sabre*, but the last issue did a feature on the new scholarship that was endowed recently in our son's name. Most Novembers they include a brief basketball preview, and I wanted to see that, too.

The "Farewells" section of the magazine mentioned that Athletic Center custodian Sal Rosales was retiring after three decades of stepladders and sack lunches. Of course that made me think about him and my own brief tenure (although we were never close). Sal was always one of the janitors working in our building, and we're approximately the same age.

The week I arrived at the university I had numerous questions about the basketball facility. One day the answer was, "Ask Sal Rosales." I found him across the concourse at the top of the arena, where he was waxing the floor. He was a short and wiry man. (Kate claims that I think anyone who is not a basketball player is short.) His skin was as tan as his work clothes, and he had rolled-up sleeves over thick forearms. I started to call to him what I needed, but the waxing machine was humming loudly. I'd have to step into his newly waxed work for him to hear me. I paced from one side to the other but the entire floor was freshly waxed with no path to approach him. The angle at which he wore his cap made it impossible to see his eyes and get his attention. I suppose that irritated me.

I stood there, waiting to be noticed, which is not something a college basketball coach is accustomed to. We were twenty yards apart, but it felt farther. I watched him work for what may have been five minutes. Lord knows I had plenty to do.

I'd been on the news all week, being introduced as the new basketball coach, and everywhere I went on campus, people I'd never met called me "Coach" and wished me luck. I believed that when Sal Rosales finally realized I was waiting, he'd be as helpful as everyone else. Except, I thought, he might have foolishly painted, or waxed, himself into a corner.

He shut off the machine, thumbed back his hat and studied his work. When he noticed me I raised an index finger, but he returned his gaze to the floor. I snapped my fingers twice to get his attention again. A mass of damp wax in front, and a row of black doors behind him, he was trapped by his own lack of planning.

I motioned for him again, and tried out my Spanish. "Hola. Señor," I said.

He grabbed hold of the wax machine and slammed his rear end into what appeared to be a solid black wall. A door opened and he jerked the machine through it and outside. The last thing I saw, he was coiling the long cord behind him as the door crunched shut. It was all in one motion and took maybe three seconds.

I stood for a moment—should I walk across his just-finished project, challenge him on his manners? I almost surely would have done that as a younger man. But the door nearest me flew open. It was Sal and his machine, which he still pulled backwards, the cord around his shoulder like a lariat. He wiped his brow with the rolled up part of his sleeve on his arm, then took off his hat.

"I speak English," he said. "What can I help you with?"

I asked him to let me into the coaches' locker room. His black hair was a little longer than I cared for, and he had a tattoo on his neck. At one time, it usually meant membership in a street gang or that someone had been to prison. Today a tattoo like that could mean almost anything.

"What keys do you have?" he asked.

An office and building key, I told him.

He turned, and walked away as if that ended our conversation. After he'd gone five paces, he called over his shoulder, "C'mon."

I hustled to catch up, not sure where he was taking me but figuring he would copy a key for me when we got there. We turned into a hallway I didn't know existed, and we suddenly arrived at the coaches' locker room door.

"I thought you had to go all the way around to get here. Up by the ticket office."

"Let me see your keys," he said. I patted myself down, and handed them over, but reminded him that Personnel hadn't given me the locker room key. Sal failed with the first, then opened the door with the second key. He flipped his left hand over, palm-side up, like the headwaiter at a posh restaurant. "The building key opens this, too," he said.

I reached out to shake his hand. "I'm Jerry Conroy. I'm going to be your basketball coach."

Without the hint of a smile, he said, "Sal Rosales," just as plain as could be. "I'm going to be your custodian."

The most positive aspect of team sports resides in the rebirth each season offers. Surely that would be true in my new position. I had served at a less prestigious college for nearly twenty years, until the late 1990s, and had a respectable record. My last year there, Lady Luck fell right into my lap—or rather, onto the shoulders and growth plates of my best player, who had sprouted three inches. John Henry Elkins measured in at 6'11" before he graduated and his maturation propelled us to the NCAA's Sweet 16 for the first and last time in my career. A month later I was offered a six-year/

six-figure contract at State. It was the grand payoff that seldom comes in this business and one that I frankly hadn't expected so far along in my career.

Coaching at a big state school brought certain perks. Some you'd expect, like an automobile and country club membership. Others were surprising. I never paid to get my car washed or to have my hair cut. I received a clothing allowance and picked the most expensive sport coats. I never seemed to buy my own lunch.

This period was also a different phase for Kate and myself, and by that I mean our marriage. We were alone for the first time in ages. Our son had graduated from NYU and moved to California, and while he leaned on us for support, he was still struggling with *personal* problems, as Kate liked to say.

"They're not personal problems. He made a choice and now he's paying for his lifestyle," I said.

She said that wasn't how HIV worked. Her calling me "judgmental" and "callous" only exacerbated the situation. None of this would keep him from dying young, of course, and that's precisely what happened although in the end it was a rare cancer that claimed him. In any event, that was the year he went to the West Coast for treatment, and we went to State.

Kate seemed to have her own agenda that first season. She was learning a new hobby, making stained glass ornaments. This project took up an entire wing in our new house, where we had more than enough space. Kate had never possessed an artistic bent that I was aware of, but she immersed herself in the stained glass, and our new home smelled of glue and soldering. Her hobby filled every window in the house, and I'll admit the stained glass was quite striking, and also that her talent surprised me.

The television exposure from coaching a team to the Sweet 16 insured that the players at State knew my face before I'd even arrived on campus. When practice started on October 15th that first autumn, I was as excited about basketball as I'd been in years.

My first few days of practice were relatively easy on the

players—primarily teaching days, explaining what was to be expected while we executed drills at a moderate pace. This was partly to avoid injuries. A long season lay ahead, and I didn't see the point of beating people down. Also, I wanted them to understand right from square one that we were going to do things my way. The right way. I also wanted them to get accustomed to reacting to my voice, and upon hearing it, to quickly focus.

This classroom-style atmosphere, along with my early emphasis on free-throw shooting, made my first practices fairly subdued. I had planned on each boy shooting one hundred free throws that first day, interspersed throughout the workout. Free throws mean quiet time at practice if they're done right, and I discourage even the assistant coaches and student managers from talking.

Maybe it was the quiet that drew my eyes upward, seeing the expanse of the arena from a different angle than the fans do. My son used to attend practice, at his own request, from the time he was four. If I halted play to emphasize a teaching point, he was careful not to bounce his undersized basketball, holding it to his chest. By the time he was eleven, though, he would discard his ball in the rack, leave the court, and climb to the top of the arena. My assistant coaches commented on how well-behaved he was as he sat quietly throughout practice. While I was happy not to have to reprimand him anymore, I thought it strange that he didn't want to stay close to the court and heave up shots each time we took a water break. Kate informed me, on his twelfth birthday, that he no longer enjoyed coming to practices. By the next season, he had stopped coming to the arena altogether.

During our free-throw break that first day, I looked around at the history of the gym. By that I mean the few championship banners. That's when I noticed Sal Rosales—heard him, actually, first. He was jogging laps around the concourse. I could only see him from the waist up, but he appeared to have his work clothes on and not a track suit. I made a mental note of the time. One thing that irked me for years was the aversion some folks have to hard work. All this is to say that I did not think Mr. Rosales should be out for a jog on company time. Every twenty minutes, we broke for more free throws, and there he was, plodding away. My aggravation built with each lap, and I continued to hear him whenever I lectured that day on ball reversal or weak-side help. When Sal Rosales finally finished, nearly an hour had elapsed, and he disappeared into the south concourse.

That evening I climbed into bed to watch SportsCenter. I set the volume low so as not to disturb Kate's reading. During a commercial, I muted the television to tell her about our jogging janitor. She lowered her glasses to the end of her nose and looked over the top at me. "Don't you have enough concerns without worrying about this Sal Rodriguez?"

"Rosales," I corrected her. "I do have enough to worry about, that's the point. I don't want to be experiencing a problem with the height of the baskets or arena lighting and spend time hunting a janitor who's off training for the Senior Olympics."

Kate shook her head and went back to her reading.

The next day I called the maintenance office at exactly 12:10, during the normal lunch hour, knowing Sal would be eating. I could prove to myself that he was behaving unprofessionally by taking two hour-long breaks a day. Maybe I could make someone else aware of his habits if he was at lunch already.

"My boys aren't getting much hot water in the locker room," I lied to whomever answered.

"Sal's around here somewhere," this other fellow said. "Do you want to talk to him?"

A wave of heat came into my face. "I thought he'd be at lunch," I said. I had merely planned on leaving him word.

"Sal doesn't eat," the man said. "He runs."

I told him to simply let Sal know, that there was no great urgency. I was wrong on that count, he was not taking advantage of the university, but I resolved to continue keeping an eye on him.

Another problem I encountered that fall were the lines on our court. Lines are significant; they naturally mark the places where defensive ball pressure is applied and help-side defense originates.

This may sound overly technical, but these are the kind of principles that are common at the collegiate level. I have always had the approach, when I teach my defensive scheme the first month of practice, to emphasize these lines as markers—lines that are on every court in America. The problem was this: lines denoting a volleyball court were on our floor, since their season was still in progress.

I should admit that none of my players claimed to be confused by the volleyball lines. I attributed this to their fear of being labeled as "bitchers," which I warned them at our first meeting was the worst label a boy on my team could have. I personally found the volleyball lines distracting, even irritating. After looking at them for a week, I decided I'd had enough.

While the players were doing their pre-practice stretching, I began my own modest routine: pulling up most of the tape that was used to mark off the volleyball court.

Because volleyball is a minor sport, they use a temporary tape that normally lasts an entire season. (I knew this because in 1986, the summer they implemented the rule, our boys wanted to experiment with the three-point line. I used the same semi-permanent tape to mark the three-point stripe that July. My team led the conference in three-point shooting the first year so I think the effort was worthwhile, despite the problems it caused my lower back.)

We practiced at two in the afternoon, just after women's volleyball finished. I had already attended two general staff meetings that October and didn't think I could stomach another. I'd heard the women's volleyball coach rise up at both meetings—when nobody else bothered to stand, unless it was to excuse themselves to use the facilities—and ramble on about equality this and equity that. She had a lack of tact that irritated me—and a haircut that would have made a Marine proud.

My new boys laughed when I pulled up the taped lines. A couple even tried to assist me, but I told them to return to their stretching, I'd handle it myself. They saw it as an example of how I would fight for them, my "circle the wagons" mentality, and they appreciated that, I'm certain. Some coaches will argue with the referee to get a technical foul called on them on purpose for the same reason. I've done that myself more than once.

The morning after taking up the lines I had a red-faced volleyball coach in my office, thrusting a roll of tape under my nose, and looking very much like a Marine.

"You go down there this instant and put those lines back," she said.

Ten minutes later, the athletics director knocked.

I knew the general rule on taking a new job: if you wanted something, get it the first year because after that you'd have to fight for every tube sock and bag of ice. I brought my A.D. to the chalkboard and showed him why the volleyball lines interfered with my teaching scheme, how important the floor markings were to my concept of team defense. He pretended to comprehend my theories on ball pressure, flat triangles, and rotations. And he genuinely understood that I would continue to take up the tape each practice until the volleyball season was over.

"I'm not asking you to apologize," he said, "just stay away from her. Stay out of her hair." We both had a good laugh over that last line.

Back at home, as Kate put the final touches on dinner, I related the story of the volleyball lines and my conversations with the woman coach. I mentioned how my lower back was sore from all the bending over the tape, hoping not so much for sympathy as for a backrub. After that day, taking up the lines became routine, the kind of mindless thing you do each day, like reading the sports section first, or calling your broker.

One morning in early December I arrived at the office before sunrise. I had in hand our players' class schedules for the Spring semester—their *proposed* schedules. A boy can get enrolled with a problematic teacher or a difficult class; perhaps a lab section might make a player late for practice. I had a policy of reviewing each schedule after advisements and making the changes I deemed necessary.

That morning there were fewer adjustments than usual. New

to the job, I still had to be cautious about overruling advisors. I was finished by eight and grew tired of waiting for someone to make coffee, so I took a notebook to the last row of the arena to get a head start on drawing up the day's practice plan.

The last row of an empty arena can give a man an interesting perspective. I've done some of my best thinking there, and I still go to the arena on occasion if events or problems need to be reconsidered. There's a quiet and expansiveness in an empty arena that I've heard some men find in the mountains of the West—or others perhaps while fishing. When Skip Johnson, a boisterous and lively point guard, died from a congenital heart defect at my previous job, Kate knew where to find me at midnight. I also sat there for several hours after my son's diagnosis. Early mornings in the arena are a time of clarity, and I find I am less emotional and more analytical at that hour. When the players grumbled about my first early practice, I presumed it was out of laziness. However, as soon as the sun was high enough, its rays shot across half the court through the huge windows over the east gate. At some angles the boys couldn't see each other, let alone the goal. We had our first and last morning practice that day.

That morning, with clipboard in hand, I sat at the last row near the windows on the east side. The court lights were off, yet the arena wasn't completely dark. Sal Rosales was bent at the waist near one sideline. I assumed he was scraping up gum or sealing a crack. However, when I looked up from my practice plan fifteen minutes later, he was still down there, on the other side, close to the ground.

The sun gradually blessed the court with a stream of light, and although Kate could verify that I am not religious, the arena was bathed in a golden aura that could only be described as heavenly. I rarely saw the court in this kind of quiet and never from this perspective in this kind of light. I put aside my practice plan to call down to Sal. I wanted to invite him up to the top row with me, to witness what I saw. The moment seemed so fine, I knew it was fleeting.

Then I realized what he was doing. Sal was putting the

volleyball lines in place, by hand. A foot at a time he unrolled the tape, squatted over the line and shuffled backwards as though he was picking onions. I sat back down to watch him work in his peculiar way. He replaced all the lines crossways, and then the lines that ran the length of the court. I remembered in that moment my own father, who was over fifty by the time I was born. He wore the same matching khaki work clothes and smelled of pork and garlic when he came home to Joliet from the sausage packing plant in Chicago. I didn't know then why he continued to work after the retirement age, but my mother told me years later: so I could attend St. Francis, a private local college that didn't offer basketball scholarships. My father's mindset—he was our family's caretaker—was one that I tried to adopt with my own team over the years. I wondered then what kind of family Sal Rosales had or if he had one at all.

Nearly thirty minutes had elapsed since my arrival. Sal Rosales collected his tape measure and scissors and seemed to have finished. He arched his back to loosen it, rolled his hips from side to side, then walked around the lines, gave it one final inspection and pressed each corner with his toe. He climbed up the arena stairs, which is pretty vigorous exercise, headed straight towards me. It could take quite a while to hike the thirty-eight rows to the top.

I did something odd then, although the reason was not clear to me in that instant. I suddenly remembered that we had absolutely no fresh fruit left in the house that morning, and I jotted a note to myself. Then I listed other grocery items we might have needed, even though I hadn't done our grocery shopping in years.

Sal arrived at my side, his breathing deep, but steady and controlled. He said good morning, with a strong emphasis on the 'good,' and thumbed his belt and surveyed his work.

"Those lines look straight to you?" he asked.

I squinted at the court. "Yes," I said. "They're just right."

Sal sat across from me on the aisle for a minute until his breathing leveled off.

That afternoon an assistant coach reminded me as practice began that we hadn't taken up the volleyball lines. There were only two weeks left in their season, although basketball was just getting started, and I told him not to bother. If the boys didn't understand defensive positioning by now it was not because of the lines.

My first season at State got off to a rocky start although we would quickly recover, and, as I like to mention, come within a basket of winning the conference championship. The boys took a couple months to wake up to my system, a typical process any new coach experiences. There's a language and philosophy players and coaches share, but like any learning process that takes some time. The boys needed to awaken from a fog of mediocrity, which I knew they had the ability to do. One reason I accepted the job at State was that I had done my research: the team had gifted young players and the potential to change for the better.

Two weeks after changing my policy on the volleyball lines, we suffered a bitter loss. I kept the team in the locker room afterward for over an hour. I could already hear the hoarseness that plagued my voice each winter from all the hollering and speeches. Although we still hadn't begun conference play, we had some issues that needed clarifying—girlfriends, parents, reporters, and wives could wait.

Every coach, from junior high to the professional ranks, battles the same cancer continuously: selfishness. I call it the "S" word. It will wreck a team if you can't get them to sacrifice individual concerns for a greater cause. My success or failure at convincing my team of this has been the single most important factor in each season's outcome.

In the locker room, shortly after the defeat that I felt was directly attributable to selfishness, I became physically demonstrative of my rage, ruining an expensive pair of shoes and breaking my big toe in the excitement. On occasion, I plan that sort of thing. Not this time. Looking back on the season, this incident may have been the pivotal moment in kicking those kids out of their slumber. The team never saw me act out again. In fact, never again in my career did I lose control as I did that night.

The next morning I again felt the need for some meditative time. Our team was at a crossroads. I knew we could go either direction, and anything I said could influence their reaction. It was during the Christmas break, and Kate was spending eight days of the holiday with our son in California. It seemed like eighty.

Her decision to travel was just as well, though, since the team was practicing twice a day for a holiday tournament, and I have trouble getting into the holiday spirit when we're losing. She was due back that evening, and I cleaned the house in the early morning, disposing of fast-food wrappers before Kate would see them.

Rather than stay around the house or sit in the office to view yet another game film, I made my way to the arena and the last row, with the hope that the sun would light the court in that same golden way again.

I wasn't certain which direction the team would go. They could fall apart. Or pull together out of respect for me. Or out of hatred. I'd seen all of these variations.

Sitting in my quiet spot, I recalled a quote that had gotten my attention. I do a lot of reading for a coach, or so I've been told, mostly American history and biographies. I often spend the last hour of each evening with a book. That morning brought to mind something Abraham Lincoln had said during the Civil War, and I started to limp over to the locker room on my swollen foot to write the quotation on our chalkboard. When the team came in to change for practice, Lincoln's wisdom would be the first thing they saw.

It may surprise you to learn that I cannot, for the life of me, bring to mind that quote now, and I have searched for it since in three books about Lincoln. What I do recall clearly is that the locker room door was propped open when I got there, which was odd for that time of day. Sal Rosales was on his knees, looking very Catholic in front of my chalkboard, repairing the hole in the wall underneath it. He glanced over his shoulder at me and went back to work.

"Somebody on your team needs to grow up," he said. I supposed from his tone that he knew it wasn't one of the players who kicked a hole in the wall. He went back to spreading the plaster mix. A can of white paint was next to him.

"We lost a tough one," I said, "and it got heated. Did you see it?"

"Fourteen bucks a ticket, family of four," Sal said. "Parking and Cokes makes it seventy bucks. I saw the highlights on television." He worked the putty knife in short strokes. "Can I help you with something?"

"I was going to write a quote on the board," I said. "It can wait."

"Why don't you tell me what to write, and I'll put it up there when I'm done." That would have been fine in most cases, but I was too embarrassed to tell him what I wanted up there—Lincoln's quote, which had something to do with grace under pressure and the survival of the Union. I told him no, thank you. Instead I found a folding chair, and sat with my elbows on my knees, as I did during a game.

I nearly asked how I could help. And perhaps I could have said, "My own father wore the same brand of work pants that you do."

That's what I was thinking. And maybe Sal would have asked me if my dad was a custodian. He might have said he had two kids, both in the armed forces. His wife maybe had a secretarial job at a trucking firm. Maybe Sal had been a wrestler in high school but had been too short for basketball. Physical labor brings that out in a man, talking about his past and his family. My own father was too tired to have much of a social life after work, and I wondered if he talked about his family—my mother and I—at his job. Sal probably had lived in town all of his life. He'd ask me how much longer I planned on coaching, something I thought about every day, but no one had ever asked me directly. I'd tell him some things about my son, and he'd listen intently when he stopped working for brief moments.

But we didn't say any of that. I sat and watched him work. Sal had lined the edge of the carpeting with newspaper.

He adjusted his clip-on light, switched it to a better angle by fastening the clasp to the other side of the chalkboard. He worked with the care of a craftsman, mixing the bag of Dura-Bond to help secure the hand-cut plasterboard he had fashioned. When he was done, he brought a small fan from his cart, plugged it in, and pointed it at the repaired wall.

"I'll paint it tomorrow," he said. "That'll look as good as new when it dries. It'll break easier next time though."

Who can explain why men do what they do? And why men incapable of bending gradually change? It is true I used to believe the work I did was important work. I'm surely not the only man who thought that, especially at a state university. I know now that everything we do has, if not importance, consequences. We make choices, and the results stick with us like a losing season in the record books. I suppose that is something each of us discovers in our own time. Undoubtedly Sal Rosales could tell you that and so could countless other men.

My broken toe caused me to hobble around like a fool for nearly a month. Maybe I needed that for some kind of lesson to sink in. I'm not suggesting I became a better coach because of this; the truth is I lost a little fire during my last seasons.

When I got home that night, after watching Sal Rosales repair my locker room wall, Kate was on the sofa. She had already unpacked from her trip, her empty travel bags in front of the closet. Her head was propped up on two pillows and Bach was playing on the stereo. She looked emaciated. A framed photograph of our son, one I'd never seen before, sat behind her head on the end table, a shot of him standing in front of a canoe with his Golden Retriever. There was also a boxed gift from him waiting to be unwrapped. Kate's shoes were off, and she had on some overly puffy slippers and a black turtleneck sweater that were also presents. Above the sofa in the window hung a stained glass Celtic cross she must have recently finished. Kate sat up. She said he was having respiratory trouble, was hardly sleeping.

"I got your message," I said. "You said he still acts optimistic."

"I don't know where he gets the strength."

I drew the drapes in back of her and switched off her lamp, but it was still light enough to see the surprise in her eyes as I tried to kiss her. She pushed me away, hard, at the collarbones.

"Our son is going to die soon," she said.

I told her not to be upset.

"You're a fool," she said. "I am too, but it's more than that. Or worse than that. Time is our enemy, Jerry. There won't be a new season for you to redeem yourself with us."

I try to take small steps forward. I'll be sixty-three soon. These evenings after the boys at State play, I'm home at a decent hour—and not with a bellyful of bourbon. Kate sets down her book as soon as she hears me climb the front steps, finds her coat, and we go to a 24-hour chain restaurant known for their pies. It was Jerry Junior's favorite spot when he was a boy. Of course this isn't the same location, but the layout and feel of the place are exactly the same.

Time is against us now, my wife was right of course, and the renewal that I depended on when I was coaching will never again present itself. I now consider myself the keeper of the family, which includes every boy who ever played for me. Most of my ex-players I have not spoken with in decades and it's rare that one of them calls, but when one does find the time, he's invariably from my last seasons. This seems to me to be some kind of improvement or achievement. More than my slightly-better-than-average win-loss record.

Yet the sport continues to have an allure, a pull, and that's something I can neither explain nor admit to Kate. After every game, I slide my legal pad of notes and diagrams into a drawer in the foyer—the "mud room," my father called it. I organize my notes the next morning while she is on her daily walk. We sit on the same side of the restaurant's booth and talk over pie a la mode and decaf coffee. If she asks who won the game, I smile and tell her I don't remember, which is what I imagine she wants to hear.

Jamal Davis
May 2004
Final Essay: *People in Conflict*
English 200 – Mr. Hartigan
Writing in the Humanities

This essay has called for me to describe a person, based on his/her actions during a conflict. The person I have chosen to write about is actually two persons: Coach Gage and Coach Pytel.

Gage and Pytel are the same age, forty. Gage is black. Pytel is white. Both work as assistant basketball coaches here, and both had been very terrible players themselves, "back in the day" (as Gage likes to say over and over and over). Like most coaches, I bet. Both are convinced that they have all the answers.

I have seen each man act when there is conflict and dramatic tension, which, as we discuss in this class, reveals their character and who they are. Yet neither man seems to be aware or maybe they don't care about how their actions are affecting people. I don't mean they're bad guys, just that they're complicated, which will make for a better essay.

While I was still in high school, I was faced with a major problem that is the emotional center and trigger of this essay. My girlfriend Vanessa turned up pregnant.

There are two other minor characters in this essay. Reverend Oliver, who you'll meet later, is one. The other is Tree Turner, my rec center coach who first connected me to the coaches here at school.

Tree is not a man of God like Reverend Oliver. They've known each other for years, but I can't talk about one in front of the other. Tree cares about me, he's helped my game plenty, and there's no way I'd have a full ride to college without him. So, that's my admission: I have depended on and trusted Tree for basketball stuff nearly as much as Reverend Oliver for life issues.

I should also say here that although my professor, Mr. Hartigan, has strongly discouraged us from writing about our religious convictions, that is part of what this essay is about. I mean my own faith, and belief in the Bible as really the only book any of us would ever need. So, while it will be a challenge to not mention the Savior by name, He was in the back of my mind during all of this time, just as Mr. Hartigan's rules are in the front of my mind now.

Mr. Hartigan's rules are detailed: avoid the cliché, try to get in scene, don't use exclamation marks and bold letters, hunt out the conflict in your writing. Look for trouble. Use some metaphors. And especially avoid the Hollywood ending, which sports movies have. Mr. Hartigan likes to look at me when he says that part, as if I was born in Hollywood because I play college ball.

The Savior's rules are also well defined and might take a while to get used to. There are two main ones to get you started: love God with all your heart, and love your neighbor as yourself.

You can see already where there's a conflict between Mr. Hartigan and the Savior (and maybe that's a whole other essay, *hah hah*). The happy ending that God offers us is too sentimental for Mr. Hartigan. The dialogue can't be fresh because we've heard things like the Sermon on the Mount over and over, or we should have. The Bible makes you think "simple is better," but we are taught in this class that complex is better. In my copy of the Bible, everything the Savior says is bolded in red ink, and I can guess what Mr. Hartigan would have to say about that.

Anyway, that conflict between God and Mr. Hartigan is brewing under the surface of this essay. I hope Mr. Hartigan won't be mad at the Savior for influencing this essay, and vice versa.

When Vanessa said she was pregnant, I felt like I was too. Not with a baby, but with the information inside me, only I couldn't wait nine months for all of it to burst out. I had to talk to somebody. Lucky for me, Coach Gage was on a recruiting trip to my hometown Detroit (shout out!).

All of us think our problems are unique, but they're not, and I was happy in a funny way to find out that Gage had also had the same problem when he was seventeen. Gage had to make a decision then too. He chose to make himself more marketable for the good of his own family, and he went away to college to play ball. As I said, he must never have been good enough for the pros or even Europe, and he wound up coaching, which is a way to stay involved in the game and make money.

After I told Gage about Vanessa being pregnant, we all sat down and had a talk about what was best for all of us. Best for my family, I mean. Vanessa got highly emotional and probably felt a little threatened, not knowing what a good person Gage was, and we discussed the situation until late.

The next day, Gage showed up at my house very early and offered to drive me to school.

"I'm going to do you a favor, Jamal," he said to me in the car that morning. "I'm going to take Vanessa to see a counselor who she can talk to about teen pregnancy."

This is where the first conflict came in. Vanessa talk to a counselor we'd never met? I knew that Vanessa and me should go to talk with Reverend Oliver instead. Not only was he a man of God, but he was an old friend of the family and a partner of my own father (RIP). Everyone says he (Reverend Oliver) was a hell of a ballplayer in his big-Afro, Converse All Star-wearing days. But he was also straight up honest and my own selfishness at that time filled me with a fear—I was afraid Reverend Oliver would tell our mothers about the pregnancy. I wasn't ready for that yet. Instead of facing up to Reverend Oliver, I agreed Vanessa would talk to this counselor. That was the smaller conflict.

I had a bigger problem staring me down with Vanessa being pregnant. I could choose between two options.

1. Marry Vanessa that winter and give up on my commitment to attend State.
2. Go on alone to college at least for the first year then bring her and the baby to school to live off campus.

Gage said that morning that I had some important stuff to think about. I didn't want to witness to Gage in that moment, tell him he did too. I mostly listened.

"You have to let the woman be involved in the decision process here. I looked up a counselor in the phone book, and talked to the nurse on the phone already."

"The nurse?" I asked.

"I mean some lady."

"Already?" By my watch, it wasn't even eight in the morning.

Gage said that this was a hotline that worked 24/7. "I just want to be up front with you and get your blessing," Gage said. "Vanessa asked me to step *in* and help by finding someone she could talk to when you stepped *out* to get her that Orange Crush last night."

"Vanessa didn't say nothing to me about it," I said.

Gage put his hand on me, and his hand was thick like a country ham. I'm half a foot taller but it seemed like that hand could crush my skinny arm. He was taking things with Vanessa in a direction I hadn't planned, and I said so out loud. But then Gage mentioned God's plan, and I had some contentment about not going to Reverend Oliver.

Before he dropped me off at school, I said I had been praying about this all night. Praying for him, too. I had hardly slept.

Gage thanked me, and said, "You're going to have to trust God to work things out for you with Vanessa." That helped. That's exactly what Reverend Oliver would have said anyway. Gage and I had never discussed God, but when he said that, I knew that there was no need to. Gage was going to help me and trust God. That was enough.

Gage told me another story from his high school days while we drove to school, then he took Vanessa to that counselor. They—the counselor and Vanessa—were supposed to talk about family issues, but also about women private things that I surely wouldn't have wanted to know anyway.

By the time I got out of school and practice, Gage was gone back to State, and my immediate worries were terminated. I went straight to Vanessa's, and she was there under her blanket just like the night before when Gage and I had showed up. She seemed happier, although she was sleepy, she said, from all the pressure and talks. Dreamy even. "You were right about Gage," she said. "He's cool."

"He talked to the counselor with you?" I asked.

"He's not that cool," she said. "I don't want him in there hearing all that talk about my uterus." Vanessa said we should wait; there was no hurry to get married that instant with all we had to think about. We had plenty enough to tell (or hide from) our mothers about without saying *Oh, by the way, we got married, too.*

At that moment, Vanessa did two things that I had never seen. First, she said, "I love you, Jamal," and that was the first time she ever said that. She wasn't no typical girl in that regard, or so I'm told, as she was my very first and only real girlfriend.

Then she smiled a smile and fell dead asleep. She looked peaceful, and who can ask for more than that? Not me, so I covered her up, cut off the overhead, locked up, and walked home. It's nearly a thirty-minute walk and it was plenty cold, but I was at peace too. There are some rough blocks to pass through on that walk, but nobody could nullify the good feeling I had, (I was thinking about "Though I walk through the valley of the shadow of death") and in that time I decided on a name for my son: *Oliver*, named after the Reverend. If she was a girl? *Olivia*.

That leads me to Coach Pytel. Reverend Oliver warned me about Coach Pytel from the start, said Pytel was a faker. He also said not to let that influence my choice of colleges because, he said, "the world is filled with fakers."

Since Pytel had discovered me, taken the trouble to drive to our summer camp, and was willing to attend our Gospel Rally, I cut him some slack. When Pytel came up to Detroit again the next spring, it was about a month after Gage had been there.

I don't care that unlikely coincidences don't make for the best stories according to Mr. Hartigan. Both of these men came to visit me during times of crisis, and that says a lot about God's will. And this was during a time when their own team was crumbling like a condemned building.

Vanessa told me the new crisis two weeks later, while she was sitting straight up on that sofa where she'd sailed off to her dreamy sleep.

"I miscarried," she said. "It's all over. The baby is gone."

I fell to her lap and cried like I hadn't since I don't know when. And this is one of the things I learned from Vanessa: that we don't always get what we expect. She was adaptable like that. Vanessa stroked my cheek while I wept. A while later, I asked her why she wasn't upset.

"I've been crying all day," she said. "You just now finding out."

Pytel was due at Vanessa's apartment soon, and I had to collect myself and be a man, with the death of my unborn child hanging around our necks.

Pytel got lost on his way, like Moses in the desert, except it was just for forty minutes. When he showed up, I remembered his way of walking—he has the knees of an old man, as if he'd spent far too much time around ball and his body said, "Hell, no." He's always pushing at his wispy hair that doesn't change its appearance anyway. Pytel was supposed to be coming to talk to us about summer jobs after high school graduation and where we might live when we got to college because you couldn't keep a wife and baby in the dorms. School rules.

Before he could get to that, I just figured I'd save him some time. I told him that Vanessa had miscarried and that there was no longer any baby to worry about. There was just the two of us. Again.

Vanessa has a tendency to come across as angry the first time she meets someone, but on this afternoon she just nodded to Pytel, pleased to meet you.

I'm not sure what I expected from Pytel in that moment. But I didn't figure he'd say what he did: "That changes your plans, I guess." As though we were switching from zone defense to man or something. No "I'm very sorry for the both of you," or anything, not that I expected him to lead us in prayer. And it did not change our plans all that much, not in my mind anyway.

But Vanessa announced, "I'm going to join the Army in August."

When the woman who was having your baby and being your wife one minute announces she's going to boot camp the next minute, man, it's a shock. I let out a cry that must have sounded like a baby, and suddenly I was arguing with Vanessa about what she was going to do with her life. She was just a junior in high school, and she needed to finish up school and not do something impulsive like enlist in the Army under duress. I was explaining all this to her when she turned around and sort of grabbed at the back of her shirt, looking for a tag she couldn't possibly see.

"Let me see," she said. "Does it say *Jamal Davis' bitch* on my shirt tag? Do you see that shit?" That was Vanessa. She could miscarry in the morning and cuss me out in the evening.

We went back and forth like that for a while as if Pytel wasn't even there, and he might as well have still been in the car for real. I needed his help, so I said, "Coach Pytel, what do you think?"

This is where Pytel showed himself different than Coach Gage.

Pytel said that he didn't think it was his job to say. I hated him right then, thought he was a coward. But that was no cause for me to be rude to him—although Vanessa sure wouldn't hesitate ever in that regard, but I'm not Vanessa. After her and I argued some more, and she suggested I go home and let things settle, I asked Pytel for a ride home.

I had enough conflict and dramatic tension swirling around in my head to write a whole semester of English essays. I didn't need any small talk. But I also didn't need any music, so I cut his radio off in his tiny rental car, one where my knees jammed against the dashboard.

Then Pytel said, "I just don't think it's my place to try to tell you how to live your life. You've got to decide." Which he'd already pretty much said at Vanessa's apartment.

But he *had* tried to tell me how to live my life, I said—he'd helped talk me into signing for a scholarship with his school a few months earlier. Wasn't that the same thing? I reminded him of what went down the first time I'd ever met him in July. He'd come to Reverend Oliver's camp way out near Freeland, just to see me. At our Gospel Rally, he fainted dead away in the middle of the service. The other kids carried him out to the river, where they revived him. Then he got in his car and drove away from the crisis, I said, just like we were doing now. That one was his crisis, but this one was mine.

I asked him a question. "When you passed out at church last summer, what happened? Were you hit with the Holy Spirit? Or was that all an act?"

He gripped the steering wheel with both hands. "It wasn't an act, I can tell you that for certain," he said. "But I don't know if it was God or dehydration that made me collapse."

"You don't know if God's hand knocked you down?" I said. "How could anybody miss that?" I never cuss, but it was hard not to then.

"I was under a lot of pressure at that time," Pytel said. "Maybe not as much as you are now, but I was exhausted and discouraged, and—" He sputtered, feeling for the words the way dudes who can't dribble feel for the ball—"overwhelmed by how pure everything seemed. Next thing I knew, I was lying at the river with that Reverend Oliver ready to kick my ass."

"But didn't you see God's plan in that moment?"

"Listen," he said. "We aren't supposed to be talking about *me*. Let me turn this around. Do you not see God's plan in what happened today?"

That was the first moment that I had been able to think about what had happened to me as God's plan. Although putting it into words made it come out ugly, which I honestly did not intend, I did it anyway. "You think God made Vanessa miscarry today? Like, God gave Vanessa an abortion?"

"That's an unfortunate choice of words," Pytel said.

"It was God's plan for Vanessa to give her an abortion," I repeated. I bit down so I wouldn't start crying again.

Pytel said that wasn't what he was saying. "Honestly, I don't think God had anything to do with it."

"Just like he didn't have anything to do with you being hit by the spirit and knocking you dead away."

"That's right."

"You were reborn in that very moment," I said. "How could you miss it?"

"Stop talking about me," he said. "We're talking about you. In any event, how could God have his footprint on me last July and not have the same footprint on you and Vanessa today?"

That was some heavy stuff for real. Like, did God want Vanessa to join the Army? Why would God want anyone to join an army? Would God want me to marry or not marry Vanessa? Could something bad that happened, or a lie, be God's will?

I didn't like any of these questions, but at least Pytel was talking to me about them. I said, "Maybe you can come with me tomorrow and talk about this with Reverend Oliver."

"Absolutely not," Pytel said. "These are things you're going to have to work out on your own."

"Coach Gage was a lot more willing to help me than you are," I said. "You should have just let Gage come back to Detroit." That was maybe a hurtful thing for me to say, but it was true. Gage was willing to help, and Pytel was only willing to talk and then drive away.

I was left floating. Vanessa would throw out the baby catalogs, and she'd replace them with a stack of enlistment papers. Our own mothers would be unaware of what happened to us, still going to Reverend Oliver's church every Sunday. I stopped going (not because I was afraid of Reverend Oliver like Pytel was) because I couldn't understand what anyone could call God's will.

Instead of telling Reverend Oliver what happened, I went to the rec center to talk to Tree. Before I had Tree on my side, little Michigan schools like Alma College and Hope College, places nobody ever heard of, were sending me postcards. With just one phone call to Pytel, Tree got a Division I school to offer me a full ride.

The next day was a Saturday, and I got to Tree's center before noon. I told Tree the whole story from the beginning: Vanessa, the baby, the miscarriage, the United States Army, the way Gage helped on his visit, the way Pytel did not, and now a university was waiting on me to enroll in the fall, a long way from Detroit. I confessed my anger at Pytel too.

"Pytel just left here," Tree said.

That made me mad all over again. Pytel visited with Tree, but not with Reverend Oliver! Then I thought, well, that was all right. That day, the same was true about me. I didn't say that out loud, because I knew Tree and Reverend Oliver hadn't gotten along for years.

Still, I asked Tree the question that maybe I should have saved for Reverend Oliver. "Do you think it's God's plan for me to attend State?" I asked.

And Tree said, "God don't have shit to do with ball, Jamal."

Tree said to go on to school at State, that Vanessa would either love me after six years in the army or she wouldn't, and either way I had a sunny future. But that one sentence is the part I remember best. *God don't have shit to do with ball.* I wrote that down on a card, which is in my wallet to this day.

I still send a letter to Vanessa every month, and I keep her letter back to me in the desk of my dorm room. That's not any kind of Hollywood cliché ending, Mr. Hartigan, so you'll probably like it.

TERMS OF THE GAME: PART I

Steve Pytel held the remote but he was not in control. Coaches-only film sessions before road games were a time warp; forty-minute basketball games morphed into four hours. Pytel had not yet called home. Although road trips were the norm, his wife seemed upset about his departure, like a soldier's bride who feared the worst.

"Stop!" Jack Hood yelled. Yelling during film sessions was a head coach's privilege. He ordered Pytel to rewind. Pytel thumbed the video of last year's Fresno game to a halt. Moments later, State's best player, Leonard Redmond, leapfrogged over a Fresno defender, legs splayed in an inverted V, and dunked.

Pytel ran the tape up and back several times. They'd forgotten about Leonard's breathtaking jump a year ago, partly because they rarely watched film of victories.

"God*damn*," said Tyrone Gage.

The three coaches were transfixed, reduced to fans, while Leonard Redmond soared, went back in time, and took flight again.

The team had flown west for a pair of games against Fresno and Long Beach, with a layover day in between. The players were safely in their rooms at the Fresno Marriott, supposedly asleep. The coaches were in Gage's room because, Pytel suspected, Hood's wife Vicky needed a quiet place to drink. The night before a game the team had an early curfew, and the lowest coach in their hierarchy, Ernie Lancha, was on bed-check duty.

The coaches had no curfew, and Jack Hood wanted to watch film. Pytel rarely thought of his boss anymore as Coach Hood or Jack, but always both names together—Jack Hood. Pytel had warned him when they scheduled the game that Fresno was a team they couldn't beat, but Jack Hood had been blinded by the chance to appear on national television. Now they scrutinized last year's game. Hood must have believed that if they rewound the tape often enough they might uncover a clue. Or a miracle cure.

Pytel let the tape advance, but soon they found another Leonard Redmond highlight. He seemed to have hydraulic springs in his legs—the inhuman ability to jump high and bounce back up quickly. When he missed a shot, he would often trampoline after his errant attempt to slam the ball home.

"We can watch game videos until our eyes bleed," Jack Hood said. "But if we lose Leonard Redmond from this team, you guys are through."

Gage smirked for Pytel's benefit, then dabbed at the corner of one eye with his wrist as though he might really be bleeding. Jack Hood had his hands clasped on the top of his gray hair, which he kept combed straight back. Pytel switched from "pause" to "stop" and nodded appreciatively, as if Hood had given him the key to a fulfilling life. Here it comes, he thought, the Leonard lecture followed by the Leonard pep talk.

"We can't outwork some mistakes," Hood continued. "Losing our only all-conference player would be that kind of mistake."

One scorching day the previous summer, Pytel had fielded a collect call at his home from Leonard Redmond's mother. Leonard had been arrested for selling marijuana, she said. Miraculously, it didn't hit the newspaper, the only explanation being that the daily arrests in Chicago might allow a black teenager to slip by unnoticed. Even the 6'8" ones. "Drug dealers wind up killed around here," his mother said, and seemed at peace with that fact, perhaps relieved that his arrest would protect him from danger. Had the crime happened in their university town it would have been splattered across the front page. Still, the coaches held their collective breaths—the story could surface at any time.

Leonard's trial was scheduled to take place in May, which meant he was playing the 2004 season with a possible prison sentence hanging over his shaved head. The team was enduring a bad year (9 wins, 15 losses, Fresno on deck), and the pressure was building. Long Beach State was next.

The team's failure was a mystery, but Pytel understood what that meant: the blame was already being assigned to the coach. Soon, Jack Hood would assign that blame to his assistant coaches. He was already blaming the players.

Their religious kid, Jamal Davis, just a freshman, was playing well. Their troubled transfer, Nate Wilkerson, should have been the best center in the league. He was not. At 6'10", he could slice through the lane like a switchblade, but he couldn't seem to get the ball in the basket, as if the trail of trouble and problems from his previous school jinxed him. In honor of his fresh start, Leonard Redmond had given Wilkerson a new nickname: "Smooth."

Despite this talented frontline trio, the team had not meshed, which left the coaches stupefied. Maybe it was because all three were underclassmen? That could turn out to be good news, and the coaches already spoke of how Leonard would dominate next year—if he was not in jail. If they could survive this messy season, they'd finally field a team that would qualify for the NCAA tournament the following year.

"We just need to survive this year," Jack Hood had been saying since Christmas. Pytel would lead the staff in nodding solemnly. Hood called the tournament "The Big Dance"—a tired expression—but making it to the dance stuck in their collective minds during this February in which they had gone lifeless. They'd all but given up on 2004, but qualifying the next year would mean a roll-over contract extension for Hood. And a death-row reprieve for Pytel and the other assistant coaches.

Jack Hood's main concern for Leonard was not jail time. Rather, it was how Leonard's problem might play out in the newspapers. The last thing Hood needed with just a year remaining on his contract was to get his name sloshed around in the paper for building his high-post offense around an accused drug dealer.

Details of the charges and mandatory sentences had filtered their way to Pytel. Once he tried to explain to his boss: "The problem is he sold it to an undercover officer and—"

"Relax for once," Hood said. He had a curious way of telling people to relax while radiating tension.

Leonard's best chance, the public defender told Pytel, was to demonstrate that he was now a productive member of society—a scholarship basketball player, staying out of trouble at a state university very far from Chicago—and throw himself on the mercy of the court. In essence, Leonard would show the judge his fall and spring term grades and pray.

Hood told Pytel to read Leonard's grades from last semester aloud. Again. Pytel carried Leonard's transcript around for this exact purpose, although he pretty much had it memorized. "Read," Hood said again when Pytel took too long.

Jazz to Rock. Minority Studies. Team Sports. Intro to Criminal Justice. Marriage and the Family. A perfect GPA.

"Fifteen hours of 'A,' which means a perfect four-point-oh." Hood held up a palm to stifle Pytel's reaction. "He'd better maintain it, or Leonard will turn out as useless to us as your Nigerian." Hood crossed his arms as if he'd just beaten Pytel in a game of checkers.

The door popped open. Ernie Lancha, the low man on the staff, stood in the doorway, a sheet of paper waving dramatically in one hand, like an annoying kid in need of attention.

"We're watching film," Pytel said and pointed to the blank screen.

"One of the players got shot," Ernie said. He quickly clarified. "Not one of ours. A Long Beach player."

Jack Hood told him to sit down and shut the door. Ernie did, but then stood again to read the fax, as if auditioning for a role.

> *Keith French, a forward for the Long Beach State University men's basketball team, was shot in the back while visiting his mother's home in South Central L.A. The bullet appears to have glanced off his spinal cord and punctured a lung, but the extent of damage is unknown—possible head injury from the fall. French is now listed in critical condition and remains in a coma at Los Angeles Children's Hospital. The shooting was described as a 'drive-by,' and appears to be a random act. The university offers its—*

"Blah blah blah," Hood said, splicing in his own conclusion. "We have the Fresno game to worry about. Fresno is good and it's on ESPN. I could give a fuck about Long Beach until after Fresno. Don't forget the first rule of coaching. *One game at a time.*" Each week the first rule of coaching seemed to change.

"Long Beach might want to cancel the game," Ernie explained.

Jack Hood looked from Ernie to Gage to Pytel. When no one said anything, Hood got philosophical. "Against some things there's no defense," he proclaimed. "Was Keith French a foreign kid?"

"I think he's the junior college guy from San Francisco City College," Ernie ventured. He didn't have a clue. Pytel's own modest playing career was not impressive, but at least he *had* played. Ernie's career, Pytel knew, involved sitting the bench at a small college and culminated in being team manager for Northern Illinois while in grad school. This background had only programmed Ernie to enjoy catering to the team's stars. Jack Hood was a prima donna and a prick, but that didn't annoy Pytel the way Ernie's *earnestness* did. Working with Ernie was like working with a fan, and Pytel hated his posturing. "Keith French is the freshman they picked up late in the summer from Manual Arts High School," Pytel said to Ernie. *Junior college from San Francisco*. Nice try.

"What was he averaging?" Hood asked.

Ernie flipped through papers. "Not much, filling in off the bench. Let's see. Two and a half points a game."

"Why the hell cancel the game if this Keith French isn't even a starter?" Hood asked.

"If they forfeit we'd win, right?" Gage said.

"Not on a cancellation," Pytel said. "Remember when we got snowed out on the way to Minnesota? Nobody got credit for a win."

Ernie said Long Beach *could* play, but according to one news source they had not yet decided. The Long Beach team met in the Children's Hospital parking lot just after they'd marched the squad in to see the wounded Keith French. Their administration wanted the game played, of course, because of ticket revenue.

"Figure seven thousand people, maybe more, now—times a twelve-dollar ticket," Hood said. "Parking and concessions."

Pytel did the math in his head. Over six figures.

"I was thinking," Ernie said, "we could let them postpone the game a few days. Come back out to Los Angeles next Sunday and play on Monday night. That would give everybody time to—"

"Are you insane?" Hood asked. "Give them a chance to regroup? We're here in California and they'd better play. Those are our terms. They'll be confused and exhausted."

"Should I tell our players what happened?" Ernie asked.

Jack Hood said what Pytel was thinking: "What for?"

Leonard Redmond had arrived on campus two years earlier, in 2001. The day he moved into the freshman dormitories at State, he appeared in Jack Hood's office doorway which interrupted the coaches' meeting. Pytel remembered it because it was the same day the assistants would lock Ernie in the vault.

Leonard looked like a sleepy-eyed child on Christmas morning. Of course, none of them understood then how good a basketball player Leonard was going to be, not even Leonard. He wanted to know if there was a pet store near campus. He wanted to get a puppy for his dorm room. The coaches were stunned, as though Leonard had presented them with a complicated ethical quandary. Pytel stopped himself from blurting out that a puppy in the dorms had to be against the rules.

Jack Hood looked at Leonard as if he were an escaped lunatic. (Later, Hood blabbed the story, cruelly, Pytel thought, and the players mocked Leonard for weeks. Then the games began and the teasing ceased.) The only thing Hood could think of was to tear the pet store listings from the Yellow Pages and give it to Leonard, who dropped down in the middle of their meeting to study his choices.

Meanwhile, the three assistant coaches—a model trio of racial balancing, white, brown, and black—slipped silently into Ernie's office. Pytel and Gage were laughing out loud, but Ernie didn't seem anxious to bite into the moment. Ernie was soft. He had the kind of bubbling enthusiasm that you'd wish for in a mascot, but not a coach. For instance, he played intramural basketball Monday nights with a scruffy collection of teaching assistants. Despite this unnecessary exercise, he was puffy with baby fat, especially in his face.

Gage, a black bear of a man, pummeled Ernie's shoulders and they laughed. *Leonard wanted a puppy!* They wrestled around until Gage hoisted Ernie in a bear hug and hauled him into the walk-in vault at the back of the office. The vault was a remnant from the days when the ticket office was inside the basketball arena. It had a door heavy enough to stop a car, and it took real strength to stop once it was set in motion. The coaches crammed uniforms, shoes, equipment, office supplies, and a library of game tapes in the vault. Because the secretary didn't have access to it, the tomb-sized space was a mess of boxes and shelves. Gage turned Ernie over and held him on the vault's floor, while Pytel got the door moving. Gage sprang free and left Ernie on his back, stuck in the vault. It was nearly soundproof, but it was obvious from Ernie's tone that he was still laughing.

Then Gage got called to the phone by their secretary. "Let him out," he said to Pytel before he hustled to his office.

That left Pytel alone to guard the muffled and imprisoned Ernie. Pytel knew he was fine, but after a few minutes Ernie's voice took on an edge of anger.

Pytel perused the photos on Ernie's walls. One was of Ernie with Michael Jordan at a kid's camp. Pytel could imagine how he cut in front of dozens of children for that one. Pytel sat down at the desk, waited for Gage to return. He put his feet up and closed his eyes for a few minutes.

Leonard Redmond tapped on the door's frame. He had his list of pet shops in hand, two of them circled. Leonard couldn't make sense of the locations. "Where's Ernie? He was going to help me," Leonard said. Ernie was the only coach the players referred to by first name.

Pytel decided to end the fun before Gage got back. He twirled the combination and hauled open the vault's stubborn door. Ernie turned from the shelves to face his liberator. Pytel held a finger to his lips and pointed to Leonard, meaning the game was over and they had work to do. Ernie brushed past Pytel and Leonard without saying a word.

The shelves had been organized into even stacks and tidy rows. It was as if Ernie had been locked into one vault but had been freed from another.

A week later, after the team's physical exams, the trainer informed Jack Hood that Leonard Redmond's pulse was forty beats-per-minute. Hood instantly dubbed him Leonard Deadman.

Pytel had gotten credit for uncovering Leonard when the kid was an unknown commodity in high school. Tired of the larger tournaments, Pytel had sat alone in a dingy southside Chicago Park District gym observing Leonard's odd sense of devotion after some pick-up games were finished. Leonard at that time was obsessed with trying to dunk two basketballs simultaneously. After thirty minutes he still hadn't done it, but Pytel was impressed.

He had not been difficult to recruit—his test scores were a disaster, and he hadn't qualified by NCAA standards until his last attempt. His questionable grades meant he was rarely listed by recruiting services, despite being 6'8". Pytel only had to believe his own eyes and sign him. Naturally, there were rumors about Leonard's sudden jump on the math portion of his SAT.

The coaches considered having Leonard sit out for a year to let him mature, but they were desperate. In fact, Leonard suggested to Pytel that the coaches red-shirt him, an unusual occurrence. Likely he had heard an upperclassman use the expression "red-shirt" and simply repeated the phrase. But Leonard took off like a 1990's dot-com stock, was sensational from the first game, the coaches congratulated themselves. The team floundered, but Leonard broke some school rebounding records. Despite their sluggish finishes his first two years, he was twice awarded the league's MVP—a fine player on a team fighting for their coaches' survival.

The morning after the loss to Fresno found Pytel with a thumping hangover. He needed to help drive the team to Long Beach. "Git your ass up," Gage had said when Pytel finally answered the phone. "We leave in ten minutes."

It was 245 miles from Fresno to Long Beach, and the athletic department had rented three Dodge vans. Pytel knew if State's record were 16-9, instead of 9-16, there wouldn't be any money-saving van rentals. On a tour bus he could sleep and nurse his miserable head. Of course, if they were 16-9, he might not have a hangover.

Road losses sometimes allowed post-game anonymity—no one in the bar had recognized Pytel. No offers to diagram a better offense or recommendations to recruit a seven-footer.

They had taken a beating from Fresno, as he had expected, live, on ESPN. Television exposure was important, but not a televised ass-kicking. Late in the game, Jack Hood had stomped around the sidelines in a frantic dance that would have gotten him restrained in civilian life.

During Stephanie's and Pytel's nightly phone call, she had spun their defeat like this: "Who knows? Maybe a good prospect saw the game and figures he can help you guys immediately."

"Nothing good can come out of a loss like that," Pytel had said.

"You don't know that."

"Trust me," he said, "I know."

With their fertility issues resolved, she was now prepared to move forward, have his child. While his emotional lifeboat centered more on the following season, Pytel was satisfied that Stephanie was ready. She was even becoming more interested in his job. "If I have to be a coach's wife," she had said, "I guess I ought to be a good one." Her phrasing had not thrilled Pytel, and her encouragement sometimes seemed more combative than supportive.

"You didn't wear that shirt I bought you," she said.

The shirt was pink, not a color for a coach on Jack Hood's staff. "I'm saving it for the Long Beach game," he said.

"Which isn't on national TV, so how will I know?" she said. "By the way, how does a new tattoo appear on Leonard immediately after he plays a great game?" He'd been sensational against Fresno and, despite being on the losing team, he did a post-game television interview. His new tattoo seemed to be some sort of predatory bird attacking a snake.

"That's not a new one," Pytel said.

"He's covered with them. Calves. Forearms. Shoulders," she said. "And that's just the places I can see." She was from Santa Cruz, California, Pytel often reminded himself. She did not know the first thing about black city kids. But in this case, she was right. Pytel had locker room proof—Leonard had more tattoos than sense.

Pytel wandered the hotel parking lot for five minutes before he found his van. Gage and Ernie had saved a spot for him, second in line, at the hotel's loop-around driveway. A simple task awaited him: fit his van into the vacant space. He rolled forward to take a stab at it. The driveway of the hotel was a semi-circle, which made parallel parking a challenge. His extra-large coffee mixed with the cool California air to fog a hoop-sized circle on the windshield.

The Nigerian player appeared in Pytel's rearview mirror—raven-black skin, strapped-on glasses, rigid posture. The coaches called him The Nigerian because his name was so difficult to pronounce. The players called him all sorts of things. The Nigerian circled his arm and nodded as he attempted to guide Pytel into the parking spot. Pytel ignored him and twisted over his left shoulder to avoid clipping the fender behind him. But he misjudged the last cut of the steering wheel and bounced up on the curb. Coffee splashed onto his pants and his yelp seemed to kill the engine. The white players on a bench looked up from their shared newspaper and snickered. Now his tilted van was on a sloping stage. The Nigerian shook his head and went inside the hotel.

Tyrone Gage stepped from the Marriott's sliding doors, approached the van, motioning for Pytel to lower his window. The plan was to stop to eat halfway to Long Beach, Gage said. He passed him a set of directions with a hand-drawn map. Pytel lifted his sunglasses.

"Keep those glasses down," Gage said. "Your eyes look like fishbait."

Pytel set his sunglasses back on the end of his nose. *Fuck you too*, he thought. Instead he thanked Gage for the morning call.

"Like waking the dead," Gage said.

Besides being away from Stephanie and marathon film sessions, road trips meant constant complaints from the players, bad buffets, and Jack Hood's unpredictable sleep patterns. Hood liked to break down postgame videotape until he was convinced that his own players were awful. Then he'd march the team in to rub their noses in it, replay their mistakes in slow motion.

Chauffeuring between games wasn't Pytel's idea of fun, either, but he appreciated any time away from the larger group. If he was lucky, he got Jamal Davis in his car. Sometimes the players slept. Leonard, for example, often dropped off instantly. "I'm not a coach," Pytel had bitched to Stephanie. "I'm a chaperone." His job was less about game-preparation, more about seeing to it that Leonard ate breakfast. Or he'd check with the tutor to make sure Leonard and Nate Wilkerson were in their mandatory study hall. Pytel might appear between classes to ask Leonard a trivial question, then walk him to his next course without saying a word. Like a mute nanny.

That night, Stephanie interrupted Pytel's bitching with her usual question. "What's the point of staying on this job if you hate it?"

Pytel came clean. "The point is that I love basketball," which sounded stupid, made him feel like a kid at summer camp. Did she understand, Pytel had continued, that he'd wept before the last game he'd ever played in college? She hadn't known him then, and she hadn't known him two short years later when he was the youngest high school coach in the state of Michigan. After winning the conference title, his all-black team (nearly every team was all-black) carried him across the locker room to ceremoniously toss him and his camel hair sport coat into the showers. Pytel still had the scar from from when he slipped in the frenzy and bashed his forehead. He kept a great photo of that celebration, with blood and what looked like sweat trickling down his face, above his office phone until recently. He took his basketball photos down because they made him feel too much like Ernie.

Stephanie said she hadn't known any of that, although she'd seen that photo.

It occurred to Pytel that if Stephanie didn't know he loved basketball, then she didn't truly know him—a jarring realization after four years of marriage.

"It's a shame that you've lost that…" She seemed to be searching for a word but never came up with one, and that had pretty much ended the phone call. Perhaps, Pytel thought now, she was right: he *had* lost something that was hard to name. His wife's concern led him to a decision. He would no longer deliberately gloss over his troubles. He would reveal to her his true feelings about the job and even admit his aspirations. He wanted to be a head coach at a big-time program. Why should he be ashamed of that? Just because Jack Hood had the ethics of an executioner didn't mean that the job required it. Yet, there was no point in rehashing his career goals after the loss to Fresno. Instead, he'd let their conversation dwindle away and headed for the bar.

Leonard came straight to Pytel's van, followed by Nate Wilkerson, who now insisted on going by "Smooth." Smooth had attempted just two shots and hadn't been much of a factor. Pytel flipped the radio to a news program in hopes that it would somehow discourage them. They piled in anyway. Leonard grunted at Pytel as he climbed aboard. The ice bags wrapped around his knees were already dripping.

The Nigerian reappeared, news magazines in hand. He was older than the others, spoke several languages, and his father was a diplomat. The Nigerian had his headphones ready in case the conversation was not stimulating. He liked his native Juju music. "That Zulu shit," Smooth called it. The Nigerian often rode with Pytel, but Pytel was not in the mood that morning for political debate. When the Nigerian opened the side door, Smooth—for once in sync with Pytel's needs—quickly reached behind and yanked it shut. He hammered the lock with his fist. Smooth popped open the side window two inches and leaned his mouth close to the gap.

"We ain't going on safari," Smooth said. "Find another ride."

"The other cars are filled," the Nigerian said. "Allow me inside, please."

"Listen to this sorry jungle motherfucker," Smooth sneered over his shoulder to Leonard. The Nigerian came around to the driver's side window to ask for help, clasping his hands together as if in prayer. Pytel was too weary to intervene. Behind them, Gage leaned on his horn for a three full seconds. The Nigerian shuffled over to Gage's van, a homeless man hustling a handout. He spoke with Gage before returning to Pytel.

"Man," Leonard said, "let him in."

Smooth unlocked his door and jerked it open.

Pytel set the cruise control to a conservative sixty-seven and took a deep breath. Smooth climbed up front from the back seat, all

6'10" of him slipping through the middle into the shotgun side. A hijacking of sorts. He turned off the news program and flipped through a CD case. He jammed in a CD, twisted the volume, then the bass. The windows vibrated. Occasionally Smooth would shout out a verse accompanying the rapper, then sink back into a bouncing silence, bobbing his head. Smooth grinned at his coach, not so much because he was enjoying the music, but likely because he knew for certain that Pytel wasn't. Each time Smooth looked away, Pytel nudged the volume down.

The Nigerian was oblivious, lost in his headphones and what appeared to be a copy of *The Nation*. Leonard wasn't asleep yet.

Something smelled bad. Pytel peeked at Smooth, then sniffed at his own armpit. Perhaps Smooth's practice jersey hadn't been washed. Or was it the Nigerian? He popped out the CD and cleared his throat. "Did one of you guys forget to turn in your wash?"

"It's me," Smooth said.

Pytel kept his eyes on the road.

"It's me for real. I decided not to shower."

"Seriously. You need to," Pytel said, assuming someone would give the gag away.

Smooth was straight-faced, as if he were standing for a police lineup. "I'm serious as cancer. Been three days. I needed to do something to get the coaches' attention." He sounded proud almost.

"You might think about getting our attention by rebounding." Pytel offered a smile, willing to believe it was all a joke. Just what a losing team needed, a shower strike.

Smooth looked out the side window and, as if reading from the pavement, said, "When y'all recruited me, I said don't bring me to no school where I won't get at least ten shots a game. I'm not showering until I get the shots you all promised me, even if we only got a few games left."

Pytel cracked his window an inch. "Have you told anyone? Besides me? What do the fellas think?"

"We behind him," Leonard answered for Smooth. "Although

we not necessarily next to him." They laughed, and Smooth turned back to knock knuckles with Leonard. Pytel lowered the window on the shotgun side.

Smooth had an audience now. "I saw that movie on Home Box. Bout those cats in Northern Ireland, the ones who starved themselves, wouldn't eat nothing. I'm a political prisoner, too. But I can't starve and keep playing. And I can't transfer again. I had to do something political to get treated equally. It's a political world," he concluded. "Ain't that the story, Jungle Boogie?"

The Nigerian took off his headphones. "Equality cannot be achieved without an assault on those with economic privilege," he said.

Leonard said, "Where'd you get that?"

"Malcolm X."

"I got a Malcolm X hat," Smooth said in agreement.

"Put the music back on," Leonard called.

"We talkin' bout politics," Smooth said.

"Fine, man. I'm not showering anymore either," Leonard said. "But I want to know when our new Nikes get here. We on ESPN last night looking like Northwest Lutheran Teacher's College."

"You got new Nikes three weeks ago," Pytel said. "For the Arizona State game." The new shoes had not helped that night.

Smooth shifted in his seat to whisper to Pytel, "Those are the *old* style, Coach. We had the same model last spring. They dumping reject shoes on us." Smooth spoke gently, as if Pytel were one of Stephanie's kindergartners. "You all got to tell Nike to quit taking us for granted. We want the latest, the LeBron James model."

"Maybe if we won more, Nike would do it. But what difference does—"

"All the difference," Leonard said.

The players would always be nineteen, Gage liked to remind Pytel. Gage would say, "If we can't outsmart Leonard and those cats, we don't deserve our jobs." These days it was getting too easy to tune the players out. Pytel had quit battling them, which was what talking to them amounted to.

"How are we supposed to feel," Leonard called out, "wearing dusty old Nikes? Don't the coaches think about our self-esteem?"

Smooth squinted and did his impersonation of Jack Hood. "You have to understand human nature!"

Leonard and Smooth howled. The Nigerian sat as still as a judge. Soon Leonard and Smooth were both mimicking Jack Hood.

"You're a selfish sonuvabitch!"

"The show must go on."

"Let's get some concentration."

Pytel shoved the CD back into the console, jerked the volume up high, and the pounding hip-hop drowned them out. It seemed to soothe them. By the third song, Leonard and Smooth began to nod off. The Nigerian sat erect, head nearly touching the roof, as though he'd been sent along to watch over Pytel.

THE JESUS OF COOL

My January project was the reenforcement of our old windows, so a sea of plastic covered the kitchen floor of the old adobe rental house. The desert gets colder than people think, and my December heating bill had convinced me to take action. I had to cut the roll of almost-clear insulation wrap with a straight razor and affix it over the single pane glass with heavy tape, then repeat the process a dozen times. Since the semester hadn't yet started, I wasn't hurrying around campus to make sure our players were in class. State had floundered through the first half of the season and there wasn't much reason to be optimistic.

Astrid walked right through the mess into the kitchen, a towel wrapped around her head. "Ernie, sealing windows on a property that's not yours is a bad investment," she said after she'd nearly tripped on a roll of plastic. She puttered around the kitchen, humming softly to herself, then paused to read the obituary I had taped to the refrigerator.

"Who was this Booker Robinson?" she asked.

I followed her back to the bedroom and explained that

Booker Robinson had been both a great ballplayer and my roommate in college. Although it was dark while she dressed, I could see her creamy skin, which had a spooky luminescence. Astrid was into ballet, not basketball. She didn't ask any more about Booker; she wasn't the inquisitive type, didn't know much about my past. I trailed her from bedroom to bathroom, back to the kitchen, and recalled some of the old stories. She raised her eyebrows but didn't ask many questions. That was her way, and I didn't mind.

For me, it's important to ask questions, be a student of something. As an assistant coach at a state university, I learned more than I taught, that was certain. I read a dozen newspapers online, and not just the sports section. That's how I came across Booker Robinson's obituary. Ten years had passed since Booker and I roomed together. He had been playing professionally in Amsterdam, where an incident occurred that involved a Dutch policeman. But the story was inconclusive—all you could take away was that Booker had died under mysterious circumstances.

After Astrid left, I exhumed my old photo album and picked out an action shot—Booker, with a serene expression as he ascended over a desperately-reaching white guy from St. Mary's College for an easy basket. I taped the photo of Booker next to his obituary.

Astrid had danced in the Chicago City Ballet, but put her career on hold to pursue a degree in Classical Dance. She was a bit older than your typical undergrad. Her goal was to be selected some day for the Joffrey Ballet, to make it big. Astrid didn't have to go to practice—she called it rehearsal—until the afternoon, but she liked to get out of the house early to get a coffee and run errands. Although we were still on holiday break, the dancers continued to practice, just like the basketball team.

I'd met her at the espresso café where she worked. We had Chicago in common, and we'd dated for half a year before she moved in. I told her she didn't have to pay rent until she could. She'd been bounced out of her last place due to money problems and planned to split our rent as soon as she got her equilibrium. The place was a little cramped for two, she said. I thought it was cozy, although our first month required some patience.

That evening she checked out that photo of Booker and read the obituary again while she peeled an orange. "How does someone go," she asked with her back to me, "from *playground legend* when you're living with him to *results of the autopsy are still pending*? Do you have that kind of effect on people?"

How could I answer that? It had been my idea to room with Booker, I said, when he needed a roommate after our freshman year. I was too short and slow for the game, even by small college standards—a bench warmer was the nicest way to put it—and the idea of rooming with a player of Booker Robinson's stature had great appeal. He was anxious not to get stuck with a religious kid or some other dud.

We were at a small church-affiliated college near Chicago, but Booker was already receiving a bit of media attention. He'd grown four inches since high school and was our league's best player as a freshman. He could have transferred to a big state university, but I think he liked the big fish/small pond thing.

Booker made great improvement playing in the off-season. The holy land for Chicago summer basketball was the Martin Luther King Jr. Boys Club on the west side, where I was often the only white spectator. The tournament featured guys back home from playing pro in Europe, a sprinkling of NBA players, plus a lot of current college standouts. Music throbbed constantly, even during the games.

The public address announcer was the first to call Booker "The Jesus of Cool." He would shout, "A soul-slam by the Jesus of Cool! Can I get an *Amen*?" And the whole gym would answer. Booker never changed expression and sometimes even looked bored, as if there was nothing unusual about a player from a small religious college taking the big boys to Sunday School. If you didn't know basketball—really appreciate it, I told Astrid—you would not understand what a graceful player Booker was. He had an innate feel for the game, as if it was all a movie he'd seen twice. Although he was 6'6", he had the body control of a guard. Booker would hardly perspire, and his cool demeanor wasn't just on the court. The way he strolled across campus was graceful. In the time it took him to get to class, I could practically complete both of our homework assignments. Even the way he salted his food was cool, never frantic, just tapping a forefinger at the top of the saltshaker.

After a game at the Boys Club, I broached the roommate idea with Booker and flipped him my keys. After I got in on the passenger side, he said, "Man, fuck no." But he smiled and I could tell he liked the idea. "I can't be listening to that weird music you listen to," he said, "and don't be leaving your shit all over the room and using my stuff," he said. Soon we were both laughing.

Booker loved to drive. He'd lean into the middle, supported by his right elbow so that his head was almost dead center, to keep the headlights of oncoming traffic out of his eyes, he said. I couldn't see over the dashboard the time I tried that.

"What are you going to do when I have LaTonya over?" he asked. "Or Patti?"

Booker had two girlfriends he juggled, trying to keep them happy but separate. Patti was aware of LaTonya, that's partly what made the arrangement so strange. Patti was married and white. LaTonya was single and black.

I lived in the dorms that summer of 1994 and was somewhat of a mystery to the gym's janitor—he'd peer through the doorway at me, wondering if there was a rule about practicing basketball alone at midnight or if the campus cops should be called. I set up our dorm room for the fall by stealing some matching bedspreads and drapes from the hotel rooms in the Campus Union. Just for fun, I hung a photograph of Booker I'd gotten from the yearbook office.

"The same picture," Astrid guessed correctly, "that's up on the refrigerator."

One night, just as the season had started, Booker forgot to leave his "keep out" signal on the door: Scotch tape over the keyhole. I burst in on him and somebody scrambling for cover. I backed out, apologizing, but he insisted I stay. My eyes leveled off and I could make out their forms in the pinkish-green streetlights that poured in through the drapes. The air was dense, soupy, and smelled of sandalwood incense and sex.

"We straight anyway, Ernie." It was LaTonya, which I figured, but I wasn't going to say hello until I heard her voice. "It only took Booker an hour," she added. He must have tickled her because she squealed and they squirmed around, the sheet flapping. LaTonya's leg fell off the side of the bed, her foot flat on the rug. As black as she was, I could still see her because of the sharp contrast with the sheets.

They whispered for a minute. She wanted to get dressed and go. I untied my sneakers and tossed my shirt into our wash basket. After more whispering, she got quiet for a minute and lifted her leg back onto the bed. Booker announced that LaTonya would stay the night. This was a first.

I stripped all the way down to my boxers and went to the bathroom to brush my teeth. When I returned, they both made fun of my shorts because the glow-in-the-dark smiley faces were now lit up. Booker clicked on his desk lamp, reached under the bed, and backhanded something into my chest—an official uniform pair of shorts from DePaul University, from a pal who played at the Boys Club summer league and was now a pro. I gave an extra yank to the drawstring so they wouldn't droop so much.

"Now you look like a player," Booker said. "Keep them."

"Wow," I said. I lofted a couple jumpshots at the ceiling and made a swish sound.

"Elbow in, baby," he said.

Our mattresses were set up in an "L" shape, meaning when we slept our heads were close. After I got in bed, LaTonya said in a singsong voice, "When you going to hook Ernie up with a sister? You ever been with a sister, Ernie?"

"He ain't ready for that," Booker said.

"Maybe *you* ain't ready, Booker," she said. More squealing.

I was in the midst of another dating slump, which LaTonya was aware of. She offered me odd tidbits of advice on how to impress girls. After each suggestion Booker would mutter, "That shit don't work," and there'd be more laughing. Booker often joked that he was going to "loan" me Patti soon—but of course he couldn't say that in front of LaTonya.

From then on it was cool for me, Booker, and LaTonya to all stay together. I'm pretty sure I fell asleep while LaTonya was still whispering advice.

The window-sealing project was nearly complete and the house already felt warmer. After practice, I'd spent the late afternoon going from window to window with Astrid's hairdryer, shrinking the plastic to an exact fit. The doors continued to leak cold air. They'd be the next project.

I had the linguini and mushrooms ready when Astrid got home that evening. I did the cooking, mostly pastas, and she was fine with that because dancers of her caliber burned carbs by the bowlful. She had a relaxation period after rehearsals, that was her rule. She went to the bedroom and didn't say a word until she'd had her quiet time. That allowed me to coordinate things in the kitchen—finish the sauce, open the wine, light candles.

"Smooth isn't coming over to eat again, is he?" she said when she reappeared. Our players weren't interested in socializing with the coaches, but Smooth Wilkerson was different. He appreciated the meals and usually left with a grocery bag of goodies and loaner DVDs to take back to his apartment.

"Smooth has lost his appetite since we started losing," I said. Although it was only January, we'd already lost more games than we had the previous year. Things were getting ugly, and Smooth caught a lot of the blame around the office. The newspapers and call-in radio shows blamed Jack Hood.

"He cleaned us out of breakfast cereal last visit," she said. "Let's not give him free reign of our pantry when he comes."

After dinner, Astrid put her bare feet up across my knees. If you haven't ever had a world-class dancer prop her legs on your lap, it's something to see. I'd learned the basics of Korean foot massage from her, and I worked away on her callused feet. She was deep into Eastern philosophy and had me reading Lao Tzu each morning after she left at sunrise. Studying it became part of my own breakfast routine. It wasn't exactly that she asked me to read it, but she often quoted him and left the book out on the coffee table. She explained a lot of Buddhist ideas to me about non-attachment and desire as the cause of human suffering.

I had became a novice ballet aficionado, sitting in the last row at our university's auditorium each month with a bouquet stashed at my feet. "The Flower Man," one of the other dancers called me. Who knew our university had one of the top classical dance programs? I even checked out an educational DVD called *Fall in Love with Ballet* from our library. Artifice plays an important role in ballet, it said, and I was intrigued by the theory that you never really dance as yourself, but rather as another character.

Anyway, I was supposed to keep quiet during the foot massage. When she opened her eyes, she said, "Did LaTonya ever find you one?"

"Find me one what?" I asked as I shook my hands out.

"A sister," she said. "Listen, the thing about Booker Robinson is this. If he was such a great player, why isn't he in the NBA? You make it sound like he was Michael Jordan but he seems like a jerk. And what's the deal with these women? How did he keep them straight?" She pulled her legs back and crossed her arms.

Booker got named "Little All-American," an honor for a small college player, just before Easter weekend. I remember because an all-day party in his honor was on Good Friday at an off-campus apartment. Booker left the celebration around midnight, and I returned to the dorms even later.

I was surprised to find Patti's long blond hair cascading off the edge of his bed. Patti rarely came to the dorm, so her husband must have been out of town. Booker usually visited her at home during what he called "business hours." Patti was kind to me, just like LaTonya, and I was the only one who knew their secret. She was an older woman, twenty-seven or so.

A stick of incense burned again in the ashtray, and this time a joint and a candle. Booker offered me some smoke, although he knew I wouldn't unless it was New Year's Eve or a birthday. This was his habit out of politeness, I think, and wanting me to feel a part of things. I undressed and pulled on those too-big DePaul shorts.

Patti mumbled a hello and pointed over Booker's shoulder. A tray of brownies was on the windowsill, which served as our refrigerator.

Booker leaned back in the bed and barred his arm, blocking my path to the brownies. "Now that you're looking like a player," he said, "let's see my Step Back."

This was his signature move to free himself, and he was teaching it to me. With a couple of dribbles, I rolled my shoulder over the imaginary ball, feinted with my left foot, stepped back, and popped a jump shot.

"Why are you fading away?" Booker asked.

I repeated the move, but tried not to fade.

"Sweet," he said. "Do a few more."

Patti rolled off Booker's shoulder to watch in the flickering light.

"That's my paycheck," he told Patti. "That's cold cash money." To me: "Now go left. Do ten more."

After I did, Booker said to begin with the behind-the-back dribble to get into the same Step Back move. I slid a chair over to make more room on the rug. He grew silent, propped up on his elbow, nodding his approval, but Patti began to call out, "Just like that!" after each shot, an encouragement she'd likely heard our players on the bench yell. I was ready to quit, but her enthusiasm kept me going.

A sudden *whomp* on the door shook us. It sounded like a horse was kicking the damn thing. More kicks followed, and just when it seemed the door might burst open, a woman's voice called for Booker, using all sorts of horrible names.

LaTonya.

I felt a panic in my gut. My bare feet were frozen to the

K-Mart carpet. Booker wasn't phased—he shook his head in disgust, mumbled something to Patti and patted her ass. They crawled out of his bed, naked as the absolute truth. Patti stepped past me with a soft smile, not embarrassed at all, mouthing an excuse me. She had a thin gold chain slung around her waist.

Patti slipped into my bed.

Booker wrapped an arm around my shoulder and calmly whispered to take five deep breaths and open the door for LaTonya. He blew out the candle and disappeared behind the sliding panel into his own closet.

My throat tightened, but I followed his instructions. LaTonya was about to take a running start when I popped open the dormitory door. She had fire in her eyes, but when she saw I wasn't Booker the meanness left her. She marched in and asked where the hell Booker was. Patti's shape in the darkness, face down, blond hair splashed on my pillow, stopped her. LaTonya whispered, "I'm sorry, Ernie," as though at a funeral. "I smelled my incense and I guess I went a little crazy."

I sat down on my bed and rubbed Patti's back. LaTonya clasped her hands like a kid saying grace, and leaned toward Patti. "Forgive me, ma'am," she said and backed toward the hallway. I jumped up, happy to escort her out. A goofy grin spread across LaTonya's face as I reached for the door. She put two fingers to her lips and inhaled before she wagged a finger to scold me. The dope was still flowering up from the ashtray next to the incense.

"You forgot to put the tape on the lock," she hissed. I grabbed the tape dispenser and followed LaTonya out. She startled me by slapping me hard on the butt. "You're sweating, Ernie," she said. "You must be gettin' it on. You don't need my advice after all." She gave me a kiss on the cheek, told me to have Booker call her, and clacked down the hallway in her heels.

I was stupidly putting the tape over the lock on the open door when the campus police officers appeared from the other direction.

"Where's the party?" one of the cops asked as he badged me.

Astrid's mother came to visit the next week from Chicago on a cheap post-holiday ticket. Her mother had been telling Astrid that she wanted to meet me. We went to pick her up for a late dinner at the Hilton. I was conscious of making a good first impression, and okay, I was agitated because I waited for an hour at the barber that afternoon despite having an appointment. Also this: while cleaning up around our bedroom I found an old article about Astrid's potential as a dancer. It was actually from her high school newspaper, and I used a magnet to put it up right next to Booker. She tore it down the instant she saw it, didn't think it was funny at all. So Astrid wasn't exactly sunshiney to begin with either.

When we arrived at the hotel, Astrid grabbed my wrist before I could shut the ignition off. She said wait here a minute, she'd be right back. She hustled up the driveway and vanished into the lobby.

I must have misunderstood—I assumed we were eating at the hotel. The car hummed blindly in the cold January night while I twirled the radio dial. She'd brought along part of the newspaper, but it was only the classifieds. After ten minutes, still no Astrid. When she finally reappeared, she was alone.

"Let's go," she said, and added that it wasn't a good night for her mom. I gave her an annoyed look because this wasn't my idea in the first place. Also, I'd traded duties with another assistant coach to cover our study hall that evening.

"What do you mean, not a good night? She doesn't want to meet me?"

Astrid didn't want to talk about it. So I sulked a while, until I got the idea to do her peaceful visualization technique, relaxing each muscle from head to foot. A rare snowfall began, so I slowed the car.

I must have been thinking of Booker again, because I knew exactly what she meant when she said, "So that's why it took you six years to finish college?" At least she'd finally started to take an interest in Booker's story. I could feel her eyes on me as I drove.

"The coach booted me off the basketball team immediately,"

I said. The next week I faced a student trial in the administration building, where one of the jurors wanted to know how often I "took pot." They asked me twice if I had anything to say on my own behalf, but I declined. I admitted I was guilty and was expelled from school.

"For Booker's sins," Astrid said.

In a strange way, I was proud to tell her this part. It gave me a history, some scars, some character. The rumors were out of control after my arrest. Here I was, Mister Dedicated, caught with dope and this exotic blonde. Patti stayed in my bed the whole time the cops questioned me, our door wide open, every light in the room on, the sheet clinched in her fist at her chin. Evidently having a naked blonde in the room was enough of a distraction to keep the cops from searching the closet and finding Booker. I had to dig out Patti's ID from her purse which was under Booker's bed. One of the cops held her license up to her cheek for a lot longer than he needed to, then handed it back to me. They made me place the joint into a plastic bag and took me away by the scruff of the neck.

Patti said, "Bye Ernie!" as if I was boarding a bus to summer camp. Just outside the room, the cop who'd studied Patti's ID bopped me on the back of the head. "You didn't even kiss her good-bye."

In the hallway stood three loser stoners, checking out Patti and the drama, offering me silent support like brothers I didn't know I had.

Astrid and I were almost home. When snow falls in the desert, the moisture mixes with the sandy streets, so you have to be careful not to spin the wheels. I stopped in front of our house but left the engine running. She was quiet for a long minute, letting my story sink in.

"I can't believe they nailed you," she said. "Why didn't Booker come forward and say it was his dope and his fault? Who cares if those bimbos found out about each other?"

"He had a possible pro career to worry about," I said. "We did what we had to do."

She was looking at me like I was her trig homework and things didn't add up. She leaned across and cut off the car's engine. "Listen to me," she said. "Ernie. You're a nice guy. I'm not saying you're not. But you can't put that kind of faith in someone. You have to investigate people before you start leading their parade. Booker Robinson wasn't the Jesus of anything, I know that." Now she sounded like she pitied me, which wasn't my intention at all. But she didn't get out of the car. Instead, she waited to hear the rest.

After my expulsion from school, I said, I went back to the dorm to load up my Maverick and say good-bye to Booker. He said he'd be waiting to hear the verdict, but there was a note taped to the door saying to call him at LaTonya's place. I tried for an hour, but never got through, and she lived way on the south side. I packed up and left Booker my parents' number.

"That was it? After the sacrifice you made?" Astrid said.

That wasn't it, I told her. The guys on the team organized a huge party for me that night at the Hollywood Tap, our local bar.

The party was unbelievable. I didn't tell her the rest, how they'd hired a topless dancer. Or that Booker didn't show. One of our guys had stolen my game jersey from the equipment room and they presented it to me near the end of the evening in a drunken ceremony. After I put it on, all the guys signed it with a permanent marker. Since I was a substitute and never took off my warm-ups, hardly anybody had seen me wearing the uniform; that was the big joke. I drank until they carried me to the car, where they threw me in the back seat and drove to our dorm room—Booker's room now. We wanted to get Booker's signature on the jersey, too, but he still wasn't around. Instead, we went to the statue outside the student union and pissed at the base of it.

I took a year off school and commuted from home to Northern Illinois for my last three years, where I began my coaching career as their team manager.

I never did see Booker again, but I didn't tell Astrid that either. Instead I told her what I'd learned that day: that he'd been killed on his bicycle when he swerved to avoid an Amsterdam policeman. And I showed her the Van Gogh postcard I'd found at the bottom of a box. He'd posted it from Holland a few years earlier.

The car was off, but Astrid had her mittens on the dash, elbows locked, as if we were going to crash. The neighbors would have thought someone was being dropped off.

After she tired of her book, Astrid went back to the bedroom to change into the loose-fitting outfit she slept in, old dancing rehearsal gear. She did her twenty-minute stretching routine. While I continued to read, she slowly went through a couple of steps that needed work.

At one point, she executed an impressive *penché*, the extreme arabesque, with her back leg all the way up and out. I complimented her on her terrific extension.

She said thanks, but froze. "Wait," she said. "Just how do you know what a perfect *penché* is?"

"Your hands were nearly touching the floor," I said. "I could really feel the energy flowing through your fingertips and toes."

Astrid stood for a second, her hands on her hips. She said, "I'm still not thrilled with it. Anyway, I feel off balance for some reason." She smiled, just for a second, and went back to working on the *penché*. But I could tell she was thinking about what I had said—she'd glance over at me from time to time. Her shoulders filled with pride and she repeated the move, and each time she put a bit more effort into the steps until she was really perspiring. "Thanks, by the way," she said after a while.

Later that night when she was asleep, I got up to get some water. I nearly broke my toe on the suitcase she'd been living out of since she'd moved in, but I stifled a yelp and hobbled down the hallway. For the first time that winter the house actually felt too warm. I went outside to sit on the back porch and take in the view of St. Jude's elementary school across the yard. The temperature was below freezing, but no wind at all, just a nativity-like winter calm. That kind of cold can feel like a slap in the face, but it was so peaceful the chill didn't bother me, even with my bare chest and basketball shorts.

When I came back inside I studied the photo on the refrigerator. Booker was still soaring eternally upward. The stuff Astrid said about Booker—and about me—kept repeating in my head like a chant. She was right, I had gotten overextended with him and things wound up a little one-sided. But what was the point of being bitter about that now? I'd learned a lot living shoulder-to-shoulder with the best player in school history. Not everything was going to end up the way you hoped. I knew that much, even in college.

TERMS OF THE GAME: PART II

Like giant magnets, towering fast-food signs pulled Steve Pytel's van off the interstate. Smooth reached back and shook Leonard awake. Pytel reminded the players to synchronize watches or cell phones and set a departure time. They could pick their own spot among the four restaurants, a policy that didn't exactly promote togetherness, but it limited complaining and allowed Pytel to slip away unnoticed.

He dug through his shoulder bag for more ibuprofen and something to read, stalling so he could select the least popular spot. The Nigerian and Smooth made off for Arby's. Pytel pulled out an *LA Times* and locked the van. When he turned around, there was Leonard.

"You guys got meal money yesterday," Pytel said.

"I know, I'm straight. Where you gonna eat?"

"I haven't decided."

"I'll go with you," Leonard said.

The more attention the coaches gave Leonard, the more he avoided them, so Pytel was taken aback. Leonard tore the plastic wrap off his melting ice bags as though they were shackles. He pitched the watery sacks underneath the van.

The Nigerian was the only player content to eat alone, his book spread open, hunched over, cleaning his glasses between bites. Oddly, the Nigerian was now chummy with Smooth. And Leonard wanted Pytel's companionship.

"You see that girl, Coach?" Leonard asked, dropping in across from him with his tray. "At the counter. See how she looked at me?" Leonard fancied himself a ladies' man. One of his tattoos boasted about it. He took a bite of Pytel's fries.

"Order your own," Pytel said and pulled them back, his voice higher than he intended.

"But did you see her check me out?" Leonard asked, his mouth full.

"Okay, how?"

"Like she's into me," he said, eyeing the girl. "Damn, now look at her."

Pytel turned. Their churchgoing freshman, Jamal Davis, seemed to be writing his phone number down for the girl. "I taught that boy too well," Leonard said.

A pile of trash grew between them: wrappers, bags, empty sugar and ketchup packets. One swift motion would wipe it clean.

Outside, the other two vans of players arrived. Any chance for a quiet lunch was gone.

Leonard said, "You think I should still try and talk to her?"

"No," he said.

"Why you coaches always gotta be so negative?"

"How's school?" Pytel countered.

"You mean my classes?"

"You've really got to hump it," Pytel said. "You can't miss. You know what's at stake."

"I'm missing classes today," Leonard said.

"Be sure to sit in the front and keep up with your assignments."

"They not giving me no homework." Leonard shrugged.

"Did you stay after in Criminal Justice and talk to Dr.

Wesson on Monday?" Pytel asked. Wesson was their ace, an older prof who liked athletes.

Leonard nodded yes. "He wants me to change my free throw." He lifted his left arm, shot an imaginary free throw. Then he launched another.

"How long did you two talk?" This was a good barometer. Wesson could be temperamental.

"Half hour, I guess."

"Great," Pytel said.

Leonard finished his food and crushed the wrappers. "What's going to happen to me?"

It took a moment to register with Pytel: Leonard was worried about his upcoming trial. "Like I said, you just need to hold up your end. Make grades."

"What if I'm found guilty anyway? What then?"

Pytel took a big bite and tried to talk through it. "A judge is supposed to use judgment. If you're found guilty, we hope the judge considers your grades."

"See, that's what I don't like." Leonard stacked his trash into two neat piles. "We *hope* the judge. We hope. I can't be hanging onto hope."

What choice do you have? Pytel thought.

Leonard said, "I heard there's countries I could play in that wouldn't care about me selling weed."

"Who told you that?" Pytel immediately figured it was Ernie. This wasn't an alternative Leonard would have come up with on his own.

"And that I could make decent money and have a real career overseas."

"That would ruin your chances at the NBA," Pytel said. Leonard was good enough to make a living in Europe or South America, as young as he was, but was not likely good enough for the NBA.

"I'm talking bout staying out of jail," Leonard said, "and you waving the NBA in my face." He rose from the table and took the trash with him.

Pytel recalled something Stephanie had said. She was home when Leonard's mother called about the arrest. Stephanie had taken an interest in Leonard's plight. "Is Leonard up for this so-called academic challenge?" she'd asked. "I mean, what did you enroll him in? *Addition and Subtraction? The Poetry of Phil Jackson?*" They had been in bed, naked, and neither of them very satisfied after a bout of perfunctory sex.

"Would you rather we let the prison system rehabilitate him?" Pytel asked.

"Don't get curt with me," she said. "I was the one who said Leonard would have a better chance of succeeding being in school, not in jail."

"He'll get off when the judge sees his grades. Maybe he'll have to do some community service next summer."

Leonard reappeared with a milkshake in hand, and slid down across from Pytel again. He pointed at the counter and said, "I hate when a bitch acts like she knows more than I do. Let's go."

The Nigerian was outside, his carryout cradled, waiting for Pytel to unlock the van. All he needed was the sign: *Will Play for Food.* A book would soon double as his makeshift table. He was a slow eater but polite enough not to make the others wait.

Leonard's dark face brightened seeing the Nigerian again. "Jungle Boogie," Leonard called.

Long Beach was less than two hours away. Pytel would be able to squeeze an hour nap in before practice.

Ernie strolled out of another restaurant with his crew of players. He laughed as if they'd beaten Fresno the night before and he'd been the hero. One of the players had his arm around Ernie's shoulder, conspiring with him. Had they been on streets of a big city, Ernie would have been having his pocket picked.

A Mercedes passed the van. Leonard came to life. "Coach Py. Speed up. Catch that Benz. That's the new model just came out."

Pytel groaned. He signaled to get over and, not trusting the side mirror, twisted back. The xeroxed directions to Long Beach fell from his lap.

Leonard and Smooth both pivoted in their seats to be his eyes as he switched lanes. "Chill. Chill," Leonard called out as cars passed. "You *got* it. Go!"

"Get on your horse, Coach Pytel," Smooth said. "We ain't gonna catch him going this slow."

Pytel gave this a half-effort, accelerated slightly to seventy-two. He wasn't going to be bullied. But the Mercedes seemed to be slowing, as if to accommodate the players. They'd catch up with it soon enough.

Pytel said, "Is this all you guys think about? There's a lot more—"

"Is *what* all we think about?" Leonard asked, feigning innocence.

"Cars. Material things."

The comment was just the kind Smooth would bite into. "You driving a new vehicle back home," Smooth said. "Which we ain't."

"They give that to me," Pytel protested. "I don't pay for that car."

The Nigerian removed his headphones. "Not paying yet advertising for the corporation," he said.

"Yo, look at that bitch," Smooth gasped. "The tail lights are different. They changed the design."

"I don't want him to think we're harassing him," Pytel said, and drifted back to the right lane.

"I couldn't have no color like that," Smooth said. "I'd get gun-metal blue. He got the wrong color leather seats, too. Black gets hot in the sun."

"Don't leave it in the sun," Leonard said. "You a mark."

"Coach, pull up some more. Let's see this stud."

Soon they were parallel. The players were nearly in Pytel's lap, straining to get a better look. He had to bar his right arm to hold Smooth away from the steering wheel. It took all his strength, forearm against ribs. Leonard pressed his forehead to the window directly behind Pytel's head.

"Look at old boy! Look at your brother, coach," Smooth shouted. Behind the wheel of the Mercedes was a man of about thirty. He had hair like—who? Elvis? His tight horizontally-striped shirt was not quite a tank top, and exposed most of his thin arms. The driver blew them a kiss and fluttered his ringed fingers, as if to say "toodeloo," and sped off.

The players howled. Leonard pounded Pytel's shoulders from behind, as if the joke were on him.

"Dude was a straight-up faggot," Smooth said.

"Catch him again, Coach Py!"

"Forget about it."

"Let's see if he'll ride with us. C'mon, Coach."

"We'll stick him in the back with Leonard. We can offer him tickets."

Pytel knew it was what coaches call a "teachable moment." What was the deal, he could have asked, with their narrow view of gay men? Oppressed minorities and all that. But he left it alone. He could just hear Leonard later, "Man, Coach Pytel was *defending* this faggot."

Leonard rolled his jacket into a makeshift pillow, leaned against the window and went to sleep, as though he couldn't be bothered with the day-to-day hassles any longer. Probably he was exhausted from carrying the entire program while his teammates and coaches struggled for breath. Instinct, that was how Leonard Redmond got by. Regardless of how much they confused him during film sessions, he continued to improve. "I'm obsolete," Pytel had told Stephanie once. "Leonard doesn't need to be coached."

"Everyone needs to be coached," Stephanie replied.

When Pytel was sure Smooth and Leonard were all asleep, he cut off the music. The Nigerian was reading.

The jolt of the driveway at the Long Beach Hilton woke Smooth, but not Leonard. Pytel ejected the CD, handed it to Smooth, then looked back at Leonard. The guy could doze off in an orgy. The Nigerian touched Leonard's shoulder, squeezed, and patted his back gently. Leonard's eyelids slid up as slowly as a sunrise.

They'd beaten the rest of the team. Pytel tried to sign for their keys but the rooms weren't yet ready. The four of them were stranded in the massive lobby. The furniture was as plush as in Jack Hood's office. He flopped onto one of the fancy sofas. He could have retrieved the *LA Times* from the van but decided not to bother. He punched Stephanie's number into his cell phone and left her a message.

Soon Ernie and Gage trudged in with their players. Ernie was loaded with luggage, probably hauling one of the player's bags. Some went into the hotel's gift shop. Ernie was at the bellhop stand near the registration counter.

In the corner, the Nigerian sat at a small table with Leonard. The Nigerian was Leonard's backup forward; they were State's version of *The Odd Couple*. Ernie approached them, gave the pair a newspaper and walked away.

The two huddled over the paper for a minute. They went back to a book the Nigerian cradled as if it were a globe. Maybe it was algebra they were working on. Or Spanish. Although there was no chance that the two would have been in the same classes. Their heads were nearly touching. Leonard would write, and occasionally the Nigerian would scrawl something too or perhaps underline what Leonard had written.

Leonard talked uninterrupted for nearly two minutes. When he stopped, they shook hands and smiled. From across the lobby that was half the size of a basketball court, it was hard to figure what they were up to.

The Nigerian—his name was Sikiru Adapaju—said something and put both his hands on Leonard's shoulders. A simple and direct gesture. Neither spoke for a moment. They went back to the book, the Nigerian leading with a long finger.

In that moment, Pytel was jarred out of his hangover. The Nigerian seemed capable of doing what Pytel could not—he could communicate with Leonard.

"The Nigerian," Jack Hood liked to remind anybody within earshot, "was a great big mistake." Hood always looked directly at Pytel when he said it. A little under 6'9", the Nigerian lacked the balance and footwork to be effective in major college basketball. Pytel had learned to keep silent whenever his boss said he wished the Nigerian would go back to Africa, "or wherever he came from." But the Nigerian didn't get his feelings hurt being ignored by the coaches or teased by teammates.

Leonard, who normally slunk down in his seat, sat up straight. Maybe the Nigerian was explaining what it meant to be African. Or introducing Leonard to Nelson Mandela's story. Or asking why Smooth wouldn't let him in the van back in Fresno. What seemed to be a large map had unfolded between them too. Perhaps they were complaining that the team hadn't taken a more scenic route. What the hell was there to see around Long Beach?

Or perhaps Pytel had things backwards.

What if *Leonard* was teaching the Nigerian? Suppose Leonard could get the Nigerian to engage in a way the coaches hadn't been able to? Was he telling him not to worry about riding the bench, just to focus on getting a graduate degree? Maybe Leonard had something to offer that was tangible, more than showing the Nigerian how to shoot a jump-hook, a lesson that could be written on paper and passed between them and discussed. Or was Leonard pointing out black neighborhoods on the Los Angeles map? It weighed in Pytel's gut like fried food. These days, even Leonard could convey something of value to the players better than he could.

Pytel was weary of the verbal jousting and logical gymnastics his job required; he couldn't give Leonard or Smooth the direction they needed. Gage was right, Pytel didn't deserve his job if he couldn't—or wouldn't—outsmart the players.

The supple leather of the overstuffed couch began to swallow Pytel. In an hour the lobby would be filled with players, coaches, and trainers ready to leave for practice. If Pytel feigned sleep, no one would bother him until it was time to depart. They'd wake him, and he'd be exactly where he was supposed to be. He reached into his warm-up jacket for his sunglasses, slid them on, then pulled the ballcap over his eyes.

On the way back from the Long Beach gym, Pytel counted: maybe ten more practices for the year. He was eager to get to his room. A quiet evening in a comfy hotel room, a pay-per-view movie, a phone call home, and he would be happy enough.

When Pytel stumbled onto Stephanie in the Hilton lobby, it didn't compute. She was sitting cross-legged on the same overstuffed sofa where he had slept, like she might have an appointment. Stephanie did not fit: hiking boots near the Persian rug, laced up tight as if she were ready for a rugged climb. She munched on an apple—eating the seeds, core, and all so as not to waste anything. She was the type who wouldn't use the clothes dryer on a sunny day. Pytel sat next to her just as she pocketed her apple's stem.

He must have given her a strange look. "You were expecting someone else?" she asked. She began to chew on a thumbnail. Already upset about something.

"What are you doing here?" he said.

"I'm ovulating," she said. "I'm just as surprised as you are." She'd done her math wrong, she said. "Tonight's our night. When I found I could fly Southwest for ninety-nine bucks, I went for it."

"Let's go upstairs," he said.

"Well, it's not that urgent," she grinned. "I'll be ovulating for another twelve hours."

Pytel simply wanted her out of sight. It wasn't against team rules, a woman in the hotel room. Not for coaches. But it wasn't something he flaunted unless he wanted to field pointed questions of a sexual nature the next day. He often lied to the players about his personal life, anything to throw them off.

On the elevator she said, "You're back early." He waited to hear if she'd say "for once." She didn't. Not this night.

Matching his hotel key to the room number—he was forever trying to open the wrong one—he shouldered the door and let her in. "I need to ditch the team now," he said, as much to himself as her. He called Ernie's room, begged out of supervising the team dinner, claiming exhaustion. They switched duties. Ernie would make sure the team didn't go wild and take over the entire

Hometown Country Buffet. Pytel would take on Ernie's job, a curfew check at 10:00 p.m. A fifteen-minute task, max.

Stephanie was in her typical get-up. Or lack of get-up. No mascara, a fleece pullover, a sad smile. She hugged him. "Also," she said, "I thought I'd offer a little moral support." When she pulled away, she asked, "How is he, anyway?"

Pytel thought, *This is a test.* But he had no idea who she meant.

"Jack Hood?" he asked.

Her nostrils flared, as if maybe now it was Pytel who hadn't showered in days.

"I'm serious," she said. "The boy who got shot. Keith French."

"Right," he said. "Critical condition."

"Are your guys upset?" she said.

"Steph, he doesn't play for us. He's not our problem."

"I know that." She found a room service menu and paced around the bed. He could tell she wasn't really reading it. She took a newspaper and a paperback from her overnight bag and slapped them on top of the television. "I can't believe you're here and not—did you guys send him flowers? Visit his mother? Or the hospital?"

"It's out of my hands," he said. "I just do what I'm supposed to. I thought you were here to make a baby." He reached for the novel she'd set down and studied the cover.

"That's for Ernie," she explained.

Pytel tossed the book at the bed, but it bounced over the mattress and dropped to the floor. He went to the bathroom to wash up. Stephanie followed him to the door. Over the splashing water, she read the latest report on Keith French from the afternoon paper. It wasn't even on the sports page, she noted. "His mother works in a high school lunchroom."

"Okay," he said, and he dried his hands on his shirt. When she didn't go on, he understood she was waiting for a reaction.

She said, "Like Leonard's mom."

"That's right," Pytel said. "How did you know about Leonard's mother?"

"I asked Leonard once," she said. "The radio is saying the boys from Long Beach don't want to play."

He knew exactly where this was headed. They should not want to play either. "It's not like the kid died," he said. "You know how our guys can be."

"What does the great Jack Hood say? He'd play even if it were his own mother. Especially another TV game."

"This one's not national TV." He had no interest in defending Hood. Maybe this could be their common ground—trashing the head coach. "Jack Hood doesn't know if they'll be motivated with this kid wounded or if they'll be in disarray."

"You're missing the point," Stephanie said and handed him a menu.

"*Christ*," he said. "What do you want me to do?"

She stared at him a long time. "I'm hungry," she said. "Why don't you start by ordering us room service?"

Pytel went to Ernie's door a few minutes early for the rooming list. He and Stephanie had eaten and watched most of a movie in the room. They had not talked about Keith French again. She had packed a sheer nightgown and it hung now on a bathroom hook like a promise.

Ernie was showing an old game tape to Leonard Redmond. It wasn't even Long Beach. *Artificial coaching*, Pytel called it. Ernie liked to spend unnecessary time with a kid and falsely build his confidence. It was irritating. Ernie was the world's youngest thirty-year-old. Pytel didn't approve of the private film sessions and had been vocal about it in the past. Now though, he just said, "Rooming list."

"Check this out, Py," Leonard said, running the tape back himself. "Watch your recruit Jamal Davis here. I know the coaches been wondering if he's too soft sometimes."

The replay showed their talented freshman throwing a vicious elbow to the solar plexus of a Fresno player. Nobody noticed that night, not the refs, not the coaches. The opponent dropped to his knees unable to breathe as the play went in the other direction. Jamal didn't even look back.

"See that shit?" Leonard asked, replaying the moment over and over. "Your church boy done growed up."

Pytel wasn't sure he wanted Jamal to grow up like that. He also didn't want to discuss it now, not with his wife in the wings. "Rooming list," he said again to Ernie.

Pytel told Leonard he'd see him in a minute and sat in his vacated chair. Leonard grabbed his shoes and split. He knew the routine.

"How was the buffet?" Pytel said. One of the players had made a waitress weep in December, and the coaches had been told to monitor the guys closely.

"Just okay," Ernie said. He fidgeted, scratched at himself, handed over the list. "That Leonard. He's such a good listener, don't you think?"

"Don't worry about what I think," Pytel said. The temptation to criticize Ernie lost out to the image of Stephanie's nightgown.

He went to tap on doors. The players were supposed to be in bed. The TV could be on, but no lights. The Nigerian was the odd-man-out, left with a cherished single room. Technically, he was violating team policy by reading a book with the lights on and not watching television. Pytel let it pass.

Leonard was in bed, covers up to his chin, hands folded across his chest, eyes shut. He looked like a corpse.

Smooth was in the other bed. The TV's sound was turned down out of respect for Leonard's sudden catatonic state. Pytel breathed through his mouth to avoid the blowback of Smooth's shower strike. He whispered goodnight and Smooth's head swiveled slightly in Pytel's direction and his eyes did a slow blink, as if practicing Morse code—two long blinks, one short. Pytel stepped back into the hallway and pulled the door shut.

Stephanie had the pillows propped up and the bed covers stripped, with just her legs under the sheets. Her nightgown tugged at Pytel in a way that made him believe this would be a good night. She thumbed through Blue Ribbon Basketball, a magazine they relied on for scouting.

He cursed—it was Smooth's copy he'd borrowed on the plane. He'd better return the magazine before Smooth came knocking at midnight, which would be just like him.

"I was reading more about Keith French," Steph said and handed him the thick publication. "Did you know he wants to be a nursing major?" She pointed to the kid's name in bold letters. "Weird karma, huh?"

"I'll be right back," he said. "Stay right there."

He took the magazine down the hallway and tapped lightly on the door with his ring. It was slightly ajar, so he stuck his head in and waved the magazine like a passport.

Smooth still lay beneath the covers, but Leonard Redmond's bed was empty. From catatonic to AWOL in five minutes. Pytel poked his head in the bathroom.

"He's probably down in the lobby," Smooth said.

Pytel took the stairs two at a time, but the lobby was empty. His breathing was labored—either from the stairs or knowing what Jack Hood's reaction would be.

Stephanie was still in bed, with her own book this time. The nightgown gaped suggestively. "Do you want to return my library book for me?" she said as she put it down. She knew he didn't like being teased about the babysitting side of his job, but in that outfit she could get away with it.

"Leonard's missing," he said.

Leonard Redmond
February 26, 2004
English 200: Writing in the Humanities
Event Essay: Scene & Dialogue

The event I have chosen to write about most people will never have to go through. I was arrested for selling a controlled substance, meaning weed, after my freshman year here at State. This occurred in the Lawndale neighborhood on Chicago's west side and caused my mother, or should I say me, many problems.

This event lead to me being dragged away from home and some dialogue from my mother that I never heard from her before, although I heard other people say those things. As I was being cuffed and read my rights, she started screaming "no good motherfucker," and went completely out of control, and I realized that she was yelling at me and not the cops. She began to slap me, and they had to restrain her. So this was another event that most people will never have to put themselves through—hearing their own mothers say motherfucker, and cops respond with laughter, as if I was not humiliated enough.

But the ripple effect that we talk about in class, what happened after the event, was even more interesting and what I have really chosen to pursue in this paper and even write a scene about. While I was gone that afternoon, my mother had to call the coaches here at State and tell them the details of what happened. Everybody knows lots of players smoke weed. I heard the NBA doesn't even test for it anymore, don't ask me why the colleges do.

This was after my freshman year (I am now a junior, and don't ask me why it took so long to take this class) when I was named the league's Freshman of the Year, the trophy of which my mom tried to hit me with too, while I was in handcuffs. I had to calm everyone down and tell my mom to put my damn trophy back on the TV where it still sits, chip and all. But I bailed out thanks to Red, an old partner of mine, and I didn't even have to spend the night, which I was thankful for.

I got home and the phone was ringing. It was my coaches who already knew what had happened, because of my mom's panicking. Glad she's not my coach, right?

So I had to explain everything to Coach Pytel, and each time I said something, Pytel repeated it to our head coach, Jack Hood, who probably thought he'd get polluted talking to a drug dealer. And I was damn near in tears, for real, because I thought that they'd take my scholarship. Until Coach Pytel said this: "Did you talk to any reporters?"

So I said, "No. This Chicago. Getting popped for weed happens every day."

And I heard Pytel say something to Coach Hood, who he always has to answer to. Pytel would get very twitchy when Coach Hood was around. One time I noticed this when Pytel was doing an internet search, with Hood standing right behind him. Pytel would click like ten times when he just needed to double click on something. Anyway, then Pytel came back on the phone and said, "Do you think there's a chance it will stay out of the papers?"

The coaches never had any experience with Chicago cops, not that I had a whole lot, so I told Pytel that, "If I go to trial and get convicted, it would have a bigger chance to make the paper."

See, I was what the coaches call a "sleeper," meaning nobody ever paid any attention to me or realized that I was going to be a great player. But in a funny way, I could tell even when I was in high school. I started seeing plays develop and I'd make my move—but it was like my body wouldn't listen to me. Not yet. Meaning that I'd miss the steal or the blocked shot, but I knew I should have had it, and in my mind I did make the play.

Once I got to college as a freshman, I guess my body started to catch up with my mind. And the plays where I used to barely be too late, now I was making them easy. Plus I gained about ten pounds eating in the cafeteria, which my mother was mad about, since she's a better cook (smile).

The next day—really, I mean the next day—Pytel called me again, but this time he was at the Midway airport, and he said to stay at home because he was coming to visit.

Pytel hadn't been to our apartment since he came that one single time, by himself, for his recruiting trip before I decided what college to attend. On that day, in my last week of high school, he said, "All we are offering you is a chance, there are no guarantees about playing time," so that day was different. Pytel was the only coach from a major college to show up, since my grades were a mess. The junior college coaches said I'd be a big star, but my mom liked that Pytel was more realistic. Me, I wanted to be a star, but I also wanted to play at a major school, so when I made my SAT test score, that was it. I signed at State.

The day after my arrest, I met a much different Coach Pytel. Here's why. Now that I was already the team's best player, he talked to me the way I wished he had before.

"You're our best player," he said. "We've never had anyone become Freshman of the Year. So we're going to do our damnedest to help you here." And he just generally made a fuss over me, saying it would be a shame if my career ended over this and that he'd already left a message for the Public Defender.

I knew what was up, but I said, "Y'all kicked Harvey Wilkins off the team last year for just smoking weed." I mean, here I was selling. Then Pytel repeated Harvey Wilkins' name, in a way that I knew we both knew the deal. Harvey Wilkins wasn't shit. I was dunking on Harvey Wilkins while I was still homesick my first week.

The next week, a miracle happened. My PD discovered that the warrant that the cops used had the wrong address, it said 832 South Kedvale. But our apartment building is 932. And 832 doesn't even exist. Also they spelled my last name Readman, which isn't right either. So the whole case was thrown out, and the cops would have to find someone else to fuck with, because that side-job career was now over for me.

"I hope you learned your lesson," my mom said, like most moms probably say all the time.

Except I did learn a lesson, another besides Do Not Sell Weed.

One day in August, I called Pytel to say the whole case had been dropped and they could stop fretting. Pytel answered and asked me to hold on a minute. He had to excuse himself from a meeting with the school's president.

And I thought—and I'm being real here—*when will this shit ever happen again*? Meaning, I didn't want the coaches to stop sweating me and treating me special. They were now worried about my life and my career and my grades.

"Sorry to keep you waiting," Pytel said. "I had to tell the president it was an emergency. What's the latest?"

"No news," I said. But it was like I heard me saying it. Because at the same instant, I was thinking, "Why are you lying to Pytel, Leonard Redmond? Why not just come out and tell the coaches that the charges were dropped?" That was the first lie I told to the coaches.

Pytel told me the plan that he and Coach Hood had cooked. They were going to put me in the easy classes, meaning Criminal Justice and the like. And I was going to just play through the year and then when my trial came, I'd have a bunch of "A's" to show the judge.

"Did you talk to Aaron Greenberg?" I asked.

He was that Public Defender. If Pytel talked to him, he'd

know the whole case had been dropped like a bad habit. But Pytel had not talked to the PD since the first time, and I told him that Mr. Greenberg had said it was better from now on if none of the coaches called ever again. Which was the second lie I told and leads me to the real conflict of this essay (getting arrested for drugs would be a more sentimental and cliché conflict that as writers we are supposed to avoid). Instead, it was telling a lie to help myself and improve my status. Even though being known by the coaches to be a drug dealer most people wouldn't think is too helpful. So, it's ironic, which means better.

September of 2002, my sophomore year, the coaches signed me up for Intro to Criminal Justice. And also Jazz to Rock. And Marriage and the Family. And two others, but not this English class (smile) so I had a very relaxed time. I was supposed to be frantic about my upcoming trial and what I was going to say to the Judge on my own behalf.

And instead it was Coach Pytel and Coach Hood that were worried, always on my tip, checking up on me. Like my mom when I had my tonsils taken out. Pytel would ask did I need anything? Had I talked to the people at the Public Defender's office? Then it was extra Nikes and sweatsuits and sometimes even single rooms on road trips. And I began to wonder if I should tell the coaches a third lie: that there had been a continuance in the trial and that the whole case might take another year and to keep those new Nikes coming.

Now I know that I pushed the whole thing too far.

I realized it one morning when I was next door at the Nigerian's apartment. He's on the basketball team, too. I named him "Jungle Boogie" but he's serious for real, although he can't play too good. It was a Monday morning, and Pytel was coming by the school apartments as usual, pretending it was something important, like where did I think the team should eat the pre-game meal, but really to find me and make sure that I got out of bed and went to class. I didn't mind because who wouldn't like being chauffeured to class three days a week?

Jungle Boogie pulled the drapes back. "Coach Pytel is here to get you. He just beeped his horn." If I wasn't in my own apartment, he'd know to check Jungle Boogie's.

But I didn't move. "Let him come up and get me," I said. I'd just put some cinnamon Pop Tarts in his toaster.

Jungle Boogie got that look on his face he gets when he's thinking about Marcus Garvey and Malcolm X. He started talking about our overdependence on the white man and the cycle of poverty that I was now party to.

"Party nothing," I said. "I'd be doing this even if Pytel was black. You seen me do this when Coach Gage comes over too."

But Jungle Boogie said that wasn't the point; the point was that all the coaches had made a colony out of me, and now I was part of their system just by playing along. And maybe he had a point, although he made almost the same statement when I was waiting for this fine girl from La Jolla to swing by the apartment in her new Altima. What Malcolm X and the coaches and some slim goodie from California have in common, I still don't exactly get.

Jungle Boogie didn't know anything about my court case, let alone the whole thing being dropped, but I started to think maybe he was right. There was only a few games left in my junior season, and the coaches thought my trial was coming up soon. It wasn't, but still I figured that this was the time for me to change.

I saw Pytel slam his car door like he was mad. He had left the windows open, his radio cranked up on my station, Hot 103, which I know he never listened to if I wasn't in his car. Just as he started to come up the stairs to get me, I was coming down from Jungle Boogie's apartment.

"I'll get to class on my own," I said. I could see that Jungle Boogie was right. Pytel needed me more than I needed him.

"It's over a mile," he said. "You don't want to be late."

I said, "I got legs."

— The End —

TERMS OF THE GAME: PART III

Steve Pytel could imagine Jack Hood smashing a hotel ashtray or highball glass when he heard the news. Still, Pytel had to tell his boss that Leonard Redmond had gone missing. Hood had derided Ernie Lancha mercilessly when Ernie covered for a player who missed curfew. In fact, Hood used it as a reason to not give Ernie a pay raise.

Stephanie, however, was amused by the news of Leonard's flight. "If I were a Leonard, where would I be?" she sang, the kids' game for finding a lost shoe.

"Not in the library," Pytel said. "Or in class. Or on time. Maybe passed out somewhere."

"Quit being so…*narrow*," she said. "Can't you try to imagine being Leonard for a minute?"

He knew the answer to that without trying: No. He could not imagine being Leonard Redmond. Being so complacent, such an air ball. And more than anything else, he could not imagine having that kind of talent, touched by the basketball gods.

"Leonard's a selfish sonuvabitch!" Vicky Hood declared minutes later. "How could he do this to our boys on the team?" A half-gallon of vodka—odorless, they liked to claim—sat perched on the dresser.

"Was he in the swimming pool?" Jack Hood asked.

"Negative," Pytel said, although he wasn't aware there was a pool. He'd have to check it, but he doubted Leonard had gone for a dip.

"On the phone in the lobby?"

"Nope."

"Who does he think he is?" Vicky said. "It's a must-win game, and he decides he's going to tour Los Angeles."

Every game was a must-win when you were collapsing and jobs were on the line, Pytel thought. He wasn't about to say it, though.

"Do the rest of the players know he's gone?" Hood asked.

"Just his roommate, Smooth," Pytel said. "What difference does that make?" Pytel winced. He knew better than to ask questions of Jack Hood during a crisis.

"If nobody knows he's missed curfew except us," he said, as if Pytel was an idiot, "we don't have to discipline him." Jack Hood smiled, the only genuine smile he'd flash: when he'd embarrassed someone. "But if the whole team knows Leonard's out partying, we have no choice."

"We'd send him home."

"Hell no!" Hood said. "That'd be all the media would talk about. We'll say he's sick, a viral infection or something. You sit outside his room, see exactly what time Leonard comes in. Stand close to him to see if you can smell anything. If he can walk on his own, we'll let him play. Call me, no matter how late. We'll be up, won't we, dear?"

Pytel was not going to spend the evening waiting in the hallway. It wasn't an option, not with his own wife visiting.

"Just say Leonard got in late," Stephanie said. The nightgown had vanished and she had put on her jeans and a fresh tee shirt. Only her feet were bare. She was arguing to ignore Jack Hood, but her clothing was making a different statement entirely. "Late is late," she went on. "Does the exact time matter?"

"To me? No. But Jack Hood needs something to drink about."

"Yeah, right." Then she showed him a soft smile. "I have an idea where Leonard would be."

How was that possible? Pytel pretended he wasn't surprised. "Okay, where do you think Leonard is?"

"For one thing, I bet Ernie knows. Ask him."

"Ask Ernie to find Leonard?" Pytel said. "Or ask where Leonard is."

"Either," she said. "Ernie would go looking if *I* asked him."

She was fond of Ernie, he knew, thought he was nice. Ernie brought the players—usually the Nigerian—to Steph's elementary school to read to her students.

She reached for the hotel phone, but Pytel didn't want Ernie to know she was here. Or why. He pushed it away. "Come on," she protested, "Ernie would appreciate having a role in this, if saving Leonard Redmond is involved."

"I'll ask Ernie myself," he said.

Requesting another favor from Ernie would be pulling rank, but Pytel would find a way to pay him back. Anyway, Ernie *would* enjoy being deputized to find their best player.

Pytel tapped, then hammered on Ernie's door. Nothing. He went back to his room and dialed Ernie's cell phone while he looked out over the parking lot and did a quick count. One of the vans was gone.

Stephanie sat on the edge of the bed, her boots laced and tied. She had been right about Ernie's desire to be involved. Ernie and Leonard were both gone.

The door to Smooth's and Leonard's room was still propped open, as if Smooth was expecting Pytel to return a third time.

Smooth had the bedspread pulled to his navel. A rich, farm odor filled the air. His attention flip-flopped between a Long Beach media guide and *Top Model*. Pytel sat on the edge of the bed, near Smooth's feet. From a distance Smooth was a good-looking kid.

At close-range the vertical scar on his cheek became prominent. The mashed nose. He had a burn mark across his arms and chest. They'd taken a chance on a problem kid, and the worst possible scenario had unfolded: he was trouble and not very good.

"You staying with me, Coach Py?" Smooth asked. "What's your woman gonna think?"

"What woman do you mean?" Pytel said. "Who have you been talking to?"

"I ain't been talking to nobody. What woman do *you* mean?" Smooth raised a crooked eyebrow.

"Look. Is Leonard with Coach Ernie?"

"Why you asking me if you already know?" He pulled the covers up higher.

"How did they get out of here so fast?"

"Leonard knows how to shake a defender," Smooth shrugged. "You been shooked."

"Where are they?" He was relying on Smooth's kindness, which could be hard to come by. Still, Leonard was already busted, and they both knew it.

"This another question you already know the answer to? They ain't out drinking. Chill. You should be worried about your boss, though. Or me, if we win tomorrow." Smooth grinned defiantly before turning serious. "They went to see that boy who got shot."

"Why didn't they just go to the hospital earlier?"

"Why didn't we take the whole team instead of that bullshit practice?"

"You guys don't even know Keith French. He's a freshman."

Smooth scrunched-up his face. "So?" He aimed the remote and turned the TV's volume up.

Stephanie was in the bathroom, but she'd left a lamp on. Pytel scanned her newspaper until he found mention of the hospital treating the wounded player. When she came out, she said, "Tell me Leonard is safe and sound."

He put down her newspaper. "Leonard is safe and sound."

"But don't lie to me."

"I've got to find him. I'll wake you up when I get back."

"I'll go with you."

This was why she had gotten dressed—she had already guessed where Leonard and Ernie had gone. Understanding this led to the next thought: she should not be here on a road trip, ovulating or not. Having her tag along while he did his duties, these stupid, demeaning things, he felt…crowded. Some things should be done in private.

"You stay," he said. "I'll be fast."

The hotel phone rang, and Stephanie sidestepped toward it as though blocking his cut to the basket. A standoff. On the fourth ring, Pytel agreed that she could come along. She reached back and handed him the receiver.

"No, I haven't," Pytel said to Jack Hood. "But I have a hunch where he might be."

Surprisingly, it was a feeling close to happiness. Stephanie beside him, cracking jokes about his driving on the expedition to find Leonard Redmond. She had the map on her knees and was comparing it to the directions she'd gotten at the front desk.

"Leonard Deadman in the hospital," Pytel said. "Can you imagine? Maybe he'll get mistaken for a patient and get held against his will."

He zipped the van in and out of the late-night L.A. traffic. This trip, this journey, was better than the promise of the nightgown. A strange thing to think, but true. Maybe this was what they needed, not only being together but paired on the same side in this mission, which was not often the case. He exited at Sunset Boulevard, pointed west, and swung the van into a *Doctors Only* spot. Stephanie didn't object.

I love my wife, he thought and took her arm. They walked briskly through the Children's Hospital emergency room lobby, slipped through the double doors marked "Restricted" on the heels of two police officers, peeked into rooms that they passed, and went for the stairway. The adventure was as precise as a video game, a quest to find Leonard, avoid obstacles, and maybe dispose of enemies. They bounded a flight of stairs. Pytel grabbed the desk phone and waited patiently for an operator. Up one more flight to ICU, she said.

The instant they walked onto the floor they came face-to-face with a squat, silver-haired nurse with a clipboard. She had thick glasses and a purposeful waddle. Stephanie knew to take the lead.

"I know it's late," she said, "but we wanted to see the basketball player. Keith French? We won't stay long."

The nurse appraised Pytel's track-suit top and sneakers. "Are you one of the coaches?"

"That's right," he answered. And that was enough. Keith French was a player, Pytel was a coach. The nurse wasn't going to ask him, *Which school?*

"Not me," Stephanie added with a smile.

"I've never seen the likes of you all bawling on each other's shoulders. So many tall boys. How you can play some game after this is beyond me." The nurse shook her head, and walked off. They followed.

"Are any of the other players here?" Stephanie called to her as they tagged along.

"Leonard," she said. "Is that his name? You could get me fired for being in here after hours. You're not even family. Although I appreciate your concern."

"It's hard not to be concerned." Pytel said.

She pointed to a door. "I'll be back soon to check his vitals.

The corner room had two walls with windows. A room with a view for a kid in a coma, Pytel thought. He half expected to find Leonard snoozing, and he was ready to wake him with a lecture. Didn't he know that the program's existence depended on him getting enough sleep and playing well? He immediately chastised himself for thinking like Jack Hood. The last thing he needed right now was to bring Hood into the room.

The Long Beach player was on the bed surrounded by machines and tubes. The room was nearly dark, but in the glow from the green and red lights, he could see Leonard on the other side of the boy's body. Keith French appeared too thin and weak to ever have been a ballplayer. Or one you could win with. Who would recruit a player so frail?

Leonard looked up from his chair and nodded. The bed was raised, almost to the level of Leonard's eyes.

"Coach Py," Leonard said. "Mrs. Pytel." He motioned toward the boy as if to say, *What about this shit?* As if they could have done something about it. Leonard looked smaller, not at all like the best player in the conference.

Stephanie stepped around the bed and hugged Leonard as if they hadn't seen each other in years. She returned to Pytel's side and looped her arm through his.

"He's in bad shape," Leonard said.

"How long have you been here?" Pytel asked him.

"Just a few minutes. Coach Ernie got us lost."

That figured. "Where is old Ernie?" Pytel felt his face get hot. There was no point in letting Leonard know how he felt about Ernie.

"I told him to wait in the car," Leonard said. "I messed up, huh? I thought you already came by to check rooms."

"It's done now," he said. "We better get back. You've got a game to play tomorrow."

Stephanie gently kicked his shin, a little tap, the smallest of warnings.

Leonard said, "The nurse thinks we all from the same team."

Pytel nearly said, *But we're not.* He did not want a philosophical discussion. He could get that from the Nigerian. Instead, he wanted to drive back across the dark city with his wife, to lie down beside her. The nightgown, of course, would not reappear, but he didn't care.

The gentle beeping and steady hum of the life-support system was hypnotizing, meditative almost, but he was too agitated to get sleepy. *I love my wife*, he thought again. That could be his mantra to get through the night. Yet there was something else here, something he couldn't get his teeth around—there was no way Leonard could know this Keith French. They were from different towns, and Keith French was a freshman. Did Leonard think he might save him? Pray for him? Did he think he was such a talent that he could redeem a human's life? It didn't matter, and yet Pytel couldn't entirely let it go.

Stephanie moved around the bed once more. She stood beside Leonard and leaned just inches from Keith French's chest. "He's not old enough to shave," she said.

Just in that moment Pytel thought Keith French, for some reason, looked left-handed. He could usually spot that in the way a lefty carried himself. Stephanie reached down and put her hand between the wounded player's shoulder and neck and kept it there, the way she did when Pytel had a fever.

"What you doing, Mrs. Pytel?" Leonard asked.

Keith French stirred slightly, and Stephanie jumped back nearly into Leonard's lap. "I don't know," she said.

The nurse came in, checked monitors, scribbled on her clipboard. Pytel and Stephanie sat on the arms of Leonard's chair, flanking him. The nurse dragged the other chair next to them and practically collapsed, leaned back, and actually put her feet on the end of Keith French's bed. She smelled of baby powder. For her, the job was manual labor. Pytel thought she might light a cigarette or take out a flask.

The four waited in a row, as though on a courtside bench. All eyes were on Keith French. He was the star this night. The bullet had pierced two organs.

"He going to live?" Leonard asked, without taking his eyes off Keith French.

"I told you yesterday he would," the nurse said. She still hadn't figured out that they were not from Long Beach. "What kind of life he's going to have is another story." Then, facing Pytel, "Are you all close?"

"Close?" he said. "I'm a coach. They're players. I guess you could—"

At that instant Keith French jerked erratically, twisted his head as if to shake the tubes loose. Pytel hadn't realized until then that the kid was held down with restraints. The nurse didn't seem alarmed. She left her feet propped up on the bed.

"Help him," Leonard said. "Call the doctor." Leonard's legs bounced up and down, the way they did during time-outs at the end of close games. He jumped to his feet.

"That's the body's instinctive response," the nurse said, "to pull those tubes out of his throat and nose. He'll get used to it."

When Keith French settled down, Leonard dropped back in his chair and the nurse rose, as if on a seesaw.

"You can talk to him," she said, "but be careful not to jostle the boy or the tubes." She picked up her clipboard and walked out.

"Talk to him?" Pytel said.

Leonard rose and moved next to Keith French, face to face, slid slowly around the bed as if he were a medical student examining a cadaver. He might have whispered something.

In basketball—in all sports, Pytel assumed—the unwritten rule was to ignore an athlete who was hurt. Walk away. Coaches never bent to console or touch an injured player or offered to help him off the court. Bad luck or something. No matter how important the guy was, the trainer helped him, or the doctor, but nobody else.

Pytel knew what he was supposed to do—what his wife thought he ought to do—but he could not bring himself to talk to or share his feelings with Leonard Redmond. He had seen all he wanted to see.

He went to one of the windows and scanned a few rows of cars for Ernie's van. The farthest lights of L.A.'s infinite sprawl vibrated, but that might have been his eyes playing tricks. He heard Stephanie go down the hall, maybe to find a bathroom. Months later, when they were having the last fight of their marriage, he'd learn she was weeping.

Leonard joined him at the window. Then he lifted one heel and put it high on the windowsill and leaned into it to stretch his hamstrings.

"Big game tomorrow," Pytel said.

Pytel's van was the only vehicle remaining in the *Doctors Only* section. He stopped with Leonard while Stephanie walked ahead to the van.

"Where did you leave Ernie?" Pytel asked Leonard.

"I'll find him," Leonard said and started towards a corner of the parking lot.

"No, ride with me," Pytel said, and Leonard did an about-face. "You and Steph warm up the van, and I'll tell Ernie to follow us. His cell phone is always off. Do you have yours on?"

"Mine's back at the hotel," Leonard said. He was forever losing his phone.

"Perfect," Pytel said. "Just show me where the van is."

Leonard pointed, reminded him that it was white, and Pytel took off at a trot. "Be right back," he called. Stephanie shouted out, probably something sensible, like why not just drive over to Ernie? She liked to say that coaches blamed problems on anyone but their good players. Maybe so, and maybe that was why he didn't want her around during the confrontation. They'd traded jobs—team meal for curfew—and Ernie had deliberately taken advantage of it. This stupid field trip had been premeditated. It was his impulse to yell at Ernie, yet he wasn't angry anymore. Soon this whole adventure would be forgotten.

Pytel rapped on the glass and startled Ernie, who frantically rolled down the window.

"Oh. Shit," Ernie said. "What are you doing here?"

"Some asshole drove our best player to a hospital thirty minutes after curfew."

Ernie stuttered something lame—"life issues"—but Pytel cut him off. "Don't ever pull a stunt like this again."

"Where's Leonard?"

"Leonard is still inside the hospital. Wait here. I've got important business back at the hotel. Don't even think about leaving here without him. Can you handle that, or is it too complicated?"

"Of course not," Ernie said. "I mean, yes."

"Leonard says he'll be out in thirty minutes," Pytel said. "He doesn't have his phone, so just be patient. Can you bozos get back without getting lost, or should I draw you a map?" He leaned forward, his hands wide on the car door, elbows bent. Head nearly in the window, he looked past Ernie in the dim light.

Somebody else was in the van. The Nigerian. The goddamned Nigerian was along for the ride.

Sikiru Adapaju looked over at Pytel innocently, as if they'd been pulled over for rolling through a stop sign.

"We're cool," Ernie said. "We'll be fine. I'll get Leonard back safe."

"My phone's not charged, so you can't call me either," Pytel said. "Just make sure Leonard wears his seat belt."

Ernie grabbed his own shoulder harness like an idiot, and he gave Pytel the thumbs up. The trip had been Ernie's idea, Pytel thought, and Ernie had talked the Nigerian into keeping him company.

He hustled back across the parking lot to his van. Leonard was spread across the back seat, staring forlornly at the hospital room, his forehead against the window, like a child who was being carted away from a swimming pool. "That boy was just a young buck," he said as they drove off. Then, catching Pytel's eyes in the rear view mirror: "Coach Ernie isn't too good with directions."

"He'll get back on his own. I told him to call me if he gets lost."

"He's not behind us," Stephanie said, looking over her shoulder.

Pytel said, "He knows the way."

The humming of the highway became a roar in Pytel's head. He thought about how Keith French had taken a bullet in the back, and how that caused Leonard's psyche to come unhinged, and perhaps killed the team's hopes for a win at Long Beach—and delayed Pytel's evening alone with Stephanie. Whatever broke inside Leonard would have to be fixed by game time, less than twenty-four hours away. He knew he ought to say something instructive, but what Leonard needed now was sleep, not a lecture. Pytel had allowed Stephanie along on this misadventure, but his serious talk with Leonard—whose foolish choice had let his team down—needed to be done without her and probably after the weekend was over. Right now, Leonard should focus on Long Beach.

"It's a crazy world, huh?" Pytel said quietly, but Stephanie was silent. She had wanted to know what his job was like, and she'd been rewarded with a front-row seat at the circus. If she longed for this kind of intimacy, here it was. All that was missing was Smooth's stinking armpits and Jack Hood's half-gallon of vodka. He didn't like her seeing all this, but perhaps now she'd be more empathetic when things went haywire.

He made another stab at conversation. "It's late for all of us." He reached over to put his hand on her knee, but she turned back to face Leonard.

"I just want to tell you, Leonard," she said, "that I am *so proud* of you for doing this."

Leonard thanked her, as if he really had done something more noble than sneaking out of a hotel.

Pytel—surprised and strangely jealous—said, "What are you talking about? Leonard has a game to play tomorrow. He's supposed to do a job."

"He's supposed to be a decent human first."

"What does visiting a kid who he's never met have to do with being a decent person? The world is full of suffering children we don't know." He cracked his window open an inch and sucked at the air. Leonard spoke, but Pytel couldn't make out what he said.

"Leonard," Stephanie said, "can you tell my husband why you visited that boy?"

Pytel said, "Because Ernie suggested it."

"Why don't you let him answer?" There was a vicious edge in her voice that he hadn't heard before, but would hear again.

They waited for Leonard to speak, as if whatever a twenty-year old proclaimed—a kid with a forty-inch vertical leap and deadly jump-hook—would prove one of them right and one of them wrong.

Leonard cleared his throat. "I don't know if I can put it into words."

Pytel let out a snort, his point confirmed—Leonard was a pawn and Ernie was a toadying clown.

Stephanie said, "You're an ass."

"I shouldn't have brought you along," he said quietly.

"I shouldn't have brought *you* along." She swiveled to Leonard again, put her hand on his knee and said, "Don't feel like you have to play tomorrow."

Pytel slammed his hand on the steering wheel. "Of course he has to play. Everyone has to do things they don't feel like doing. It's called being an adult."

"And you," she said, "don't have to shout."

Pytel had the opportunity to destroy Ernie the morning of the Long Beach game. Instead, he put aside his anger and tried to save Ernie's pathetic ass, which he figured Stephanie would want him to do. He told Jack Hood that Leonard had merely gone out for a fast-food fix.

"Cheeseburger, huh?" Jack Hood said.

Pytel would learn later that Ernie had been to see Jack Hood minutes before to confess his misdeeds in the kidnapping of Leonard Redmond. Pytel tried to salvage Ernie, but screwed himself by lying on Ernie's behalf. Hood had been ready to fire Ernie; instead, he directed his remaining venom toward Pytel.

Against Long Beach, Leonard Redmond played like a man reborn. He scored at will and snuffed out their inside game, until, with three minutes remaining, he fouled out. The Nigerian took Leonard's place, and while his contribution wouldn't have been apparent from the stats, his lurking presence on defense helped the team win. Smooth couldn't seem to make a basket until it mattered, but he got plenty of shot attempts and his shower strike would be called off.

"Keep the inmates from celebrating like idiots," Hood said in Pytel's ear as the clock expired. "It's not like we won the goddamn NCAA title." But the players ignored Pytel and raced onto the court at the final horn to celebrate. The Nigerian did some sort of dance with the team urging him on. Even Stephanie seemed happy—she came down to the court to kiss Pytel on the cheek, accepted hugs from the players, as if maybe everything would turn out fine.

THE JACK HOOD REPORT

If *The Jack Hood Report* aired today, it would show a man mumbling to himself in the high school gym office in Putnam County. Chipped red paint would flake from the office walls. The star of the show would chant, "What the fuck am I doing here?"

ESPN would not be airing another episode, though. Hood now lived in a remote Nebraska town, and his ex-wife Vicky's favorite line echoed in his head. "Don't forget," she used to crow after every win, "it takes a lot longer to claw up the ladder than it does to tumble down." She'd taken her share and moved to Colorado rather than help him resurrect his career.

After less than a week at Putnam County High, he found himself choking down that wisdom, like a teenager trying liquor for the first time. He'd sworn he'd never subject himself to coaching in a town where a store clerk asked if you wanted a "sack" instead of a bag. Yet, here he was, and in three short years he'd gone from a state university, to a smaller college, to obscurity.

The first official basketball practice was normally a time of optimism, but not today. Finished with classes, he was alone for one period in the gym office he shared with the other phys ed teacher—

and the biggest bugs he'd ever seen. Hood was a man of habits and already had a new one: a large Styrofoam cup sat on his desk, which he used to collect the roaches he'd killed. The back of a pink absentee slip served as the stat sheet. Jack Hood was up to twenty.

At 2:35 p.m. Hood was summoned to the main office by the principal, a man named Bill Tracey. The hallway's crush of students made Hood skittish, so he walked a loop outside, around the building. He knew the Nebraska weather would get nasty soon enough, but on this day it felt like spring. Everyone was still in shirtsleeves. Yellow school buses lined up and brought traffic to a halt. Back inside, he strode past the meek protests of the secretary and plopped down across from Tracey. "How many days left until summer vacation?" he asked.

"Too many to count," Tracey said. He closed his office door, the noisy teenagers in the hallway reduced to a palatable hum. "What's on after practice today? Let's get a beer."

Hood waited for the joke that wasn't coming. Tracey knew a drink was out of the question. "What are you, testing me already?" Hood asked. He hadn't even begun to figure out his new boss. Was Tracey's offer a joke? A genuine attempt to be friendly? Either way, it was an odd suggestion.

"One or two wouldn't hurt," Tracey said. "I've had my own little battles with the bottle, you know. Moderation is the key. I thought it would be something we could work on together, but suit yourself." Tracey said he'd be at a tavern called The Spot for a few hours. Hood could meet some of the folks from town, he added. "To gather a little support."

The last thing Jack Hood needed was to get back on the sauce and loll around with a bunch of townies. *Are you a fast-break coach or slow-down coach?* he could imagine them asking. He'd been forced to endure that from college boosters, guys in fancy suits—not farmers in overalls. The best thing about this job, he'd already decided, was that he didn't have to talk to anyone.

Just two years earlier, every college hoops junkie in the nation knew *The Jack Hood Report*, a weekly feature on ESPN. It wasn't that Hood's team was terrorizing the modest Ohio Valley conference. Or that he'd been fairly well known from his previous job, a few seasons at Southern Arizona State. Rather, it was because of what one of the announcers had observed when the University of Kentucky was hammering Hood's team: The coach was going crazy. And not just regular crazy, but entertaining crazy, his career a strange sort of slow-motion crash landing.

With his slicked-back gray hair and sumo-wrestler's build, he was instantly recognizable. He'd gained seventy pounds since he'd lost his job at State, where he was fired due to unreasonable expectations. That's what got him. The expectations. Also, a disloyal assistant coach named Steve Pytel, chickenshit administrators, and the entire African-American community.

He lasted two seasons at the next college, where his antics would become sound bites for insanity. The first ESPN spot featured Hood appearing to faint dead away after a referee's horrendous call. Play continued, but he laid courtside like a corpse. For five minutes. It prompted so many phone calls that ESPN sent their own cameraman out to cover their next game, just in case they were on to something.

Jack Hood didn't disappoint.

Hopelessly behind with just two minutes left in the contest, he instructed his 6'9" center to closely guard one of the referees for the length of the court. The ten-second slice of a gawky player guarding a grizzled basketball official, then Hood's quote—"I told Brandsky to cover the guy that was hurting us the most"—secured his status among cultish college basketball fans. Thereafter, the station would devote sixty seconds a week to Hood's latest behavior.

He claimed his antics were to take pressure off his team and keep an assured attitude in the face of the weekly disasters. Later it evolved—degenerated, really—into a personal obsession. This was his show. Eighteen spots of *The Jack Hood Report* ran over the next two years. In one, Hood dropped to his knees, eyes shut and palms glued in prayer. His team needed both free throws to tie the game with 0.7 seconds left. When the home crowd groaned, he looked upward and shook his fist at the basketball gods.

At the Aloha Classic, he wore mirrored sunglasses the entire tournament. At a game in Idaho, he tried to bribe a referee with a potato. After a rare victory, he ran to the water cooler at the end of the bench, ripped the top off, and in a solo imitation of the football tradition, dumped icy Gatorade over his own head.

The first few ESPN spots quickly became an embarrassment for his school, a celebration of failure. Soon Hood's only remaining joy was to belittle his players during timeouts. This led to an unheard of situation in college ball—a coach revered on the road, but despised at home.

At what turned out to be his last home game, Hood strolled to half-court, uninvited, as the National Anthem concluded. The featured eight-year-old twin sisters squeaked out, "home of the brave!" and Hood stepped in front of them to the microphone. The girls didn't even have a chance to wave, bow, or say thank you. Attendance was so poor, Hood announced, that rather than introduce the players, as was customary, they should just introduce the fans "because it will take up less time." Boos rained down from the inconsiderate crowd. One of the twins tried to kick him in the shins.

The school president came grim-faced to the locker room after that contest to personally fire Hood, face to face. That showed something on the president's part, he sometimes reminded himself. Guts maybe. The final *Jack Hood Report* ran that evening.

It was a chicken-or-the-egg thing with his drinking. He hit it harder with each loss and there were enough losses to drive a nun to drink. What Hood called his "year-and-a-half sabbatical" was called a "downward spiral" by doctors. The stats, the ones he could recall, were ugly: five detox centers in eight months. A bitter wife. Soon, a bitter ex-wife. Financial ruin. Some reporter got wind of his last stay in rehab and an AP story titled, "Jack Hood's Not So Good" ran nationwide.

Hood was on his deathbed—that's what the doctor said,

"deathbed," as motivation—when Putnam County's principal read the article. Bill Tracey was in a bind, too. He showed up unannounced at the rehab center after driving from central Nebraska to interview Hood for the vacated coaching job. Hood had never heard of the town, hadn't applied for the position. But Tracey was an alumni of the college that had dumped Hood, and he must have found something alluring in the article. Tracey got on his good side right off by calling the president who fired Hood a "dimwit."

Administrators liked to take credit for a prestigious hiring. Or firing. Maybe Tracey needed a feather in his cap to calm a dissatisfied school board. Corralling a name coach with college experience to a tiny high school would be quite an accomplishment, even if the coach was on Antabuse.

The rehab room was a mess when Tracey arrived. He looked wobbly, on the verge of collapse himself. He had a shock of uncombed grey hair. A matching growth sprouted disturbingly out of his ears. He was painfully thin. Bad investments or maybe alimony payments must have kept him from retiring. Tracey seemed pretty comfortable in the rehab clinic, Hood realized weeks later.

Vicky Hood, her fashion magazines at her feet, held court. "He's not an alcoholic," she said to Tracey, as she insisted to every nurse and doctor. "Alcoholics go to meetings. He's a drunk." She'd hide from Hood's retaliatory barrage behind her magazine. Later he'd learn that she was already packed and had decided to move to Denver.

"This gentleman needs me, Victoria," Hood said. "Would you please be quiet so we can hear what he has say?"

Putnam County hadn't had a winning season since Eisenhower was president. Tracey mentioned the movie "Hoosiers," and talked about what a dramatic comeback it would be. He looked around at all the charts and tubes, and he told Hood he was a "courageous sonuvabitch."

"Courageous!" Vicky laughed. She liked to say rehab was for quitters.

Hood told her to fuck off. Tracey's last comment sealed the

deal. He'd driven all that way from Nebraska, and at his age? Hood didn't even ask about salary, it was so nice to be wanted again. What was it about coaching he missed exactly? There'd be no glamour, little power, a paltry paycheck.

Hood arrived at Putnam County at the start of the school year. He was disappointed to learn that hardly anyone had even heard of him. Some townspeople didn't yet have cable TV or ESPN. Nebraska was football country, anyway. Basketball was number three, one teacher told him. Corn was number two. And Hood learned why Bill Tracey was looking for a coach in September: the man Hood replaced had skipped town with a cheerleader from the senior class.

Jack Hood carried a laminated wallet-sized Prayer of St. Anthony, the saint of all things lost, a card his own college coach had given to him. The gift came after Hood's sixth year, when he finally graduated. Hood kept St. Anthony next to the 3x5 cards he normally used to plan practice. He wasn't planning practice on that October day, however.

Finally sober enough to think clearly, minutes after leaving Bill Tracey's office, and just before his first practice, Hood came to a realization. He'd gotten desperate and sentimental in the hospital. And he missed Vicky, who made it clear she would never move to Nebraska. "What's that old saying," she said of his suggestion to join him there, "about the snowball in hell?"

A year or two without booze or basketball, that's really what he needed now. Then maybe he could return to coaching. He hated this new town already, with its one stoplight and four taverns. He hated his office, hated the other teachers, their looks of judgment or apathy. He hated his cheesy apartment, the plywood furniture. If he hadn't felt sorry for Bill Tracey, he wouldn't be in Putnam County. Now he was stuck.

Or was he? He wiped the sweat from his hands on his mesh shorts, sat up straight, and took a deep breath. He'd made this career move on instinct, and now he needed to consider what the hell he was doing. What if he stalled to see if his team was any good, played games up to Thanksgiving, then decided? But he'd be called a coward if he walked away mid-season. That would be worse. Now was the time to quit, if he was going to quit. He didn't like the word "quit,"—how about "put his career on hold"?

At the 3:00 bell, Hood felt like the married guy turning in his key at a cheap motel—the walk of shame. Embarrassed yet relieved. He'd write a memo for Tracey, informing him of his decision in the morning. Hood had nothing in the gym office except the Styrofoam cup and two letters from Ernie Lancha, the only former assistant of his who'd bothered to keep in touch. He trashed the letters.

Against the rush of kids in the hallway, Hood sidestepped his way to the faculty parking lot. He felt light and springy, as though he could jump up and grab the hoop with both hands. He climbed into his car, and calculated how long it would take him to clear out of the duplex. Before dark? Maybe, but he'd still have to return with his letter of resignation. But when he put the car into reverse, he realized he'd be snared in parking lot traffic, a dozen yellow buses in front, parents behind him. Stuck for at least forty minutes, he figured.

As his Putnam County job sputtered to a merciful death, he recalled how his last job had ended. The university president at least had balls enough to look him in the eye. Hood cursed, jerked the car back into place, and went in to say hello and goodbye to the Red Raven varsity hopefuls, the team he hadn't yet met. Nobody could say that Jack Hood didn't have the fortitude to do this man-to-man. Or man-to-boys. After that he might even march down to Bill Tracey's office and say thank you. Leave with a bit of dignity for once.

Twelve kids stood at one end of the gym, which was painted the same hideous red as Hood's dingy office. This wouldn't have been a tryout—you couldn't even cut the worst kids, not with twelve players total. No basketballs were out. Why would there be? He was the coach, and it was his job to do everything here, like roll out the rack at the start of practice. He recognized some of the taller boys from around school, but he had only met a handful through his gym-teaching assignment. Dumb farm kids, two of them pretty good sized, all of them wearing their P.E. uniforms and socks that didn't match. Acne, crooked teeth, wide-eyes. They hopped in place or leaned their weight on one leg, trying to look relaxed yet coachable.

He gathered the team to the center circle and told them to put their toes on the line. The boys silently encircled him. This had been Jack Hood's pre-practice ritual for as long as he could remember. Alone but surrounded, he turned slowly, made eye contact with each player.

"I'm not going to talk long," he said, "and I'm damn sure not going to repeat myself. After a lot of thought—" he paused. They looked like a teenage basketball version of *One Flew Over the Cuckoo's Nest.* He bit his lip to keep from laughing. It wouldn't have been funny to be their coach, though. He might not have won a game all year.

How to put this, to tell kids he'd just met that their season together was already finished? He finally said, "Which of you guys can tell me why Jack Hood is your coach?" That wasn't great but it would get things moving.

The shortest kid said, "Because Bill Tracey had to save his own self on account of our last coach and that slut Tiffany Evans."

Hood smiled, but none of the players did. They nodded solemnly.

"But," the short kid continued without being prompted, "now my Dad says Bill Tracey's realized he's made a worser mistake."

They nodded at that, too. Kids could be so refreshing.

"My Dad says you used to be a helluva coach," a boy behind Hood broke in, and the coach pivoted to face him now. This kid had a hooked nose and cut-off sleeves, his arms folded across his chest. Hood nodded to the admiring boy, then squinted at his own shoes. When he raised his head dramatically to affirm that he was indeed still one hell of a coach, he caught the hook-nosed kid pantomiming a drinking motion—fist and thumb as the beer bottle. The bastard was mocking him. One boy hissed, "Goddammit, Zarucki."

Hood felt his face get red-hot. "Everybody over here!" he bellowed, and led the team to the sideline. He returned alone to the center circle, like the demented opposite of a firing squad. He'd address the little shits one last time before their punishment, and he'd get the last laugh before the school busses and parents cleared out of the parking lot. He had to be somewhere for the next thirty minutes, after all.

"How many of you know what a Suicide Seventeen is?" he asked.

The boys were contrite as they awaited their sentence.

"What about you, Zarucki?" Hood asked. "What kind of name is Zarucki? You seem to know everything." He didn't wait for an answer, then he explained the torturous wind sprint drill: sixty seconds to go sideline-to-sideline, seventeen times. He had once taken a player to his knees, an Army veteran in fact, with just the threat of yet another. "We're gonna do a bunch so you'll know who's in charge here." *You'll remember who Jack Hood is even after he's gone,* he thought. He looked down at his watch that hadn't worked in years.

"Go!"

Pounding feet and frantic breaths filled the dank gym, but there wasn't the normal squeak of sneakers because the floor was so dirty from gym classes. As the first boy approached the finish, Hood counted off "fifty-four, fifty-five." When he looked up from his broken watch, there was Zarucki, well ahead of the others. Zarucki thrust his fists into the air as though he'd won the fucking Olympic Gold Medal. What an asshole. The other players bent over, hands on knees, but Zarucki was doing some deep-breathing technique that sounded like a vacuum cleaner being shut on and off. The other boys hated him, too, Hood was certain.

After the next set of sprints, Zarucki ran the final forty feet backwards and still came in first place. On the third round, he winked at Hood as he finished and did jumping jacks until it was time to run again. His behavior was becoming more erratic by the minute.

After the tenth sprint, a couple boys wept openly. One cried something about "not fair," and was quickly shushed. Another kid seemed to be having an asthma attack. Hood could almost hear their hearts pounding. "Rest time," he said. "We're halfway there. Ten more to go."

Hood figured he had ten minutes left before the busses were gone, yet now he was no longer in a hurry. This part of coaching, he realized, he missed a great deal. The control, the absolute abruptness with which people moved at his command. Vicky had never quite bought into being around a strong leader. "I'm your wife, not your bartender," she'd begun to say.

He checked his watch and blew his whistle. The boys groaned and lined up again. Except for Zarucki. He walked away, toward the exit.

"I figured you'd be the first to quit, Zarucki," Hood called out. "An alligator mouth and a hummingbird heart. You couldn't even make it to last call." It felt good, and it occurred to Hood that this was the first time he'd smiled since arriving at Putnam County.

But Zarucki stopped short of the exit. He staggered and gripped the steel rim of the waist-high trash barrel, then drank in a huge gulp of air. He leaned forward and his head disappeared, as if he'd dropped his keys in the garbage. Leaning back again, he steadied himself on the edge of the cylinder, and he gave Hood a terrible, hateful glare.

Zarucki faced the barrel again and puked with such force that a "ping" sound resounded, and it pinged again each time he sprayed vomit against the sides. He was a broken spigot. When he finished the fourth eruption, Zarucki turned back to his teammates and Hood. "Taco Bell!" he declared. As if for a sobriety field test, he steadied himself, wiped his mouth, and swaggered back to the sideline to join the others. He let out a roar and pounded his chest with both fists.

Hood was nearly too stunned to blow has whistle and start the humiliation all over again. It was a peculiar display of—well, what exactly? Zarucki's conduct was the kind of things he and his assistant coaches would have talked about for years. Hood had no help now though, nobody to talk to. And no Vicky.

After a half-dozen more of the brutal sprints, the kids appeared to be running in mud. Hood stopped them, unlocked the equipment closet, and rolled out the rack of basketballs. He told the boys to "pair up in threes" at each hoop. This created a mild panic. One boy abandoned his two to join another couple, thought for a moment, and ran back.

Hood tossed each group a ball, which they held like eggs while they awaited their orders, not daring to bounce them. He said he wanted ten free throws apiece, to check out who was man enough to make shots while exhausted.

Zarucki was the only one Hood kept track of. He made his first eight before he missed. Two minutes into the free throws, Hood noticed somebody, through the chicken-wired glass of the door, shuffling toward the gym. Bill Tracey.

Hood turned his back to the door and blew his whistle, just moments before his principal would appear, and paused to listen for the clink of the door behind him. Hood would never lose his sense of drama or timing.

"Hold the basketballs!" he said when he heard the door close. He raised both hands. The gym was silent. The boys probably feared the worst: an angry coach and the school principal.

"I know I've said this ten times already," he announced, "but schoolwork is more important than basketball will ever be." The kids looked at each other, confused, but most of them nodded anyway. "That's one thing we're going to learn this year if we don't learn anything else. None of you will amount to—to crap, if you don't hit the books. Don't let me hear about any of you guys screwing off in class ever again." The gym door shut moments later. Bill Tracey must have been duly impressed and was already on his way back to his office.

Zarucki was an obnoxious prick, of course, but what heart he had. He was tough. Beyond tough, even. Hood could mold him into their leader, and maybe the team would deduce that they should all be more like Zarucki. Hood caught himself and laughed. Was this what he really wanted to do, coach these fucking farm kids? The players, who had gone back to their free throws, stopped and considered him until Hood stopped laughing and pointed them back to their task. He called out for ten more free throws apiece. Of course this job wasn't exactly what he wanted. Still. Running back to Vicky wasn't the answer, either.

What he ought to do, the instant practice ended, was go bitch at Bill Tracey about getting the floor swept before practice each afternoon. How could you practice on such a filthy floor? The coach had more important things to do than sweep the court. Hood took out his 3x5 cards and scribbled a reminder to recruit a freshman student manager who could do that for him. He started to put the cards away, and then he added a reminder to work with Zarucki on getting arch on his shot. The kid would never evolve into a good shooter without more arch.

The principal wouldn't be in his office in two hours, which was when they'd finished practice. Maybe Hood would just wait until morning to complain. He definitely was not going to The Spot, where the Happy Hour crowd was probably already congregating. Or, if he did go to the bar, he'd stand. He would not sit down, he would not remove his coat. Jack Hood blew his whistle, waved his team over. Helping each other on defense, he'd start with something simple. Would they ever be unselfish enough to learn that? One thing was certain: this was going to be an awful goddamn season.

WORLD UNIVERSITY GAMES

That summer, Jamal Davis, of all people, was arrested for stealing a car.

Steve Pytel sped back from the July recruiting showcase in Phoenix, the lucky recipient of Jamal's one allotted phone call. He arranged bail while on the interstate, although Jamal still had to spend a sleepless night in lock up.

The administration would be desperate to locate a bonded-out Jamal, so Pytel insisted he not return to his dorm or answer his cell. He wanted to get Jamal alone, learn exactly what had happened, and run interference. Jamal agreed to hide out at Leonard Redmond's empty apartment.

Jamal and Leonard Redmond had grown close, an interesting development because just one week into his freshman year, Jamal had come to Pytel's office to complain about Leonard.

"Nicknames are between you and the team," Pytel told Jamal. Leonard had begun handing out nicknames as a twisted sort of revenge, after he learned that Jack Hood referred to him as Leonard Deadman. "What did Leonard name you?" Pytel asked.

"Church Boy."

"Tell him you don't like it," Pytel said, wondering if Leonard had given him a nickname too. He knew that the players called Ernie "Baby Brother," for the way he tagged along behind Pytel.

Be somebody else then, Leonard had responded to Jamal's request. Then he suggested "Sweet Jamal." Jamal okayed that one. It didn't stick.

Once the games started, the two developed a strong on-court connection, and they were the only reason State avoided a total meltdown. The relationship grew away from the court, as well—Jamal and Leonard shared DVDs, sweat suits, and even (Pytel had heard) a ZTA sorority sister. They cut each other's hair, gushed about new Nikes, cars, and the future of the team. Pytel had heard the duo discuss "next season" with ten games still remaining.

Pytel was responsible for Jamal Davis and Leonard Redmond choosing State. Maybe that explained their loyalty to him, as lukewarm as it seemed. Neither Jamal nor Leonard had been highly regarded in high school, which gave Pytel cachet as a shrewd evaluator. Conversely, any player who flopped—or got arrested—stuck to his recruiter like a rash. "Smooth" Wilkerson, for instance, had turned out to be a bad gamble, a kid whose mean-spirited aggression Pytel had assumed would surface at game time, but never did.

Also, Pytel had set up Leonard's class schedule the previous spring, the academic equivalent of a picnic. Leonard owed him for that, because he made the Honor Roll at a time when he desperately needed the grades, weeks before his hushed-up court case was set to commence. The fifteen hours of "A" also meant he was a sure bet to remain eligible. He was popular with the fans, but the media depended on Jamal because Leonard was a bit coarse—he had too many tattoos to be a spokesman.

The truth was that most of the players disliked Pytel because he reported weekly to their mothers, and his calls focused on missed classes, missed study halls, or misdemeanors. The calls to Jamal's mom were unique, though, because Jamal was never late, never cursed the cafeteria ladies or parked in the handicapped spot—he had a bicycle. Jamal was a semi-serious student who declined to take the typical route of the Criminal Justice major. Although Pytel seldom clashed with Jamal, he still worried about him, but in a different way than he worried about the other knuckleheads.

In December, with hope for a decent season still alive, Pytel suggested Jamal to the sports marketing office as State's poster boy for a campus-wide campaign. Marketing agreed and used their star freshman: *You Don't Have to Drink to Have a Good Time* posters were plastered all around the university.

But it helps! somebody had scrawled at the bottom of nearly every poster. Leonard liked to say that Jack Hood wrote the postscript. Pytel thought that was funny and maybe even true. It could have been Hood, or his wife.

Just before the conference tournament, when Pytel thought things couldn't get worse, two scrubs got arrested for lifting lunchmeat from a grocery store. The newspaper used mug shots of the morons under the headline "Hood's Hoods." The article, of course, did not mention Leonard Redmond and his little problem from the past. But an editorial that day called not so much for the basketball coach's resignation as for his head—and hinted Hood would be terminated, after just two years at State, when the season concluded.

It was obvious to Pytel which way the wind was blowing. "Start looking around for a job, boys," Pytel advised his fellow assistant coaches. The timing would be ironic if Hood got axed. He had a year left on his three-year deal, and if the administration left him alone, the squad (with a handful of freshmen, and the entire front line to return, including Jamal Davis and Leonard Redmond) could be vastly improved, possibly even qualify for the NCAA tournament. But if that happened it would be impossible for the university not to offer Hood an extension.

Hood dismissed the lunchmeat larceny culprits from the team immediately, an addition-by-subtraction move. Then State won two games in their conference tournament. That impressive little surge was not enough to get them an NCAA bid, but the administration seemed to change course: they were willing to allow Hood to fulfill his final year.

Jamal and Leonard were named All Conference the following week, something Pytel knew Jack Hood had tried to veto with his vote. Two all-league players and a losing record? They might as well give Hood a plaque that read "This Man Cannot Coach."

"He *can't* coach," Pytel heard Leonard say more than once. Jamal might have thought the same thing, but he was polite enough not to say it.

By June, the coaches had stopped meeting as a staff, fractured by different duties—preparing for their summer camp for kids, recruiting trips, or, in Jack Hood's case, sipping vodka tonics. For Pytel, it also meant two days of lugging boxes into a U-Haul. His wife had abandoned him for California, although, as Pytel reminded himself, they were still legally married. And the team had a good season on the horizon, if they didn't lose Jamal Davis over this mysterious stolen car.

Jamal cracked the apartment door an inch, realized it was Pytel, and unhooked the chain. Pytel handed him the certified letter from the university that he'd taken off his dormitory door. Jamal was holed up, alone, because Leonard Redmond was in Colorado.

Before Pytel drove that morning to Leonard's place at the Sunset Villa complex, he'd phoned Ernie and Jack Hood. Neither had spoken with Jamal, couldn't find him, they said. Pytel didn't let on that knew where he was stashed.

He smiled at Jamal and said, "Who are you hiding from?"

"Everybody," Jamal said. The other fuckups on the team would have been annoyed or defensive, but Jamal was relieved and happy to see Pytel. He said he had a dozen phone messages from the university lawyer, nearly as many from Jack Hood.

Pytel sat, tried to relax. This was going to take a while to get the entire story and come up with a plan. His impatience with the players was sometimes obvious—*What you mad at now?* they often asked when he approached.

"Tell me what happened," Pytel said.

"I got high on pot the last day of school," Jamal said, as if that explained anything.

"That's why you stole a car in July?"

"No. This isn't a simple story." Jamal said that a month ago he'd bicycled to Leonard's apartment, stoned on weed for the first time in his life after a white kid had smoked him up that afternoon at a fraternity beer bash.

"Tell him to leave you the fuck alone," Leonard said when Jamal showed up with red eyes. Leonard's tone meant he was serious, and Jamal agreed to blow off the entire fraternity. Jamal locked Leonard's doors and windows like he was back in Detroit, then fell asleep on the couch for two hours.

"Peep this out," Leonard told him when he awoke. "Nobody even knows I smoke. I tell people, I don't *take* pot. Everyone thinks you're a buster if you say it like that."

"When did you start worrying about your image?" Jamal asked, assessing Leonard's tattoos.

"I'm worried about you. Smoking with white boys you just met?" Leonard made Jamal promise they'd only get high together. "Sit your ass up, you're falling asleep again," Leonard said, and poured him a Red Bull over ice.

That was when Leonard told Jamal his own story. He said he nearly got stuck playing only home games. "That means doing prison time," he added.

Jamal was surprised—nobody on the team even knew Leonard had been arrested in Chicago for selling marijuana after his freshman year. All the coaches knew, though. That was precisely why Pytel had enrolled Leonard in the easiest classes a year ago, so he'd have something to show the judge when asking for leniency.

"My English teacher knows, too," Leonard admitted. He'd written a long personal essay about his arrest. The players often recycled school papers within the team, but Leonard said he shredded that one. "I was lucky," he added. "My case got dropped after a couple of weeks."

Pytel interrupted Jamal's story. "Actually, Leonard's case didn't get dropped that soon," he said. "The case got dropped just a few months ago." It took two years, although Pytel never really understood exactly why.

Jamal said he was simply repeating Leonard's explanation.

Despite the problems that came from selling weed, Leonard confessed to a single positive. He'd made a lot of money, kept the cash in his closet now, and he'd hardly touched it. Sixteen thousand dollars. He'd planned to use it for a real lawyer if he lost his court case and needed to appeal. But now? He thought about buying his first car and had been combing through the *Wooden Nickel's* ads. "That's where you come in," Leonard said.

Jamal had found his used mountain bike in the *Wooden Nickel*, gotten a great price, and he'd turned Leonard on to the weekly trade paper. Leonard didn't want to buy his vehicle from a local dealership because car dealers were university boosters. They knew the coaches, knew everybody in town. State's best player buying an SUV with cash? There'd be too much talk. So Leonard asked Jamal to help him sift through the weekly paper.

The next day, by chance, Leonard got selected to try out for the World University Games. He'd be flying to Colorado Springs in a week, at the end of June.

Jamal felt a jolt of jealousy—he was already stuck working as a counselor at the Jack Hood Basketball Academy, where the camp's namesake hardly made an appearance. Leonard quit his counselor's post the minute he got the invitation for the tryout.

Pytel, for his part, was thrilled not to have to work that camp anymore, although Hood still cut him in on the profits a bit. Babysitting kids with basketballs wasn't any fun—"Hold the ball!" was Pytel's summer camp coaching philosophy. And his main teaching tool was something he'd come to despise during the season. "Here's a video I'll bet you kids have never seen," he found himself saying every afternoon.

But Leonard said that the easy work was precisely the point. He had once used up an entire afternoon helping his team of twelve-year-olds pick their own nicknames. All white kids, they wanted to sound "street." Leonard was happy to comply—*Gangsta Boy, Pimp Thang, Smooth Ride*. He wrote their new names on the back of their camp shirts in flowing cursive. His group even invented an elaborate handshake. All season those kids had loitered on the concourse after games, waited patiently for Leonard so they could perform their handshake. *Remember me? Mack Daddy?* In fact, one of the camper's mothers called Pytel to complain. Her son had used a Sharpie to tattoo *Bad Nigga* on his forearm.

To celebrate his invitation to Colorado Springs, Leonard decided to splurge, to finally spend his sixteen thousand. But the search stalled. He couldn't decipher the *Wooden Nickel* ads; the terminology and abbreviations frustrated Leonard. This was typical—he found the Internet, in fact all technology, perplexing. He said he had over two thousand unopened emails.

Jamal figured it was the end of the semester, that kids needed to pay off their debts, this was a good time to buy. A few days before Leonard was to leave, they sat at his kitchen table and sifted through the weekly. "We're late," Jamal said finally. "You have to get the paper at noon on Fridays, right when it comes out, because stuff moves fast. And if something gets listed two or three weeks in a row, make sure the price is going down."

Leonard became anxious as his departure for Colorado closed in on him. When Jamal pointed out a steal on a 2002 Mitsubishi Endeavor they had overlooked the week before, Leonard got angry. "Look man," he said, "anyone can point out mistakes after the fact. That's Jack Hood. He panics at game time, but he's got it all figured out during films two days later. Tell you what. I'm leaving for my tryout tomorrow. Come look here." He walked Jamal to his closet, which was stacked, top to bottom, two deep, with Nike boxes. "Too bad we're not the same size, huh?" he said. He slid a box out of the center and revealed the contents.

"Holy Jesus," Jamal said. He'd never seen that kind of money. Rolls of hundreds were stuffed inside a pair of shoes Leonard had never worn. Jamal reached without thinking, but Leonard slammed the box back in.

"Don't start, Church Boy," Leonard said. "That's not the collection plate." He hadn't called Jamal "Church Boy" in six months, and it stung, more than it should have. "I wasn't going to rock those shoes anyway," he said. Leonard would only appear publicly in sneakers that were new releases or retro classics. The overflow dictated that he give some shoes a few years to "marinate."

Pytel felt queasy when Jamal described the towering Nike boxes. The shoes must still be there, in the apartment.

Leonard said, "You hook me up when I'm gone, Jamal. Find the right car, pull the trigger. I trust you, so surprise me. Anybody will take cash."

Jamal was silent.

"Come on, man," Leonard continued, "I'm not playing you, there's no risk. Tell you what, we'll get two sets of keys and you can use the car whenever you get ready. But not to go to no fuckin' frat boy parties."

Jamal reluctantly agreed. The Jack Hood Basketball Academy ended Friday at noon. He could be waiting when the *Wooden Nickel* was dropped off at a convenience store. "But I'll call before I buy anything with your money," he suggested.

Pytel interrupted the story again. "Leonard *did* play you," he said. "He shouldn't expect you to cart around his drug money. You took a big risk for Leonard."

Because Pytel was in Phoenix, on the lookout for the next Jamal Davis, he missed the camp awards ceremony. But Pytel knew the routine: every child got an 8x10 of Jack Hood, the autograph forged by Ernie.

Jamal said he'd hurried through the final formalities, the autographs and photos, and cornered Ernie for his paycheck.

"And Ernie gave you a hug, too," Pytel suggested. He knew it was true when Jamal ignored the jab.

Jamal said he'd ducked out of the arena, cycled down the

street to the PicQuik, and waited for the *Wooden Nickel's* delivery van. His pacing in front of the store window must have made the clerk nervous because the kid stuck his head out the door. "You have to buy something or leave," he said meekly. "We had a stickup this year."

Jamal apologized and bought a bucket-sized soda. He sat on the curb and pictured Leonard's giant wad of cash in the shoebox, sipping endlessly while he waited.

The van arrived and Jamal grabbed a paper before they were racked. He laid it across his handlebars, poised for action. A 2003 Escalade, low miles, grabbed his attention. The asking price was $17,000, "cash discount, must sell." Somebody was in trouble. He pedaled furiously to Leonard's apartment to look up the Blue Book price online—and collect the money—sensing this was the right deal. He called Leonard to get the go-ahead. But Leonard's cell phone rang on his own kitchen counter, where it sat charging.

Jamal decided he'd do nothing at all. He'd tell Leonard it was his own damn fault that he forgot his phone.

But he began to imagine Leonard talking smack, maybe even giving him a new nickname. *Fraidy Boy. Big Pussy*. Something like that.

The Escalade owner said, in broken English, he'd only take cash. Jamal kept the phone shouldered to his ear as he pulled the shoebox out and jammed the money into a baggie and then into his shorts. He'd be a thousand dollars light, but anyone who saw sixteen thousand would have to bite. "I got cash, don't worry," Jamal told him, and the man suggested they meet right then at a Target parking lot. The store was within biking distance so despite the heat, Jamal agreed.

As a negotiating ploy, Jamal put one thousand in a different pocket. He'd start by offering fifteen, unfurl it like a winning poker hand, claim that was all he had. He could bring out the other thousand if need be.

The little man was all smiles, kept calling Jamal "my friend."

Jamal took a test spin around the parking lot after he adjusted the seat and mirrors, checked under the hood as if he knew what to look for. He signed both sheets that read "Bill of Sale." The man asked Jamal to write down his address, then to sign a copy of the title. He said he'd get it notarized and mail it in to the DMV, and the state in turn would mail it back to Jamal. The man counted the cash quickly and handed over the keys, didn't even notice the payment was two thousand dollars light. He disappeared into the Target store.

Jamal felt high. He hoisted his bike into the hatchback. On his return to Leonard's, dickering with the radio, he blew through a stop sign.

"I didn't steal the car," Jamal said to punctuate his story. "I bought it."

Pytel cradled his head in his hands. "You left the Target without the car's title?"

"My ass was on TV, huh?" Jamal said, ignoring Pytel's question. "At least nobody will ever call me Church Boy again."

Jamal's arrest, his hands spread across the hood of the nearly-new Escalade, had been caught on camera by a curious passerby. Local television had broadcast a file tape of Jamal, peddling his beloved bike in one sequence, in handcuffs in front of the SUV the next.

The episode had played repeatedly on ESPN and was splashed across the local newspaper. Jamal told the cops he'd paid cash for the car. That made the paper too, even the dollar amount. The university issued a statement that somehow distanced the school from Jamal Davis, yet also embraced him.

Pytel's cell phone went off. It read "Southern AZ State."

He had been screening Jack Hood's calls for the last twenty-four hours to allow time to protect himself, get things straight with his recruit. The greatest advancement for college basketball coaches in the last few decades was Caller ID. You wouldn't miss a recruit's call, or, for that matter, have to coddle one of your own player's parents after you'd been drinking. Pytel spent a quarter of his waking hours on the phone, maybe a third.

Pytel let his phone ring out, but it started up again. Maybe this was Jack Hood on a school line, although he rarely made it to the office before lunch. Pytel couldn't keep ducking Hood, who always had inane questions—"Why does Smooth Wilkerson like to overpower his girlfriends but not the other team's center?" was one he asked Pytel constantly.

This call could also be Ernie or Tyrone Gage calling with valuable news. Pytel picked up. It was the fucking university's attorney, summoning him back to campus. Pytel said he could meet in twenty minutes.

Nothing good could come of a stolen car or unaccounted-for-cash, not for Jamal's recruiter, and Pytel feared that he'd be a prime suspect for the origin of the cash. If this got pinned on him it wouldn't be fair, not at all. Yet he couldn't just point the finger at Leonard, or blame Jamal, not without losing perhaps both of their best players.

"What'd you have to tell the cops the dollar amount for, anyway?" Pytel said as he pocketed his phone.

"It was the truth," Jamal said. "Everything happened the way I said. You believe me, right?"

"Sure," Pytel said. He hoped that knowing Jamal's version before the lawyer might somehow be an advantage. "The school lawyer is waiting for me. Stop crying, I'll be right back. He'll want to talk to you next."

"Nobody is accusing anyone at this point, this is all preliminary," the university attorney said, but he pushed the tape recorder close to Pytel. The man had the gaunt frame and unhappy face of a marathon runner. He said he had not yet interviewed Jack Hood about the vehicle, was saving the head coach for last. That meant the school was either building a case against Hood or shielding him, Pytel didn't know which.

"We don't believe Jamal Davis is really stealing cars," the lawyer said through a forced smile. "Or we hope he is not. But it's a strange coincidence that Mr. Davis paid cash for this vehicle on the final day of your basketball camp."

"It's not *my* basketball camp," Pytel said. The last two weeks, he reiterated, he hadn't been in town. Although Pytel did keep close tabs on the camp's attendance figures. The income was yet another perk of being a head coach, something he still longed for. Three weeks of camp, so nine hundred kids total this year. Multiplied by three hundred bucks apiece. Anyone could do the math. Hood paid a pittance to his camp staff, but kept a fortune for himself. Summer camps were like offshore banks because nobody bothered to check account levels, and if you played smart, nobody could.

"It's possible Mr. Davis really did steal that car," the lawyer said. "Worst case. But let's assume the young man did as he claimed to the arresting officer, bought a stolen car."

I know more than this guy does, Pytel thought. He sipped at the Diet Coke that the lawyer's secretary had fetched, said he wasn't aware that Jamal had that kind of cash until he saw the news. He also knew to be careful of questions the attorney already had the answer to. Sure enough, here came one, as big as a basketball.

"What was Jamal's salary at the basketball camp?"

Pytel had forgotten to ask Jamal that. "You'd have to ask Ernie Lancha," he offered. "Jack Hood made Ernie the camp director three years ago."

The lawyer's face lifted at the mention of Jack Hood and Ernie. "We interviewed Ernie earlier," he said, "but, again, we've yet to speak to Coach Hood."

The revelation about Ernie angered Pytel. Ernie had made no mention of meeting with a school lawyer.

"We'd like to get this settled," the lawyer continued, "so we can clean things up and the NCAA doesn't have to come to town. You recruited Jamal, right?"

Pytel said, "I haven't done anything wrong." He knew instantly that he'd reacted badly at exactly the wrong time, when Jamal's recruitment was mentioned. But it was due to learning that Ernie had been questioned already and could possibly know things that Pytel did not.

"Nobody is saying that, Mr. Pytel," the attorney said.

"Yeah, Jamal was my recruit."

The attorney wrote something down, flipped a page on his yellow pad, and studied it. "Ernie claimed that you told him how much to pay the summer camp counselors."

Pytel nearly jumped at the mention of Ernie's accusation too, but he quickly regrouped. He had made some suggestions about Jamal's salary, sure, but nothing concrete, nothing written down. "I may have told Ernie *which* players to hire," he said. "But I don't control the camp's purse strings."

"Who does?"

Pytel was supposed to just come out and say it, but he wouldn't—out of some kind of misplaced loyalty or a code he could not name. He might piss off the attorney by bouncing questions back, but Pytel did it anyway. "What's the name on that camp brochure?" he said, and he nodded at the glossy tri-folded pamphlet on the table.

"Jack Hood's Basketball Academy," the lawyer said.

"And who signs the checks?" he said, getting bolder.

"Jack Hood. And Ernie," he said, playing along.

"There you go," Pytel said. "You're talking to the wrong cowboy."

That ended the interview, and Pytel hadn't told the lawyer anything that wasn't already in black and white. His soft drink was still cold, an indication of the meeting's brevity. He knew he'd crossed some kind of line, not covering for the man who'd hired him a couple of years ago. But should he have lied and said it was the Steve Pytel Basketball Academy, that he endorsed the checks?

The attorney showed Pytel out, said something about carelessness, but Pytel was distracted by the realization that this guy—and maybe the entire administration—believed Jamal Davis had been handed fifteen grand from Jack Hood's summer camp coffers.

Now, in July, the administration might understand that this was their window to dump Jack Hood.

Pytel came to another realization almost the instant he stepped into the desert sunshine: he could be named head coach if Hood was fired.

Maybe only as an interim, but the school wouldn't have time for a lengthy list of interviews, not in early July. By the time the controversy settled, it might be August. Even September. His mood brightened at his good fortune and timing—anyone could coach next year's team to a winning record, and when he did he'd likely get a multi-year contract.

During Pytel's time in the administration building, it had both poured rain and cleared up. No real sewer systems existed on the desert campus, so puddles were everywhere. A car blaring rap music drove too close to him and sprayed a muddy mess on his shirt. The kids looked back and laughed but he couldn't make out their faces.

Pytel needed to talk to somebody, but not Jamal Davis again, not yet. With his wife apartment hunting in California, who could he confide in? Not Tyrone Gage, who would also be after Hood's job. State had a black coach for three years in the 1980s, and it didn't work out—boosters still complained about that era. That would spoil Gage's chances.

Pytel remembered that Jamal had never told him exactly what he had been paid from the camp. He phoned Jamal but it went to voicemail. Would talking to Hood at this point be foolish? Pytel noticed several new calls from him, and he had to do something to distract him, pacify him. Pytel took a chance and called Hood at his home.

"You're not going to believe it," Pytel said. "Ernie gave Jamal all that money from your summer camp account."

"That stupid son of a bitch," Hood said. Then, "I don't believe it."

"I didn't either, at first," Pytel said. "But what other explanation is there?"

Hood demanded that Pytel set up a meeting with Jamal, bring the kid to the office later that day.

"I haven't talked to Jamal since he called me from jail," Pytel said, but he promised to go by the dorms and find him. Both Jack Hood and the school's lawyer wanted Jamal Davis, but Pytel knew he'd better keep him hidden at Leonard's for the time being.

But Pytel couldn't resist making a point with Ernie, so he drove across campus to the basketball office, the lawyer's business card between his fingers like a burning cigarette. The attorney's words echoed in his head. *Ernie led me to believe that you told him what to pay the players who worked at the camp*. If Ernie blamed him for Jamal getting that kind of cash, he wouldn't feel bad about reversing the charges. Yet Pytel had to be cautious about what he said. Ernie would repeat it one day.

Ernie was in his office, thumbing through a *Sports Illustrated*. For some reason, that set Pytel off. "You told me you were still in Phoenix," Ernie said. "Jack Hood is looking for you. What happened to your shirt?"

Pytel took the magazine from Ernie, flipped through it, and flung it into his face. The pages fluttered like a wounded duck. "Hey," Ernie protested.

"You didn't tell me you'd talked to the school's lawyer."

"He told me not to discuss it with anyone. Not even Jack Hood."

"How long was your interview?"

"An hour, I guess," Ernie said.

"You paid Jamal in cash and tried to finger me? And you said that I decided what the players got paid?" Pytel was leaning over the desk and some spit flew from his mouth.

"Coach Hood told me to ask you about salaries," Ernie said. "I gave Jamal a check for seven-fifty. And seven-fifty in cash. That's what you told me to do," he said decisively, as if he'd suddenly been to see the Wizard of Oz for courage. "But that's fifteen *hundred*," Ernie said, "not fifteen *thousand*. Calm down." He wiped his face. "Anyway, you always say we've got to *take care of Jamal*."

Overpaying a player—in this case, by twice as much—was against NCAA rules. "Taking care of Jamal doesn't mean to give him fifteen thousand," Pytel said, sticking to his script. "That's what you gave him, and you tried to pin it on me."

"I didn't pay him that much. It's just a coincidence that

it sounds the same. I'm the low man," Ernie reminded him needlessly. "They don't think I set the salaries myself."

"Well, my signature isn't on anything," Pytel said. "Is yours?" Pytel picked up a leftover stack of autographed photos of Hood meant for the campers. "Have you ever forged Hood's signature before?" he asked. Ernie had probably signed Hood's name to the checks, too. Ernie's shoulders sagged, and Pytel came to an odd understanding—what he'd initially feared to be a personal disaster might instead be the perfect convergence of evidence and circumstances, if he could protect Jamal and Leonard from blame.

"Anyway," Pytel continued as he rose, "where was Hood on the last day of his own camp?"

"He doesn't come because the campers make him nervous," Ernie said. "You know that. He's like you, kids annoy him."

I like kids, Pytel thought, but there was no point in arguing with Ernie now. He was through with him.

Local police were quoted the next day as saying that the SUV had been stolen from Yuma, Arizona, a Wild West noonday carjacking in the hundred-degree heat. But not by Jamal Davis. The gunman had been arrested but the car had made it across the state. The police believed that Jamal Davis had indeed foolishly given a lump of cash to the gunman's brother. The brother, investigators theorized, probably took a bus after unloading the car on Jamal and crossed into Mexico with the money. The charges against Jamal Davis were dropped.

Pytel was calculating his next move when the school's lawyer phoned again, this time from a private number. Pytel felt a sense of dread, but the lawyer asked for an "unofficial" meeting, suggested a tiny Mexican café far from the university. In fact, he said, he was already there waiting. But what could this mean? Was it possible that Jamal Davis had met with him? Pytel knew precisely where the café was, but he drove slow as he tried to connect the pieces.

They were the only customers. If this were a mob movie, it would be the perfect setting for a hit. But the lawyer said, "I don't have the tape recorder with me," and he raised his hands as if Pytel might want to frisk him. Everything was off the record, he added and smiled at Pytel for the first time, gushed about how good the basketball team could be the following season, a strange topic under the circumstances. Or was it? He smacked the menu down and said, "I'm not even hungry. Are you?"

Pytel knew to wait this out, keep quiet.

"Some higher-ups at the university aren't at all happy with Jack Hood," he said. "He's worn out his welcome in just two years. He's abrasive."

No shit, Pytel thought.

"His players are bad actors," he continued. "They get arrested. His contract is a huge burden. The school is ready to make a change in leadership, and if a major rules violation is found, we can justify it."

Pytel had grown to hate Hood and wasn't shocked to hear administrators disliked him. But he almost said something in defense of the charge that Hood's players were bad actors. Not all of them. Not Jamal Davis, for one, despite recent events.

The lawyer dropped his voice, although nobody was around, and the implication was obvious—it was time to trust each other. "Just as you suggested, Ernie admitted he gave Jamal too much money, but he says it was fifteen hundred, not fifteen thousand. Still, it's inconsistent with the other counselors' salaries and that's a major violation."

"Okay," Pytel said.

"But Ernie claimed that you pushed him—and I'm quoting here—to take care of Jamal."

"That's not true," Pytel said.

"The point is," he said reassuringly, "that your fingerprints, in a figurative sense, aren't anywhere to be seen." He paused while the waitress refilled their coffees. "Coming right out," she said, although neither of them had ordered breakfast.

"It's obvious where that cash came from," the lawyer continued. "This basketball camp brought in nearly three-hundred-thousand dollars, gross. The administration didn't have a clue how much money is floating around this camp, although you can be sure we'll take our share from here on. Anyway, it's apparent that Hood had authorized Ernie to forge his signature." He grinned at Pytel as though he'd just told a dirty joke.

Pytel smiled. "That's right."

"It's your word against Ernie's. We've got Jack Hood trapped because it's his camp, his responsibility to oversee the money."

Pytel said, "What do you want me to do?"

The lawyer said, "What do you suppose Jamal Davis would say if we asked him who authorized his cash bonus from camp?" He said it in such an off-handed way that Pytel sensed it was the real reason they were meeting.

"I don't know for sure," Pytel said. "Jamal might be wrestled into saying anything."

"Fine. Let me rephrase that," the lawyer said. "Is Jamal closer to you or Ernie?"

"I recruited him. He trusts me. Do you want me to try to find Jamal, to ask him everything that happened?"

Jamal's interview, the lawyer said, was scheduled for ten the next morning, and the pressure was mounting to locate him. "We need to know who to believe, and, frankly, we want to believe you."

"I understand," Pytel said. "Maybe I can track down Jamal for you."

On the drive to see Jamal, the radio claimed more good news for State basketball, besides the fact that Jamal Davis was innocent.

Leonard Redmond had played well enough at his University Games tryout to be selected. A great break, but bad news for Jamal—Leonard wouldn't be home any time soon to advise him. Pytel could capitalize on this; he could coach Jamal, prepare him for the lawyer's questions. For the first time since he arrived at State, he had been given a strange advantage: he could peek at everyone's cards before he made his next move. He parked two blocks from Leonard's apartment and hurried to the door.

"Ernie just came by," Jamal said. "I wasn't sure if I should let him in."

Pytel made himself smile.

"I didn't though," Jamal added.

"Good move. And did you hear the great news?"

Jamal hadn't turned on the TV or read the paper.

"The cops found the car thieves, or one of them. They're brothers. The charges against you were dropped."

Jamal appeared to relax at this information. He said he was tired of hiding out at Leonard's, and the news at least proved he was not capable of car theft. "But they didn't recover the money," Jamal guessed.

"No, not the money," Pytel said. Yet, that was a small problem compared to explaining to the school lawyer—and probably the NCAA—where that cash came from. The police, though, would have no interest in the source of the money Jamal claimed to have paid.

"And Leonard made the team in Colorado too."

Jamal looked at Pytel, digested this bit of news. "I'll have to repay Leonard someday. I need some advice. I was wishing Leonard would twist his ankle, just bad enough to be sent home."

"You want Leonard to get hurt?"

Jamal said that wasn't what he meant; he wanted guidance about what to tell the school's attorney. Pytel saw his opening in Jamal's admission.

"I know what you can't say," Pytel said. "You can't say Leonard gave you the money." That could lead the media to the old charge of Leonard selling drugs in high school, something that nobody but the coaches—and now Jamal— knew. If school officials did their homework, learned Leonard was once arrested for dealing, they might take his scholarship. And they surely wouldn't be sympathetic about Jamal buying a car with drug money.

"You've got to leave Leonard out of this," Pytel said. He knew what weighed on Jamal as much as losing his friend's money—Jamal couldn't tell the truth this time. "I'm going to level with you," Pytel said. "The school thinks that you got the money from our basketball camp. The lawyer is going to accuse you of that tomorrow. At ten in the morning, by the way. They're certain Ernie gave the money to you." Pytel waited for that to sink in.

Jamal got up to pace. "They think Ernie gave me fifteen grand from camp?"

"Exactly." Pytel knew what came next. He'd have to convince Jamal—if the school's people think that already, why not just ride along with it? Why try to force the truth into this and screw up Leonard, Jamal, the whole team? A greater good was calling, calling both Jamal and Pytel. He had to help Jamal to hear that call.

"Maybe since the cops are dropping the charges," Jamal said, "the university will too. Leonard said his drug case got dropped immediately."

"You keep saying that about Leonard's case, but it's not true," Pytel said. Continuance after continuance; the proceedings went on for two years before the charges got dropped.

"You won't believe where Leonard kept the money," Jamal said. He showed Pytel into the bedroom, the closet devoted to Leonard's shoe obsession, the place that had housed the hoard of bills. "Look," Jamal said, sliding out the exact box, "there's still a thousand left that I saved Leonard."

"Sonnuvabitch," Pytel said. The orange boxes rose to the top of the closet like the Great Wall of China. "There must be a hundred pairs here."

"A hundred and six," Jamal said.

"Leonard told you his charges got dropped immediately?" Pytel asked.

"Yup," Jamal said. "Why would he lie to me about that?"

Four times since the arrest Leonard had told Pytel there'd been a continuance for his trial. It hadn't made sense, but Pytel put the trial out of mind because it was nerve-wracking. Pytel *had* wished the whole case would just go away, disappear. In the meantime, he'd been passing Nikes on to Leonard, like the absentee father trying to placate a neglected son. Pytel didn't think he'd slipped Leonard this many pairs—Leonard had stopped accepting the shoes and his chauffeuring to class back in February—but here was the embarrassing proof of both Pytel's guilt and gullibility. He found himself angrier about the shoes than Leonard's lies about his trial status.

"Fucking Leonard has been playing me," Pytel said. "I gave him these shoes because I was worried about him and his stupid charges." Pytel got a sudden jolt of fear—all these free shoes were an NCAA violation, too.

"There wasn't no charges, I told you," Jamal said. "They got dropped."

"But that's not what Leonard told me. He kept saying there was another continuance, up until the case was dropped right after this last season." Pytel decided he'd load as many of the boxes as he could fit into the trunk of his car. He chinned a stack and wobbled towards the door.

"What are you doing?" Jamal said, and blocked his way. "They're just shoes, the money's almost gone." Jamal helped him ease down the boxes. "I figured it was Ernie who gave him these shoes," he added.

Pytel crossed his arms and cursed. Jamal smoothed the boxes back into tidy rows, and put his arm around Pytel's shoulder, directed him away from the closet. Pytel whirled, punched the door in disgust, and some of the boxes tumbled and jammed it so that Jamal could no longer slide it open.

Back in the TV room, they sat on opposite ends of the couch. Jamal reminded him of the obvious dilemma at hand: what to tell the school lawyer about where the cash came from.

"Oh, tell him the goddamned truth," Pytel said. "You used Leonard's savings from his marijuana enterprise. Hey, maybe Leonard could go into the shoe business now," he added sarcastically. "He'd have the only store in America with just size sixteens."

Jamal laughed, but turned solemn. "I could end Leonard's career if I tell the truth."

"And ruin our chances for a good team next year," Pytel said, thinking out loud, finally under control. He studied Jamal. The kid was eighteen going on thirty—he'd been through a lot. The usual single parent upbringing, but also his high school girlfriend's miscarriage, and getting dumped by that same girl for the U.S. Army. The catch with college sports was that it ended by the time these kids were twenty-two. In Jamal's case, he'd be twenty-one. Events simply unfolded too quickly for a young kid to learn much, the window was too small. The players got one chance, while coaches could recycle themselves, learn something, come out brighter in the wash, and start again.

Pytel decided in that moment that the world would be better off without Jack Hood coaching. That simple thought spawned this one: if this Escalade episode indeed cost Hood his job, a promotion was Pytel's destiny. He *would* step forward, take over the team, and he'd do really well. And this was his first duty as the coach—Jamal Davis needed Pytel's guidance, a freshman all over again. "Yeah, you can't say you got the money from Leonard," Pytel said, a new confidence in his voice. "Leave his name totally out."

"What do I say then? Anything bad about Jack Hood means Ernie is going down, too."

"Listen," Pytel said, "Ernie wrote the camp checks, right? He already admitted to the lawyer that he overpaid you. You can't save Ernie now, even if you wanted to."

Jamal brooded. He began flipping through muted cable channels.

"Ernie is young," Pytel said. He took the remote away from Jamal and cut off the TV. That was all Jamal needed, to see himself in handcuffs again. "Ernie's career will recover. In a way you'll be doing him a favor, getting him away from Jack Hood."

"So I should say Ernie gave me all that money?"

"Yes, but be sure to say the money was from camp. Tell them only Hood and Ernie knew about it, and you were surprised it was so much, and you figured if you put all that money in the bank, people would ask questions. So you jumped at the first used car you could find. You just picked the wrong car dealer."

"But they'll fire Ernie," Jamal said. He was close to tears.

"Sure, but Jack Hood, too," Pytel said to balance things.

"Here's your choice. Listen. Do you want Leonard to get in trouble, end his college career? Or would you rather play with Leonard, under a new coach next year?"

"Play with Leonard. And a new coach. But what about Ernie?" Jamal asked.

"Ernie's going down anyway for giving you fifteen hundred. Can't you see? He confessed to that, the amount doesn't matter. You can't save him, so admit it was fifteen thousand he gave you, and you bought the stolen car."

Would Jamal have to find a way to pay fifteen thousand back to the camp? Maybe not. Maybe just half of the fifteen hundred. Still, Jamal might have to repay Leonard. But how could he? No way could he do that. Pytel would worry about it later, when Leonard got home from Colorado. He'd get Leonard alone and think of something.

"If we lose Leonard," Pytel said, "can we still win without him?"

"No," Jamal said.

"But can we win without Jack Hood and Ernie? I'm asking you to think about our team."

"Won't they hang me, too? I'm the one who got caught, not Leonard."

"I'll take care of you," Pytel said. He had an idea. A plan.

It happened two days later. *Hood is History!* the newspaper headline gushed. The administration also released Ernie, and Tyrone Gage too, just for good measure, although Pytel learned that they agreed to pay Gage for a year to avoid a race-based lawsuit.

Pytel phoned California to tell Stephanie the good news. He had done some research on her new school, a community college, and laughed at the irony when he learned their sports teams' nickname: the Claimjumpers. He knew she'd found a rental house—she didn't buy—and was preparing to begin her instructor's job in Early Childhood Development. Yet maybe she'd rethink things if she knew Pytel's slog through college basketball was on the verge of paying off big, and that he was in line for Hood's job—and a hefty raise.

But she seemed to know more than she should; she accused Pytel of advancing his chances for Hood's job with school administrators by strangling Ernie. "You squashed him, I bet," she said, "the way Jack Hood would step on a bug." That ended their conversation. Might she have already spoken with Ernie? How else could she imagine what had been going down? He'd think of her status as "undecided" until he could talk to her again at length. For now he had to focus on how to figure out the situation at hand. If she would not consider a return in a year, he'd have to force himself to think of her status as a recruiting issue: another body needed to be replaced.

State liked Pytel's idea: for the school to use one set of evidence at hand to create a groundswell on campus to fire Jack Hood—and a week later, to use a different set of evidence to save Jamal Davis in response to the NCAA's preliminary inquiry. Jamal had admitted to the school's attorney, after Pytel's push, that he got fifteen thousand dollars. But with that same lawyer by his side, Jamal later denied that amount to the NCAA. The attorney showed NCAA investigators the summer camp accounts, which Ernie had turned over just before he'd been fired. The totals were close to legitimate. Jamal had been slightly overpaid, and the ledger was, in fact, short just $750—still a major NCAA violation, but hardly enough to wreck three careers. There was no indication that $15,000 was missing from camp, but that dollar amount seemed to evaporate. By then, Hood *was* history. So were Gage and Ernie.

And if Jamal had no car, what harm had been done? None, not that anyone could prove.

The NCAA and the university agreed that Jamal needed to sit out one game and return the missing $750 to put him on par with the other counselors' salaries. The NCAA backed off, and the school wouldn't press Jamal to return more than what their official records showed was missing. Leonard Redmond's old summer vocation and arrest were never brought up.

The university's acquiescence showed their confidence in Pytel, in his capabilities to be the head coach. Recruiting was a young man's game and he was in his forties now, too old to be an up-and-coming assistant. But wasn't he the right age to be named a head coach?

That still left Leonard Redmond and his devastated shoe closet depository. Would Leonard lash out at Jamal? Would the car problem and missing money ruin the chemistry they'd been building? Pytel fretted. He tried to set up a meeting a few days after Leonard returned from Colorado—he didn't want trouble between his two stars, not while he was on the verge of taking control of the team.

"We're cool, we worked it out," Leonard told him. "We don't need you."

That gave Pytel an odd feeling. How could Leonard be fine with losing that kind of money? He'd planned on negotiating some vague settlement to be worked out if Jamal wound up playing in the NBA or Europe. Had they done that without Pytel?

A week later, Pytel interviewed for Hood's vacated head job. Somehow the committee knew about his marital situation—one woman offered Pytel her condolences—and Pytel believed he was eliminated from the search due to Stephanie's departure.

But the director of athletics asked him to remain on staff yet again to assist the new coach, who was coming from a New York state university. Initially devastated by not getting Hood's job, he quickly figured out that with their good team in place—many of the players his recruits—they were on the verge of having their best team in decades. And Pytel would be the dean of assistant coaches for the top team in the conference.

We'll be even better when Jamal Davis is a senior, he thought. In three seasons, Pytel and Jamal would each move on to bigger things—Jamal to the NBA. And Pytel could trampoline into his first head-coaching job. The stolen car controversy would have quieted down, and if Stephanie had not returned perhaps he'd be remarried by then.

He could already imagine Jamal's final home game of his senior year, the pageantry. Jamal's mother would have flown in from Detroit for the event, and two cheerleaders would escort their star to midcourt for the ceremony. The ovation would be deafening, but it would fade, be as quiet as a church when a tearful Jamal finally spoke. He'd invite Pytel out from the bench to mid-court in order to publicly thank him in the blazing spotlight. "Join me over here, Coach Pytel," he'd implore. Pytel would decline, but he'd rise and wave modestly to the crowd.

Pytel had become a member of Jack Hood's staff unexpectedly and with trepidation. This time he could be proud, though—he was highly regarded by his university, valuable.

The new head coach brought his entire staff from New York to Southern Arizona. Even a strength coach and video coordinator came along, so Pytel felt like the odd man out, especially when they argued about the Yankees or degraded the local pizza that he brought into the office. His new colleagues were younger, twenty-somethings, and that didn't help Pytel to feel a part of things.

In November, State made an enormous splash—they signed the top junior college recruit in the country, a point guard from Eastern Utah. Pytel was as surprised as anyone by the coup, wasn't even aware they'd been recruiting the kid. The point guard hadn't visited their campus before he'd signed, an unusual occurrence.

One morning, eight games into the new season, with Christmas days away and State still undefeated, Pytel was taken aback to find a young man with spiky hair leaning back in his office chair, his tasseled loafers propped up on Pytel's desk. He was studying a scouting report. Pytel kept a meticulously organized desk and more was out of place than just the occupant.

"If you want to steal my job," Pytel said with a grin, "you don't need to, it's yours for free. Take it."

"Somebody misspelled *strategy*," the young man said in a friendly tone as he swung his feet down and waved the report at Pytel. They introduced themselves, shook hands—this was the junior college coach from Eastern Utah, the coach whose top player was going to enroll at State.

"Let me fix it and bring you a clean copy," Pytel joked. He sat on the visitor side of his own desk for the first time, and they talked about the prized point guard recruit, their seasons so far, and their own career trajectories. "You've had quite a history," the young man said, but Pytel shrugged it off. After a few minutes, Pytel learned why State had an "in" with his coveted player. Just twenty-seven himself, this coach had played at the same New York university where State's new head coach had done so well.

"Is this your first time in Arizona?" Pytel asked.

"It is," he said, "but I can already tell it'll be a great place to live. And coach."

Pytel studied him. The young man kept his face frozen in a smile as he dropped Pytel's scouting report, dropped it next to a copy of *New Homes* magazine, the local real estate profile. Pytel got lightheaded. He put a hand on his desk to steady himself.

Stephanie was in California, maybe permanently. Even so, with a good team finally in place and Jack Hood departed, Pytel had been consoling—no, congratulating—himself because he'd kept his job yet again. Now Pytel understood, and he was certainly the last person on staff to get it: he was coaching this season on borrowed time. This guy who now sat at Pytel's desk had delivered his great guard to State in *exchange* for an assistant's job at State—Pytel's position—and he'd be arriving that spring. Pytel would not be cashing in on State's success.

The junior college coach stood to offer Pytel his desk back, but Pytel excused himself, said he had an errand to run. But what was that errand? The only pressing duty he could think of was updating his CV, and he'd have plenty of time, the remainder of their games, to do that.

ACKNOWLEDGEMENTS

Versions of this book appeared as short stories in *The Southern Review*, *Colorado Review*, *Aethlon*, *Freight Stories*, and *Puerto del Sol*.

I met Robert Boswell by chance in the autumn of 1994. He had a lifelong love of college basketball and was interested in a window into the game. I was anxious to find a door out. In many ways this book is the rebound of that long shot meeting. For nearly two decades, he and Antonya Nelson have been generous friends and patient teachers, not to mention exceptional writers. Thanks so much, Boz and Toni.

Barry Pearce has kept a close watch on this book, which at times must have felt like watching a blank wall while standing in the rain. He's a fine writer, editor, and pal.

John Conroy, the courageous Chicago journalist, provided inspiration and smart edits.

Big thanks to Andrew Blauner: friend first, agent second.

Special thanks to Kevin McIlvoy for his help and encouragement in the early years.

Thanks to Dagoberto Gilb, David Shields, Tony Hoagland, Kath Lee, Lillie Robertson, Mike James, David Meggyesy, Doug Harris, Dave Zirin, Tom Spieczny and Kitty Spalding, Steve and Tracey Yellen.

Thanks to Rob Wilder, Andrew Scott, Bernadette Smyth, Duncan Hayse, Victoria Barrett, Alexander Parsons, Tripp Hartigan, Henry Shukman, Jeff Vance, Greg Hammond, Gina Colantino, Evan Lavender-Smith, Eric Moir, Franklin Tate, Carol Capatani, Becky Hagenston, Phil Hurst, Candice Morrow, Jay Ponteri, Steve Green, Casey Grey, Tim Floyd, Larry Gipson, Tom Bennett, Joe and Jill Somoza, Mark Medoff, Sheila Black, and Mike Austin.

Big thanks to fellow New Mexican Lee K. Abbott for his sage advice.

Thanks to my colleagues at NMSU.

Thanks to Don Kurtz, Tony Judge, and Alex Shakar for their support.

Thanks to Tom Russell, whose songs seem to be the best kind of short story.

Thanks to Lou and Mary Henson, who opened the door and encouraged me.

Thanks to Dick Versace and Jon Ferguson, renaissance coaches.

Thanks to Craig Holden for his grace and dignity.

Thanks to Don Johnson, Scott Peterson, and the Sport Literature Association.

Thanks to Alexander Wolff, Bobbito Garcia, Dan McGrath, and *SLAM* Magazine editor Ben Osborne.

Thanks to the team at Cinco Puntos Press: Lee Merrill Byrd, who is not afraid of tough decisions or ex-coaches. Also Johnny Byrd, Jessica Powers, Elena Marinaccio, and Mary Fountaine. And, of course, thanks and love to the Buddha of the Border, Bobby Byrd, for his patience and friendship.

Finally, thanks and love to my wife Connie Voisine and our daughter Alma.

Handbook of

Clinical Skills

A Practical Manual

Handbook of Clinical Skills

A Practical Manual

Balu H Athreya, MD

Thomas Jefferson University
University of Pennsylvania School of Medicine
Alfred I duPont Hospital for Children

NEW JERSEY • LONDON • SINGAPORE • BEIJING • SHANGHAI • HONG KONG • TAIPEI • CHENNAI

TOMBSTONE OF JASON

Published by

World Scientific Publishing Co. Pte. Ltd.
5 Toh Tuck Link, Singapore 596224
USA office: 27 Warren Street, Suite 401-402, Hackensack, NJ 07601
UK office: 57 Shelton Street, Covent Garden, London WC2H 9HE

British Library Cataloguing-in-Publication Data
A catalogue record for this book is available from the British Library.

Book cover image: Marble tombstone of an Athenian physician called Jason, shown examining the swollen belly of a patient, who appears to be a child with an unnaturally enlarged stomach. Jason is shown seated on a cushioned stool, bearded and draped. An egg-shaped object resembling a cupping vessel is seen on the right.

In translation the inscription reads: 'Jason, also known as Decimus, of the Archarnian deme [an administrative division of Athens] a physician ...'. It then goes on to mention other members of his family. © **Trustees of the Bristish Museum**

HANDBOOK OF CLINICAL SKILLS
A Practical Manual

ISBN-13 978-981-4277-07-5
ISBN-10 981-4277-07-X

Typeset by Stallion Press
Email: enquiries@stallionpress.com

Printed by FuIsland Offset Printing (S) Pte Ltd. Singapore

To “ANNA”

Preface

This book is based on a course on "The Art of Medicine" which I had given every year at the Children's Hospital of Philadelphia for over 20 years to medical students, pediatric trainees, and the staff. I have presented portions of this course at other medical centers in U.S.A, India and Italy. The topics included are skills required of a clinician — listening skills, observational skills, diagnostic skills, problem solving skills, communications skills, and just plain helping skills. Several students and physicians who have attended the course suggested that I put the material together as a book. So here it is.

I wrote this book primarily for medical students and trainees (residents, house officers) in various medical subjects — generalists and specialists. Most of the examples are from pediatrics since that is my area of experience. However, the contents and references should be useful to trainees in other medical disciplines. Other health professionals may also find this book useful.

The purpose of the book is to share practical ideas on how to observe, how to listen, how to help and how to communicate. These skills are important in many other fields and professionals in these disciplines have developed tools to improve these skills. Physicians should feel free and comfortable to borrow these ideas from other professions. Therefore, you will find references from disciplines as varied as Art History and Semantics. Initially I wanted to include classic articles such as *Social Contract* by Talcott Parsons, *Illness Behavior* by David Mechanic and *Helping Relationship* by Carl Rogers as part of the book. Since copyright issues made it difficult to accomplish this goal, I have listed these articles and books as references or as part of the "Reading List" at the end of each chapter.

Most educational programs do not address the topics covered in this book in a formal and systematic manner. That was the reason why I organized this course many years ago. Now these topics have become more and more relevant because of the emphasis on communication and human relation skills in the training and evaluation of physicians for both board certification and recertification. Therefore, this book can be used as a Primer for the newly emerging competency based medical education courses for medical students and physician trainees. I have added specific exercises on clinical skills in the final chapter on *How to Organize a Course on Clinical Competency Skills* to help you get started.

The numbers of people I am indebted to are in the hundreds, starting with the many children who helped me grow as a pediatrician and the many pediatric trainees at The Children's Hospital of Philadelphia and at the A. I. duPont Hospital for Children who helped me grow to be a teacher. My brother, Professor N. H. Athreya and Doctor Lewis Coriell have been my mentors and role models. My interest in human relation skills and communication came from my brother. He is also responsible for most of the ideas in Chapter 10 on learning and teaching. Doctor Coriell gave the foundations for my scientific attitudes to medicine.

Doctor Henry Cecil gave me an opportunity to practice what I had learnt in books and gave me practical pointers. The course I developed and this book are the results of application of clinical skills under Doctor Cecil's watch and support.

Many of the ideas presented in this book were polished during the discussions I have had with Ramaa, my wife, also a physician. She knew of my love for teaching and writing. Without her understanding and support, I could not have become a better teacher. My children Bama, Hari, and Sheela knew my strengths and weaknesses, indulged me a lot and taught me about "knowing myself" first.

I received considerable support and invaluable editorial suggestions from two seasoned academicians in medicine — Doctor Abraham

Verghese of the Stanford University School of Medicine and Doctor Peter Dent at McMaster University, Canada. I acknowledge their help with thanks. I also acknowledge the editorial help I received from Mr. Hiran Ratnayake, Ms. Michelle Stofa and Ms. Kim Eissman with thanks. Mr. Gerald Murray drew Figs. 4.2 and 4.3.

Angela and Richard Hoy of Booklocker.com helped me publish this book in e-format and publish-on-demand schedule. They gave me invaluable suggestions to popularize the book. Without their ideas and help, this book would not have seen the light of the day. I thank them for their support and encouragement.

Following the publication of the e-edition, I received feedbacks from several colleagues. Many ideas from these feedbacks have been incorporated in this book. I wish to give special thanks to two in particular: Doctor James Johnson of Chappaqua, NY and Doctor Bud Weiderman of Washington, DC.

I greatly appreciate the interest and enthusiasm of Ms. Ang Ching Ting and Ms. Shelley Chow of World Scientific Publishing/Imperial College Press. They kept me on schedule with gentle reminders. Their responses were always timely, their support unflinching and their approach always professional.

My sincere thanks to all of these significant people and many more I have not mentioned individually.

Although it is obvious that physicians may be males or females just as patients may be males or females, I have used the word "he" exclusively for the sake of simplicity. Please read he/she wherever you see the word "he". Thank you.

Finally, I have a request for the reader. Please share your ideas and experiences with me, if you wish. I may like to include some of them, with your permission, in future revisions.

Balu H. Athreya, M.D.
A. I. duPont Hospital for Children
1600 Rockland Road
Wilmington, DE 19899
E-mail: bathreya@nemours.org

Go and learn what you do not know; after you learn, *practice!*

Sanskrit Poem

Contents

Part I

Transition To The 21st Century

Chapter 1

Introduction

Why This Book?

I entered medical school in 1951 when adults and children were dying of small pox, measles, and poliomyelitis. Besides a good history and physical examination, the only available diagnostic tools were bedside laboratory procedures such as blood count and urinalysis, and plain roentgenograms. The only available antibiotics were sulfa, penicillin and streptomycin. There was no CT scan or MRI, no cardiopulmonary resuscitation (CPR) and no intensive care unit (ICU).

Medical science and technology have advanced so rapidly in the past 60 years that we can see things our eyes cannot see; hear sounds our ears cannot detect; touch parts of the body we could never have hoped to touch. It is now possible to perform robotic surgery, surgery on the unborn fetus and surgery through natural orifices without any external incision. There is no more smallpox in the world. Poliomyelitis is almost gone. Certain forms of cancers can be cured. It was exciting to be part of this adventure.

My training had a strong scientific foundation. After entering actual practice, I rapidly learned that medicine is more than science. Scientific training is the foundation; but without a personal, human touch in its application, it falls far short of its potential. In the words of one observer, "…the art of medicine lies in the promotion of productive doctor–patient relationships."[1]

I soon realized that in my enthusiasm to "cure" diseases, I had forgotten how to hold hands with the patient, give comfort and "care" for them. I realized that the way patients show their illness, seek help, follow advice, react to stress, and learn to cope depend on several non-medical factors such as their age, sex, belief systems, support systems, social status in life, and economic condition. I realized that I did not have to be an expert in cultural anthropology, sociology, behavioral sciences, and psychology to be able to help my patients. However, I had to develop wider sets of skills and attitudes so that I could treat the whole patient — not just the disease.

I realized, too, that medicine is primarily a helping profession.[2] Therefore, in addition to understanding the latest developments in the pathophysiology of the disease and the individuality of the patient, I have to understand myself and my own needs, beliefs, and motives. Then, and only then, can I become effective in listening, solving problems, making decisions, connecting, communicating, convincing, and becoming worthy of the patient's trust. These are the non-scientific components of the practice of medicine. I had to learn these mostly by myself, although I was fortunate to have had a few role models.

In order to address these issues, I developed a course in the 1970s for pediatric trainees at The Children's Hospital of Philadelphia. I emphasized several topics, including the development of skills in listening, observing, communicating, problem solving, decision making, and negotiating. I introduced several classic articles and books not known to many physician-trainees. These include Talcott Parsons' paper on *Social Contract*, David Mechanic's article on *Help-Seeking Behavior*, Carl Rogers' paper on *The Helping Profession*, Tolstoy's novelette on *Death of Ivan Ilyich*, and poems by William Carlos Williams. I have presented this course, called "The Art of Medicine", to medical students and practicing physicians at the The Children's Hospital of Philadelphia, at the Alfred I. duPont Hospital for Children in Wilmington, Delaware, and at several other medical centers. Several medical students, trainees, and physicians who attended the course implored me to put the ideas into writing. This book is my response.

The purpose of this book is to broaden the horizons of the young physician by showing the spectrum of non-scientific issues that impinge on the clinician's work. The idea is to show that members of other professions also have thought about observing, listening, problem solving, and communicating and have written extensively on these topics. We have a lot to learn from them. One special feature of this book is the reference to classic articles at the end of each chapter and the brief presentations of ideas from original thinkers in several fields such as art history, semantics and educational psychology. I hope that exposure to these ideas helps future physicians to develop better clinical skills.

The Art in Medical Practice

"The practice of medicine is an art based on science," said William Osler. How do you define "art" in the practice of medicine? Webster's Universal Unabridged Dictionary defines *art* as "the modification of things by human skill to answer the purpose intended." A synonym for *art* is *skill.* The word "art" implies that there is opportunity to practice skills which leads to excellence in one's field.

Science allows us to analyze a problem, tease it to pieces, look at it objectively, and help "explain" the problem. Arts and humanities allow us to synthesize the various pieces into an aesthetically sensible whole to which we can relate. Science is analytic, left-hemisphere–dominant. Art is synthetic, right-hemisphere–dominant.

While science can help investigate the mechanism of diseases, it cannot help solve problems of how a patient responds to the disease, stress, and special circumstances of his life. While these problems have to be solved by the affected person, they have to be perceived and understood by the physician so that he can help the patient heal. These considerations demand that the physician uses both halves of the brain in managing his patients and make the practice of medicine scientifically, artistically, and aesthetically complete. It is the art aspect that allows a physician to help patients "feel better even when science cannot heal them."[1]

Science is evidence-based and objective. In accord with the scientific method, a scientist abstracts pieces out of the whole and studies them with certain tools. For this reason, the scientist is looking at only a fragment of the truth from a narrow angle. When he tries to extrapolate from this one fragment to the whole (this is called "misplaced concreteness"), the pieces may not fit together.[3]

Clinicians, on the other hand, are like artists. They will use any tool, any bit of evidence, and any prior experience that will help them create a full picture. Therein lies the danger for the artist. It is easy to stray away from critical thinking.

However, by emphasizing the importance of its methods, namely objectivity and measurement, science relegates knowledge obtained by other methods such as reflection and personal experience as less important or outright trivial. Intuition is considered irrational. Feelings and sentiments are considered anecdotal and unreliable.

In real life practice of medicine, the technical knowledge based on universal phenomena cannot help when applied to solving problems for individual people with unique circumstances. Individual values and judgments, which are not within the sphere of science, have to be taken into account. We need the science of medicine to solve problems at a fundamental level and to advance our knowledge on a solid foundation. We need the art of medicine to apply that knowledge to individuals and to society, to make it practical and useful. How can we merge these two? That is where the word *prudence* comes in.

Art is skill. The root word for skill is *techne* in Greek. In Latin it is *ars* and in English *art*. The skillful way a clinician practices his profession is the art of medicine. Knowledge is the prime requisite. But the skills needed to apply specific knowledge and technical rationality to solve the problems of a single patient includes an ability to take into account the complexity, uniqueness, and unpredictability of the disease in individual patients, the position of the patient within his family and the community and the values, preferences, fears and expectations of the patient.[4] A good clinician will be intuitively considering all these factors even as he is seeing the patient and formulating diagnostic hypothesis and a treatment strategy. This "reflection-during-action" is the process used by the practitioner to deal with specific, unique, uncertain and complex situations.[4] This is the art of medicine. Prudence is a big part of it.

Perhaps we should consider the "art of medicine" as composed of two components. One is subjective, physician-centered and explains the skills of the physician in using professional knowledge to arrive at a medical diagnosis and treatment plan. The other component is patient- and society-centered and defines the factors related to the psychology and the sociology of the patient. The word "*prudence*" is better suited for the first component and the word "*humanities*" for the second component.

Prudence in Medical Practice

In the future, we may have to consider dropping the term "*art of medicine*" to explain the non-scientific aspects of the clinician's work and replace it with the term "*prudence*". Subjective aspects of decision making include the training, personal beliefs, motives, bias and judgment of the physician. Subjective aspects also include the individual variations of patients, their values and preferences and personal station in life. All these go under the heading of "art" and have not come under adequate scrutiny until recently. When these variables lead to variations in patient outcomes, the public, policy makers, and insurance companies want an adequate explanation. They want to know why some physicians and some hospitals do better in managing certain problems. They do not want to hear about the difficulties of practicing the "art of medicine".

Prudence may be a better word since physicians do use this virtue when choosing between alternatives. The root word for prudence is *prudentia*, which comes from *providere*, which in turn stands for foresight and for providing for eventualities.[5] Prudence in making decisions implies attention to the present while being careful about the consequences of present actions. Prudence differentiates the reflexive from the reflective action, judiciousness from recklessness.

Stoic philosophers defined prudence as a science of what to do and what not to do. The term presupposes uncertainty, risks, chance, and the unknown. These are exactly the conditions of medical practice, even with all the advances in knowledge. It will always be so. Since "prudence is not science; rather, it replaces science where science is lacking"[5] and since prudence considers the future when choosing between alternatives where "no proof is possible or adequate," it is an ideal compliment to science.

Pellegrino[6] suggested several rules as part of clinical prudence. They are:

- Act to optimize as many benefits, minimize as many risks as possible.
- The serious treatable diseases *must* not be missed; the non-serious and non-treatable diseases *may* be missed.
- Use the clinical Ockham's razor; don't multiply causes, diseases, tests or treatments without justifiable necessity.
- Only reluctantly rest the case for any diagnosis or treatment.
- Clinical skepticism is the only guard against the tyranny of the "established" diagnosis, ancillary data, and the findings of colleagues (lab results, X-ray, etc.).
- Maintain a high degree of skepticism for uncommon manifestation of the common diseases. "Hoof beats don't mean zebras," unless zebras are in the vicinity.
- Even after all the data are in, continuing debate is the safeguard against error.
- Recognize your own clinical style, prejudices, and beliefs about what is good for patients.
- Be wary of hunches, intuitions, E.S.P. — gamble with your own fate, not the patient's.

I would like to add the following additional rules:

- Patient's needs and anxieties come before physician's conveniences.
- Moral relationships come before legal relationships.
- Logical reasoning alone does not assure favorable outcome.
- Patients often need solutions to their day-to-day problems of living before referral for mental health.

Major Message: This book is about the exercise of prudence and clinical skills in the practice of medicine, the elements of medical practice relevant for all times. Since prudence replaces science where science cannot help, the word "*prudence*" may be more appropriate than the word "*art*" to describe the non-scientific aspects of medicine.

- "...art of medicine lies in the promotion of productive doctor–patient relationship."
- Science is analytic; art is intuitive.
- Prudence stands for foresight and providing for eventualities.

References

1. Bates RC. *The Fine Art of Understanding Patients*. 2nd edn. 1972. Oradell, NJ; Medical Economic Press.
2. Odegaard CE. *Dear Doctor: A Personal Letter to the Physician*. 1986. Menlo Park, CA; The Henry J Kaiser Family Foundation.
3. Schwartz MA, Wiggins O. Science, Humanism, and the Nature of Medical Practice: A Phenomenological View. In White KL (Ed.). *The Task of Medicine*. 1988. Menlo Park, CA; The Henry Kaiser Family Foundation.
4. Schon DA. *The Reflective Practitioner*. 1983. USA; Basic Books Inc.
5. Comte-Spanville A. *A Small Treatise on the Great Virtues*. 2001. New York; Metropolitan Books.
6. Bulger RJ, McGovern JP. *Physician Philosopher: The Philosophical Foundations of Medicine: Essays by Dr. Edmund Pellegrino*. 2001. Charlottesville, Va; Garden Jennings Publishing Co.

Reading List

Balint M. *The Doctor, His Patient and the Illness*. (Churchill Livingston 1963) 2nd edn. 2003. Philadelphia; Elsevier Publishers.

Mengel MB, Holleman WL, Fields SA. *Fundamentals of Clinical Practice: A Textbook on the Patient, Doctor and Society*. 2002. New York; Kluwer Academic/Plenum Publishers.

Chapter 2

Clinical Competence and New Directions in Medical Education

Abraham Flexner (1866–1959) started as a teacher and principal of a secondary school. He became the first director of the Institute of Advanced Studies at Princeton and had a profound effect on medical education in the United States and Canada. In 1910, he wrote a paper entitled "Medical Education in the United States and Canada" (later known as the Flexner Report) that laid the scientific foundation for the teaching and practice of medicine during the 20th century. The results are self-evident. We are starting the 21st century with a strong scientific foundation, exciting new possibilities, and hope for real cures for many currently incurable diseases. However, we are also starting the 21st century with several new issues and a broken patient–physician "dyad".

Why did the "dyad" break? How did the covenant between a physician and his patient that once governed their relationship get diluted? Is it because physicians have become so enamored with medicine's advances, gadgets, and inventions that they have forgotten the person behind the illness? Is it because physicians have become technicians, as perceived by the public? Is it because of distractions presented by all the regulations and paperwork?

Or is it because patients have changed in their outlook and expectations? Is it because patients do not accept the help that physicians are so eager to give without questioning and double-checking? Is it because patients are ready to sue physicians even after receiving the best of care delivered in good faith?

The problems lie with both parties.

Physicians face a dilemma, because of the complexity of the systems of delivery of medical care and competing pressures.[1] In the old "compact" with the society, the doctors sacrificed early earnings, studied hard and long, and madc sure that patients were provided with "good" care. The physician received a reasonable income, autonomy, job security, and respect from the patient and the public.

Things have changed. In the current climate, physicians are still motivated to do their best, spend several years in training, put in long working hours. But they do not get the same respect as they used to and indeed there is a good chance they will be sued even if they did everything correctly. There is no more job security. Many physicians are concerned about loss of control over clinical decision making, increasing pressures on their time, threat of malpractice suits, and the cost of malpractice insurance. There are demands for greater accountability and external monitoring of time spent and "quality" of work. As Kassirer pointed out, "disgruntled, cranky doctors are not likely to provide outstanding medical care."[2]

Patients are unhappy because of increases in the cost of care, inability to access care when needed, unreasonable expectations, and unfulfilled promises. They are not sure whether their welfare is the physician's primary focus. Patients also have unreasonable expectations of what medicine can and cannot do. From the society's point of view, what is the use of boasting about the best medical care in the world, if it is not available to the needy and if, when available, it bankrupts the family's resources?

Overemphasis on the strengths of science has raised unreasonable expectations on the part of the patients and the public. Physicians are partly responsible for this expectation by making people believe that every symptom is always due to a disease; every disease can be diagnosed if only we have the right test; every disease can be cured if only we have the right specialist and more research, and so on. When things do not go well, we tell the public belatedly that medicine is an art and an imprecise science. For the public, that is a lame excuse.

The medical profession has to do a better job of educating the public on science and pseudo-science and on the limitations of what medicine can and cannot do. Until this gap between expectation and reality is closed, there will be stress on the "dyad".

The enormous progress we have seen in medical science during the past century is directly related to changes made in academic medicine based on the recommendations of the Flexner Report. The challenges facing the medical profession today are related to both these advances in medical sciences and to the changes in the socio-political climate of medical practice. In my mind, the three most important changes are: (1) Explosion of scientific knowledge resulting in new technologies and specialization; (2) Patient autonomy, patient rights and the public demand for a voice in medical decision making and on allocation of resources; (3) Cost of care and a complicated administrative structure directly related to items 1 and 2. These changes are discussed below in more detail.

Technology and Specialization

Increase in medical knowledge has created several new technologies and specialties. This has resulted in better and earlier diagnosis and prolongation of life for those who are sick and can get access to these specialties and technologies. It has not necessarily improved overall health or health care and has caused social inequities. As Odegaard pointed out, the primary goal of medicine is "caring", not necessarily "knowing".[3] That does not deny the fact that knowing clearly makes caring better. However, the current trend has tilted too much towards "knowing" and not enough towards "caring". The public resents that trend.

Every time there is a new technology to diagnose a condition, the demand for its use increases. When someone gets a headache, he goes to the doctor not only seeking help and relief from pain, but also with a request (or a demand) for an MRI. If after a good history and physical examination the physician does not think an MRI is needed and the patient insists on getting it, what is the ethical responsibility of the physician? And who should pay for it? Some physicians may feel a subtle pressure to prescribe an MRI even if they know that there is no indication. The physician knows that if he does not give what the patient wants, the patient will go somewhere else. There is also a remote possibility that this headache is ominous. This starts a fear of litigation and leads to a decision to obtain an MRI. It is easier and less time-consuming to order the test than to withhold and try to convince the patient. Both the physician and patient usually know that, at least in the American system, someone else will pay for the test. The physician can always send the patient to a specialist. However, the specialist will most likely order an MRI to definitively rule out a brain tumor or other problems. Therefore, why spend time examining, discussing, and referring, particularly when time has become a commodity to be charged per minute?

This is exactly how technology has come between the patient and the physician. In place of the warm, comforting touch of their personal physicians and their personal attention, patients have to experience the impersonal solitary confinement inside the CT scan and MRI, the cold paste of ultrasound, and the invasion of their interiors with various scopes that create anxiety, discomfort, and, sometimes, complications. Justifiably, the patient feels that he has been dehumanized, even though the patient has to take part of the blame for this situation.

Several new tests and medical instruments are added each year. Every time a new test comes along or a new machine is available, the industries advertise them directly to the public. The public is sold on "new ideas" before all the advantages and disadvantages are worked out and before all the risks and benefits of the new technology are defined. There is an instant demand, and since insurance pays for most of the tests, one more technology is given a code number and added for reimbursement. How many more new technologies can the society support before it gets bankrupt paying for tests?

Increasing emphasis on the biology of medicine and subspecialization brought great dividends to the society, but at a cost. There is a specialist for every organ, but often there is no one in the patient-care team who knows the patient as a whole person. This is a particular problem for people with chronic illness and functional disorders. All that the specialists can say to them is, "It is not in my specialty." That leaves no one to look after the whole person, who is still hurting. *"Even if the patient's illness has been negotiated out of medicine by other physicians, someone must remain who can help."*[4] This is not what is happening now.

All these developments influence medical education and give a skewed view of the real world to physicians in training. Following the Flexner Report, science and objectivity were emphasized in medical education, and the medical curriculum was devoted entirely to biology and scientific methods. Most of the teachers in medical schools were leading investigators in their fields. Most of them emphasized objective, hard data to the exclusion of the subjective, and, therefore, "soft" data. Rapid development of their subspecialties with associated high technologies and a narrower focus added to this trend. Yet, they were the teachers of medical students. Procedure-oriented specialists brought in more revenues to the hospitals than cognitive specialists and generalists. Generalists were barely tolerated in medical schools. The reward system in the academics was for the specialist and the physician scientists, not for clinician role models as pointed out by Doctor LaCombe. These "dinosaurs," as they were called, were appreciated by medical students but were shunned by the administrators of medical schools.[5]

Fortunately, this is changing, and enormous progress has been made toward introducing humanities and bio-psychosocial models of illness in medical education. Primary care physicians and generalists are given the recognition they deserve and are now playing a greater role in the education of current physicians-in-training. This trend has yet to catch up with the need, but it is a hopeful sign for the future.

Patient Autonomy

The basic relationship between the physician and patient has also taken a dramatic and crucial turn in the past 50 years. Patients are better educated and better informed. The informed public is increasingly skeptical of authority and power. Patient rights and informed consent are the norms. Patients do not want to be passive and comply with doctors "orders" and recommendations. They want to be partners in decision making. These are positive developments.

In the patient–physician relationship, the physician has all the information. Even after many years of training, it takes skill, time and effort of the physician to make sense of the vast amount of medical information and adapt it to individual needs. The patient does not have the knowledge and experience to make a rational judgment particularly when he is anxious and is under stress. Even though it is the patient's right, I often wonder whether the exercise of "autonomy" to decide on matters requiring technical knowledge is of value to the patient, particularly at a stressful time.

An informed patient is an asset, but problem arises when the patient wants to read "all about the illness" before making a decision. It is even worse when the information is obtained from internet forums. In such cases, the patient is jeopardizing his own care by relying on opinions and unverified claims and second-guessing the physician. Much energy and precious time are spent in "negotiating". Negotiation is part of the process; but carried to excess, it creates tension and at times to adversarial relationship. It shows a mistrust of the professional. We do not expect patients to trust their physicians without any reservation. But would it not be better for the patient to choose someone whom he can trust, ask all the questions needed to be asked and allow to be helped, rather than constantly act as if he is alone in this world and there is no one to help make a decision?

The reality is that patient autonomy is a good thing and is here to stay and requires different sets of responses and skills in future physicians. Academic medicine has not done a good job of preparing physicians for this task. In order to do this we need scientifically trained clinicians with human relations skills as role models.

Cost of Care

We all know that the cost of medical care continues to escalate. There are several causes and effects to this phenomena. This is too complicated a subject to deal with in this book. It is clear that the economics of medical care are creating another dilemma for physicians who are torn between their innate desire to help people and the realities of economics. There are too many players in this field, including regulatory agencies, insurance companies, pharmaceutical companies, and lawyers. Therefore, the physician finds it difficult to focus on the best interests of the patients in the midst of competing pressures.

Profession or Trade? "Dyad" or Myriad?

The profession itself is increasingly looked upon more as a trade than a profession. Too many "others" have entered into the "marketplace". Too many interested parties are breaking the sacred bond between the physician who sees a "moral" obligation to care for the sick and the patient, who is in need of help. A "dyad" has become a "myriad" and a "covenant" has become a "contract".[6]

I am using the word "covenant" in the Biblical sense, although my intention is "not to analogize the physician with the Almighty". In a covenant, the relationship is between two unequal parties. One party has more knowledge (as in medicine), or more power (government), or more money. The other party is weaker or at a disadvantage. In a contract, the involved parties are supposed to be equal in power. In a covenant, the stronger party, notwithstanding its strength, promises to keep the welfare of the weaker party in focus all the time. In a contract, each party looks after itself; each party is interested in its welfare only. A covenant, therefore, is a helping relationship; a contract is an adversarial relationship. A covenant is based on trust; a contract is based on mistrust. All the current social and economic forces have gravitated toward the contract as a basis for health care and patient–physician relationship. That is part of the dilemma.

How did a "dyad" become a myriad? How did so many players enter into the patient–physician encounter? What are the forces involved? How did they come to be? A partial answer is that this is the nature of a complex society. The situation is not going to change. The players are here to stay. They all have their own spheres of influence to protect. It will be easy if every interested party realizes that "it" is part of the problem. It will be easier if all involved parties realize that they have a common interest in solving the problem and therefore will have to be less rigid and give up something for the welfare of the whole. However, so far, it has not happened.

How did all these "significant others" arrive on the scene? As pointed out at the beginning of this chapter, several critical developments in the past century have made medical encounters a complex process. New technologies brought in specialists and subspecialists such as "interventionalists," pharmaceutical industry, manufacturers of medical equipment, and insurance companies. Ideologically motivated "experiments" done on a whole society and good research performed on vulnerable people without their knowledge went against basic human values and respect for the individual. The society had to intervene and establish the primacy of "patient autonomy" and "informed consent". This, in turn, brought in legal experts, regulatory agencies, ethicists, and clinical investigators. Increasing costs of medical care stressed the health care resources of individuals and the governments had to intervene. National Health Services were developed in many countries and Medicare and Medicaid arrived in the USA. All of these developments are important and needed. However, these developments come with the disadvantage of a complicated system of medical care delivery.

What is the role of pharmaceutical industry in this scene? The industry has done a wonderful job of developing remarkable new drugs that have clearly improved the quality of life for many patients and for some made a difference between survival and death. At the same time, it is a business, and why would anyone want to start a business but for making a profit? In a free-market atmosphere with no external control, greed takes over. Loyalty to the shareholder takes precedence over loyalty to the society's needs. The recent trend in direct advertising to the public adds another layer of interference to the patient–physician relationship. The problem is that there is an uneasy alliance between physicians, who have a covenant to keep, and the industry, whose motive is sale of its products at a profit. By accepting favors from the industry, physicians and medical organizations are placing themselves in a vulnerable position.

The relationship between the pharmaceutical industry, physicians and academic centers has come under increasing scrutiny in recent years.[7,8] Is it really possible for physicians to keep objectivity while accepting gifts from drug companies? What is the effect of company-sponsored clinical research on the veracity of conclusions? Do drug companies suppress unfavorable data or modify them for publication? What is the role of individual physicians in this collusion?

The outcome of all of these developments during the past 100 years is a changed relationship between the patient and the physician. A helping relationship has become adversarial, with each party approaching the other with caution, doubt, and mistrust. How does the medical profession adapt to these changes and preserve what it thinks is important? This is the challenge. Physicians cannot solve all of the problems alone. However, they can do so with the support of the public. Indeed, the public is demanding a voice in many of the decision making processes. That is a good sign.

What are some of the things that are under the control of the medical profession? Physicians can show the public that we consider medical practice a "moral" activity, that we are primarily a helping profession, and that we are not in it for self-aggrandizement or money. We can do all we can to build trust by being honest, open, respectful of the patient's needs and concerns, and unattached to any organization with a profit motive. We can make patients equal partners in decision making, when appropriate. We can be prudent. We can educate the public on the limitations of medical science. We can make sure that every time a major policy decision is made on health care delivery, we remind all parties involved to keep the focus on strengthening the physician–patient "dyad", the main functioning engine of good medical care.

Fortunately, efforts are under way to face these challenges and to bring about changes in the practice of medicine and, more importantly, in medical education. One of the most important efforts is a study of the health care system as a whole by the Institute of Medicine. This study was summarized in a report entitled "Crossing the Quality Chasm",[9] an important document that will impact the way medicine is practiced in the 21st century. The report points out the need for continuity of care, sharing of information with patients and making them the source of control of care, evidence-based decision making and emphasis on patient-safety. The report provides both a rationale and a plan of action. It suggests that the involved parties adopt a shared vision of six

Table 2.1: Six specific aims for improvement.

Health Care has to be:
1. Safe
2. Effective
3. Patient-centered
4. Timely
5. Efficient
6. Equitable

From the IOM Report on *Crossing the Quality Chasm.*

specific aims for improvement (Table 2.1). The emphasis is on patient-centered, evidence-based care that is "respectful of and responsive to individual patient preferences, needs, values, and ensuring that patient values guide all clinical decisions."

The report also points out that the "fundamental nature (of health care) is characterized by people taking care of other people in times of need and stress. Stable, trusting relationships between a patient and the people providing care can be critical to healing and managing illness. Therefore, the importance of adequately preparing the workforce to make a smooth transition into a thoroughly revamped health care system cannot be underestimated. One approach is to redesign the way health professionals are trained to emphasize the six aims of improvement." Subsequently, the Institute of Medicine published another report (Project: Behavioral and Social Sciences in Medical School Curricula — March 24, 2004) emphasizing the need to equip future physicians with "knowledge and skills from the behavioral and social sciences needed to recognize, understand, and effectively respond to patients as individuals, not just to their symptoms."

Even before these reports, the American College of Graduate Medical Education (ACGME), the accrediting body for continuing medical education, opined that education of physicians in specialties with a focus on knowledge, skills, and attitude was not adequate for the practice of medicine in the future. The ACGME recommended that future physicians be trained and evaluated in six new areas of competency (Table 2.2): patient care, medical knowledge, interpersonal and

Table 2.2: Core Competencies.

Trainees must obtain competencies in the following six areas to attain the level of a new practitioner:
1. Patient care that is compassionate, appropriate, and effective for the treatment of health problems and the promotion of health
2. Medical knowledge about established and evolving biomedical, clinical, and cognate sciences and the application of this knowledge to patient care
3. Practice-based learning and improvement that involves investigation and evaluation of their own patient care, appraisal and assimilation of scientific evidence, and improvement in patient care
4. Interpersonal and communication skills
5. Professionalism
6. System-based practice

From http://www.acgme.org/acWebsite/RRC_280/280_coreComp.asp, last access: July 2009.

communication skills, practice-based learning, professionalism, and systems-based practice.[10] The ACGME also recommended that the training curriculum must include provisions for the trainees to receive instructions and feedback to master their skills in interviewing, communication, and interpersonal relationship. It further demanded that the training programs establish effective programs to evaluate the competency of the trainees in these areas. Both the American Board of Internal Medicine and the American Board of Pediatrics have agreed that assessment of knowledge through examinations alone is not adequate to assure competency to practice and have agreed to evaluate future candidates and existing diplomats using this same list of competencies.

These policies have impact on practicing physicians as well. Board certification in the USA is undergoing major changes because of the IOM reports and the actions of the ACGME. All Boards have now agreed to issue time-limited certification. This necessitates recertification at 7- to 10-year intervals. In addition to passing a test once in 7 to 10 years, a more continuous process of competence will be included. This will require physicians in practice to take part in self-evaluation and the documentation of performance in practice, including technical competence and patient satisfaction with care.[11]

Systems of Delivery of Care

Education of future physicians in principles of patient centered care and professionalism alone are not adequate when the systems of delivery of care are so unfriendly to these concepts.

In response to declining public trust and competing pressures on the medical professionals, the American Board of Internal Medicine Foundation, American College of Physicians Foundation, and the European Federation of Internal Medicine collaborated on a project and prepared "Medical Professionalism in the New Millennium: A Physician's Charter" in 2002.[12] While the motivation behind this charter is laudable, the altruistic principles outlined in the Charter cannot be viewed in isolation. Physicians practice in a society and within a system of delivery of care. Physicians cannot apply their altruistic principles without support from the public and the policy makers. With this in mind, another conference was held in 2005 to discuss the ramification of the Physician Charter, which resulted in a recent publication.[13] This publication suggested changes in the system of delivery of care to ensure that all members of society have access to a basic set of preventive and medical services, construct and maintain a medical liability system that encourages wide dissemination of lessons learned from medical errors, align payment system with professional values and performance, and to recognize and minimize opportunities for conflicts of interest. It is obvious that effective alliance between the medical profession and members of the society is necessary to implement these changes. I am not aware of any forum to implement these ideas.

Several other changes have been proposed to the current system of medical care. One of them is based on successful chronic care models with proven benefits and well-known common sense concepts such as *continuity of care* and *one person for the patient to relate to*. Also included are ideas such as templates for patients to make an agenda for their clinic visits in which they can write their specific concerns and internet-based tools for self-management.[14]

These are important developments that will change the way physicians are prepared and expected to practice in the future.

Major Message: The 20th century started with the Flexner Report that radically changed the way medicine was taught and practiced. The impact on the scientific aspects of medical practice was enormous. The report on "Crossing the Quality Chasm" by the Institute of Medicine and the ACGME report will have an equally major impact on the way medicine is taught and practiced in the 21st century by reemphasizing the humanistic and professional aspects of medical practice.

1. Physician–patient "dyad" has been broken.
2. Three important changes in the past several decades have contributed to some of the problems in the health care systems: explosion in medical knowledge resulting in technologies and specialization, greater patient autonomy and greater role for the patient in making decisions, and cost of care.
3. The reports from the IOM and ACGME will drastically change the way physicians will be trained and practice in the future.
4. Effective alliance between physicians and societies is urgently needed to implement several new ideas that have emerged to strengthen the physician–patient "dyad".

References

1. Edwards N, Kornacki MJ, Silversin J. Unhappy doctors: what are the causes and what can be done? *BMJ* 2002; **324**:835–838.
2. Kassirer JP. Doctor discontent. *N Engl J Med* 1998; **339**(21):1543–1544.
3. Odegaard CE. *Dear Doctor: A Personal Letter to the Physician.* 1986. Menlo Park, CA; The Henry J Kaiser Family Foundation.
4. Bulger RJ, McGovern JP. *Physician Philosopher: The Philosophical Foundations of Medicine: Essays by Dr. Edmund Pellegrino.* 2001. Charlottesville, Va; Carden Jennings Publishing Co.
5. LaCombe MA. In a stew. *Amer J Med* 1991; **91**:276–278.
6. Li JT. The patient–physician relationship: covenant or contract? *Mayo Clin Proc* 1996; **71**(9):917–918.

7. Miller LG, Cleary PD, Blumenthal D, Campbell EC, Gruen RL, Mountford J. A national survey of physician–industry relationship. *N Engl J Med* 2007: **356**:1742–1750.
8. Fugh-Berman A, Ahari S. Following the script: how drug reps make friends and influence doctors. *PloS Medicine* April 2007; **4**(4):e150. (www.polsmedicine.org)
9. Institute of Medicine. Crossing the Quality Chasm: A New Health System for the 21st Century. Corrigan JM *et al.* (Eds.). 2001. Washington, DC; National Academy Press.
10. ACGME: Outcome Project–The Common Program Requirements Document. http://www.acgme.org/outcome. Accessed March 26, 2009.
11. Steinbrook R. Renewing board certification. *N Eng J Med* 2005; **353**:1994–1997.
12. Medical professionalism in the new millennium: a physicians' charter. Medical Professionalism Project. *Lancet* 2002; **359**:520–522.
13. Cohen JJ, Cruess S, Davidson C. Alliance between society and medicine: the public's stake in medical professionalism. *JAMA* 2007; **298**:670–673.
14. Bergeson SC, Dean JD. A systems approach to patient–centered care *JAMA* 2006; **296**(23):2848–2851.

Chapter 3

Getting to Know the Patient — Disease, Illness, and Illness Behavior

There is no universally accepted definition of the word "disease".[1] Disease is a concept that combines a description of a physical or physiological state with a judgment that this state is abnormal or dysfunctional requiring competent care. This, in turn, provides a conceptual basis for medical intervention, but the concept may differ between different societies and cultures and may change over time.[2]

Based on the foundations of organ pathology of Morgagni and microscopic pathology of Virchow, the idea of disease classification arose during the past two centuries. Clustering of clinical findings into definable diseases led to a better understanding of their pathology and etiology. Recent advances in molecular biology, genomics, and other biological disciplines have made it even more important to classify diseases into homogeneous subsets. The best recent example of the importance and usefulness of such an organized, scientific study of a defined disease category is the story of Lyme disease.[3]

Polly Murray and Judith Mesch of Old Lyme, Connecticut, mothers of two children diagnosed with juvenile rheumatoid arthritis (JRA), knew of 12 other children in their small town with the same diagnosis. Four of them lived in the same street. The mothers guessed that this was not JRA (currently renamed as juvenile idiopathic arthritis or JIA) but some other epidemic form of arthritis and called for help from the State Department of Health. Dr. Alan Steere, who was at the Yale University, was assigned to study these patients, and he agreed with the suspicion of the mothers. Based on the epidemiology, Doctor Steere thought that this was a disease caused by an arbor virus and named it after the town where these patients resided. This was in 1977. The entire spectrum of the disease was fully defined very soon thereafter, and the relationship of this disease to skin conditions and neurological conditions described in Europe during the late 1800s and early 1900s was recognized. Once the arthritis of Lyme disease was distinguished from JRA and rheumatoid arthritis, modern tools of medicine and public health helped discover the etiology, pathogenesis, immunology, and rational treatment of this disease within a span of 10 to 12 years. This is the best demonstration of how scientific definition and analysis give us the most effective and efficient way to study human diseases.

Illness is a subjective sensation described as a symptom or symptoms by the patient. This may or may not indicate the presence of a treatable medical condition/disease. Textbooks of medicine describe diseases as if they have an existence of their own outside of a person. From the scientific point of view, this approach to defining diseases has yielded the most useful understanding of human ailments. However, people with diseases have their personality, cultural background, social responsibilities, and economic realities, all of which modify the way the diseases are manifested in any one person. This is illness (unique manifestation of the disease in a person).

Physicians use the word "illness" to include both physical and psychological disorders. They also classify illness as organic or non-organic. When a physical or biological explanation can be found for the patient's symptoms and illness behavior, an organic illness (disease) is said to be present. If the patient's illness seems to be due mostly to psychological factors such as anxiety, depression, or the desire to manipulate others, it is said to be non-organic illness or a functional disorder. (Primary mental illness is not part of this discussion.)

Applying the name of a disease to a cluster of signs and symptoms is a clinical endeavor and is based on the physician's scientific understanding of what disease is. However, the diagnosis of a disease in a person assigns a social "sick" role to that person.[4] It allows some privileges to the person with the disease, such as excuse from usual roles and responsibilities in the society. It also expects the sick person to seek appropriate help, get well, and return to his role. What kind of help is appropriate? Who is the person to be sought? Answers to these questions have changed over the centuries depending on the prevailing concepts of disease and illness.

Clinical Scenario 1

A six-year-old girl from rural New Jersey developed a swelling of the right knee in early September. This was associated with mild pain and a limp. On examination, she did not appear to be ill. There was no fever. The right knee was moderately swollen with mild flexion contracture. The left ankle also showed mild swelling. Complete blood count was normal, but the sedimentation rate was elevated (38 mm in 1 hour). Antibody to *Borrelia burgdorferi* was present in the serum as shown by both ELISA and the Western blot methods.

Clinical Scenario 2

A 14-year-old girl from the same geographical area came with a history of pain for several months all over the body. The pain was said to be so severe that she missed school often. The pain in her wrists interfered with her playing a flute. She had been treated twice with amoxicillin for presumed Lyme disease. There was no benefit. An orthopedic surgeon and an infectious disease specialist had seen her earlier. They did not notice any objective findings. All of the laboratory studies were negative except for a marginally positive ANA (1:40). There was a history of fibromyalgia in the mother. Physical examination did not show any swelling or restricted range of movement of the joints, but she had tenderness in several locations all over her body. These tender points did not correspond to the classic tender points associated with fibromyalgia. Antibody to *Borrelia* was positive by ELISA at 1.1 units but was negative by Western blot. Complete blood count and sedimentation rate were normal on more than one occasion.

These two case scenarios are examples of what David Taylor, a thoughtful pediatrician, outlined in his Point of View on "The Components of Sickness: Disease, Illness and Predicament".[5] Taylor's guidelines on what constitutes a disease are outlined in Table 3.1. When these concepts are applied to the case scenarios, Patient 1 has Lyme

Table 3.1: Disease, illness and predicament.

Diseases

1. Diseases are discernible as physical reality. They are therefore amenable to scientific study.
2. Disease requires specific changes in the structure of tissues but is not necessarily organ-specific.
3. Disease may be trivial. The changes in the body may not be severe.
4. Disease is valid without illness. "Although disease and illness are conceptually separate, the name of a disease is often used carelessly to describe the way someone is being ill."
5. Person with disease is not judged for being unable to carry out his responsibilities.
6. Space, place, and time are irrelevant.
7. Systematic study of a disease leads to discovery and therefore offers scope for specific therapy.

Illness

1. Illness is an experience which may or may not be referable to disease. "Disease is about things but illness is about experiences, about processes."
2. Illness is a social manifestation. An ill person with or without a disease may exhibit "illness behavior."
3. "Illness can be overplayed, stoically borne, or foolishly denied."
4. Illness is valid without discoverable disease.
5. Illness will probably be judged morally.
6. Illnesses vary through space, place, and time.
7. The diagnosis of illness is description in the language of medicine which is a diagnostic label. "By describing an illness the physician is creating a model. The model may be capable of being validated, or not be worth validating, or not yet technically possible to validate. Or it may be purely conceptual and have the function of standing for disease."
8. The treatment of the person with an illness is empirical and palliative.

Predicaments

1. The predicament is the complex of psychosocial issues which impinge on the individual.
2. "The predicament is more personal than the environment."
3. The predicament is diffuse and multifactorial.
4. Predicaments have a very unstable structure.
5. Predicaments can be painful without disease or illness.

(*Continued*)

Table 3.1: (*Continued*)

6. Predicaments are charged with moral and ethical implications.
7. Space, place, and time are paramount.
8. Knowledge of predicaments grows with understanding.
9. Predicaments contain scope for social and political remedy.

Modified from Taylor DC, The Components of Sickness: Diseases, Illnesses and Predicaments, *Lancet* 1979; **314**:1008–1010. (With permission from Copyright Elsevier.)

disease. There is sound scientific basis for this diagnosis. It is an objective entity that will behave true to its form for the most part in boys and girls, men and women, in New Jersey or New Mexico. The diagnosis is valid regardless of the severity of illness. (In other words, some other patient with this same disease may not feel ill.) The disease does not depend solely on the subjective experience and testimony of the sufferer. Specific therapy is available. If untreated, the disease may have serious consequences in a proportion of infected individuals.

Patient 2 has subjective symptoms that are important since they interfere with daily functions. However, there is no objective evidence of any derangement of any of the organ systems. The patient has an illness. There is no disease diagnosis and no specific treatment exists that can *cure* her of her symptoms. Some symptomatic *relief* is possible with prescription medicines, but complete relief will require the personal efforts of the sufferer.

Patient 1 was treated with oral antibiotics and recovered fully. She is back to school and resume normal activities. Patient 2 was disappointed that there was no medical cure, refused to follow suggestions for pain relief, and was last seen "doctor-shopping", probably for someone who will make a disease diagnosis and give her a prescription.

What are predicaments? The individual lives in a particular family with its own strengths and weaknesses. Each family has its own special constraints on time (both parents working), place they live (poor and/or dangerous neighborhood), financial resources (poor or no income), and belief systems (Christian Science, Seventh Day Adventist, etc.). For example, a patient with bone marrow failure may have severe anemia or thrombocytopenia but cannot accept transfusions because of religious beliefs. Or a 22-year-old mother may have her first child with serious illness requiring ventilator support. She may love the child but cannot take the child home because of lack of physical and financial resources. These are the predicaments in life.

It took many years for me to recognize that when I get frustrated with the care of a particular patient, it is often due to my inability to separate the disease from the patient's personality (illness component), to recognize the predicaments of the person with the disease, and my inability to help the patient change his life situation or the coping style.

Acceptance of the individual's sick role is a social contract,[4] and society does not always accept emotional disorders or illness without a disease diagnosis as an acceptable entry into the sick role. What is a sick role? How does a society assign this role? What are its implications for the person with a disease or an illness?

Talcott Parsons[4] re-formulated the *concept of social contract* between a sick person and the society in the mid-1900s. When someone has a disease, the society agrees that the sufferer is not just "acting" sick but is actually feeling sick, that he cannot help being sick nor can he get better just by wishing, and that he needs appropriate medical help. The sufferer is excused from daily duties but is expected to seek competent help. Social and cultural differences do exist on what types of diseases and illnesses are acceptable for the privileges assigned to a sick person and what competent help means. However, the need for help is a constant factor. The cost of care will be assumed by the society by one method or other. (We also have to remember that this concept was made for the 20th century and for acute medical conditions. It was not intended to apply to chronic illness and mental illness and will have to be modified for the 21st century.)

How does society deal with those who have annoying symptoms interfering with their lives and those "worried well" people with no respectable diagnosis of a "disease" to explain their symptoms?[6] As pointed out by Parsons[4] and Taylor,[5] society will judge them morally. Although we know that illness is a valid state of loss of health, even without a disease, if a person suffers from a prototypic disease he is considered a victim, but "when patients' suffering cannot be understood in biological terms, they are held more responsible for the illness." Since there is no medical diagnosis, the message these sufferers get from their family, friends, and physicians is often unsympathetic. This, of course, is cruel and infuriates the victim. Those with chronic illness are also often left to their own resources to cope with their illness.

Since there is always a possibility that vague symptoms are forerunners of a more serious disease, the pressure is to diagnose a disease, and with the fear of litigation in the background, physicians order more and more unnecessary tests. If there is an abnormal laboratory value, and often there is, more tests are ordered. This gives the impression to the patient that there is indeed something wrong and "no one is able to figure it out". They continue to feel sick and seek medical help.

Many parties want to meddle with the scientific aspects of defining and studying diseases. This includes patient advocates, pharmaceutical companies, and insurance companies, among others. If there are adequate numbers of patients with similar symptoms, a word is coined to describe this cluster. Once a name is coined, it becomes a reality just on the basis of the fear it evokes among the public and the number of times it gets repeated, as it happened with chronic seronegative Lyme disease. Both patients (understandably) and physicians (not so understandably) cling to that word. Direct advertisement to "consumers" by pharmaceutical companies linking one of their products to a specific "condition" adds to the anxiety. In their desire to be helpful to the patients and placate them and to stop patients from doctor shopping, some physicians are willing to give a label to the sufferers even when there is no scientific validity to the existence of that condition as an identifiable disease with a medically treatable cause.

For emotional and economic reasons, sufferers of symptoms without disease diagnosis organize online chat rooms and publish newsletters to legitimize their "condition". Advocacy groups and issue-based groups start putting pressure on insurance companies and legislators to help pay for tests and medicines, as it happened in the case of chronic seronegative Lyme disease.

In response to pressures from advocacy groups, the Connecticut legislature passed a bill in 1999 mandating that health insurance companies pay for intravenous antibiotics for adults and children with presumed Lyme disease for no less than 30 days. By itself, this sounds benign. But the surprising element in this legislation was that objective findings and/or positive serology for *Borrelia burgdorferi* were *not* required.[7]

Finally, drug companies have a say in this matter, now that they can advertise directly to the public. Indeed, "disease mongering" is a term being used to refer to this situation.[8] Drug companies support disease awareness campaigns directly or indirectly. This then becomes a part of their marketing strategy. Moynihan and his colleagues investigated the role of a pharmaceutical company in promoting a product through another company specializing in corporate-backed "medical education". According to a leaked document, the education program's key aim was that, "Irritable bowel syndrome (IBS) must be established in the minds of doctors as a significant and discrete disease state." It is obvious how such a continuing medical education program aimed at the physicians combined with a media blitz can lead to establishment of any ailment as a dreaded disease in the minds of the lay public.[8]

Pressures from various directions have resulted in the naming of several new "diseases" in recent years without adequate scientific evidence. My intention is not to belittle the seriousness of these illnesses. Patients with these conditions suffer and they need our care and support. However, naming diseases without scientific evidence is not likely to be helpful to individual patients or to the society over the long term.

If a physician names a disease when none exists, he becomes part of the problem. The dangers are abandonment of scientific approach and procedures and treatment of a non-existent disease with unnecessary and dangerous drugs. The more serious problem is a closed mind and lack of attention to other serious mental health and psychosocial problems in the patient's lives. The most memorable example in my practice was a young girl who was being treated with anti-depressants for fibromyalgia when the actual problem was sexual abuse.

There is one other disadvantage. The implication of diagnosing a disease in a person who does not have one is that a physician can relieve the symptoms with medicines. The reality is that prescription drugs alone cannot relieve the symptoms of a person whose symptoms do not arise from a known biological process. The patient has to take personal effort to change attitudes and lifestyle to get better. As long as physicians treat illnesses as diseases, patients will continue to expect prescription medicines to cure their symptoms and will not take sufficient efforts to change their lifestyle or attitudes.

Conversely, refusal to accept grouping of symptoms as a separate disease entity until all proofs are received is unfair to the patients. By taking this position, the physician is likely to be judgmental and label patients with vague symptoms as "hypochondriac". Even patients with cancer have been shown to delay their initial visit to the doctor because of concerns of being labeled as anxious.[9] It is no wonder that patients with vague symptoms feel helpless and start drifting to available unconventional remedies. This position is also not scientific since there is a possibility that the particular symptom complex is indeed due to a specific defect in the function of organ or organs and more research is needed.

Predicament and help-seeking behavior: A simple working mother brings her child to the walk-in clinic of a big city hospital at 10 p.m. for a minor illness because that is the only free time she has. Another mother brings in her child for a serious illness at 4 a.m. because that is when she returned home from the bar and found the child on the kitchen floor. (Both are from my personal experience.) In both instances, the method of seeking treatment was hinged on the personal predicaments of the mothers.

Illness Behavior

Any illness, with or without a disease diagnosis, can lead to illness behavior and help-seeking behavior. Illness behavior refers to "the ways in which given symptoms may be differentially perceived, evaluated, and acted (or not acted) upon by different kinds of persons".

For example, when I am sick, I do not like to complain about every symptom, ignore some, and keep working until I cannot carry on any further. When someone offers to help me, I feel embarrassed since I like to take care of my own needs. In my own extended family, there are others who will complain about every ache and pain everyday, several times a day, and go to bed at the slightest sneeze or a cold.

Some will assume sick role or maintain sick role to get relief from demands placed on them and their responsibilities. For example, I once saw a girl with severe wrist pain. Even after extensive investigations, no definable cause was found and she was diagnosed as having reflex neurovascular dystrophy. During counseling, this girl said that her mother wanted her to learn piano but she hated it. After this insight, the child got better very quickly.

Some may not like the dependency role of the sick, but may accept help when offered. Others may behave rudely to those who want to help, like Ivan Ilyich in Tolstoy's novel.[10] They often reject help even while they are longing for a hug.

Age, sex, position in the family and in society and at work, economic conditions, and the individual's learned behavior are known to affect illness behavior.[11,12] Perceived importance of the symptom is also a major determinant. For example, most people will ignore symptoms of cold but not chest pain. Very young children usually respond to their illness more naturally than adults do. A father who is the only wage earner with a large family is likely to ignore abdominal pain until it is unbearable. However, a middle-aged individual with a whiplash injury after an accident is likely to stay dysfunctional if there is a possibility of an insurance claim.

Finally, the way people behave individually and as a group is culturally determined.[13–15] This is particularly so with respect to illness behavior and help-seeking behavior. Many years ago, as a trainee in Pediatrics, I worked in the Emergency Room of The Children's Hospital of Philadelphia. The hospital was located in the center of Philadelphia, close to the various ethnic neighborhoods including Italian, Polish, Irish/Catholic, and African American. I could not help noticing the way symptoms were noticed, interpreted, and acted upon in different cultural settings. Later, when I returned to India to practice, I was able to appreciate the cultural aspects of illness behavior even more.[14]

Illness does not necessarily lead to help-seeking behavior. Why is it that some patients rush to the physician for the slightest of symptoms, and others bear them stoically or avoid seeking care altogether? There are several reasons why patients, even with suspected cancer, postpone their medical visit (Table 3.2). Fear of embarrassment is one of them. Some may be concerned about medical procedures or the cost of care. Some may be suspicious of physicians in general. Some may deny their illness or postpone the visit hoping that symptoms will go away. Some cannot afford to stop working or take time off. This is common in countries with poor socioeconomic conditions

Table 3.2: Reasons for delay in seeking medical help among cancer patients.

I. Recognition and interpretation of symptoms

- Delaying factors in recognition of illness
  - Vague and mild symptoms
  - Absence of pain
  - Belief that symptoms will go away
  - Intermittent symptoms
  - No awareness of cancer symptoms or risks
  - Previous benign diagnosis for symptoms by doctor

II. Fear

- Fear of embarrassment
- Fear of being seen as a time-waster or as neurotic, especially for those with diverse mild symptoms
- Fear that even the patient's family thinks that the symptoms are psychosomatic
  - Men help-seeking as unmasculine
  - Embarrassment of sensitive and sexual areas
- Fear of cancer
  - Serious and painful symptoms, fatal incurable disease
  - Previous negative experience with cancer
  - Fear of unpleasant treatment
  - Loss of sexuality after treatment
  - Shame associated with dirt and uncleanliness

Modified from: Panel 1: Reasons for delay in Smith LK, Pope C, Botha J, Patient's help-seeking experiences and delay in cancer presentation: a qualitative synthesis, *Lancet* 2005; **366**:825–831. (With permission from Copyright Elsevier.)

where the breadwinner has to work for mere subsistence. A person's religion, social class, dependency on others, and the magnitude of the stress are some of the factors known to be related to when and how patients seek medical help. People under high stress in life are more likely to use a medical facility for minor symptoms. They are also more likely to consider the symptoms more serious than they indeed are and to use emergency services more often. Symptoms associated with conditions that are a serious threat to life (e.g., chest pain or lump in the breast) will make the sufferer seek help immediately. All of these will be modified by the economic condition, access to care, and ability to pay.

One other point of importance in help-seeking behavior is the time at which the patient chooses to seek medical advice. One of my favorite questions is as follows: "You have had these symptoms for so many days (or months). What is it that made you come today instead of yesterday or tomorrow or next week?" Answers to this question have opened several fascinating windows into patient's lives. Some were humorous such as "This is the only day I could get an appointment with you." Some were revealing, such as "I could not tolerate my mother-in-law's pestering any more."

Finally, the stated reasons for the patient's visit may not always be the real reason. This is particularly true in pediatrics.[16] The symptoms may be associated in the parents' mind with a family history of serious life-threatening illness related to similar symptoms, fear of loss of the child, or fear that the child may lose major organ function. Very often, a grandparent or an ex-spouse is pressing for an answer for the symptoms. If these concerns are not addressed, parents are not happy even when the outcome is likely to be a good one. They may "doctor-hop" until someone answers their concerns adequately.

Physicians learn about human behavior during illness all through their professional careers. In addition, one can learn a lot from classic articles and books such as Tolstoy's *The Death of Ivan Ilyich*,[10] David Mechanic's "Illness Behavior",[11,12] Norman Cousins' "Anatomy of an Illness",[17,18] a chapter on *Illness and Help-seeking Behavior* by Leigh and Reiser,[19] and others.[20,21] There are several papers and books on cultural aspects of medicine; I refer to only a few.[13–15,22]

Major message: Differentiating between disease and illness is not a mere semantic exercise. Diseases can be approached objectively, diagnosed, and treated with medical and surgical interventions initiated by the physician. However, illness and predicament are subjective and unique to each individual patient. The illness component cannot be "cured" or relieved without help from the sufferer and from society. An effective treatment plan cannot be established without knowing the disease, the illness, and the life situation for each patient. Therefore, clinicians have to be capable of diagnosing not only diseases with names; but also illnesses and predicaments without names. In addition, an awareness and understanding of illness behavior and help-seeking behavior should help physicians become more effective.

- Disease is objective, based on scientific understanding of human physiology and pathology.
- Illness is a subjective experience and may or may not be related to a medical condition.
- Making a diagnosis in a person is a scientific activity.
- However, the diagnosis of a disease in a person assigns a social role for the person.
- It is essential for the physician to understand the disease, illness, and predicament of his patients in order to be an effective and compassionate clinician.

References

1. Humber JM, Almeder RF (Eds). *What is Disease*? 1997. Totowa, NJ; Humana Press.
2. King L. What is disease? In *Concepts of Health and Disease*. 1978. Caplan A, Tristram Engelhardt Jr H, McCartney JJ (Eds). Reading, MA; Addison–Wesley Publishing Co. pp 107–118.
3. Steere A. Lyme disease. *N Engl J Med* 2001; **345**:115–125.
4. Parsons T. The sick role and the role of the physician reconsidered. *MMFQ/Health and Society* 1975; **53**:253–278.

5. Taylor DC. The components of sickness: diseases, illnesses and predicaments. *Lancet* 1979; **2**:1008–1010.
6. Meador C. *Symptoms of Unknown Origin*. 2004. Nashville, TN. Vanderbilt University Press.
7. Feder HM. Differences are voiced by two Lyme camps at a Connecticut Public Hearing on insurance coverage for Lyme Disease. *Pediatrics* 2000; **105**:855–857.
8. Moynihan R, Heath I, Henry D. Selling sickness: the pharmaceutical industry and disease mongering. *BMJ* 2002; **324**:886–891.
9. Smith LK, Pope C, Botha J. Patient's help-seeking experiences and delay in cancer presentation: a qualitative synthesis. *Lancet* 2005; **366**:825–831.
10. Tolstoy L. *The Death of Ivan Ilyich*. 1981. New York; Bantam Books.
11. Mechanic D, Volkart EH. Stress, illness behavior and the sick role. *Am Sociol Rev* 1961; **26**:51–58.
12. Mechanic D. The concept of illness behavior. *J Chronic Dis* 1962; **15**: 189–194.
13. Galanti G-A. *Caring for Patients from Different Cultures*. 3rd edn. 2003. Phildelphia, PA; University of Pennsylvania Press.
14. Athreya BH. Cultural factors in pediatric practice. *J Pediatr* 1971; **78**: 547–548.
15. Kleinman A. *Patients and Healers in the Context of Culture*. 1976. Berkeley, CA; University of California Press.
16. Bass LW, Cohen RL. Ostensible vs actual reasons for seeking pediatric attention: another look at the parental ticket of admission. *Pediatrics* 1982; **70**:870–874.
17. Cousins N. Anatomy of an illness (as perceived by the patient). *N Engl J Med* 1976; **295**:1458–1463.
18. *Physician in the Literature*. Cousins N (Ed). 1985. Philadelphia, PA; WB Saunders.
19. Leigh H, Resier MF. *Illness and Help-seeking Behavior in the Patient*. Leigh, H and Reiser MF (Eds). 1980. New York; Plenum Medical Book Co.
20. Williams WC. *Doctor Stories*. Compiled by Robert Coles MD. 1984. New York; New Directions Publishing Co.

21. Aronowitz RA. *Making Sense of Illness. Science, Society, Disease*. 1998. Cambridge MA; Cambridge University Press.
22. Spiegel JP. Some cultural aspects of transference and counter transference. In *Individual and Family Dynamics*. Masserman H (Ed). 1959. New York; Grune and Stratton. pp 160–182.

Part II

Clinical Skills

Chapter 4

Listening Skills and Observational Skills

The word "clinical" is derived from the Greek word for "bed," *klinikos*. The Latin equivalent is *clinicus*.[1] The skills used by the physician at the patient's bedside are clinical skills. They include listening skills, observational skills and human relations skills. I would like to add a few more items to this list. They are problem solving skills, decision making skills, communication skills, negotiation skills, helping skills, and caring skills. Doctor James Frye adds two more: common sense and uncommon sensibility.[2]

Inspection, palpation, percussion, and auscultation used to be the mainstay of clinical medicine. Several new technologies are replacing, supplementing, or augmenting these modalities. Auscultation is used less effectively. The stethoscope may not be around the physician's neck or in the coat pocket in the future. In our obsession with achieving absolute certainty in medicine and zero tolerance for error, we are relying on technology increasingly. Consequently, many of the new graduates may be losing basic clinical skills.[3–6] For example, in one study from an academic medical center, approximately one-third to one-half of the residents failed to make the correct diagnosis after listening to heart murmurs.[4]

Physicians suspect the diagnosis based on history and physical examination. Laboratory tests and imaging studies confirm or refute the primary hypothesis and help exclude other possible diagnoses. In this process, listening skills are essential for obtaining a good history and for building a good relationship. Observational skills are needed during physical examination and throughout the clinical encounter.

How important are history taking and physical examination? In an interesting study conducted at the general medical clinic of a university medical center in England, the physicians were asked to enter their diagnosis, based strictly on the referral letter from the general practitioner. They were then asked to take a history and perform a physical examination and then write their new diagnosis. At this time, they were asked to make a management decision from one of five options. The charts of these patients were reviewed later after a diagnosis had been firmly established. Table 4.1 summarizes the outcome. In 37 patients, the referral diagnosis was not changed. In 34 patients, the diagnosis was changed after history was taken. Only six patients needed a change in diagnosis after physical examination. Finally, laboratory testing was necessary to make the diagnosis in only seven patients and essential in only four.[7]

Even more interesting was the fact that when the laboratory tests were considered "essential" by the examining physician, 64 out of 160 were positive; when they were not considered "essential" on the basis of history and physical examination, only 21 out of 202 were positive. This is not surprising, since the pre-test probability determines the positive predictive value of any test. Since then, there are other similar studies with similar results.[8,9]

Table 4.1: Effect of history, physical examination, and laboratory investigation on the diagnosis.

	Number of Patients
Referring practitioner's diagnosis unchanged	37
Diagnosis changed after history taking	34
Diagnosis changed after physical examination	6
Diagnosis changed after laboratory investigation	7

From Hampton JR, Harrison MGJ, Mitchell JRA, Prichard JS, Carol Seymour, Relative contribution of history–taking, physical examination, and laboratory investigation to diagnosis and management of medical outpatients, *BMJ* 1975; **2**:486–489. (Reproduced with permission from the BMJ Publishing Group.)

There are other benefits to this initial interaction. Deep and active listening during the process of taking a history helps build rapport with the patient. The process of physical examination, done with sensitivity and respect, provides the "healing" touch, which so many patients crave. History and physical examination also give an estimate of pretest probability for a specific diagnosis.

The reader is referred to standard textbooks on physical diagnosis for time-honored and well-tested techniques of interviewing, history taking, and physical examination. In this chapter, I plan to discuss some topics not discussed in standard texts.

When taking a history, interviewing techniques developed by psychologists, psychiatrists and mental health professionals are emphasized. This includes open-ended questions, not interrupting, free-associating, etc. As important as these techniques are to understand the psychological make-up of patients and their needs, they are not helpful to retrieve important clinical clues. Patients do not know which symptoms are important and which detail is important from the diagnostic point of view. To arrive at the correct diagnosis, physicians will have to ask probing questions. This is particularly important when asking about the presenting symptoms. It is acceptable to interrupt gently with questions to clarify the details of the symptoms so that an initial hypothesis can be generated.

A good clinician should develop a list of different diagnoses in his mind as soon as he hears the initial symptoms. Further questions should be directed at clarifying specific features of these symptoms. As this is done and as new symptoms are elicited, the clinician's mind should be rearranging the initial list of diagnoses. It is important to sniff out all the clues, but without being sidetracked. As my professor used to say, physicians will have to "go after the presenting complaints like a hound dog".

It is not necessary to let patients free-associate during the early stages of history taking. We need to let them do so after we have done the initial job of finding out whether their symptoms lead us to a diagnostic hypothesis. The following example shows why.

A 10-year-old boy was seen with a history of polyarthralgia and swelling of hands. There was a history of an infection during the past month. The trainee obtained a complete history. However, the mother started talking about many of her own personal complaints and family problems. The trainee let the mother speak freely and did not probe to find out what the infection was, what antibiotic had been used, what the time factor was between the antibiotic and the current symptoms and what the location of the swelling was. He did not arrive at a working diagnosis. When the senior physician obtained answers for those specific questions, the diagnosis of serum sickness was obvious.

Good history taking should help accomplish the following additional tasks[10]: make it easy for the patient and family to relax and communicate; locate barriers to communication and minimize or eliminate them; and get a picture of the patient's life at home, work and in the society; clarify and explain the disease and management plan; assess patient's strengths and weaknesses; assess patient's coping style; evaluate social, economic and family relationships; and reassure the patient, even in the midst of uncertainty.

Another important goal in taking history should be to understand how the patient experiences his illness in his specific predicament and how he feels about it. Some of the questions that may help get a description of how a disease or illness is experienced by the patient are: "What do you believe is the cause of your problem?"; "What do you think this disease is doing inside your body?"; "What do you fear most about this disease?"; and "What do you fear most about the proposed treatment?".[11]

In the 21st century of genomics, taking a good family history is very important.[12] In a little-known article written in 1972,[13] Richard Juberg suggests a three-tiered approach: minimal, detailed, and maximum family history. Minimal history including information on age, date of birth (age), history of illness, and date and cause of death of first-degree relatives is adequate for most situations. Based on this information and the clinical setting, if a detailed history is deemed necessary, a set of five questions should be asked: (1) Is there a relative with an identical or similar illness? (2) Is there a relative with a possibly causally related illness? (3) Is there a relative with a trait that is recognized to be genetically determined? (4) Is there a relative with an unusual disease or a difficult-to-diagnose disease? (5) Is there consanguinity? This will be necessary in genetically determined diseases. Finally, it is up to the geneticists and genetic counselors to obtain a comprehensive family history. This will include a detailed pedigree tree.

In any encounter, the first contact is the most important. It is the best time to establish good relationship. Therefore, I prefer to take my own history. That allows me to initiate a positive relationship with the patient. Time spent in taking "routine" history is not a waste of time. It is a critical time because this is when the patient tells the physician what is bothering him physically and emotionally and shares the details of life that have not been shared with anyone else. It is a time to hear not only what the patient says but to see how he says it. It is a time to build trust. I certainly do not want computers taking history.

Listening Skills

It is not enough that physicians ask good, relevant, and important questions. Physicians have to learn to listen. They have to learn to listen more than to talk. They have to listen to the patient's needs, concerns, and fears *before* giving advice. They have to listen with their ears and the heart and listen actively. At the end of the encounter, the patient has to feel that the physician listened.

> Walker Percy said: "…if you listen carefully to what patients say, they will tell you not only what is wrong with them, but also what is wrong with you." Plutarch is credited with having said: "We have two ears and one mouth so we can listen twice as long as we talk."

It is obvious that patients need information to suit their needs and abilities. We cannot know what their needs, abilities and constraints are unless we LISTEN carefully.

It is not adequate that you think you are truly listening. It is how the parents (patients) perceive that counts. Their perception depends on your listening habits and body language. It also depends on what you do with what you hear. If you do not address their concerns specifically, they go away thinking that you did not listen.

How do we know what the concerns of parents are? An essay on "Listen to the parents — They may know best" refers to the information needs of parents of children with recent acute illness.[14] In a related article on the information needs of parents of preschool children with acute illness, the following questions were identified[15]:

1. How can I gauge the severity of illness?
2. How do I know when to seek advice?
3. What do you mean by virus? Where does it come from? In other words, could I have done something to prevent it? In other words, was I a bad mother?
4. How do antibiotics work?
5. What is the experience of other mothers?

I would have thought that physicians would be in the forefront of research on listening. Unfortunately, physician educators have not focused on this area until recently.[16,17] At present, most of the literature on listening comes from industries and business organizations.[18,19] Some ideas on good listening developed by Dr. Ralph Nichols are given in Table 4.2.

Some listening techniques used by good clinicians are listed in Table 4.3.

Table 4.2: Ten ways to improve listening skills.

1. **Find areas of common interest.** Listen with an open mind. Keep your attention focused on the topic. Poor listeners prejudge topics as uninteresting or a waste of time, and this serves only to block effective listening.
2. **Judge content, not delivery.** It is much easier to follow an effective speaker. Be aware that some speakers can charm an audience with a speech that has minimal content; while a poor performer may have good ideas. It is very easy to distract ourselves by focusing on the speaker's delivery.
3. **Withhold evaluation.** Don't jump to conclusions until you hear the whole message. Many listeners do not follow the message and resort to taking short cuts by categorizing what is being said. Effective listeners have learned to stay with the speaker and hear everything being said.
4. **Listen for central ideas.** Most of us have been taught to listen only for facts. However, if we only listen to facts we may miss the more important message that might be nonverbal. The effective listener focuses on central ideas to get the whole message.

(*Continued*)

Table 4.2: (*Continued*)

5. **Stay flexible when taking notes.** Effective listeners respond to each speaker's style, using note taking as an aid in understanding and retaining the message.
6. **Overcome distractions by concentrating.** Distractions may be external such as noises, or internal such as our own thoughts. Most physical distractions can be eliminated, but internal distractions have to be overcome by concentrating and focusing on the content.
7. **Check your emotions.** Know your own biases and personal prejudices. It is impossible to listen when you get angry. Speakers should know their audience and not tune them out by using "red flag words." It is up to the listener not to allow emotional flare ups to take away from understanding and hearing the central message.
8. **Challenge yourself by exercising the mind.** Poor listeners often respond to difficult subjects by tuning them out or refusing to make the extra effort. Effective listeners view difficult subjects as a challenge to exercise the mind.
9. **Use that extra energy.** While the poor listener is distracted by day dreaming or going off on a mental tangent, the good listener stays with the speaker, interpreting and focusing on the central ideas.
10. **Be an active listener.** Listening is a very active, complex intellectual and emotional process that requires hard work. It takes more energy to listen effectively than it does to speak. It is easier to be a passive listener.

Modified from: "Ten ways to improve listening skills" in newsletter of International Listening Association, April 1982. (Reproduced with permission from the International Listening Association, PO Box 164, Belle Plaine, MN, USA.)

Table 4.3: Listening habits of good clinicians.

- Let the patient talk without interruptions
- Probe the hints and nonverbal cues
- Acknowledge that you are listening
- Ask open-ended question — Listen
- Do not prejudge
- Check for accuracy
- Know the expectations
- Validate patient perspective
- Maintain body and eye posture
- Ask: "What else is on your mind?"

Modified from: Appleby C, "Getting doctors to listen to patients" in *Managed Care*, page 28, December 1996. (Reproduced with permission from Managed Care Magazine.)

In 1982, I was asked to talk to the International Listening Association about listening in the medical setting. Since this material is not available in print anymore, I am reproducing it here.

The Importance of Listening for the Medical Professions: (Summary of a seminar presented on March 4, 1982 to the International Listening Association in Washington, D.C.)

The major functions of a physician include diagnosis of disease, illness, and predicament in a person, and management of the disease and illness. The disease is the biological component, the illness is the personal component, and the predicament is the social component of illness. For a physician to be effective, he has to collect data about the disease, the illness, and the predicament. Collection of data in a medical setting requires looking and listening. It is impossible to make a proper diagnosis without adequate data on the disease and the illness. It is impossible to be a good doctor and help manage an illness unless the advice given takes into account the patient's illness and the predicament. This, again, requires asking questions and listening.

Physicians, in general, are trained to give advice. But they are not adequately trained to listen. In addition, there are many built-in blocks to communication between physicians and patients. These built-in blocks are: (1) the expectations of the patient are often different from the expectations of the physician. It is not enough if the physician takes care of what he thinks is important. He has to the extent possible take care of the patient's expectations. (2) The fears and anxieties of the patient color the presentation of the illness. For proper management it is essential that the physician find out what those fears and anxieties are. (3) The current appointment system is the single most important deterrent to physician–patient communication. The "most common complaint of patients is in regard to the inordinate waiting time in the doctor's office.

(*Continued*)

(*Continued*)

The patients are so angry because of this waiting that when they really get an opportunity to talk to the physician they are unable to express themselves completely. (4) Even the time that is spent with the doctor is interrupted with paging systems and telephone calls. This makes the patient wonder whether the physician is listening. (5) When a diagnosis is made and the patient is told about the disease, the patient goes into a state of shock, anger/or dismay, and very often the information does not get through during this initial period of shock. The physician may have to repeat the information on a number of occasions before the patient really listens. (6) Patients who can afford to pay obtain their own physician. But patients attending clinics get different doctors at each visit. Therefore, these patients feel that there is no one person they can talk to who will listen to them. (7) With the current trends and specialties, both in medicine and allied health personnel, there are a number of people involved in managing patients. Unless there is one person coordinating all these consultants and therapists, there is usually more than one message given to the patient, which, in turn, confuses the patient. (8) Physicians have a problem in talking in lay language. Patients tend to misinterpret technical statements. (9) The first contact with any person is the most important contact. Often this contact is over the telephone, and frequently with a medical secretary. Even when the physician talks directly with the patient, it is often hard to judge over the phone how important and urgent the situation is.

Some recommended solutions to improving communication between patients and physicians and allowing a better listening situation are: (1) Physicians turning off all telephones and the paging system while they are with patients. (2) Keeping appointments as close to the scheduled time as possible and respecting

(*Continued*)

(*Continued*)

the value of the patient's time. (3) Listening with the eyes and with the ears. (4) Reviewing at the end of the session what the patient has said, so that together they agree on what the major concerns, fears, and anxieties are. (5) Remembering crucial points from the history, so that during subsequent visits the physician can, if appropriate, inquire about events of importance in the patient's life. (6) The physician demonstrating that he heard the patient's concerns by acting on them — which is the only proof the patient has of knowing that the physician indeed listened to his major concerns and complaints.

Observational Skills

When I was a house officer at the Wadia Hospital for Children in Bombay, India, one of my favorite teachers recognized that a child with thalassemia had been admitted to his service without having been told about it. All the junior physicians were impressed. When asked how he came to that conclusion, he said that he saw a new patient who was pale and yellow suggesting probable hemolytic anemia. The large skull suggested the possibility of chronic hemolysis. The mother's dress suggested an ethnicity in which thalassemia is known to be high. Those kinds of observations are great, not just to impress the lowly medical students, but to better manage clinical problems.

Physical examination requires visual observational skills. How does one learn to observe and practice observational skills? When I was organizing a course on physical diagnosis for medical students, I found two groups of people who practice observational skills in their work more than physicians do. They are artists and plastic surgeons.[20] A professor of art (Doctor Charles Stegeman) and a plastic surgeon (Doctor Linton Whitaker) taught me most of the following points.

Dr. C. Stegeman is an artist, an art historian, and teaches art at Haverford College. He teaches medical students how to observe and how to *think visually*. In the process of teaching undergraduate liberal arts students how to observe, he has developed some techniques and vocabulary that are useful in teaching observation skills to medical students. They are easy and you can practice them yourself.

(1) *Yo-yo technique*: In this exercise, one stands at a distance from the painting and looks at the whole picture first. Then one "zooms in" on one aspect of the picture, looks for details, "zooms out" placing the close-up details on the big picture, "zooms in" again and so forth (Figs. 4.1A and 4.1B).

(A)

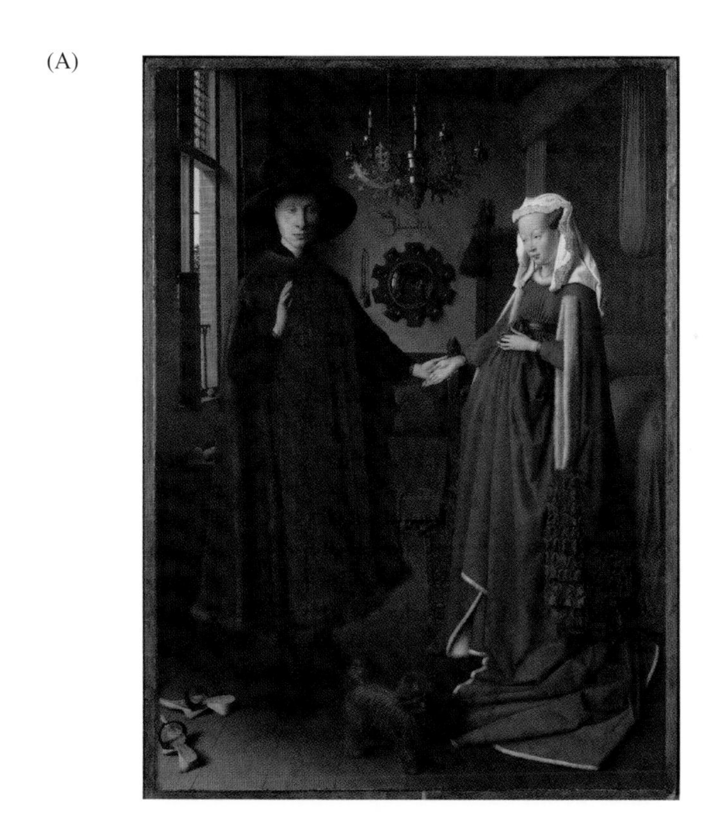

Figs. 4.1A and 4.1B: Portrait of Giovanni Arnofini and his wife by Jan van Eyck. From the collections of The National Gallery Picture Library, London, England. © Copyright, The National Gallery, 2009. (See text for details.)

(B)

Figs. 4.1A and 4.1B: (*Continued*)

To practise this yo-yo technique, look at the entire picture (Fig. 4.1A) for a view of the global scene. Look at the man and the woman. Is the woman pregnant? Or is it the nature of her gown? Then zoom in above the main subjects and observe the chandalier and the mirror behind. Zoom out and then zoom in below the subjects and observe the wooden sandals and the dog. Zoom out and zoom back in on the window next to the man. Do you see the oranges? (Fig. 4.1B) Did you observe them during your global view of the portrait?

This method is particularly useful in gait analysis. For example, when you observe an abnormal gait, the initial global impression may suggest that the patient walks with a hip-hike. However, on scrutiny, you "zoom in" on the hip and look for stiffness or weakness (absence of flexion); you go back out again to observe the whole gait before zooming in on the knee. You then look to see whether the knee is stiff or flail; next, you zoom in on the ankle to see if there is anterior tibial weakness. In essence, you alternately "zoom in" and "zoom out".

(2) *Squinting*: This technique is useful to look at paintings that are drawn to give an impression of hazy borders. Next time you go to an art museum, practice this technique when looking at paintings by

Claude Monet. The edges may appear fuzzy with no clear outlines of the structure. However, when you squint your eyes and look at the painting, margins become more defined and the shape of the structure is clearer. This technique is useful in clinical medicine, when examining a diffuse swelling. Squinting helps define the characteristics and the border, particularly when examining the thyroid or a joint. It is also useful when examining skin rash.

(3) *Abstraction/pattern recognition*: In abstract paintings, the artist is painting a tree but may show only the concept of branching in the painting. From the strokes and brushes, one can also guess whether a painting is by Normal Rockwell or by Picasso. Though not identical, the corresponding concept in clinical area is "pattern recognition". For example, when a child is seen with coarse facial features and a large tongue, one thinks of hypothyroidism or mucopolysaccharidosis. Children with Down syndrome can be identified purely on pattern recognition.

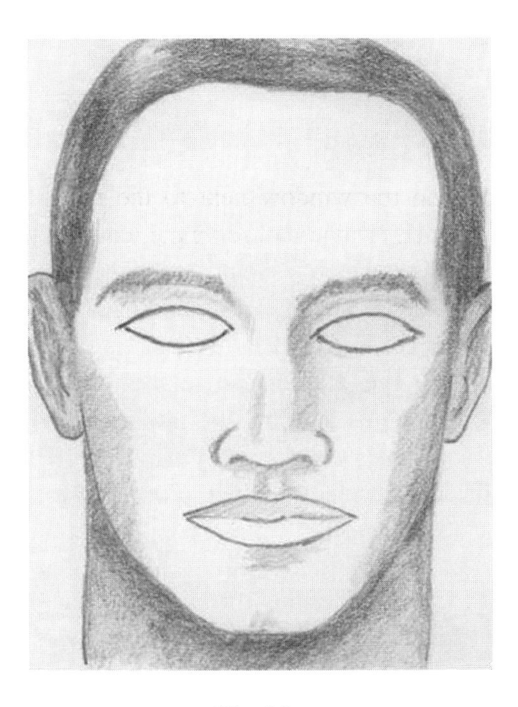

Fig. 4.2.

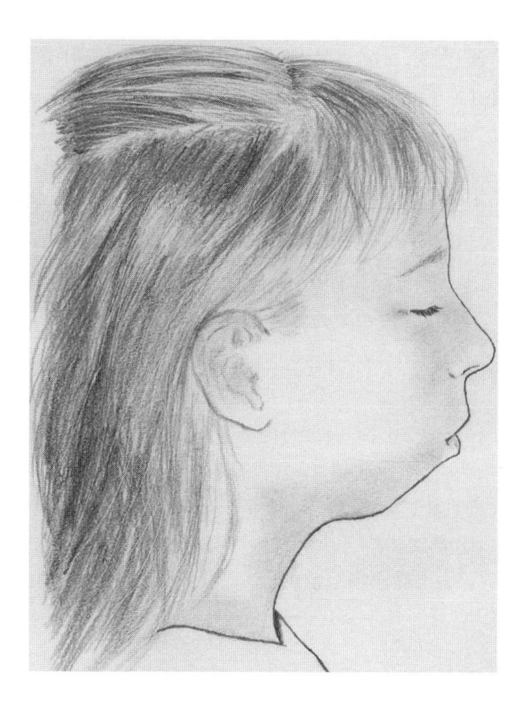

Fig. 4.3.

(4) *Visual logic*: Great anatomists and plastic surgeons practice this technique. For example, are the eyes in Fig. 4.2 normally placed, or are they closer together than they should be? Is the profile of the patient in Fig. 4.3 normal? If not, what is abnormal? In answering these questions, one has to know what "normal" is. What criteria should be used to say that eyes are normally placed, too crowded, or wider apart? What makes one say that the jaw in Fig. 4.3 is small? To define these abnormalities, normality has to be defined. Once the parameters of normality are defined, one can use "visual logic" to recognize the abnormality.

For example, Fig. 4.2 defines the distance between the eyes in normal children. Artists suggest that there is one eye's width between the two eyes. If the space between the eyes is too narrow to accommodate another eye, there is crowding of the eyes (hypotelorism), and if there is more than one eye's width, the eyes are too far apart (hypertelorism). Similarly, in the profile of a face, a perpendicular line drawn from the bridge of the nose should touch the tip of the chin. If the chin is too far behind, it is hypognathism, as seen in JRA (JIA).

Until now, the discussion focused on the techniques the *observer uses in observing an object*. We can also categorize the components of *what is being looked at*. This is not new to clinicians. For example, there are certain general headings under which clinicians have always described a swelling — location, size, shape, color, texture, edge, consistency, adherence to adjacent structures. Similar headings are used to describe ulcers, rash, heart murmur, etc.

Another logical way to define and recognize abnormality is to define the components of normal structures and physiology, and then describe their variations.[21] This requires the division of each organ and its functions into their component parts in a logical fashion followed by definition of normality for each component. The focus is on the components of the organ and its function (Table 4.4) and not on what modality the observer uses (observation, palpation, percussion and auscultation).

This discussion on abnormality should lead one to an understanding of normality.[22,23] Edmond Murphy points out that the word "*normal*" is ambiguous.[22] The meaning of the word "*normal*" will vary depending on the purpose of its use. It can be precise as in mathematics or vague as in behavioral sciences. Definition of normal requires two conditions: (1) that the attributes fall into classes, (2) that there is a need to decide which of those classes is to be designated as normal. This becomes a problem when the characteristic involved is not an attribute (e.g. short or tall) but a continuous measurement or variable (e.g. blood pressure, cholesterol level).

Dr. Murphy points out seven different meanings of the word "*normal*".[22] They are: "Gaussian" as used in statistics, "most representative of its class" including the words average, median and modal as used in descriptive sciences, "commonly encountered in its class" or habitual, "most suited for survival" or optimal as used in genetics, "carrying no penalty" or harmless as used in clinical medicine, "commonly aspired" or conventional as used in politics and sociology and "most preferred in its class" as used in metaphysics and morals.

Table 4.4: Defining normality: What is normal?

One way to systematize our observations of normal structures and functions is to define the variable under the following headings: Anatomic Variations and Physiologic Variations.

The following must be considered in describing an anatomic structure: size, number, shape, position in relation to itself, position in relation to other structures, color, texture, continuity, and alignment. An anatomic description of normality gives a logical basis for describing abnormality. Such a base is applicable to all anatomic structures.

Alterations in physiological functions can be grouped under the following headings: presence of, loss of, partial loss of, function present but painful, function present but difficult, abnormal function of, function reduced or excess in number, frequency or duration, and irregular function.

Examples of Logical Description of Symptoms and Signs

Traditional term	Structure/Function	Alteration(s)
Dyspnea	Respiration	Difficult
Hyperpnea	Respiration	Rate-fast Depth-increased
Tachypnea	Respiration	Rate-fast
Diarrhea	Bowel movement	Rate-increased Consistency-decreased Volume-increased
Polyuria	Urine	Volume-increased
Melena	Bowel movement	Color-black
Hematochezia	Bowel movement	Color-red (bloody)
Hypertelorism	Eyes	Position-far off (in relation to each other)
Proptosis	Eyes	Position-forward (in relation to itself)
Ulcer	Skin	Continuity-loss of
Jaundice	Skin	Color-yellow
Papule	Skin	Extra growth-elevated-smooth
Purpura	Skin	Extra growth-flat-red (blood)

For further details see Ref. 21.

Examples of the use of the word "normal" in clinical medicine include measurements of height and weight to decide whether the patient is too tall or too short or overweight or underweight in comparison with the average, the *most representative of its class*. When metabolic measurements such as serum potassium or oxygen saturation levels are made, these numbers are compared with "normal" *values compatible with survival*. When the eyes and the ears are reported to be normal on physical examination, we mean that the *features carry no penalty* or are *harmless*. An understanding of the concept of normality is likely to be even more important with the increasing sophistication of imaging, and biochemical and immunological methods. Developments in neurobehavioral science and genomics will test the concepts of normality even more in the coming decades.

Physical Examination

Some physical abnormalities, such as a cleft lip or a pronounced limp or hemiplegia, are clear to everyone, including non-medical people. Some findings such as mild jaundice are visible only to an observant eye. Some findings require careful examination, since the organs involved are hidden: for example, heart murmur, splenomegaly, or rectal mass. Finally, some findings have to be elicited by examination of the patient. For example, you have to tap the knee or ankle with a percussion hammer to elicit tendon reflexes.

To recognize abnormal physical findings, one has to know what to look for, how, and when. One has to have knowledge of anatomy and physiology. The patient has to be cooperative. The setting has to be conducive for a good physical examination. Clinical disagreements occur even with the best of knowledge, subject, setting, and practice. Failures to detect signs that are present (error of omission) and reporting of signs that are not present (error of commission) are common errors made by beginners and experienced clinicians alike. How can one improve?

Earlier, we said that history and physical examination help make more than 75% of the diagnosis. The other side of the coin is that in some conditions (such as mitral valve prolapse and breast cancer) require the use of new technologies for early detection. For example, only 9% of patients with mitral valve prolapse will be diagnosed if we rely on physical findings alone.[24] An echocardiogram is needed to detect these lesions. The use of imaging modalities to detect breast cancer in early stages is well known. We do need these technologies, and have to use them wisely.

The presence or absence of specific physical findings can help determine the probability of a specific diagnosis. If laboratory and imaging studies are ordered only when certain clinical criteria are met, the probability of finding an abnormality gets higher (pre-test probability), and the tests become cost effective. This requires that the findings on physical examination be accurate.[25] It will be necessary to know likelihood ratios and odds ratios of not only laboratory tests, but also of clinical findings.[26]

Accuracy, as applied in clinical epidemiology,[27,28] refers to the probability of a diagnosis, given the presence of a clinical feature in history and/or physical examination. In other words, it is the positive predictive value of that finding for that particular diagnosis. For example, in a patient with jaundice (given the age, sex, habits, and geography), what is the probability that the diagnosis is hepatitis C? Alternatively, what is the probability of finding ascites in a 60-year-old male with ankle swelling? Efforts are underway to answer such clinical questions.

It is common to see clinicians disagree on the presence of specific physical findings. It is important to study these variations and the reasons for these variations. When the agreement between two different examiners on the presence (or absence) of a symptom or sign is measured, it is called precision. It is humbling to learn that agreement (k values) between physicians on recognition of cyanosis, tachypnea, and pectoriloquy were 0.36, 0.25, and 0.11, respectively.[29] There are some simple calculations one can use. Excellent reviews and textbooks on these subjects are available.

Why are there so many errors in documenting physical findings, other than lack of experience? Why are there variations between physicians in recognizing the presence or absence of findings? If we do not carry an otoscope to a pediatric examination, we will obviously miss all cases of otitis media. All of us know the problem of listening for soft

Table 4.5: Classification of errors in physical diagnosis.

Technique
1. Poor ordering and organization of the examination
2. Defective or no equipment
3. Improper manual technique or use of instruments
4. Performance of the examination when inappropriate
5. Poor bedside etiquette leading to patient discomfort, embarrassment, or overt hostility
Omission
1. Failure to perform part of the examination
Detection
1. Missing a sign that is present
2. Reporting detection of a sign that is not present
3. Interpreting normal physiological or anatomical variant as abnormal
4. Misidentifying a sign after detection
Interpretation
1. Failure to understand the meaning in pathophysiological terms of an identified sign
2. Lack of knowledge or use of confirming signs
3. Lack of knowledge of the value of a sign in confirming or ruling out diagnostic entity
Recording
1. Forgetting a finding and not recording it
2. Illegible handwriting, obscure observations, improper terminology, poor grammar, and incomplete record of findings
3. Recording a diagnosis and not the sign detected

From Weiner S, Nathanson M, Physical examination: Frequently observed errors, *JAMA* 1976; **236**:852–855.

aortic diastolic murmur in a noisy outpatient department. Weiner and Nathanson classify reasons for errors in physical diagnosis based on direct observation of trainees in a university hospital (Table 4.5). Many of these apply to errors made by physicians at all levels.[30]

In addition, we need greater emphasis on how to elicit physical findings, how to measure reproducibility of these findings, and how to use these findings in clinical reasoning. It is important to remember that even after recognizing abnormalities in physical examination, wrong conclusions may be reached due to faulty logic.

Fortunately, there is increasing emphasis on making sure that the trainees are supervised during physical examination of patients. In the future, the training program director will be required to assure the competency of trainees to perform a thorough physical examination based on actual observation of the trainee. The technique of videotaping students during interviewing and examining, followed by critique by a member of the faculty, is a standard practice in many medical schools. Hopefully, this will become part of graduate training programs as well.

If we cannot minimize observer variations, how can we agree on the diagnosis or management? Supporting this concern, the public is increasingly impatient with differences in the ability of physicians to recognize and act on important clinical clues. Fortunately some of the earlier lack of interest in studying particulars of medical history and physical examination has passed. Several investigators are applying tools used in establishing the usefulness of laboratory tests to physical examination as part of evidence based medicine.[25]

Finally, I believe in the therapeutic value of a physician's touch. This mystique is fast disappearing. However, there is value in touching patients appropriately with care, concern, caution, and compassion. Care, because we do not want to touch the painful part first. Concern, for the comfort of the patient, so that we do not touch the abdomen with a cold hand or put a cold stethoscope on the chest. Caution because we do not want to touch members of the opposite sex at vulnerable spots or in compromising positions without someone else in the room. There is so much more to touching than just touching.[31]

Major Message: Before taking medical history and performing a physical examination, physicians should learn listening skills and observational skills, and sharpen them throughout their lifetime.

- Great clinicians teach us listening skills and observational skills.
- One can also learn listening skills from managers and administrators in industry.
- One can learn observational skills from artists and plastic surgeons.
- Once you acquire these skills, you have to practice them.

References

1. Lawrence C. Keywords in the History of Medicine: Clinic. *Lancet* 2004; **363**:1483.
2. Fry J. *A New Approach to Medicine — Priority and Principles of Health Care*. 1978. Baltimore, MD; University Park Press.
3. Fletcher RH, Fletcher SW. Has medicine outgrown physical diagnosis? *Ann Intern Med* 1992; **17**:786–787.
4. St. Clair EW, Oddone EZ, Waugh GR, Feussner JR. Assessing housestaff diagnostic skills using a cardiology patient simulator. *Ann Intern Med* 1992; **117**:751–756.
5. Mangione S, Nieman LZ. Cardiac auscultatory skills of internal medicine and family practice trainees: A comparison of diagnostic proficiency. *JAMA* 1997; **278**:717–722.
6. Anderson R, Fagan MJ, Sebastian MJ. Teaching students the art and science of physical diagnosis. *Am J Med* 2001; **110**:4419–4423.
7. Hampton JR, Harrison MJG, Mitchell JRA, Pritchard JS, Seymour C. Relative contributions of history-taking, physical examination, and laboratory investigation to diagnosis and management of medical outpatients. *BMJ* 1975; **2**:486–489.
8. Peterson MC, Holbrook JH, Hales DV, Smith NL, Staker LV. Contributions of the history, physical examination, and laboratory investigations in making medical diagnosis. *West Med J* 1992; **156**:163–165.
9. Reilly M. Physical examination in the care of medical inpatients: An observational study. *Lancet* 2003; **362**:1100–1105.
10. Novack DH. Beyond data gathering: Twelve functions of the medical history. *Hospital Practice* March 30, 1985. pp 11–12.
11. Kleinman A, Benson P. Anthropology in the clinic: The problem of cultural competency and how to fix it. *PLoS Medicine*. 2006; **3**(10):1673–1676.
12. Guttmacher AE, Collins FS, Carmone RH. The family history — more important than ever. *N Engl J Med* 2004; **351**:2333–2336.
13. Juberg RC. Making the family history relevant. *JAMA* 1972; **220**:122–123.
14. Roberts H. Listen to the parents — they may know best. *BMJ* 1996; **313**:954.
15. Kai J. Parent's difficulties and information needs in coping with acute illness in preschool children: A qualitative study. *BMJ* 1996; **313**: 987–990.

16. Bergman A. Learning to listen. *Arch Pediatr Adolesc Med* 2003; **157**:414–415.
17. Kvalsvig A. Ask the elephant. *Lancet* 2003; **362**:2079–2080.
18. Geeting B, Geeting C. *How to Listen Assertively*. 1976. New York; Monarch Prcss.
19. Nichols R. *Are you Listening*? 1967. New York; McGraw Hill.
20. Broadbent RT, Matthews VL. Artistic relationships in Surface Anatomy of the Face: Application to Reconstructive Surgery. Plastic and Reconstructive Surgery 1957; **20**:1–17.
21. Athreya BH. *Pediatric Physical Diagnosis*. 2009. Kent, UK; Anshan Publishers. (in print)
22. Murphy EA. *The Logic of Medicine*. 1976. Baltimore, MD; The Johns Hopkins University Press.
23. Davis P, Bradley JG. The meaning of Normal. *Perspect Bio Med* 1996; **40**:68–77.
24. Levy D, Savage D. Prevalence and clinical features of mitral valve prolapse. *Am Heart J* 1987; **113**:1281–1290.
25. McGee S. *Evidence Based Physical Diagnosis*. 2001. Phildelphia, PA; WB Saunders.
26. Grimes D, Schulz KF. Refining clinical diagnosis with likelihood ratios. *Lancet* 2005; **365**:1500–1505.
27. Sackett DL. A primer on the precision and accuracy of the clinical examination. *JAMA* 1992; **267**:2638–2644.
28. Sackett DL, Drummond Rennie. The science and art of the clinical examination. *JAMA* 1992; **267**:2650–2652.
29. Spiteri MA, Cook DG, Clarke SW. Reliability of eliciting physical signs in examination of the chest. *Lancet*. 1988; **1**:873–875.
30. Weiner S, Nathanson M. Physical examination: Frequently observed errors. *JAMA* 1976; **236**:852–855.
31. Older J. Teaching touch in medical school. *JAMA* 1984; **252**:931–933.

If you want someone to listen to you…
You need to know the person well
You have to know yourself well
You need to know the situation well, very well
You need to know what makes a person want to listen —

Is it because he/she is afraid (of authority or power)?
Is it because he/she has a need or want (that you can fulfill)?
Is it because he/she wants to please you?
Is it because he/she is truly interested, just for his/her own sake?

You need to know whom he/she would listen to. It will be

Someone he/she respects
Someone he/she trusts
Someone who listens to him/her.

Patients in the 21st century are partners in decision making. They are well informed. They are not interested in ALL of the facts, but in relevant ones specific to them. They are interested in what is being done to them. Therefore, they need individualized information first.

You have to address their needs and fears, then only you can suggest, convince, and negotiate.

Chapter 5

Diagnostic Skills

The meaning of the word "diagnosis" is "to know through". The word implies differentiation. In usage, however, the term *diagnosis* denotes the initial impression based on the presenting symptoms and signs. The term that describes the process of establishing a specific cause out of a list of possible causes is *differential diagnosis*.

One of the challenging, stimulating tasks of a clinician is to arrive at a diagnosis. He has to diagnose the disease, illness, and the predicament. In this process, the clinician gathers evidence (by history, physical examination, laboratory data, imaging studies), sifts the evidence, prioritizes, analyzes each piece, and synthesizes from the pieces. He may or may not arrive at a final diagnosis; but will have to arrive at a working hypothesis to make decisions on the management of the patient.

While managing the patient, the clinician's eyes have to be open for new clues all the time. As more evidence accumulates, the hypothesis has to be re-evaluated. Medicine is the art of making decisions on incomplete evidence under uncertain conditions. That is the challenge and the thrill.

Some clinicians are good at diagnosing. They are like Sherlock Holmes, or the legendary Zadig.[1] Zadig is an imaginary character in Voltaire's novelette "*Zadig or Destiny — An Ancient Tale*." In this story, Zadig gets into considerable difficulty because of his uncanny ability to draw inferences from seemingly trivial details. It is worth quoting one passage, where Zadig is able to guess that the Queen's dog is a female that had recently given birth to a litter. He is also able to guess that it was a lame dog. He did this without ever setting his eyes on that dog. Here is the passage: "I saw on the sand the footprints of an animal, and easily decided that they were those of a little dog. Long and faintly marked furrows, imprinted where the sand was slightly raised between the footprints, told mc that it was a bitch whose dugs were hanging down, and that consequently she must have given birth only a few days before. Other marks of a different character, showing that the surface of the sand had been constantly grazed on either side of the front paws, informed me that she had very long ears; and, as I observed that the sand was always less deeply indented by one paw than by the other three, I gathered that the bitch belonging to our august queen was a little lame, if I may venture to say so."[1]

This type of observation to reconstruct the past was originally developed by an Italian physician by name Giovanni Morelli. He developed it in order to distinguish fake paintings from the originals of master painters. Insurance inspectors use this technique to analyze the cause of fires. This method was called "retrospective prophecy" by Thomas Huxley first and then popularized in clinical medicine by William Osler.[2] Retrospective prophecy is the stuff of the legendary detectives like Sherlock Holmes. This is also the method used by great clinicians.

Good clinicians use Zadig's method, observing closely, taking in the crucial points, and reconstructing the past events leading to the current observations. They observe keenly, sense acutely, arrange facts in a neat package and in order of importance, and use their book knowledge (memory and ability to recall help) and past experience. Observing such clinicians in action and understanding how they function should help others learn some of their techniques.

Good clinicians make their initial hypothesis within the first few minutes of history taking. Obviously, the initial symptoms that bring the patient to the physician trigger a set of possible diagnoses. The clinician then starts asking questions to clarify these initial possibilities. The clinician's mind is shuttling between various possibilities and specific diagnoses; between the generalities of what is written in textbooks about diseases and the specific clinical finding in the individual patient. With each additional piece of information, the clinician is reformulating the possibilities and their priorities. A seasoned clinician may take two steps to get to the critical question, whereas a novice may take ten steps to get there. However, the process is the same.

What is the mental process that clinicians use to solve complex diagnostic problems? Eddy and Clanton used the clinicopathological conferences published in the *New England Journal of Medicine* between 1974 and 1979 to analyze the mental process involved in making a clinical diagnosis.[3] At the outset, we learn that this clinicopathological exercise had its inspiration from the case method of teaching instituted at the Harvard Law School in the 1870s. (Physicians do owe some gratitude to the lawyers after all.) Massachusetts General Hospital introduced this concept to medicine in 1910.

The authors reviewed the reasoning used by the discussants in 50 case analyses and found a common pattern of reasoning used by most clinicians, most of the time. More importantly, in cases where the clinicians did not use this model, no other pattern was observed. It appeared that physicians face three major obstacles in arriving at a diagnosis:

1. The amount of information to be handled by the clinician is often too voluminous to be processed efficiently. Information overload makes it difficult to separate the "signal" from the "noise".
2. Textbooks are written on the etiology, pathology, pathogenesis, signs and symptoms, laboratory features and treatment of individual diseases; whereas patients come with their unique signs and symptoms that have to be related to the textbook knowledge about specific diseases. One of my professors used to say: "Children do not read the *Textbook of Pediatrics* before they show up in the clinic."
3. After all the facts have been entered and analyzed, there remains the need to manipulate probabilities. This includes the probability of a diagnosis given the symptom or sign and the probability of specific signs and symptoms in each disease under consideration. For example, when a patient is seen with jaundice in a big city hospital such as in New York, what is the probability of the diagnosis being hepatitis A or B or C? If one looks at all patients with hepatitis C in New York, how many of them are likely to present with the initial symptom of jaundice?

Eddy and Clanton noted six steps used by clinicians to deal with these issues and arrive at the correct diagnosis:

Step 1: List all the individual findings, called the *elemental findings* or combine them in several different ways until an *aggregate* of findings is developed as a starting point for the diagnostic process. For example, if a child has polyuria, polydypsia, and nocturia, it is better to combine them into an aggregate finding that points to the possible diagnosis of diabetes (mellitus or insipidus), rather than dealing with each symptom separately. Obviously, book knowledge and experience are required to recognize such helpful patterns of findings.

(There are two related areas of interest, namely problem solving skills and the ability of the human brain to manipulate more than one or two items at a time. These will be discussed in the next chapter.)

Step 2: Decide on the most pivotal finding or aggregate of findings. This could be a pathognomonic finding or one with the least number of possibilities in the differential diagnostic list. Examples are the cough of whooping cough or the peeling of skin in Kawasaki disease. These types of findings are, however, rare. Therefore, the clinician has to choose one *pivotal finding*, or a group of pivotal findings that is most likely to lead to the correct answer and develop a differential diagnostic list. In this process, the clinician has to temporarily ignore other findings. For example, if a child comes with fever and facial palsy, it is better to choose facial palsy as the starting point since the list of differential diagnosis of fever will be long and non-specific whereas the list for facial palsy will be shorter and more direct.

Step 3: Move forward from a sign, symptom, and laboratory finding, or imaging study that has been chosen as a pivot, to a *list* of possible diagnosis. At this level, the clinician is not concerned with how probable any disease in the list is, but only with the fact that it could have caused the pivotal finding.

Step 4: *Prune* the list by comparing the important findings in the particular patient against the known features of each disease in the list. Some diseases are eliminated immediately. Sometimes, only *one* possibility is high on the list. However, most of the time, the clinician has to "compare one by one the patient's findings with the signs and symptoms that characterize the diseases" in the list. If any of the diseases in the list are rejected, they are unlikely to be reconsidered unless there are other developments.

Step 5: Take two diseases at a time from the list of differential diagnosis and compare the findings in the case with the expected features of the diseases under consideration. The idea is to find a disease that will *explain most of the features* of the case. Sometimes, the clinician may ask for another imaging or laboratory study to get more information that may help narrow the possibility. For example, if the final two diagnoses on the list are Kawasaki disease and erythema multiforme, the clinician may obtain an echocardiogram. The presence of coronary artery abnormality will eliminate erythema multiforme with certainty.

Step 6: Make sure that the chosen diagnosis at this step would explain ALL the findings in the case. If not, the clinician may have to take other findings that he did not include in the list of pivotal findings and *start all over again*.

I described the details of this paper completely because this analysis of the mental process may help other clinicians develop a method when faced with tough clinical situations.

There are several other techniques used by experienced clinicians in solving diagnostic problems. For example:

1. When presented with a symptom, a sign, or a symptom-complex, a clinician has to ask three basic questions[4]:

   - *What is it?*
   - *What is it not?*
   - *How do you know?*

What is it? Let us take two examples to explain mental processes: Assume that a patient comes with pain in the joints (arthralgia). The first question is: *What is it?* The obvious initial assumption is "arthritis". However, to be sure of this, the physician has to define the word *arthritis*. Arthritis is defined as a non-bony swelling of the joint or the presence of two of the following three findings: limitation of passive movement of that joint, tenderness, or pain on motion, and heat. If only one condition is present, the patient does not have arthritis. The first mental step assumes that the physician knows the definition of the condition he is naming.

You can rewrite the first question as: "*What is it — define*."

Here is an example. The condition of a 12-year-old girl was diagnosed as acute rheumatic fever. She was put on penicillin prophylaxis and bed rest for 2 years. The diagnosis was based on joint pains, elevated sedimentation rate, and a high ASO titer. She had joint pain but no true arthritis. If the physician had used the criteria for arthritis appropriately, he would have known that the patient had arthralgia and not arthritis and would not have subjected this child to unnecessary treatment. If the physician's first impression is wrong, the entire problem will be mishandled.

What is it not? In other words, what are the conditions that may give symptoms easily confused with those of arthritis? Bone pain is one. Tendon pain is another. Periarticular pain is a third. In this step, it is important to exclude conditions that may mimic the symptoms of the disease the clinician is considering.

This question can be rewritten as: "*What is it not — exclude*."

How do you know? The third step is, "*How do you know that the initial impression is correct?*" In this hypothetical case of arthritis, the ideal proof is to show that the synovial fluid from the affected joint has all the characteristics of an inflammatory fluid. This, of course, is clinically unnecessary in many situations. However, there should be other evidences of inflammation locally (such as warmth) or systemically (such as fever or elevated sedimentation rate). If one or both of these factors are positive, we are more certain that the patient has arthritis and can proceed with the differential diagnosis of arthritis to establish the cause.

The third step may be rewritten as: "*How do you confirm?*"

Take another example of a patient who has a history of yellow skin and highly colored urine. The initial question is, "What is it?" The answer obviously is "jaundice". The next question is "What is it not?" Conditions to be excluded are carotenemia and discolored urine due to ingestion of certain food or drugs. The final step is urinalysis to look for bilirubin.

2. Given the clinical situation, think about the most likely explanation (most common) and the most serious (emergency) explanation. The first portion of the statement is well known to clinician ("*When you hear hoofbeats, think of horses, not zebras.*") The second portion allows clinicians to be prepared to deal with the most urgent situation, even if it is uncommon. For example, if a patient with systemic lupus erythematosus comes with chest pain, the most likely cause is flare of the disease and associated myositis, pericarditis, or pleuritis. However, the most serious problem to remember is pulmonary embolism. The history and physical examination should be directed to rule out these possibilities.
3. Another method useful in certain situations is pattern recognition. Radiologists use this technique frequently. Clinicians use it too, less often. For example, a three-week-old male with projectile vomiting is most likely to have congenital pyloric stenosis. A 17-year-old sexually active girl with papules and arthritis most likely has gonorrheal arthritis–dermatitis syndrome.
4. I am impressed with the fact that there is always one *crucial point* in any given situation that demands an answer in any decision making process. If this crucial point is recognized and accounted for, the final decision is more likely to be correct. If not, the decision will invariably be wrong, however well all other points are handled. Here are some examples from personal experience:

Example 1: A three-year-old girl with arthritis was seen in our clinic. Two of her siblings also had arthritis. All the children had been treated for rheumatoid arthritis for about 16 years. Indeed, all the features these children had were identical to what one sees in rheumatoid arthritis. The mother casually remarked that all three children were born with "bent fingers". This history of congenitally flexed fingers is the crucial point in this child's history. No child with rheumatoid arthritis has been known to be born with bent fingers. Therefore, unless this particular feature is taken into account, the final diagnosis will be wrong. Indeed, an investigation of this crucial point led to the fact that all these children had a rare familial form of arthritis and not rheumatoid arthritis.

Example 2: A boy with severe head injury was a patient in our hospital. The nurse and physician in contact with the family found it extremely hard to deal with the mother of this boy. She appeared to be unreasonable, constantly demanding attention. Although any mother is likely to act unreasonable after a tragedy such as this, there was a particular pattern. It was obvious that to this mother, time was an obsession. If anybody told her that he would meet with this mother at 10 a.m., he had to be there precisely at 10 a.m. If he came even one minute late, she became so furious she could not even talk. Even if one gave her warning of a delay, she could not handle it. Given this personality, it was obvious how important it was for health care professionals to keep appointments with her and how it would be foolish to give prognostic information to this mother about her son's recovery. It became clear that this mother earned her bad reputation because of her obsession with time and the usual problems health care professionals have in keeping appointments. Once everyone coming in contact with her was asked to keep promises dealing with time, or not make promises they could not adhere to, the interactions became smoother and it was easier to communicate with her.

On reviewing these examples, one can see that to an untrained eye the crucial point will look like any other point in a given problem. However, a sensitive, experienced, or intuitive person will quickly recognize that one of the points demands the most attention for the successful solution of the problem. In example number one, it is the "bent finger". In example number two, it is the mother's obsession with time.

It is easy to recognize the "crucial" point after the problem is solved. However, how does one recognize it before the problem is solved? Experience helps, but there are also elements of logic and

Table 5.1: Iron-deficiency anemia.

Lack of financial resources to get iron-containing food
Lack of iron-containing food in the region
Cooking habits making iron unavailable
Inability to access iron-containing food — age or mental ability
Inability to chew and swallow iron-containing food
Inability to retain
Inability to absorb
Inability to transport
Inability to store
Inability to utilize for primary function (e.g. making hemoglobin)
Excess loss

intuition. There is no known way to teach this concept. However, people working as problem solvers should try to apply this concept in their daily work and serve as role models.

5. Logical sequencing of known physiological or biochemical facts can help arrive at a diagnosis. For example, Table 5.1 summarizes various steps that can lead to iron deficiency. Obviously, iron-deficiency anemia can result from defects in any one of these steps. This logic can be applied to any other nutrient. Similar logic can be used to develop a list of differential diagnosis for metabolic diseases, hormonal diseases, receptor defects and immune deficiency diseases.
6. When there is a new symptom in the presence of a chronic illness, it is useful to consider three possibilities:

   a. The new symptom belongs to the spectrum of the chronic disease already diagnosed. For example, headache in a patient with Systemic Lupus Erythematosus (SLE) may be due to involvement of the central nervous system.
   b. The new symptom represents an independent problem. For example, headache in a patient with SLE may be due to an intercurrent "flu-like" illness or meningitis or reactive depression.
   c. The new symptom is related to the treatment for the disease. For example, if the patient is on steroids, the headache may be due to steroid induced hypertension or a pseudo-tumor.

7. All diseases evolve over time, some over a period of a few hours (meningococcemia), some over a period of days (Kawasaki disease), and others over years (Alzheimer). Therefore, it may be wise to let the disease evolve, but with empathy and careful follow-up of the patient and symptomatic treatment. The patient has to be kept comfortable and supported through this period of uncertainty. This is true of neurological diseases and rheumatic diseases. Rushing to perform laboratory tests may be necessary in emergency situations but is not necessarily productive always as was my experience with a teenage girl with erythema nodosum. Initial workup for infectious diseases and small and large bowel studies were negative. Almost a year later, she developed abdominal pain and slight fall in hemoglobin. At this time, the same tests gave positive results for inflammatory bowel disease.

A method suggested by Paul Cutler in his book on *Problem Solving in Clinical Medicine*[5] is "suppression of information". Clinicians use this method particularly with patients who have symptoms referable to every system. It becomes necessary to ignore several subjective symptoms and focus on objective findings to point towards a diagnosis.

The other is a concept introduced by Alvan Feinstein, called the "lanthanic method".[6] This term is applied to situations in which an abnormality is recognized during a routine examination of a non-symptomatic patient. For example, a heart murmur or scoliosis may be recognized in a child during a routine school examination. A lump may be detected in the breast during an annual check up. Another common situation is the detection of a mild anemia or an elevated cholesterol level during a routine examination of the blood.

Use and Abuse of Laboratory Tests

At present, in the United States, many circumstances have conspired to encourage the indiscriminate use of medical technology. The public has come to believe that imaging studies and blood tests makes diagnosis. The physicians have also fallen into this vicious cycle, ordering tests reflexively for each complaint regardless of what the history and physical examination indicate. Physicians do so to allay the anxiety of patients and for fear of malpractice. Besides, the payment system favors laboratory tests and not the time of a physician who takes a good history and performs a thorough physical examination. Time has come for us to change our ways.

The physicians have to convince themselves that a good history and a thorough physical examination are still the primary steps for a correct diagnosis. They have to be convinced that a laboratory test is not meant to give absolute certainty, but to minimize uncertainty. They have to re-educate the medical students and the public. The public attitude towards the appropriate role of testing and technology has to improve. The legal system has to change so that thoughtful physicians, who are diligent, are not penalized for not ordering the latest tests. Until then, it will be difficult to follow the advice from John Stone: "*After deciding what to do, and when to do — whether to do it*."

There are several books and papers on the use and abuse of laboratory tests. I refer to two. The first one by Joseph E. Hardison is a humorous editorial on all the excuses given by house staff when they order unnecessary laboratory tests.[7] The next is an editorial by Jerome Kassirer on the quest for diagnostic certainty.[8] He lists the various well-known reasons for this obsession, including categorical thinking emphasized in textbooks, pressure from peers and supervisors, patient demands, and threat of litigation. He points out that our task is "not to attain certainty, but rather to reduce the level of diagnostic uncertainty enough to make optimal therapeutic decisions", and he suggests several ways other than ordering more and more tests to reduce this uncertainty.

Contrary to public perception and what the media portray, tests do not help separate the well from the sick. In people who do not have any symptoms, no doctor will ask for a test to be done. Presence of signs and symptoms suggests the presence of an illness. It is possible that the signs and symptoms of the illness are due to a disease process. In this situation, the physician makes an initial hypothesis about the organ system involved and the nature of pathology causing the signs and symptoms. He prepares a list of differential diagnosis and this is where tests are useful to rule in or rule out the list of possibilities. This is the proper use of laboratory tests, and not for what we call "fishing expeditions" in an asymptomatic individual or in one with vague undefined symptoms and no consistent, objective findings on careful examination.

In people who do not have symptoms or signs, test results alone cannot help diagnose a disease. This will only lead to "wild goose chase", unnecessary anxiety for the patient and even unnecessary complications because of invasive procedures. However, tests do have a part to play as screening tools in public health and preventive medicine (e.g. cholesterol screening and mammogram).

Major Message: Clinicians use one of several strategies to think through differential diagnostic possibilities and come to a final diagnosis. Laboratory tests help to confirm the diagnosis made by the clinician and help rule out conditions with similar signs and symptoms.

- During clinical examination, THREE questions the physician has to ask oneself: What is it (define)? What is it not (exclude)? How do you know (confirm)?
- When ordering laboratory tests, the physician has to ask oneself the following FOUR questions:

1. What am I ordering this test for?
   a. Is it to help in the diagnosis?
      Is it a sensitive test? Or a specific test?
   b. Is it to monitor the course of the disease?
      If so, is it the best marker for acuity, or severity, or chronicity?
      Am I measuring process or outcome?
   c. Is it to assess the prognosis?
   d. Is it for screening?

(*Continued*)

(*Continued*)

   e. Is it for exclusion? If so, is the exclusion list reasonable and sensible, given the symptoms?
   f. What is its positive predictive value?
   g. What is the negative predictive value?
2. What will I do if the test is positive? What will I do if it is negative?
   If the answer to the above question is vague, the test was probably unnecessary.
3. What is the cost? What is the cost–benefit ratio?
4. How often do I have to repeat the test — and why?

References

1. Voltaire. *Zadig in Candide and Other Stories*. 1980. Oxford, UK; Oxford University Press.
2. Belkin B, Neelson FA. The art of observation: William Osler and the method of Zadig. *Ann Intern Med* 1992; **116**:863–866.
3. Eddy DA, Clanton CH. The art of diagnosis: Solving the clinicopathological exercise. *N Engl J Med* 1982; **306**:1263–1268.
4. Athreya BH. *Pediatric Physical Diagnosis* 2009. Kent, UK; Anshan Publishers. (in print).
5. Cutler P. *Problem Solving in Clinical Medicine. From Data to Diagnosis* 1979. Baltimore, MD; Williams & Wilkins.
6. Feinstein AR. *Clinical Judgment* 1967. Baltimore, MD; Williams & Wilkins.
7. Hardison JE. To be complete. *N Engl J Med* 1979; **300**:193–194.
8. Kassirer JP. Our stubborn quest for diagnostic certainty — A cause of excessive testing . *N Engl J Med* 1989; **320**:1489–1491.

Chapter 6

Problem Solving Skills

I was caring for a girl with systemic lupus erythematosus. While she was taking glucocorticoids for her hemolytic anemia, she developed fever and flare of her arthritis. She was not acutely ill but looked "miserable". She looked pale, had an inflamed left ear, and arthritis of several joints. My thoughts included, among others: "Does she have a middle ear infection, flare of SLE, or both? How many objective facts do I need to make the decision? What tests do I order immediately and which ones can wait? If the initial tests show abnormalities, I may have to do more blood tests. Should I go ahead and order those tests now, so that we do not have to take blood twice? Am I sure, she is not bacteremic? Is steroid masking her sepsis or symptoms of SLE or both? Is it safe to send her home? If I send her home, do I give her antibiotic only or should I increase the dose of glucocorticoids?" The major issues to be addressed are obviously related to medical management. In addition, the final plan had to include management of other issues.

The mother of this girl also had lupus with involvement of the CNS. Therefore, she did not come with the child. Subsequently, I had more questions to consider: "If I find that the mother's lupus has affected her mental functions, what kind of advice should I give to the child and to the family? How will I make sure the advice will be followed? If the family does not have a car and relies on public transportation, will it affect my decision to send this child home?"

A physician's professional life is packed with moments like this. In addition to solving problems and making decisions on medical matters, physicians have to work with the public health systems, social service agencies, government agencies, and insurance companies solving different sets of problems. Even a physician working solo in office practice will have to work with a receptionist, a clerk, or a nurse. In a larger setting, he will have to work with other health professionals as a team member, team leader, or as a consultant. Physicians are increasingly taking administrative roles in hospitals, industries, insurance companies, and government agencies. Even if physicians are not involved in these activities, it will be wise to learn problem solving skills in areas other than medical decision making.

There are several sources to learn from. Educational psychologists, educators, academics, and CEOs of big companies have been working in this field for several decades. Edward De Bono, who conducted research on thinking patterns and problem solving skills and taught at Oxford and Cambridge, is the creator of many concepts, including "lateral thinking", and "Six Thinking Hats". He defines "lateral thinking" as "a way of looking at the world which is different from the way other people see the world". He prefers the term "lateral thinking" to "creative thinking" since the word creative implies value judgment.

"Problem solving is operating skill with which you use your intelligence to solve practical problems in real life," says De Bono. His book *De Bono's Thinking Course* is particularly useful since he summarizes most of his concepts in this small book[1] and gives a list of references at the end.

"If one cannot have complete information, should we spend time on (getting) more information or on thinking skills?" asks De Bono. Physicians ask themselves these questions several times a day. The answer is "yes" to both. Collection of data never stops in patient care. However, physicians have to know when to stop insisting on more information and start acting. Further information may not be available, may not give relevant information, may not be helpful, and may even confuse the issue. In addition, physicians have to consider the cost and discomfort to the patient and delay in management.

In the physician's work, information itself requires evaluation for its source, reliability, accuracy, and relevance before it can be used to make a choice, to plan, to decide, and to act. This is where problem solving skills come into play. These are skills one can learn, but they have to be practiced and perfected like any other skill.

Clever and intelligent minds can come up with quick answers. Creative minds are equally intelligent, but place emphasis on taking the time to consider alternatives, think deliberately, and come to prudent conclusions. Creative minds do not jump to conclusions. Unlike critical thinking, creative thinking is positive and practical. It values wisdom more than clever solutions. It takes into consideration mental blocks caused by perceptions, emotions, feelings, and value systems.

In his introduction to the book on the *Thinking Course*, De Bono comments, "A good doctor wants to diagnose the illness and get on with treatment. This doctor metaphor illustrates the dilemma. As a patient, which would you prefer: a doctor, who rushed in, came to a rapid diagnosis based on his considerable experience, insisted arrogantly on that diagnosis, and treated you with immense confidence? Or, a doctor who examined you carefully, generated as many possible alternatives as he could, checked these out with tests, finally came to a diagnosis and treated you accordingly? In practice, you might actually prefer the first doctor with his great confidence. You certainly would not want the second doctor to tell you all the possible alternatives and you would not want him to be tentative or dithering. Intellectually you would appreciate, however, that the great confidence of the first doctor would equally apply when he was making a terrible mistake."

The mind tends to work like the first doctor because we have to get on with life, and a flurry of alternatives too often means indecision. Because of this natural tendency of mind (to jump to conclusions), we need to develop a conscious "tool".[1]

In one study in which the authors analyzed 100 cases of diagnostic errors, faulty or inadequate knowledge was only a minor problem. Sixty-five percent of the causes were system related (e.g. faulty test instruments, failure or delay in communication, inefficient processes, etc). Cognitive factors contributed to 74% of errors. Among the cognitive problems, the single most common cause was "premature closure".[2] In other words, physicians failed to consider other reasonable alternatives once their minds latched on to the "initial diagnosis".

Our mind tries to find an explanation for everything. That is its strength. But it tends to "shut down" as soon as it finds "an" answer, "any" answer. That is its weakness.

Table 6.1: Problems and problem solving techniques.

Problem	Method
Unknown cause	Root cause analysis
Known cause or cause irrelevant	Creative problem solving (several methods)
Decision among solutions with certain outcomes	Matrix decision analysis
Decisions among solutions with uncertain outcomes	Decision tree (based on probability theory)
Jumbled list	Analytical hierarchy
Adversarial	Explanatory coherence

From: Howard PJ, *The Owner's Manual for the Brain: Howard PJ*, 1994, Austin TX, Leornian Press, page 290. (Reproduced with permission from ray@bardpress.com)

There are several well-tested tools to solve problems in business and industry. In his book with the interesting title, *The Owner's Manual of the Brain*, Pierce Howard lists several of them, with different ones for different purposes.[3] His general principles for solving problems are as follows:

1. Ask an expert first, if there is one available. He or she is the best problem solver since he or she will have the background knowledge and repertoire of experiences with similar situations.
2. If you do not have an expert available and for problems that stump the experts, first decide as to which category given in Table 6.1 the problem belongs. Then choose the corresponding tool. For problems with unknown cause, root cause analysis is the appropriate tool. For problems in which the cause is known or is irrelevant for the solution, one of several problem solving techniques can be used. Matrix decision analysis is the tool to use to decide upon the best solution among several alternatives with definite outcomes. To decide among solutions with uncertain outcome, decision analysis based on probability theory is the tool to use.
3. If you are an expert and are stumped, you can use a heuristic approach. Some examples are:

    a. Use a solution that works on a similar problem
    b. Reframe the problem — a different definition can yield a new solution

c. Remove unnecessary details
d. Simplify
e. Break the problem into simpler ones
f. List your assumptions and challenge them
g. Let ideas simmer for while; sleep on them for a day or two and think
h. Try an algorithmic approach.

In addition to learning problem solving techniques, it will be very useful to think about the mental process in "thinking". Humans can think. It appears that animals think, too. The difference is that we can think about how we think. We can think about the tricks our minds play on our thinking. At least, we should.

Why does the mind play tricks on so many of us? What are the blind alleys and traps in our mental process? To understand this, we have to look at the process of thinking itself. One major source of our problem is our formal education that is based on the classical dialectic method. It is based on refutations and arguments in search of truth. Formal education, in its emphasis on what is known and how we arrived there, tends to restrict the horizon. For creative problem solving in a clinical encounter, the physician has to deal with the uniqueness of the situation and the priorities and values of the patient. Therefore, he needs an unfettered, free mind that is positive.

The rest is related to the way information is received and processed by the human brain. Incoming information is perceived through "built-in" and "learned" filters. This is the first hurdle. Unless we are aware of our own special filters, we do not even get the incoming information correctly. If the perception of information is wrong or incomplete or if it is not even registered, a problem cannot even be recognized. In the language of the computer age, it is "garbage in, garbage out".

The information, once received, is organized into patterns. Is the pattern within the thing perceived or in the mind of the perceiver? Since the purpose of thinking is to solve a problem or answer a question (and thus stop thinking), the mind tends to go for the easiest answer. It grabs the most familiar pattern. The problem is that the mind stops thinking and refuses to let in any new input. It swears that it has found the answer and becomes possessive of its conclusion. This happens even if the pattern the mind latched onto is incomplete or irrelevant and the conclusion is wrong. The ego takes over and tries to defend the conclusion, rather than allow other points of view or even an easier solution. We can recognize this pattern in ourselves and in others. What can we do about it?

First, think about your own fixed patterns and filters. Then, stock your brain with several patterns by reading widely, listening to others (even your juniors and students), and seeking out opinions of other experts and master clinicians. It has been shown that the more patterns we can perceive in a situation, the better we will be in abstracting them, classifying them, and analyzing them. Some of it will come over the course of time by working in the field and experience. However, learning from experience "may lead to nothing more than learning to make the same mistakes with increasing confidence", unless we have an open mind.[4]

Edward De Bono points out that one of the essential characteristics of good problem solvers is their ability to reflect on their own thinking process. There are several other qualities of good thinkers and problem solvers, which may help us all. Good thinkers have a clear focus. They see the tree *and* the forest. They have *breadth* of vision in addition to *depth* in a single field. They go for a methodical approach, even if it takes time, rather than rely on their intelligence alone. They avoid theoretical blind alleys; they are practical. They are open to ideas — the more, the better. They seek out more ideas. They accept criticism. They are *humble*. They appreciate new ideas. They enjoy the time they spend thinking how their mind works.

There is one other interesting concept when the mind is trying to deal with multiple facts. It is called the *channel capacity*. In an extremely interesting paper in *Psychology Reviews*, George Miller discusses the limits of human capacity for processing information.[5] The title of the paper is "The magical number seven, plus or minus two: Some limits on our capacity for processing information". By citing a series of experiments using auditory, visual, and gustatory stimuli, he concludes that the number of items to be remembered limits immediate memory, and absolute judgment is limited by the amount of information.

When you give increasing amounts of alternate stimuli to an observer, among which he must discriminate, and then provide sufficient time to do so, there is always a point at which confusion begins to occur. This point is set at different numbers for different stimuli. This is called "channel capacity" by Miller. There seems to be a built-in limitation that keeps our channel capacity in the general range of 6.5 items.

It is interesting that the brain can work comfortably with only a limited number of items at a time (unlike computers, which can deal with millions of items at a time). This is why it is important for physicians to develop skills in gathering and analyzing information and use the computer to deal with issues requiring memory and manipulation of several facts at a time. We should not use our brain like a filing cabinet.

However, we can and do use several mental devices to deal with this limitation. Indeed, clinicians use these mental processes intuitively. Two of these are (1) making relative judgments rather than absolute judgments between stimuli or facts, and (2) arranging the facts in such a way that we can sequentially make absolute judgments about two or three items at a time and narrow down the possibilities in a step-wise fashion. As pointed out in an earlier chapter, this is how the clinician's mind works while solving clinicopathological problems.

Once we perceive and process the information, the mind abstracts it into patterns for classification and final analysis. Without going into the psychology of these processes, it is important to be aware of these simple mental processes, so that when the brain plays its usual tricks, we can recognize them.

One of the most important aspects of problem solving in medicine is the knowledge base. A main source of our knowledge base is the medical literature. However, it is getting increasingly difficult to keep up with the medical literature and know the latest concepts in diagnosing and treating even common diseases. Fortunately, developments in medical informatics have kept pace with biomedical advances. Information is available anytime, anywhere at the click of a mouse. However, one has to know how to access and use the medical literature.

On the Use of Medical Literature[6–8]

Medical knowledge has exploded in the past 50 years. All of us know the problems of keeping up with the stacks of weekly journals, monthly journals, reviews and meta-reviews, current opinions and updates, electronic journals, and instant publications. How can one keep up with this information load? Even more importantly, how does one assess the quality of the papers?

It has become imperative that physicians learn how to evaluate medical literature. Even when one knows how, no one has adequate time to read and evaluate all articles. When the lay media publicize new tests and drugs as breakthroughs (the media have made the word "breakthrough" all but meaningless), and patients come to their doctors with requests for these tests and drugs, how can physicians be prepared to give advice?

In addition to the website of the National Library of Medicine (PUBMED) there are several other websites and search engines to access a vast amount of literature. There are several excellent sources, in both print and electronic, to learn how to read medical literature critically and evaluate the validity and usefulness of various tests, drug therapies, and procedures.

Some helpful tips in the use of medical literature:

1. Keep a set of core reading journals that you read routinely.
2. "If you want to learn about a new disease or finding, read the most original description; then read the latest review." (Wm. Osler)
3. When you are looking for one article in a bound volume of a journal, browse quickly. You will be surprised to find some gems you missed or an article on a subject you have been thinking about lately! This is one advantage of prints over the online journals.
4. Always read some non-medical literature, such as novels, philosophical works, etc. (if you can read in more than one language, it is even better!)
5. Have a healthy skepticism of what is published.
6. Learn to read critically.

Major Messages: Problem solving skills, like any other skill, can be improved. The most important requirements for being a successful problem solver are an open mind, inquisitiveness, persistence, and attention to details. One should be able to look at a problem from different angles and think in different ways. Some call it "thinking out of the box". Some call it "lateral thinking" (also called *De Bono thinking*). It is also well known that the best problem solvers are those who rearrange the facts in different ways and sequences and try to find a useful pattern others do not see.

References

1. De Bono E. *De Bono's Thinking Course* 1982. New York; Facts on Files Publications.
2. Graber ML, Franklin N, Gordon R. Diagnostic error in internal medicine. *Arch Intern Med* 2005; **165**:1493–1499.
3. Pierce HJ. *The Owner's Manual for the Brain* 1994. Austin, TX; Barth Books.
4. Skrabanek P, McCormick J. *Follies and Fallacies in Medicine*. 1990. Buffalo, NY; Prometheus Books.
5. Miller GA. The magical number seven, plus or minus two: Some limits on our capacity to processing information. *Psychol Rev* 1956; **63**:81–97.
6. Sackett DL, Haynes RB, Guyatt GH, Tugwell P. *Clinical Epidemiology. A Basic Science Primer for Clinical Medicine.* 2nd edn. 1991. Boston, MA; Little Brown Co.
7. *User's Guide to the Medical Literature*. A Manual for Evidence–Based Clinical Practice. The Evidence–Based Medicine Work Group. Guyatt G, Drummond Rennie (Eds). 2002. Chicago, Il; American Medical Association.
8. Greenhalgh T. How to read a paper–The Medline database. *BMJ* 1997; **315**:180–183.

Part III

Human Relations Skills

Chapter 7

Communication Skills

Physicians spend a vast amount of time interacting with patients, face-to-face, over the phone, and even through e-mail. They do so to collect information to make a diagnosis and to make therapeutic and management decisions. Collecting information is only part of the task. Physicians have to give information too. Young physicians do fairly well in collecting information, but not so well in giving them.

Skills in receiving and giving back information to patients are the foundations of good medical care. Physicians usually learn these skills "on-the-job" by observing their seniors and mentors. In addition, they should learn from psychologists, counselors, clergy, and professionals who work in industries. Courses in effective communication are essential part of training of employees in industries. Experts in consumer relations and advertising agencies have been studying communications skills as a special field of applied psychology. The medical profession has to borrow ideas from these professionals.

We can also learn from police officers. In a study conducted in the United Kingdom, parents of children who died in accidents rated police officers as superior to physicians in giving bad news with sensitivity and effectiveness.[1] It is humbling. Police officers are trained for all aspects of their job. Physicians get formal training mostly on hard science.

In a study on the communication skills of house officers, ten specific skills were considered important in medical encounters. These were chosen since they can be observed and can be corrected, if necessary. The house officers were found to be good in history taking, listening, assessing compliance, and talking about therapy. However, they were not adequate in obtaining social history, recognizing the level of understanding of illnesses by the patients, explaining the illnesses to the patients, and eliciting the details of the emotional response of the patients to their illnesses.[2]

Due to the nature of the doctor–patient encounter, it requires skill to reassure patients about problems, even simple ones. It requires even more skill to discuss complicated medical problems and discuss goals of care. It appears that the State of California even has a law on communicating goals of care to patients.[3] The task becomes especially difficult when the physician has to give information to patients and families before all the data are available and before all evidence has been sifted through.

There may be impediments to communications in the doctor's office. The patient may have to wait for hours to see the physician. When the physician comes in, he may be constantly interrupted. There may not be adequate space for privacy. The physician may use long medical words, interrupt constantly, or not listen to the patient's answers. In such a state, the patient does not grasp most of what was said and when he goes home, is not sure of what to do. The patient is angry, afraid, anxious, and may feel embarrassed to call the doctor back and ask for clarification.

In addition, there may be individual hurdles unique to each patient. For example, most patients are afraid that the symptom may be serious. They may not even want to see the physician, hoping the symptom will go away. They have to take time off from work or arrange for someone to pick up a child from the school at the time of the appointment. Prior experience with doctors might have made some patients nervous.

Other hurdles to effective communication include patient concerns based on wrong or irrelevant information obtained over the internet, public misunderstanding of what medicine can and cannot do, sensational news in the media, and direct advertisement to the public for drugs and whole-body scans.

For all these reasons, it has become imperative that we teach our young physicians how to overcome these barriers and communicate effectively. Table 7.1 summarizes essential elements of communication in medical encounters.

Table 7.1: Essential elements of communication in medical encounters.[29]

The Kalamazoo Consensus Statement
1. *Build a relationship*: Strong, therapeutic, trusting relationship.
2. *Open the discussion*: Elicit the patient's full set of concerns.
3. *Gather information*: Listen actively; structure, clarify and summarize; use open ended and closed ended questions as appropriate.
4. Understand the patient's perspective.
5. *Share information*: Use language patient can understand; check understanding.
6. *Reach agreement*: On problems to be addressed and plans.
7. *Provide closure*: Ask for additional concerns; summarize; discuss follow up plans.

In this section, I will first summarize my thoughts on communicating with patients and then give a brief review of some articles dealing with communication in special situations. The special situations are: initial interview, reassurance, communicating with patients on risks and benefits, disclosing medical errors giving bad news, referral for mental health, request of autopsy, meeting with family members after death of a patient, keeping patient's secrets, e-mail communication, and being a consultant.

In my professional life, I worked with parents of children with chronic illness, life-threatening disease with dangerous or unknown forms of treatment, and functional disorders. Most of the time, I had to reassure patients and parents without being dishonest and without crushing their hope. I had to manage patients with ill-defined, multi-system diseases when the diagnosis was not known to me or to anyone else. Still, I had to help the child and the family to lead as normal a life as possible. I have felt helpless many times, but I still had to keep my faith so that I could help the children keep their faith and hope. I had to start with models of behavior I had noticed in my mentors and then build my own ideas and values in practice.

I learned that it is not what I say that matters, but how I say it. Both the content and the style are important. The content has to be based on the knowledge of the patient's disease, illness and personality, beliefs, expectations, fears, and hopes. I have to constantly remind myself that I am in the helping profession and what I say and how I say it have to be helpful to the patient. The patient has to perceive the message in the way it was intended. My manner should express my true feelings and convince the patient of my sincerity.

In this process, I have had to ask myself several questions: Do I talk to my patients *after* I have listened to their question? Do I try to understand the patient's questions and concerns before formulating an answer? Do I know what *really* worries them? Do I talk clearly, in simple language? Do I speak with compassion and understanding? After I talk to them, do they feel comforted or agitated? How much time do I spend talking to them and listening to them? Am I standing next to the door, flipping the chart, and looking at my watch when I talk? Am I sitting next to them and holding their hands, if need be and appropriate, when I talk? If I look at them, do I do it without making them self-conscious?

Initial Interview

Techniques of interviewing are covered well in several textbooks. One area that needs emphasis is the initial interview when the reasons for the visit and what the patient expects from the visit should be clearly understood.[4] The general headings the physician should keep in mind are: (1) What are the patient's main concerns today? (2) What are the physician's concerns in terms of their priorities? (3) How can the discrepancies between the concerns of the physician and the patient and the prioritization be negotiated? (4) What are the patient's specific requests? (Table 7.2).

Reassurance

One of the important functions of a clinician is to comfort and reassure. Statements such as "There is nothing wrong", "Don't worry", and "It will be all right" are meaningless words. Most of the time, they do not reassure and sometimes it can be wrong. To reassure is to "restore a person to confidence". Effective reassurance is a form of psychotherapy that will help patients cope better.[5–7]

The most important step in reassurance is listening to the patient. The physician should try to find out the specific fears and the questions

Table 7.2: Setting the agenda for the visit.[4]

What are the patient's main concerns?
"What brings you to us today? Why this time as opposed to earlier or later (other than available appointment time)? What else do you want to take care of today?"
"What concerns have you written down in your list?"
"What is the one thing you want to make sure we address today?"
What are my concerns for today?
(These may be different from those of the patient, at least in priority)
What do I have to be sure of checking or discuss today?
What are the issues most important to the patient?
Go over my list with the patient
What items have to be addressed today and what can we postpone for future visits?
How can we realign our priorities in terms of importance and discuss options?

of the patient. In addition, he should be looking for non-verbal clues to the patient's fears and anxieties. A complete and thorough physical examination has been found to be one of the most important elements in reassurance therapy. I have heard patients say: "This is the first time any one has asked me these questions", or "This is the first time anyone did a complete examination".

A systematic approach to "reassurance therapy", as proposed by Joseph Sapira, includes the following[7]:

- Eliciting a detailed description of the symptoms.
- Eliciting the affective meaning of the symptoms. It is not what the patient says that counts; but his tone of voice, manner of speech, and body language.
- A through examination, with special emphasis on areas of special concern to the patient to show that you listened.
- Making a diagnosis — reassurance cannot be effective without this step. At least we should tell the patient what ailment is excluded, including (if true) the ailment about which he is most worried. The diagnostic list should include among other things, patient's own diagnosis (concern), psychosomatic illness, and "non-disease".
- Explaining the pathophysiology of symptoms. For example, in patients with chronic pain syndrome, it will be important to explain

the mechanism of pain and pain perception using diagrams, if necessary. In this process, the patient should know that the physician understands the problem, that the physician is not worried about this symptom, and that the physician is sympathetic towards the patient's personal experience of pain and other symptoms. The patient should know that the physician will suggest several approaches to get relief from pain and will be there to help when needed.

Communicating with Patients on Risks and Benefits

Educating patients on risks and benefits of investigations and of treatment is a formidable task. This applies both for clinical choices and obtaining informed consent for experimental protocols. The patients have to understand not only the options, but also the risks and benefits of those options. How can we educate them on risk stratification, data interpretation and statistical analysis? What are some of the major issues in this patient education process?

In a paper on explaining risks and benefits to patients and obtaining informed consent,[8] the authors point out that the most important issues are: (1) provide the individual with sufficient information using appropriate language so that he can understand the risks involved. The "framing" of the risk is an important step in this process; (2) be truthful and realistic, given the uncertainties and the unknowns. Even after getting and understanding all the information, the patient has to trust his physician before giving a truly informed consent.

This article has a small section on trust and lists the following requirements to develop a trusting relationship: truth-telling, openness, respect for the view of others, accepting the rights of others to make decisions, doing your best in the best interest of the patient, not doing harm and keeping promises.

In another study, the authors prepared a general education primer on the ability of patients to interpret medical data and understand risk and tested this primer on patients from high and low socioeconomic groups.[9] The authors showed that the booklet improved the ability of both groups of people to interpret medical data. The authors outlined some key concepts from the primer in a tabular form. Although this was a research study and although the booklet is not for routine use, the questions listed in this table will be of great use to clinicians when they educate their patients on understanding risks. Therefore, I am reproducing these questions from the article on "The effectiveness of a primer to help people understand risk: Two randomized trials in distinct populations" by Steve Woloshin *et al.* in the *Annals of Internal Medicine*, February 2007, on page 146, with permission from the American College of Physicians. Remember that these are questions for patients to ask.

Questions to ask when interpreting risks

Risk of what? Understand what the outcome is (getting disease, dying from disease, developing a symptom) and consider how bad it is.

How big is the risk? Understand the chance that you will experience the outcome. When you hear about the number of people with the disease (or whatever outcome you are discussing), always ask, "Out of how many?" so you can learn the chance of the disease. Also determine the time period of the risk (over the next year, 10 years, a lifetime).

Does the risk information reasonably apply to you? Understand whether the message is based on people like you (people of your age and sex, people whose health is like yours).

How does this risk compare to other risks? Ask for some context so you can develop a sense of just how big (or small) the risk really is.

Things you (patient) should do to better understand risk

Get the risk information into a user-friendly format. Make the numbers as easy as you can by translating "1 in 100" to "1 out of 1000".

Try framing the risk in different ways. If they tell you that the chance of dying, rewrite it as the chance of living to see if this changes how the information makes you feel.

Questions to ask when interpreting benefit

Change in risk of what? Understand what the outcome is (getting disease, dying from disease, developing a symptom) and consider how bad it is.

How big is the change in risk? Whenever you hear about changing risk (e.g., "42% lower"), ask "Lower than what?" Learn what your risk is if you do something (e.g., take a drug, change your lifestyle) versus if you don't.

Does the change in risk information reasonably apply to you? Understand whether the people the message is based on are like you (people of your age and sex, people whose health is like yours).

How does this change in risk compare to other changes in risk? Ask for some context so you can develop a sense of just how big (or small) the change in risk really is.

Things you (patient) should do to better understand benefit

Get the bottom line. Learn what your overall chance of dying is if you do something versus if you don't.

Learn the downsides (e.g., possible side effects) that come with the benefit. Understand what the side effects are, how often they happen, and how bad they are. Find out the source of information, the kind of research and what is being measured.

Be wary of information from scientific meetings, from sources with other interests besides your health (like money), from animal research or studies that just describe what happens to people.

Disclosing Medical Errors

External pressures and internal changes within the medical profession have facilitated the development of standards for disclosing medical errors to patients.[10] The Joint Commission has issued a nationwide disclosure standard. Some key elements in this process are:

- Provide facts about the event
- Express regret and give formal apology (if appropriate)
- Establish disclosure coaching methods and support system
- Provide emotional support for health care workers, patients and families
- Track and enhance disclosure methods.

Recently I attended a talk by Mr. Bill Taggart of University of Texas (at Austin) on "Lessons learned from aviation — practical skills that actually work". Mr. Taggart is the developer of Crew Resources Management Program that is used routinely by major airlines in US and abroad. More recently, he has started applying lessons learnt in aviation industry to patient safety issues (http:// homepage.psy.utexas.edu/homepage). There are two reasons I refer to this site: (1) Here is an excellent example of learning from another profession or industry. (2) In data collected between 1995 and 2005 by the Joint Commission on Accreditation of Hospitals (JCAH) on the root causes of sentinel events, surgery at wrong sites and perinatal injuries and deaths, **communication failure** was on top of the list of causes for errors. Based on this data and Mr. Taggart's talk, here is a list of suggestions to improve communication and minimize errors, particularly in the operating room and in emergency situations such as during a "code" and in the ICU.

- Focus has to be on the patient, but physician must be fully aware of the big picture.
- Pay close attention to what the patients (and parents in pediatrics) have to say.
- Describe what you see (not impressions and interpretations).
- Be clear and precise with the words you use to describe (no euphemisms, vague remarks).
- Use the correct words to show the urgency of the situation.

Giving Bad and Sad News

It is possible to give bad news and not shock the patients. It is possible to give sad news without knocking out all hope. It is often difficult to strike a balance between being honest and being hopeful. Ideally, one should be honest and gentle, neither paternalistic nor too sensitive to issues of "patient autonomy", appropriate to the occasion, and not make everything look artificially rosy or paint a dark picture and "hang the crepe".[11]

Giving news of serious illness or death is always stressful to the physician. It appears that sometimes physicians cannot anticipate or understand how the patient will perceive the information. Many physicians have problems dealing with their own sense of guilt (for not being able to help), sorrow, identification with the patient, and a sense of failure. This can interfere with how comfortable and able they are in giving bad news. Hospital systems are not set up to train physicians in giving bad news. Very few hospitals provide an organized system of support to physicians who have to give sad and bad news often in critical care, trauma service, and cancer center.

From the patient's perspective, several steps are crucial. The manner in which the message is delivered will have a major impact. It is also important to use words patients can understand. Patients' own situations, stress, expectations, personality, mental state, spiritual beliefs, and social support will affect the way the bad news is perceived.

There are several studies on what patients and relatives expect when receiving bad and sad news.[12–14] These patient preferences can be grouped under three major categories: content (what is told), context (settings and style of delivering), and emotional support during the process.

The following guidelines based on these studies should be helpful for most occasions: The knowledge of the physician and his ability to give various treatment options truthfully, in a simple language and in a way that allows the patient to ask questions and to clarify, are the most important components. Patients prefer hearing the news from their own physicians or physicians who knows the patient than from several people or from an expert. They want the physicians to be caring and compassionate. They want to hear the news as soon as possible and with both positive and negative details. There should be privacy and adequate time to absorb the impact and ask all their questions. The presence of another member of the family or someone close who can lend emotional support is essential, particularly in pediatrics.

On the negative side, patients do not want to hear conflicting stories from different people. They criticize physicians who speak rapidly, are flipping through the chart (that meant the physician was not fully aware), and are standing during the interview (this meant they were in a hurry).

One other dictum I have used for myself is, "Before you answer, be clear about patient's questions." A physician's agenda often seems to be different from that of the patient. Even when the agenda is the same, the focus may be different. For example, when parents ask what caused Johnny's arthritis, it is tempting to start a discourse on the etiology and pathogenesis of arthritis in children. However, the mother is not interested in the T cells, B cells, and cytokines. Her hidden question is: "Did I do something wrong?" When she asks, "Is this hereditary?" she is asking, "Did I give it to him?" Until her real hidden concerns are answered, the communication is not complete.

Several years back, I conducted a survey of the most common questions parents ask in a rheumatology clinic. The questions that patients asked most often were similar to those of patients attending an adult clinic for rheumatic diseases[15]: *What is the diagnosis? What is the cause? Is it genetic? What can I expect? What can be done positively? How much exercise can be done? How much rest should I take? What should I avoid? Is there any dietary restriction? Can some specific diet help? What medicines are available and how do I take them? What are the side effects? Why so many blood tests? Why do they have to be repeated? How much will this cost?* These questions are universal and not confined to pediatrics or rheumatology.

There have been several professional groups and patient support groups working on physician–patient communication and on ideal ways to give bad news. A Consensus Statement developed by the Cancer Education Research Program, from the New South Wales Cancer Council, Australia[16] has summarized the principles involved in breaking bad news to patients. The recommended steps in implementing these principles are as follows:

- Ensure privacy and *adequate* time. (I should add, make sure that it is an *uninterrupted* time.)
- Assess understanding. In any human relationship, this is the first and most important step. First, know what the patient knows already.
- Provide information simply and honestly.

- Encourage patients and parents or spouses to express their feelings. We have to allow them to react, accept them as a starting point. We also have to respond appropriately with compassion, empathy, and understanding.
- Reassure without giving a definite time frame but with realistic expectations. Do not say, "Nothing can be done", but say, "It is a very grave situation; but we will do everything to make him comfortable and not suffer too much pain."
- Arrange for a review of the situation, as the situation changes, or within a definite time frame.
- Discuss all treatment options — with their pros and cons. Make sure the patient will be involved in the final decision making.
- Offer assistance in speaking with others in the family (beware of Health Insurance Portability and Accountability Act of 1996 (HIPAA)).
- Provide information about support services in the hospital and the community.
- Where fitting, document the information and report it accurately and succinctly.

There are special courses available to train physicians and allied health personnel on communication skills, particularly in the fields of oncology and birth defects. Some of the websites I accessed are:
http://www.apply2medicine.co.uk;
http://www.medicalcommunicationskills.com;
http://www.connected.nhs.uk. Also, look at the website for the American Board of Genetic Counseling Inc.

One other tool that utilizes established principles of communication and counseling is SPIKES, a six step protocol developed for helping oncologists to deliver "bad" news (Table 7.3). The principles utilized in the construction of this protocol can be applied to other situations as well.

Mental Health Referral

Referral to a psychiatrist or counselor can be emotionally charged (Table 7.4). It is particularly so in pediatrics.[17] The physician has to be sensitive and knowledgeable. When someone is clearly psychotic or

Table 7.3: SPIKES — A protocol for delivering bad news.*

Setting up the interview	• Mental rehearsal • Paying attention to the physical environment that includes privacy, uninterrupted time, not being in a hurry, and including other family members of the patient's choice
Patient's perception	• Eliciting patient's perception of the illness, fears and expectations
Information	• Drawing the patient to discuss the kind of information they need
Knowledge	• Imparting knowledge at a level the patient can comprehend using the information gathered at earlier steps, using non-technical words without being too blunt or too optimistic
Empathy	• Being prepared for patient's emotional reactions. Ability to observe and identify the patient's emotional response and make a connection with the patient.
Summary/**S**trategy	• Discuss a treatment plan making sure the patient understands the risks and benefits and is able to share responsibility in decision making

* From: Baile WE, Buckman R, Lenzi R, Glober G, Beale EA, Kudelka AP, SPIKES — A six step protocol for delivering bad news: application to the patient with cancer, *The Oncologist* 2000; **5**:302–311.

Table 7.4: Some personal thoughts on counseling and psychiatric referral.

Most people can take care of themselves; they just need a "listener".
Most people do not necessarily want help when they tell you of their problems.
Most people's problems are problems of living — money, work, living conditions, physical needs, transportation; they need practical help — not another professional consult.
Some families function in a pathological way — but it is a "functioning unit". Think before you interfere.
Remember the story of the frog and the caterpillar. The caterpillar was moving slowly, but still moving until the frog asked "Hey, which leg of yours moves after which?" The caterpillar started analyzing, and could not move!

depressed, there is little need for discussion. However, when mental health problems co-exist with some other illness or when the symptoms are due to somatization, referral to a psychiatrist may be difficult and often resisted. The perceived social stigma, cost of care, time constraints, and wrong impression about what psychiatric referral means create tensions in communication.

Once the physician recognizes that there is a primary mental health problem or a mental illness interfering with the treatment of a medical condition, the physician's main task is to convince the patient that referral to a psychiatrist or a mental health counselor is needed. In children, the problem is often the parents' refusal to consider that mental issues may be the cause of symptoms. After convincing the patient, parent, or spouse that a psychiatric consultation is desirable, the next step is to help the patient agree on the area where help is needed. Unless the patient is clear on what is wanted and is interested in the consult, the referral is not likely to be useful.

In psychosomatic problems and in pediatrics, there has to be good communication between the primary physician and the psychiatrist. A planning conference including the primary physician, psychiatrist, the patient and a family member should be organized to set the goals and define the roles for each member of the team. The impact of the consult on the family dynamics, available free time, and financial resources has to be discussed. Periodic meetings will be useful to examine progress and rearrange the goals.

Requesting an Autopsy

Asking for an autopsy and organ donation is a delicate task.[18,19] First, it is necessary to make sure that this is not a case for the medical examiner. The family should not be made to feel guilty or afraid to refuse permission. Facts should not be distorted; nor should the cause of death be presented as a mystery to make families agree to the autopsy. Once an autopsy is recommended, one specific physician should be assigned to meet with the family and ask for permission. Ideally, this should be a physician who knows the family the most.

The first step should be to listen to the family's grief and sorrow, guilt, and relief and support them through their feelings. The chances are that they will go through every detail of the final illness and every remark that was made by the deceased. There may be recollections of previous incidents with sadness or sometimes recollection of funny or tender moments. There has to be time for all of this.

When the time comes to discuss the funeral arrangements, the subject of autopsy is likely to be raised by the family. If not, this is the time to gently approach the subject with tenderness and respect for their feelings. The autopsy procedure should be explained truthfully and completely without frightening them. It can be explained as surgery performed after death. The family should know that they could restrict certain portions of the autopsy. This is the time to dispel any misconceptions about autopsy.

The autopsy should be conducted with due respect for the deceased and the family concerned. The autopsy should be performed in a timely manner to satisfy the family's religious preferences for early burial or cremation. There should be effort to get as much information as possible, and the autopsy should not have been in vain. It is important to coordinate with the funeral director so that there is no inconvenience for the family or the funeral director.

After the autopsy, the family should be informed of the preliminary findings. Later, there should be a meeting to go over the complete details after all the studies are completed.[18]

Meeting with Family Members After Death of a Patient

Most of us learnt how to comfort those in distress by just observing a few sensitive clinicians. This leaves teaching and learning an important skill to chance. It is important to develop tools that help young physicians learn principles of communication under different circumstances, particularly after death of a patient.

In a prospective, controlled trial, 126 family members of patients dying in ICUs were randomly assigned to a formal intervention group or routine care group.[20] The intervention group received care according to detailed guidelines developed specifically for end-of-life care. This included a tool for care givers with points of reference for their discussions. This was called VALUE. In this mnemonics, V stands for **V**aluing and appreciating what the family members have to say; A stands for **A**cknowledging the emotions expressed by the family members; L stands for **L**istening; U stands for **U**nderstanding who the patient was as a person, by listening to family members; E stands for **E**liciting questions from the family members. The authors conclude that "using a proactive communication strategy that includes longer conferences and more time for family members to talk may lessen the burden of bereavement".

In another study in which bereaved parents took part, most parents expressed a desire to meet with their physician and a willingness to come back to the hospital for such a meeting.[21] Reasons given by bereaved parents for such a meeting were to gain information about the cause of death and results of autopsy, to learn about circumstances surrounding withdrawal of life support if there was one, to ask about genetic risk for siblings, and to learn what to tell other family members. In addition, the families wanted to help the health professionals by providing feedback to the staff on communication styles, conflicting information, and administrative issues, to express gratitude and to obtain emotional support.

Keeping a Secret

What do you do when a patient tells you a secret and wants you to keep it?[22,23] This is not a problem for pediatricians, although children do give us secrets about their parents and pets. Teenage pregnancy and HIV infection are special situations in the pediatric age group, and there are legal guidelines that vary from state to state. In matters that involve law enforcement, such as crime-related injuries and sexual abuse, the physician's duty is to treat the individual *and* to comply with the law.

There are many other situations where family members tell us secrets about the patient or the patients tell us about their family members. The easiest way to deal with them is to deflect them and tell the person carrying the secret to tell the involved party directly and refuse to be the middleman. The other course of action is to *never* agree to maintain secrecy, so that the physician has the option to divulge information if it is in the best interest of the patient or legally required to do so.

Communication Through E-mail

Physicians have always had several lines of communication with patients. Now we have to add one more, namely online or electronic communication.[24] Like any innovation, it is a good thing, when used appropriately. It can be a major source of problem, when done without some forethought and guidelines. Although patients have been ready to use e-mail to ask some simple questions or to make appointments, the health care system has not been ready because of concerns about privacy and legal liabilities. Besides, no one is paying for the time spent by the physicians on this task. Now, things are changing. However, there are a few more hurdles to clear before communication with patients through e-mail is fully accepted by physicians and the health care system.

It is easy to respond to requests for appointments, prescriptions, and referral letters by e-mail. When specific clinical questions are asked, the physician will have to think before giving a quick and easy response since he cannot make clinical judgments based on personal observations and physical examination. Unlike what is possible in a phone conversation, the physician cannot ask clarifying questions. The choice of words may not express the problem accurately or adequately. The physician cannot listen to the tone of voice and discern the concerns. The physician will still have to decide whether to answer or insist on talking with the patient on the phone or seeing the patient before answering the question. If one decides to answer, one has to be careful with the choice of words.

In short, the ability to communicate effectively becomes even more important in the era of internet communication. With the use of online chat rooms, twitter and video-camera talks, things are changing rapidly. The health care system will have to respond rapidly to lead the way with appropriate safeguards and guidelines. Some hospitals have instituted such guidelines on e-mail communication.

Consultation[25–27]

Physicians act as consultants or request consultation several times a day. It is important that the primary physician communicates directly with the consultant to express the reason for the consultation and to clarify whether the consultation is to the physician or to the family. If the physician asks a specific technical question, the consultant's duty is to give the recommendation to the physician. When the patient requests the consultation or the primary physician gives clear guidelines, the consultant is at greater liberty and has a greater obligation to discuss directly with the patient.

At the end of the examination, the consultant should give some information to the family, even if he is consulting to the primary physician. Otherwise, the patient and the family will be left worrying. It is best to tell them what was found in the examination and to answer some of the questions without frightening them. My practice is to say: "It is not appropriate for me to go into the details without thinking about the situation and discussing it with your doctor. In addition, if everyone that comes to see your child talks with you, you will get different pictures and you will be confused. I promise to talk about my ideas with your doctor and I will let him talk with you about all of my ideas together with his ideas and those of others. For the present, I can tell you that there is nothing dangerous going on (if that is true) and we are considering the various possibilities." I find this satisfying to parents most of the time.

As physicians we are often asked for curb-side consults. This happens most often in family and social gatherings. If the matter sounds serious, the person should be directed to go to an emergency room or to his doctor immediately. Otherwise we can be sympathetic and be general with our recommendations. Even then, there are ethical and legal responsibilities.

What about a situation in which the physician encounters an individual in a casual setting or in a public place and suspects a medical disorder? Does one give unsolicited advice to a stranger? Does one express his concern to the individual and face the possibility of a wrong diagnosis and creating unnecessary anxiety? Or, does one not communicate one's suspicion knowing that the individual may face a serious medical problem in the future?

In his essay on "The ethics of passer-by diagnosis", Doctor Edward Mitchell gives a few guidelines.[28] He suggests that we take into account the following factors: prior relationship between the physician and the subject, urgency of the situation, accuracy of the diagnosis and the risks of harm likely to be caused by the diagnosis.

Those in academics get phone calls and e-mails from physicians asking for advice. It is a privilege to help one's colleagues take better care of their patients. However, the responsibility does not diminish. If the question is strictly a technical one, it is easy. For example, if a colleague asks questions about the adverse reactions of a specific drug and how to monitor for drug toxicity, the answer is straightforward.

The problem is with clinical case scenarios. When the generalists give a brief sketch and ask a specific clinical question, the consultant should ask for more information before giving an answer. If it is not urgent, it is perfectly reasonable to ask for a full summary of the case together with results of laboratory tests and imaging studies before giving an opinion. Sometimes the consultant may have to insist on examining the patient personally and reviewing the laboratory studies. Giving opinions on "list-serves" and "online chat rooms" should be done with caution.

A common error on the part of the generalist who asks for a consult is not preparing the family adequately. I have seen puzzled looks on the faces of parents when I ask the purpose of the consult or second opinion.

One of the common error consultants make is to belittle or disagree with the referral physician's diagnosis without adequate consideration. It will be important to know what the findings *were*, and some of the special circumstances that were present earlier when the original diagnosis was made. Without that information, it is not fair to jump to conclusions.

If the consultant sees a patient for a second opinion, or if the patient initiated the consult directly, the physician is a consultant to the patient. The consultant has to know the entire history in all the finer details. Also required is a review of all the records and of all biopsies and imaging studies personally. Then, and only then, the consultant can help the family sort out differing opinions so that they can make a decision. Even then, if the family is going back to the primary physician, the consultant has to keep the primary physician included in these discussions.

If the consultant feels he should talk with the earlier consultants or the primary physician before giving an opinion, he should feel free to do so with the consent of the family. At the end of the consult, the consultant should sit with the family, give an opinion, and explain why it may be different. It may bc hclpful for the family to go back to their primary physician and get help in making a choice between the various recommendations.

If the patient came for a second opinion and with the consent of their primary physician, the consultant can talk more freely without necessarily checking with the primary physician. Even then, with the patient's permission (sometimes the families do not want this), the primary physician should be informed about the details of the discussion by phone and later by letter. This is important, since the family may call their physician for clarification. If the family does not want this, it is important to obtain permission from the patient to send the information to a physician the family chooses. Sometimes the family may want to receive a copy of the summary.

In writing a consult, if the consultant feels extremely strong about his recommendation, it is important to indicate it clearly. He should make it clear that he cannot be responsible if the family or the primary physician chooses not to follow his recommendation. However, in most other situations, it is reasonable to write in such a way that the physician caring for the family does not feel bound if he disagrees with the recommendation. There should be option and freedom for the family physician to take several opinions, synthesize them, and help the family come to a decision.

Major Message: Communication skill is the foundation of patient–physician relationship. Even the simple act of asking for the history of what is ailing a patient requires finesse and sensitivity. Helping patients make difficult decisions, giving bad news, asking for autopsy are situations that are even more difficult. Fortunately, there is sufficient body of literature and consensus guidelines and special courses to help the young physician deal with these matters.

References

1. Finlay I, Dallimore D. Your child is dead. *BMJ* 1991; **302**:1524–1525.
2. Duffy DL, Hamerman D, Cohen MA. Communication skills of house officers. *Ann Intern Med* 1990; **93**:354–357.
3. Pantilat SZ. Communicating with seriously ill patients: Better words to say. *JAMA* 2009; **301**:1279–1281.
4. Baker L, O'Connell D, Platt FW. "What else?" Setting the agenda for the clinical interview. *Ann Int Med* 2005; **143**:766–780.
5. Apley J, MacKeith R. *The Child and His Symptoms*. 2nd edn. 1968. Oxford, UK; Blackwell Scientific Publications.
6. Waserman M. Relieving parental anxiety: John Warren's 1792 letter to the father of a burned child. *N Engl J Med* 1978; **299**:135–136.
7. Sapira JD. Reassurance therapy: What to say to symptomatic patients with benign disease. *Ann Intern Med* 1972; **77**:603–604.
8. Kalman KC. Communication of risk: Choice, consent and trust. *Lancet* 2002; **360**:166–168.
9. Wolosin S, Schwartz LM, Welch HG. The effectiveness of a primer to help people understand risk: The randomized trials in distinct populations. *Ann Intern Med* 2007; **146**:256–265.
10. Gallagher TH, Studdert D, Levinson W. Disclosing harmful medical errors to patients. *N Engl J Med* 2007; **356**:2713–2719.
11. Siegler M. Pascal's wager and the hanging of crepe. *N Engl J Med* 1975; **293**:853–857.
12. Fallowfield L, Jenkins V. Communicating sad, bad and difficult news in medicine. *Lancet* 2004; **363**:312–319.
13. Krahn GL, Hallum A, Kime C. Are there good ways to give "bad news"? *Pediatrics* 1993; **91**:578–582.
14. Parker PA, Barle WF, deMoor C, Kudelka AP, Cohen L. Breaking bad news about cancer: Patient's preferences for communication. *J Clin Oncol* 2001; **19**:2049–2056.
15. Wright V, Hopkins R, Burton K. How long should we talk to patients? A study in doctor–patient communication. *Ann Rheum Dis* 1982; **41**: 250–252.
16. Girgis A, Sanson Fisher RW. Breaking bad news: Consensus guidelines for medical practitioners. *J Clin Oncol* 1995; **13**:2449–2456.

17. Hodas G, Honig PJ. An approach to psychiatric referral in pediatric patients: Psychosomoatic complaints. *Clin Pediatr* 1983; **22**:167–174.
18. Berger LR. Requesting autopsy: A pediatric perspective. *Clin Pediatr* 1978; **17**:445–452.
19. Schneiderman H, Gruhn J. How — and why — to request an autopsy. *Postgrad Med* 1985; **77**:153–156, 160–164.
20. Lautrette A, Darmon M, Megarbane B, *et al.* A communication strategy and brochure for relatives of patients dying in the ICU. *N Engl J Med* 2007: **356**:469–478.
21. Meert KL, Eggly S, Pollack M, Anand KJS, Zimmerman J, Carcillo J *et al.* Parents' perspectives regarding a physician–parent conference after their child's death in the pediatric intensive care unit. *J Pediatr* 2007; **151**: 50–55.
22. LaCombe MA. Privileged information. *Amer J Med* 1991; **91**:648–651.
23. Burnum JF. Secrets about patients. *N Engl J Med* 1991; **324**:1130–1133.
24. Stone JH. Communication between physicians and patients in the era of e-medicine. *N Engl J Med* 2007; **356**:2451–2454.
25. Tumulty PA. *The Effective Clinician.* 1973. Phildelphia, Pa; W.B. Saunders Co.
26. Manian FA, Janssen DA. Curbside consultation — A closer look at common practice. *JAMA* 1996; **275**:145–147.
27. Goldman L, Lee T, Rudd P. Ten commandments for effective consultations. *Arch Int Med* 1983; **143**:1753–1755.
28. Mitchell EW. The ethics of passer-by diagnosis. *Lancet* 2008; **371**: 85–87.
29. Essential elements of communication in medical encounters: The Kalamazoo Consensus Statement. *Acad Med* 2001; **76**:390–393.

Reading List

Communicating with children and families: From everyday interactions to skill in conveying distressing information. A Technical Report by Levetown M and the Committee on Bioethics of the American Academy of Pediatrics. *Pediatrics* **121**:e1441–e1460 (May 2008). (An essential reading.)

Curtis JR, Patrick DL, Shannon SE, Treece PD, Engelberg RA, Rubenfeld GD. The family conference as a focus to improve communication about end-of-life care in the intensive care unit: Opportunities for improvement. *Crit Care Med* 2001; **29**:(Suppl 2):N26–N33.

Lilly C, Daly BJ. The healing power of listening in the ICU. *N Engl J Med* 2007; **356**:513–515.

Plat FW, Gordon GH. *Field Guide to Difficult Patient Interview*. 2004. Philadelphia; Lippincott Williams Wilkins.

Give me a Doctor*
W.H. Auden

Give me a doctor, partridge-pump,
Short in the leg and broad in the rump,
An endomorph with gentle hands,
Who'll never make absurd demands,
That I abandon all my vices,
Nor pull a long face in a crisis,
But with a twinkle in his eye,
Will tell me that I have to die.

Chapter 8

Physician–Patient Relationship

When a patient seeks medical help, it may be for a minor illness, for a life-threatening disease, or just because he is worried about a symptom. It may be because he is scared or worried or under stress at home and at work. It may be because the only person to seek help from without losing dignity is often the medical professional or a clergyman.

Hidden fears and anxieties often lurk behind seemingly simple questions of patients. Until these hidden concerns are addressed, the patient may not feel well, even if the original symptoms abate. Here is an example. A mother was taking her four-year-old girl to different consultants for "colds" and "pneumonia". No one could document any unusual infections or immunodeficiency. During discussion with a sensitive and patient clinician, the hidden anxiety came out. The mother said that the child had exchange transfusion as a newborn; and since the blood that was used came from a refrigerator and was cold, the mother thought that the child had a "tendency to catch cold". Physicians should probe such concerns, but gently. If pushed hard, some patients may feel threatened and go shopping for a doctor who will leave such concerns alone.

The experience of physicians with their patients is extremely satisfying and enriching most of the time. However, a small group of patients will be difficult to handle by even the best of clinicians.[1] They are not difficult just to be difficult. They are anxious, afraid, upset, or confused. Labeling them as "difficult" does not help. It makes the patient angry, blocks the physician's effectiveness, and leads to a worsening relationship. Patients who do not follow advice but keep coming back, who refuse treatment, or are disruptive, the irate patient, and those who demand constant attention belong to this category. In addition, a group of patients request or demand specific medication or test even if not indicated.

Adherence to Treatment

When a patient does not cooperate with suggested therapy, the problem can be on either side. It is unfair to always assume that the patient is not compliant or not cooperative. The physician's role and the structure of the medical care delivery system should also be examined. That is why the term *adherence* is preferred over *compliance*.

There is a vast body of literature on patient compliance.[2–4] When the causes for non-adherence (non-compliance) are analyzed, they fall under several headings. These include several factors related to the patients, such as their cognitive abilities, emotional status, socio-economic conditions and cultural attitudes and beliefs. Other factors that influence adherence refer to the disease condition, therapy and systems of delivery of medical care.[2]

For example, the patient may not have been given adequate information, or there may be lack of understanding on the part of the patient. Because of the anxiety generated by learning about a new disease, the patient remembers very little of what is said during the office visit. If, in addition, the patient is depressed or cognitively impaired or has a cultural or language barrier, these become additional reasons for lack of adherence to instructions.

Some blocks are behavioral, as in adolescents with chronic diseases or as with a well informed adult with cancer who has lost the will to live.[5]

Cultural attitudes and beliefs about the nature and cause of diseases will also influence adherence. Family structure and dynamics will also have influence. For example, if a child of divorced parents lives with one parent during the week and with the other over the weekends, there may be disruption in following medical advice. If the mother goes to work and the grandmother or another caretaker in the house who is babysitting does not favor medicines and prefers natural remedies, there will be problems with adherence.

Patients with chronic illness who need medicine every day and those who have to take several doses a day will try to break the routine and see what happens. There will be poor compliance with drugs that have too many side effects, particularly those that cause weight gain or skin rashes (e.g., prednisone).

The cost of the medicine is another major factor. Elderly patients on several medications are known to buy medicines on a rotation to stretch their budget.

Finally, organizational issues may interfere with adherence. If there is an adverse reaction and the physician does not pay attention to the patient's complaints and address them, patients will often stop taking the medicine. If phone calls are not answered promptly by physicians or if appointments are difficult to schedule, patients may stop the drug until the next visit.

It is, therefore, important to analyze the entire situation, look at the major causes for poor adherence, and address them. Strategies suggested for better compliance with treatment regimen include informational handouts; cues and reminders using e-mails or form letters; positive feedback to the patient; steps to minimize discomfort and inconvenience (for example, in adolescents with rheumatic diseases, drugs given once or twice a day are clearly more convenient than those to be given 3 or 4 times a day); monitoring the disease for changes so that management can be altered and unnecessary drugs stopped; dealing effectively with patient complaints about adherence, such as taste of the medicine, timing of the dose, etc; recognizing serious behavioral issues; and obtaining counseling, if appropriate.[4]

Patients Who are Difficult to Relate To

In dealing with patients who are difficult, my own guidelines are as follows: (1) understand the patient's perceptions, expectations, hidden questions and anxieties, strengths and limitations, and (2) understand how my own conflicts, bias, strengths, and weaknesses contribute to this difficult relationship.

Some questions to ask ourselves: Is the patient too demanding or am I being unfairly restrictive? Is my judgment of the patient as difficult preventing me from seeing a solution? Am I too controlling and too demanding which is clashing with the patient's need to control? Is this becoming a fight of our wills rather than a helping relationship? If the patient is "upsetting" me do I recognize it? Should I be honest with the patient, express my frustration and ask him for clues? Should I gently suggest to the family that they go to another doctor or get a second opinion? If I cannot solve the problem, whom can I go to for help? Can I talk to one of my colleagues? Should I take formal help from a behavioral psychologist or a psychiatrist?

The other approach that has helped me is not to get angry and start arguing about who is at fault. Such arguments only make matters worse. Nothing cools the situation better than the doctor saying, "I am sorry", if that is appropriate. Even if I am not sorry for what happened, I could be sorry that the patient is upset about the situation interfering with our relationship. I realize that such a statement may be misused by a few as admission of a non-existent fault or guilt. It is unfortunate that human relationships have been vitiated by the doctor's fear of being sued. One has to be prudent, while still dealing sensitively with the patient.

More formal writings on this subject suggest the following steps: Identify the conflict; verify it with the patient; acknowledge the view of the patient (you are not agreeing with it by acknowledging it), define the rights and duties of the patient and the doctor, negotiate a mutually agreeable plan and set up a method of monitoring execution of the plan, and provide an efficient way for the patient to reach you any time there is another conflict.[1,6] I would add one more item: Do all of these with sensitivity, without hurry, in privacy, and in the presence of another person, someone from the family and some other health professional. Finally, document accurately. *When you document, describe exactly what happened and not your judgments and editorials about what happened.*

Patients on Alternative Medicines

Most patients with chronic illnesses are trying or have tried an alternative form of therapy, even if they did not tell you. Physicians have to encourage patients to talk about them. Patients will discuss this topic if they trust the physician and are not afraid of being embarrassed or reprimanded. My own practice is to ask about any non-prescription medicines they are taking and tell them that some of them may interfere with my prescriptions. I ask them to bring the bottle and read the label. (It is now possible to get information on any of the ingredients of the herbal and other compounds through the Internet.)

There are conflicting claims about the usefulness of several modalities of alterative and complimentary therapies. A recent report from the American Academy of Pediatrics states that pediatricians should provide evidence-based information about relevant therapies and that pediatricians should make practitioners of alternative and complementary medicine part of care-coordination activities.[7] On the other side, Doctor Edzard Ernst, Professor of Complementary Medicine at the University of Exeter in UK, and Doctor Simon Singh came to a different conclusion in their book on *Trick or Treatment*.[8] These authors reviewed critically all available publications on several alternative forms of therapy and concluded as follows: "Having sought to be both open-minded and skeptical, and having relied on all best available evidence, our broad conclusion is fairly straightforward. Most forms of alternate medicine for most conditions remain either unproven or are demonstrably ineffective, and several alternative therapies put patients at risk of harm."

Parents and patients do use all alternate forms of treatment whether physicians approve or not. That is the reality. We should be sympathetic to the plight of the patients and their good intentions. But we do not have to go along. It is our duty to point out without being confrontational, that there is no basis for the claims. We need to point out that they are at risk of being exploited and even damaging their health due directly to some forms of therapy such as megavitamins and cervical manipulation and also by delaying proper care.

There are also other conflicting pressures. We want our practitioners to practice evidence-based medicine on the one side. Then, we ask them to use whatever seems to "work" or go along with the flow. In addition, there is the cost of care issue. Third party payers may not pay for treatments not backed by evidence for their usefulness, even within conventional medicine. However, they are pressured into paying for alternative therapies that have not been shown to work when rigorously tested.

What is even more important is to look at the reasons for so much currency for these ideas among the public and answer them. We have to address factors that drive patients to unproven remedies. For example, the alternative medicine practitioners clearly spend more time with patients and listen to them. The so-called conventional system does not support this simple step. These practitioners are more easily accessible. Western medicine practitioners are not. These and other reasons for the popularity of alternative medicine are well-explained in the book by Ernst and Singh and should be on the reading list of all physicians.

The following ideas may help during discussions with patients and their families: (1) Be open and non-critical of parents and patients so they will inform you of all other forms of therapy they are using. (2) Tell them that you understand their need to do everything they can to get better. At the same time tell them that your duty is to protect them from false hopes and extra expenditure on treatments not proven to be beneficial or shown to be harmful. (3) Find out about the exact items they are using and warn them if they are using dangerous forms of therapy such as mega-doses of Vitamins A and D, manipulations of the neck and unknown formulations with contaminants. (4) Take this opportunity to educate patients about how scientific treatments are developed, tested and regulated and how alternative forms of therapies are not.

Patients Who Refuse Treatment

Informed consent is absolutely essential for good medical care, even for standard treatment. A refusal is very rare for a surgical procedure unless it is surgery for inoperable cancer. Refusal to take particular medication is more common. The refusal may be well thought out or irrational. It may be one of denial, or it may be suicidal. The patient's age and mental status will also have to be considered.[9] What one does will depend on acuteness of the condition and whether there is time for negotiation. It will also depend on whether the refusal is for a test, a procedure, surgery, or medication.

In one study on refusal of treatment in a hospital setting, refusal was rarely found to be due to one particular cause. Most often, the situation was complex, and multiple factors came into play. The most important problem was with communication. The patients were given either inadequate information or conflicting information. The patients were not given a good explanation of why a procedure or a test was needed, and often the risks were not adequately explained. Some of the refusals were the result of prior bad experience with tests or medications or lack of trust in a particular doctor. Sometimes the patient was depressed, afraid, or in denial.

In this same study, a surprising finding was that the physician's response was more often coaxing, persuasion, and forceful presentation and not a response based on the patient's reason for refusal. Sometimes there was not even an attempt to reverse the patient's refusal.

When a patient refuses treatment for life-threatening conditions or psychiatric illness as a result of which they may harm themselves or others, there are legal and ethical issues. It will be necessary to get a court order for treatment. One has to be aware of the local laws and support systems.

However, in most of other situations, listening to the patient's concerns, trying to answer them, reasoning and negotiating should work. It may be helpful to enlist the help of a family member or someone whom the patient trusts, loves, or respects. Referral to another consultant for another opinion may be appropriate in some situations.

Patients Who Leave the Hospital Against Medical Advice

This, fortunately, is not a big problem in pediatrics. In adults, often it involves patients who are very anxious or those with mental health problems and poor judgment. Interestingly, patients who sign out against medical advice are different from those who refuse treatment.[10] However, the problem is similar to those who refuse treatment, and many of those same techniques of handling may be used.

Disruptive Patients

In both the office and in the hospital, a patient or a relative may become disruptive and becomes a threat to other patients.[11] They are usually violent and psychotic, and law enforcement officers may have to be called in to help. However, every medical facility has *to be prepared for such an event*. A plan must be in place for such a contingency. Every member of the staff should be aware of this plan and be able to implement it as soon as needed. As part of the planning, the staff should rehearse how disruptive patients should be restrained and disarmed without hurting them. A team leader and a backup member have to be designated. There is nothing to deter a violent person if he sees that there is no one in charge.

Other simple, common sense approaches are as follows: Do not aggravate the situation by arguing with the patient or going too close to him, give the patient room and try to calm him with a soothing non-threatening voice from a distance, and inform the security officer or the police as appropriate. The person should be isolated so that he will not hurt himself and others. If it appears that a tranquilizer will be needed, ensure that a quick history and physical examination are completed and documented. It will be necessary to collect data to convince legal authorities that the patient is likely to harm self or others. Information has to be collected on history of seizures or other neurological disorders, medications being taken, and psychological status. It is best to inform the hospital administrators and the police before applying restraints and using medications. There may be an accusation for negligence if you do not, and for battery and assault, if you do. As Perry and Gilmore[11] point out, it is best "to act as a physician and not as a lawyer", inform the hospital administrator of the situation, and try to obtain informed consent from the person's closest available relative.

Irate Patients

More common in pediatrics is an irate parent who is upset and complains loudly.[12] The most important step is not to aggravate the situation by arguing in public. It is better to gently lead the parent to a private room for a full discussion. These situations have to be dealt with at once, and everything else has to wait. Listen to the complaint; admit error if there was one. Alternatively, tell the parent that you will look into the matter and report — and make sure you do follow through on the promise. If possible, have another person, a family member, or a health professional, present during the conversation. Make sure you document it.

Patients with Unreasonable Requests

Increasingly, patients come with a request for a specific test or specific treatment. Patients get information and misinformation from friends and relatives, the Internet and the news media. Direct advertisement to the public on television causes more anxiety in patients. As pointed out by Brett and McCullough, patients may ask what they think is important or what they want,[13] but physicians have a responsibility not to order unnecessary tests or give unnecessary prescriptions, to both protect the individual patient and conserve the resources of the society.

In situations where objective criteria are needed for treatment (e.g., antibiotics for bacterial infections), the physician is not obliged to give the prescription unless there are objective indications. There are situations, such as pain, where the patient's subjective complaints may not correlate with objective findings. In such cases, individual judgment is required. If the patient requests daily physical therapy and there is no proven medical benefit from this approach, the physician is not obliged to prescribe. However, the physician can and should *suggest alternatives*. If the requested intervention has benefits and risks, there should be a discussion with the patient so that the risks are understood. Economic issues cannot be used as reasons *per se* to refuse or accept a patient's demands unless society has established formal guidelines. If the physician decides not to oblige, the reasons should be given, and alternatives, including referral for a second opinion, should be offered.

Patients Who Make Physicians Afraid

There are groups of patients who are in need of unending attention.[14] They have profound dependent behavior, which exhausts the energy of even the most tolerant physician. James Groves classifies them as "dependent clingers, entitled demanders, manipulative help-rejecters, and self-destructive deniers". The best way to recognize them is to recognize the emotion they elicit in you, as a physician. Your personal emotional response may give a clue to the behavior of the patient and help in the development of a management strategy. For example, if the physician feels aversion, he is probably dealing with a "clinger" and should learn to set limits. If a physician feels like mounting a counter-attack, he is probably dealing with a "demanding personality". In this situation, the physician has to set realistic expectations and help the patient refocus on the good care he is receiving. The patient's focus on attacking the people who are trying to help has to be shifted. The patient must be assured that the physician will still provide care even after the symptoms are gone. If a physician feels guilty or inadequate, then he is probably dealing with a manipulative "help-rejecter". The patient must be made to get involved in decision making and held accountable for his decisions or be referred to another physician or counseling.

"Self-destructive deniers" may make the physician wish the patient would disappear and go away. When such a feeling takes hold, the physician must realize that the patient is probably in need of urgent attention. Such a patient needs help and not rejection. The physician has to look for help from psychologists and psychiatrists or from other specialists.

Gorlin and Zucker[15] also emphasize the need for physicians to recognize the types of emotional responses generated in them by patients. For example, in dealing with a terminally ill patient, the physician may be overwhelmed and frustrated and avoid meeting with the family. Alternatively, when dealing with a non-compliant family, the physician may become hostile or reject the patient. Once the physician recognizes his own natural but inappropriate responses, a strategy can be developed to cope with this negative attitude and act in the best interest of the patient. Sometimes, it is necessary to take counseling from a senior colleague or a mental health professional. In some cases, it will be best to transfer the patient to another physician.

Recognizing feelings generated during patient encounters and reflecting on them may be helpful to all physicians. That is what William Carlos Williams did when faced with a young child who refused to open her mouth for a good examination. This essay is worth reading by everyone in medical practice. (See Reading List at the end of this chapter)

Major Message: The patient–physician "dyad" is a unique institution. Problems in relationships can be caused by the personalities of one, or the other, or both. Since the patient is in a vulnerable position because he is the one in need of help, it is up to the physician to analyze the situation and take necessary steps to move the relationship in the right direction. This is as important as making the proper diagnosis and prescribing the right medicine or surgery.

References

1. Difficult Relationships. In Billings AJ, Stoeckle JD (Eds). *The Clinical Encounter*. 2nd edn. 1999. Chicago; Year Book Medical Publishers.
2. Jin J, Sklar GE, Min Sen Oh V, Chuen Li S, Factors affecting therapeutic compliance: A review from the patient's perspective. *Ther Clin Risk Manag* 2008; **4**:269–286.
3. Vermeire E, Hearnshaw H, Van Royen P, Denekens J. Patient adherence to treatment: Three decades of research. A comprehensive review. *J Clin Pharm Ther* 2001; **26**:331–342.
4. Rapoff MA, Lindsley CB, Chrstophersen ER. Parent perception of problems experienced by their children in complying with treatments for juvenile rheumatoid arthritis. *Arch Phys Med Rehabil* 1985; **66**:427–429.
5. Hutschnecker AA. *The Will to Live*. 1986. New York, NY; Simon & Schuster.
6. Heaton PB. Negotiation as an integral part of physician's clinical reasoning. *J Family Prac* 1981; **13**:8845–8848.
7. Kemper KJ, Vohra S, Walls R and the Task Force on Complementary and Alternative Medicine; Provisional Section on Complementary, Holistic,

and Integrative medicine of the American Academy of Pediatrics. The use of complementary and alternative medicine in pediatrics. *Pediatrics* 2008; **122**:1374–1386.

8. *Trick or Treatment*? Ernst E, Singh S (Eds). 2008. New York. WW Norton.
9. Appelbaum PS, Roth LH. Patients who refuse treatment in medical hospitals. *JAMA* 1983; **250**:1296–1301.
10. Schlauch RW, Reich P, Kelly MJ. Leaving the hospital against medical advice. *N Engl J Med* 1979; **300**:22–24.
11. Perry SW, Gilmore MM. The disruptive patient or visitor. *JAMA* 1981; **245**:755–757.
12. Schulman JL. The management of the irate parent. *J Pediatr* 1970; **77**: 338–340.
13. Brett AS, McCullough LB. When patients request specific interventions — Defining limits of the physicians' obligation. *N Eng J Med* 1986; **315**: 1347–1351.
14. Groves JE. Taking care of the hateful patient. *N Engl J Med* 1978; **298**: 883–887.
15. Gorlin R, Zucker HD. Physician's reactions to patients. *N Engl J Med* 1983; **308**:1059–1063.

Reading List

Conrad P. The meaning of medications: Another look at compliance. *Soc Sci Med* 1985; **20**:29–37.

Trostle JA. Medical compliance as an ideology. *Soc Sci Med* 1988: **27**: 1299–1308.

Wiliams WC. *The Doctor Stories*. Compiled by Coles R. 1984. New York; New Directions Publishing Corp.

Can We Agree on the Fundamentals?

Patient (as in *pati* — to suffer) is the one who is suffering.

Therefore, patient is the primary focus.

Patient is NOT a *customer*; NOT a *consumer* either.

Patient is NOT owned by anyone — not by the physician, not by the HMO, not by the national health systems.

Physician is called a *clinician* because he works at the bedside (*klinikos*, bed) of the sick person.

Patient and the physician make a *dyad*.

The patient–physician relationship is a *covenant*; not just a *contract*.

Medicine is a Profession with focus on healing and helping, caring and counseling.

Medicine is NOT a business.

Medical care is NOT a commodity to be traded.

Chapter 9

Caring and Connection

In his landmark article on "The Care of the Patient" in 1927, Francis Peabody stated, "one of the essential qualities of the clinician is interest in humanity, *for the secret of care of the patient is in caring for the patient*".[1] Even with all the advances in scientific medicine, this statement is true. Dr. Fry listed the characteristics of cure and care as shown in Table 9.1.

Caring is doing for others what they cannot do for themselves. The caregiver has to convince through actions that all the duties entrusted will be carried out with diligence and compassion.[2–4]

When a patient seeks help from a physician, obviously he is in distress physically, emotionally, or most often, both. The patient feels vulnerable. He is seeking someone who is knowledgeable and can be trusted. He is looking for comfort and peace of mind.

How can a physician build a trusting relationship? The physician can do so by caring and by being trustworthy. Meyerhoff's comments may help start a caring relationship: "To take care of someone, I must know many things. I must know, for example, who the other is, what his powers and limitations are, what his needs are and what is conducive to his growth; I must know how to respond to his needs and what my own powers and limitations are".[3]

In general, patients expect technical competence as the most important requirement in their doctor. In addition, they want a physician who is compassionate, treat them with respect and dignity, give relevant information in a timely and understandable fashion, and be responsive to their concerns and constraints.

Table 9.1: Factors in cure and care.

Cure	Care
Disease	Person
Physical	Emotional
Body	Soul
Biological	Behavioral/Social
Clinical	Pastoral
Science	Art

Modified from Fry J, *A New Approach to Medicine — Priority and Principles of Health Care*, 1978, University Park Press, Baltimore Md, page 71.

The physician has to make the visits as non-threatening as possible. He has to listen to the patient's problems, fears, and expectations. He has to find out how the patient and family members are reacting to the illness and how well they are coping. The physician may have to probe deeper to uncover the patient's unstated worries.

In my own professional life, I realized I have to take a genuine interest in the person and respect him as an individual regardless of age, social status, and appearance. I have to be truthful in my statements and keep my promises. I have to be prepared to accept the possibility that the patient may not reciprocate my goodwill. Above all, I have to be patient.

It is not enough that I understand and accept. I have to let him know by my words and my deeds that I understand. Even my non-verbal behavior has to show that I care. For example, I can make a phone call when I do not have to and show I care. I can remember what he said during the last visit and ask whether that problem is solved. I may share in his happiness by asking about a major event in the family that he told me about during the earlier visit. Being interested is not being intrusive.

How can one make this concept of care practical? How can we remind ourselves about the core values of compassion, respect and dignity of the individual inherent in caring for others? How can medical teachers impart these values to students and trainees?

Professor Chochinov of Manitoba, Canada has developed a framework to guide healthcare practitioners and this framework can be applied to teaching and to clinical practice and across all medical specialties.[5] He calls it the "ABCD of dignity conserving care". "A" stands for "Attitude"; "B" stands for "Behavior"; "C" stands for "Compassion"; and "D" stands for "Dialogue". Learning this framework will require self-reflection about our own attitude towards patients and our assumptions about their motives. Such reflection should help us examine how well our behavior towards the patient and our discussions with the patient are reflective of our respect for the individual.

The medical profession is primarily a helping profession. Therefore, we have to know what the components of a helping relationship are and what the characteristics of a "good helper" are. Psychologists, nurses, counselors, and educators have been exploring these issues for many years. One of the best thinkers on this topic is Carl Rogers,[2,6] and his talk to the American Personnel and Guidance Association in 1958 on the characteristics of a helping relationship should be required reading for all.[6]

A sequence of ideas, as suggested by Carl Rogers, is listed in the following paragraphs. These are questions for the caregivers and helpers to ask themselves.

1. *Am I available when people need me? Am I available when they perceive that they need me? Am I available only if I think they need me? Do I have someone intervening?*
2. *Am I listening? Do they know that I am listening? What can I do to show that I am aware of their concerns and am listening?*
3. *Do I behave in a non-threatening way? Is it possible that I am threatening by my tone of voice, the way I dress, stand, fold my hands, or by other gestures?*
4. *Will my patients consider me as trustworthy? People perceive you as trustworthy if they feel or sense that what you say agrees with what they think you actually feel. This in turn has something to do with your getting in touch with your own feelings and being consistent with them. Carl Rogers calls it "congruence".*

Let us take an example. A patient calls a physician at 2 a.m. with a "silly" concern. The physician gets angry and does not conceal it. The patient is told in an irritated voice to call back the next morning. This physician was congruent with his or her feelings. The physician was angry and let the patient know about it. The physician responded to his perception of the situation, which was different from the patient's perception. Therefore, the physician was not helpful to the patient.

After a few years, a similar call still causes anger, but the same physician has learned to respond differently. He suppresses the anger and talks in a calm voice to determine what the problem is and allays the anxiety. This is not congruence, because the physician is still angry but is better at controlling it. Eventually, patients will sense that the physician is not congruent (not sincere) and will loose their trust.

Finally, the physician's response reaches a mature stage. When he now receives a similar call, he is both congruent and appropriately responsive. The physician has assimilated the fact that people's needs are based on their perception of the facts, not on the physician's appraisal of them. Therefore, the physician is *not angry* and truly wants to help. People sense this, even over the telephone, and will respond because the physician is genuinely understanding and congruent with his inner self.

These remarks are based on those of Carl Rogers and personal observations. They are supported by studies for more than 30 years. To quote Rogers, "I have come to recognize that being trustworthy does not demand that I be rigidly consistent but that I be dependably real. The term "congruent" is one I have used to describe the way I would like to be. By this I mean that whatever feeling or attitude I am experiencing would be matched by my awareness of that attitude. When this is true, then I am a unified or integrated person in that moment, and hence I can be whatever I deeply am. This is a reality which I find others experience as dependable".[6]

5. *Am I learning and growing? If I wish to help others grow, I have to grow myself. Do I know why I am in this profession? Do I know what annoys me and what stimulates me? If items that bother me*

are important roadblocks to helping relationships, what am I doing to correct them? If I am annoyed with another person, am I aware of it? If so, can I let it be known without making the other person feel small? If I am not even aware of it, isn't it likely that my communication will contain contradictory messages?

6. *Can I develop a genuine positive attitude towards this other person by showing an interest, warmth, and respect? Or, am I having negative thoughts?*
7. *Can I accept the other person, as he is — depressed or exuberant, cold and remote or overly friendly? Or, am I trying to make him over to fit my mold so he becomes acceptable to me?*
8. *If I can be gentle, non-threatening, non-judgmental, congruent, and therefore trustworthy, the other person will let me enter the world of his meaning. Isn't it necessary for me to see the world the way he does, with all the special meaning and inner values, before I can truly help? Will I be able to help without passing judgment on his inner feelings and values?*
9. *If I can and do enter this private world and see it the way he does, will I be prepared to change my attitudes and beliefs?*

If I can be successful in the above steps, I know who I am and why I am here. I know that I can acknowledge others as they are. I can relate to the other person without any fears of being drawn into conflict between our emotions and values.

In summary, caring and helping involve genuine interest in and respect for the other person. Caring involves honesty and unconditional non-judgmental acceptance. It is hard to maintain this high standard all the time with every patient. There will be a small minority of patients who will not respond to caring. The response of others and the outcome are not in one's hands and not always predictable.[7]

Suffering

One of the primary functions of the physician is to relieve suffering. Suffering is universal and part of the human condition. It is intensely personal. When someone falls ill, suffering is inevitable. Some of it is physical and some is emotional. The way suffering is handled will vary depending on the patient's age, intelligence level, education, individual personality traits, cultural and religious beliefs, and available support.

Suffering is a subjective state.[4,8] It cannot be predicted or measured. A physician may not even recognize it unless he is sensitive to facial expressions, casual remarks, and non-verbal cues. The physician's first response should be to acknowledge that the patient is suffering, even if the illness is a minor one. Complete information on the illness given in a sympathetic way will help reduce suffering. Anticipating future events based on knowledge of the disease and sharing them with the patient may help, but not always. Some people like to be told everything ahead of time. Some want to know in increments and just before the event. Telling patients what to expect and how long it will last, how much it will cost, and what other options are available will remove many of the fears and reduce suffering.

The next step is to find whether the focus of suffering is physical, emotional, social, familial, or financial. If the focus of suffering is physical pain, the physician can treat the pain adequately. If it is due to nausea and vomiting, anti-emetics can be used. For some, good sleep will reduce their suffering. If the suffering is from emotional, social, or family issues, physicians can help find resources in the community for counseling or group support. It is not possible to relieve *all* of the patient's suffering. However, physicians can find resources that will help reduce it. He can conduct his patient visits in such a way that the patient feels helped.

One other source of suffering is based on personal perceptions of life. This can be altered but personal effort is required. Cognitive psychologists, support groups and Buddhist meditative practice groups may be of help to bring about changes in perception. Support groups can also help develop coping mechanisms from others who are more resilient.

Medical Decision Making

There are many articles and books on how physicians make decisions[9,10] but very few reports on how patients make decisions.[11,12]

Szasz and Hollander[10] recognized three types of doctor–patient relationships: activity–passivity, guidance–cooperation, and mutual participation. In acute and emergency situations, the physician takes an authoritative role. In most of the medical situations requiring medical and surgical intervention, the patient has to take part and cooperate for the treatment to be successful. The third model is of mutual participation and negotiation, which is most appropriate in chronic diseases and conditions where no cure is possible or the outcome is uncertain. It is also becoming a major model in most situations since patients are better informed through education and the availability of medical information on the Internet.

As pointed out by Brody, patients and physicians approach decision making from different viewpoints.[11] Physicians will be thinking about what investigations to do and what treatments to choose. Patients will look at these options in terms of the cost, discomfort, and inconvenience. These differences in perspectives have to be considered during discussions and negotiations. The positions of doctor and patient should be complementary and parallel to the extent possible.

Ideally, one should make a decision based on information, experience, and imagination. The physician should collect all available information; sift through evidence; and calculate pros and cons, risks and benefits, gains and losses; and then decide on an "optimal" course of action appropriate for the patient's specific circumstances. The physician then offers his recommendations to the patient who has to act on them. This process is difficult for the patient, who does not understand the pros and cons of available options. In addition, he has to make decisions while under emotional stress. Sometimes, the problem is one of information overload. In reality, decisions are often made on impulse and based on recent memory.

Many branches of psychology are studying the cognitive and emotional aspects of decision making. In discussing how cognition and emotions affect decision making, Redelmeir, Rozin and Kahneman point out how people reach judgments based on simple rules and reach for an *acceptable* solution, not necessarily the *best* one.[12] It is important to remember that people generally prefer the status quo. Patients are generally risk-aversive and are more likely to be conservative when

Table 9.2: Communicating with patients about risks.

People's fears, wishes and priorities differ greatly and unpredictably.
Three major issues in helping patients with making decisions are: obtaining *reliable* information about benefits and harm; effectively communicating probabilities of both; determining how to minimize and treat adverse events.
Present outcomes in natural frequencies (e.g. 1 in 10 chance, etc); not in percentages and odds ratio.
Remember that patients need information on risks applicable to their *unique* situation.

Sources:
Alaszewski A. A person-centered approach to communicating risks. *PLoS Medicine* 2005; **2**:e41.
Herxheimer A. Communicating with patients about harms and risks. *PLoS Medicine* 2005; **2**:e42.

compared with physicians. Recent studies suggest that people adjust to ambiguities, although slowly; but do not adjust to risk.[13]

There are many ways we can help patients make important decisions. Some ideas on how to present the risks and benefits of therapeutic and experimental laboratory tests, imaging techniques, and surgery are presented in Table 9.2 (also refer to Chapter on Communication Skills).

Patients often tend to categorize risks as all or none. They also tend to consider losses as more significant than gains. The perfect example is the fact that most people, including physicians, are unenthusiastic about receiving the yearly influenza vaccination. There is often an emotional block to following instructions that restrict lifestyle at present for some potential good in the future. This is particularly true for children who want fun *now.* They cannot understand the availability of benefit in the *future*.

When asked to choose between alternatives, some patients are more comfortable doing so than others.[14] Even for those who prefer choices, too many choices cause worry about the "road not taken". Patients' choices will also depend on how the scenario is presented. For example, if the physician says that a particular treatment reduces the mortality by say 20 or 30%, it is less likely to be enticing to the patient than if he said it increases survival rate by 70%. That does not mean that the physician should use a language favorable to his own point of view. For this reason, it is important to be aware of how the data are presented to the patient. It is important to discuss absolute risks and not relative risks. Efforts should be made to reduce or eliminate any mismatch between the actual level of danger and the intensity of the patient's worry.

Brody[11] suggests the following steps to facilitate mutual participation in decision making: establish a cooperative atmosphere for open-ended communication and discussion; ascertain the patient's understanding, goals, and expectations; discuss all available alternatives with pros and cons; if appropriate, express your recommendation and the reasons for it; elicit the patient's preferences to each of the alternatives; and negotiate any disagreements. If necessary, a second opinion may be suggested.

Major Message: Caring and helping are the hallmarks of a clinician. There is no one standard method of caring since patient personalities differ so widely. In the current era of patient autonomy, it is essential to know how patients make decisions on medical matters and to help them make decisions that are in their best interest that do not compromise the physician's integrity and values.

References

1. Peabody FW. The care of the patient. *JAMA* 1984; **252**:813–818. (Reproduced from *JAMA* **88**:887–882, 1927).
2. Rogers Carl R. *On Becoming a Person*. 1961. Boston, Ma; Houghton Mifflin Co.
3. Meyerhoff M. *On Caring*. New York, NY; Perennial Library, Harper and Row Publishers. p 13.
4. Cassell EJ. *The Nature of Suffering and the Goals of Medicine*. 1991. Oxford, UK; Oxford University Press. pp 237–250.
5. Chochinov HM. ABCD of dignity conserving care. *BMJ* 2007; **335**: 184–187.

6. Rogers CR. The characteristics of a helping relationship. *Personnel and Guidance Journal* 1958; **37**:6–16.
7. Easwaran E. *The Bhagavad Gita*. 1985. Tomales, CA, USA; Nilgiri Press.
8. O'Brien ME. Relief of suffering — where art and science of medicine meet. *Postgrad Med* 1996; **99**:189–208.
9. Sox HC, Blatt MA, Marton KI. *Medical Decision Making*. 1988. Woburn, MA; Butterworth Publishers.
10. Szasz TS, Hollander MH. A contribution to the philosophy of medicine; the basic model of the doctor–patient relationship. *Arch Intern Med* 1956; **97**:585–592.
11. Brody D. The patient's role in clinical decision-making. *Ann Inter Med* 1980; **93**:718–722.
12. Redelmeir D, Rozin P, Kahneman D. Understanding patient's decisions: Cognitive and emotional persepctives. *JAMA* 1993; **270**:72–76.
13. Rustichini A. Emotion and reason in making decisions. *Science* 2005; **310**: 1624–1625.
14. Scwartz B. The tyranny of choice. *Scientific Amer*. April 2004. pp 71–75.

Chapter 10

Learning and Teaching Skills

I have to be a good learner to be a good teacher. That is why I like teaching. What is learning? What is teaching? During discussions with an educator, a new definition of the word "learning" emerged. Learning, according to this definition, is a shift from what you are, to what you can be. It is an energy shift.

Animals have built-in systems of learning for survival. Some animals can learn a few more skills to please the master, to earn a few more peanuts, or to avoid punishment. Humans learn for these reasons and more. Human beings have a need and an urge to know. Aristotle included man the learner and knower in his three dimensions of man.

An even more important difference is that animals can learn. Humans can learn how to learn.

Although humans can learn, that does not mean they do learn. Most of us are handicapped by the educational system, a system that does not prepare us adequately to be life-long, active learners. Active and dynamic learning is demanded by the fast developments and enormous growth of knowledge. Physicians must master this kind of learning if they are to keep up with the vast amount of information produced by and for their profession.

Continuous learning has become a situational necessity. Knowledge is exploding at an exponential rate, and it is unsafe to be uninformed, particularly in medicine. Much of this knowledge is available to the public as well. Our patients expect the professionals to know more than they do.

In medicine, there is a need and push for continuous life-long learning. The need to be re-licensed every seven years is a push. The recent emphasis of documentation of self-improvement as a requisite for recertification is another push. They are sources of external push. We need an internal push, a thirst for learning, as well.

For effective self-learning, a few conditions must be met. These include: a desire to learn, ability to seek knowledge, time to learn, ability to learn facts and truth from *any* source, and a sense of humility.

Once there is a thirst for knowledge, time to learn can be found, and the mode of learning will not matter. Yet, we spend too much time learning about the techniques of learning, not about the attitudes toward learning. Some learn by listening, some by reading, some through computer interaction, and some by interaction with experts and colleagues. One can choose one of these methods, but can do so only if one is motivated.

You cannot truly motivate anyone. By definition, motivation is self-generated. However, one can facilitate. For example, if you involve the person in setting the goal or the curriculum or the mode of learning, there is a stake for the individual and thus a greater chance for motivation. A necessity to pass an examination, get ahead in academic life, or acquire a coveted job may be the motivation for some. A dynamic teacher may be able to excite some and make them learn more about a particular subject.

Too many distractions and constraints make learning difficult. The unrelenting demands on the physicians' time are major constraints. There are environmental temptations and family pressures. There are no easy answers. Each one of us will have to develop our own system of choosing the subject matter, mode of learning, the place, and the time. Whatever method is used, one thing is certain. Without self-discipline and a routine, it will be impossible to keep up.

The following steps may help guide your efforts to hone your skills in learning to learn.

1. *A sense of urgency.* Whether for professional or personal reasons, for functional or fun reasons, when we have a sense of urgency, things get done.

2. *An awareness of possibilities.* Organized knowledge, available resources and facilities and above all, role models, give us the hope that we too can pick up the skills.
3. *An understanding of principles.* Researchers have assiduously identified principles and practice in all branches of knowledge. Varieties of publications, books and reviews — both in print media and digital media — are available with synthesized knowledge on what to do under what circumstances and why. They are *easily* available at the click of a computer mouse.
4. *A commitment to action.* Physicians have to commit a certain amount of time and energy to acquire, enhance and update their skills.
5. *A mastery of techniques.* In converting knowledge into results, mastery of techniques is essential. Techniques have to be acquired from masters and practiced under guidance.
6. *A set of integrated habits.* In order to move from conscious mastery to unconscious mastery, practice is needed. This requires a set of integrated habits.
7. *Constant upgrading.* Physicians have to consciously, consistently and continuously upgrade their skills. They need to upgrade their knowledge, skills, attitudes and values. Eastern thinkers will describe these dimensions as: head, hand, heart and the spirit!

The good news is that resourceful people are building tools to acquire knowledge in all these domains and most of these tools are even free.

Teaching

The word *doctor* comes from "*docere*", which in Latin means, "to teach". A major function of the physician is to teach the patients. In practice or in academics, physicians teach other health workers, office staff, and the public. In a medical school and in hospitals, physicians teach students, trainees, and junior staff. Teaching is a natural part of a physician's work.

Teaching comes naturally to some. For others, observing recognized masters are the best method to learn the art of teaching.[1] I was very fortunate to have worked with some of the greatest teachers. Each one had a different style and was good in a special setting. Some were great at the bedside with the patient. Some were great in the laboratory. Some were excellent on the podium. Others were great in small group discussions. All of them had some common features.

First is a passion for teaching and for the topic. That passion translates automatically into infectious enthusiasm in the audience. The passion has to come from within. Passion alone is not enough, however, if your knowledge is shallow and the understanding of the subject is superficial. Just listen to some of the fiery speakers on religious and political platforms. They are passionate, too.

A good teacher has to know the subject matter thoroughly. Obviously, to teach someone else, you have to know the subject and know it well. When the teacher understands the concepts, it is easier to make the topic understandable, even to a novice. In addition, mastery of knowledge gives confidence on the stage. Adapting to the needs of the recipient and their style of learning is another major characteristic of a good teacher.

For interested teachers, I recommend a book by Doctor Richard Feynman on Quantum Electrodynamics.[2] It is a small book and is based on lectures given by this master teacher to non-science students. His mastery of the topic and passion can be felt in each page. It is amazing how Dr. Feynman can make his concepts (for which he received the Nobel Prize) understandable to students with very little background in physics.

Interested teachers are referred also to several articles on the details of preparation for a talk, poster presentation, writing an abstract, etc.[3–7] But, the most important step is an ability to reflect on why you wish to be a teacher, what you want your legacy to be and what your own strengths and weaknesses are.[8,9]

It is important for physicians to take some time off from their routines. Obviously time with the family is the primary need. In addition, physicians need time to reflect on one's values, goals and direction in life and in the profession. It is part of self-healing and personal growth, so that he can be a better human being and a better physician. Even though sabbatical,[10] as it was known during the earlier era, does not exist any longer, it is important for department heads to provide time for members of the faculty to reflect on their work and life.

References

1. Highet G. *The Immortal Profession — The Joys of Teaching and Learning* 1976. New York; Wybright and Talley.
2. Feynman R. *QED: The Strange Theory of Light and Matter* 1985. Princeton, NJ; Princeton University Press.
3. Yurchak PM. A guide to medical case presentation. *Resident and Staff Physician*. September 1984; pp. 109–115.
4. Wright V. How to speak at international conferences. *Ann Rheum Dis* 1992; **51**:1259–1260.
5. MTS. On writing the synopsis — abstract. *JAMA* 1972; **222**:1307.
6. Wolman IJ. What makes a good medical book review. *Clin Pediatr* 1962; **1**:29A–32A.
7. Squires BP. Editorial and platform article: What editors want from authors and peer reviewers. *CMA Journal* 1989; **141**:666–667.
8. Schon DA. *The Reflective Practitioner.* 1983. Basic Books, USA.
9. Palmer PJ. *The Courage to Teach* 1998. San Fransisco, CA; Jossey-Bass Publishers.
10. Reuler JB. Sabbatical. *JAMA* 1989; **261**:408–410.

Who am I?

To you
I am whatever you have judged me to be
Come what may.

To me
I am whoever I truly am
Whatever you say.

Balu H. Athreya

Chapter 11

Physician, Know Thyself!

Traditional learning and teaching methods emphasize scientific tools of observation, measurement, reasoning, and analysis (*sensory knowing and rational knowing*). Traditional learning methods also emphasize discussions, arguments, and counter-arguments to reach conclusions and to sway another's point of view (*dialectics*). These time-honored methods contributed enormously to our understanding of the universe. *Contemplative knowing*, a third time-honored method of acquiring and consolidating knowledge, deserves greater attention. In this process, the learner learns more by reflecting on self and on the knowledge he has acquired. The learner tries to assimilate the acquired information into a coherent whole. He tries to integrate his book knowledge with personal values and with the reality of the world in which he lives.

It is essential, therefore, that physicians find some time every day for self-reflection. This could be a quiet time for reflection, at least once a week, if not everyday. Writing a journal is another useful method. The idea is to reflect upon what one has learned from specific encounters with patients and from new knowledge acquired that day or that week.

Based on *The Book of Questions* by Zimmerman,[1] I wrote several questions for myself to answer. Whenever I shared these with young physicians, the response was positive. Therefore, I am reproducing them (Table 11.1). Maybe, you will reflect on some or all of these questions.

Table 11.1: Physician, ask thyself.

1. Why are you in medicine? Your immediate response? Your considered response?
2. Do you like people?
3. If so, what is it about people that you like?
4. Are you afraid of being lonely?
5. Do you want to be liked? Why?
6. Do you want to be respected? For what?
7. Do you offer to help when there is a need or at your convenience?
8. How do you feel when talking to an angry person? What do you do about that feeling?
9. Do you accept sublimation of feeling as an acceptable method of handling unpleasant feelings?
10. Do you like to help on conditions or without conditions?
11. When there is a crisis, do you face it or try to run away?
12. Do you like everything neatly explained or can you tolerate ambiguity?
13. If a patient does not follow your advice, what do you do?
14. Can you recognize when a patient is "using" you? Can you tolerate it?
15. What is your definition of a "helping profession"?
16. Do you think people are inherently good or inherently bad?
17. Do you like to show that you are the "boss"? Why?
18. Tell me about Death.
19. Have you attended a patient's funeral? Tell me about it.
20. Can you take criticism?
21. Do you like giving bad news? How are you handling it so far?
22. Do you think you are a good listener?
23. Do others think you are a good listener?
24. If these two assessments do not match, what is the reason?
25. Who should decide what death is, what life is?
26. Should care be based on the need or ability to pay or on perceived importance of the person?
27. Who should decide on allocation of resources in medicine?
28. Do you think that everything that can be done should be done all the time?
29. Do you have a life away from medicine? What is it?
30. What do you do for rest and relaxation?
31. What do you do for self-renewal?
32. Are you "growing"? Is your "significant-other" growing? Are you growing in the same direction?

Another area requiring the attention of physicians is their personal life. They need to reflect on the effects of their long hours on other members of their family. The rewards in the profession are important but short-lived. Family responsibilities are much harder to fulfill, without any "awards ceremonies". This is a particular problem for women in medicine, who are torn between their professional responsibilities and goals and family needs.[2] As Robert and Lillian Brent pointed out, medicine should not become an excuse *from* living.[3]

Major Message: Self-reflection is an essential requirement for personal growth. Time spent on this activity will pay great dividends in all aspects of one's life.

References

1. Zimmerman W. *A Book of Questions* 1984. New York, NY; Guarionex Press.
2. Klass P. Where's my medal? *N Eng J Med* 2005; **353**:2107–2109.
3. Brent RL, Brent LH. Medicine as an excuse from living. *Resident and Staff Physician*. December 1978.

Part IV

Appendix

Chapter 12

How to Organize a Course on Clinical Competency Skills

The word *clinical* has its root in the Greek word *Klinikos* meaning "the bed". Therefore, clinical medicine is bedside medicine and clinical skills should include all the skills required of a clinician at the bedside. In my view, the list should include: listening skills, observational skills, diagnostic skills, caring skills, problem solving skills, communication skills, human relations skills and negotiation skills.

What is clinical competency? In order to give focus to this book I prefer the simple dictionary definition of competence as "**capacity equal to requirement**". What are these requirements in clinical medicine? The first requirement is sound, scientific knowledge of the subject. Immediately after, or simultaneously with knowledge, is the ability to relate to people in distress and make them comfortable. In other words, a good clinician needs human relationship skills. Knowledge without human relation skills is of no use; great human relationship skills without sound knowledge may be dangerous.

In its much broader definition of competence, ACGME includes six domains: medical knowledge, patient care, professionalism, communication and interpersonal skills, practice-based learning and improvement, and systems-based practice.

A good clinician needs listening and communication skills. He needs procedural skills and clinical reasoning skills. Above all, he has to reflect on daily experiences and keep improving all his skills, all the time.

All of us know that these skills are important. But how do you teach them? At present, medical students learn these skills mostly by observing master clinicians who act as role models. There are not adequate numbers of such role models in medical schools. Only recently have medical schools come to recognize the importance of master clinicians in their academic ranks. Even when such masters are available, learning by observing is a passive method.

How can one teach clinical skills using active, practical methods? One method is to observe students interact with patients directly or through a video and then discuss the techniques. Another method is to use seminars and workshops developed by industries in listening skills, communication skills, negotiation skills and problem solving skills. Some of there programs are available in medical field also.

It will be best if medical schools organize specific courses or seminars on each of the skills required at the bedside. These can be conducted by one of the staff members using materials available from variety of sources, including this book. Alternately, a specialist in listening skills from industry or in communication skills from a management consultancy firm may be invited to conduct these courses.

I have found that organizing a seminar lasting 2 to 3 hours is a practical way to introduce students to some of the techniques in each of these skills. Using well known principles of adult-learning, I divide my session into 4 segments. The first segment is for *Introduction* of the participants and of the topic. This should last for about 20 to 30 minutes. I often ask the participants what each of the participants hopes to learn in the session. I, then, summarize my plans and align their expectations with what is planned for the session. The second segment is to provide *Information*. I give a talk summarizing what is known about that topic. This talk lasts for about 20 minutes. The third segment is for *Integration*. This consists of one or more exercises to explore the main topic. Students are divided into groups of 3 or 4 and asked to think about a particular topic or problem. This should last for about 30 minutes. This is followed by a group session lasting about 15 minutes when the students present their ideas and recommendations. The final segment is for *Implementation* of ideas generated. During this session, students spend a few minutes individually or as groups, writing down how they plan to implement the ideas they learnt.

Ideally, a follow-up session should be planned to find out how well the ideas were implemented, what the blocks to implementation were and what the outcomes were.

Alternately, the table of contents of this book may be used to start a discussion group. The participants can read an assigned chapter (or chapters) before the session. One participant can be chosen to read, in addition, one of the articles or books from the list of references given at the end of that chapter. This participant may also choose one of the appropriate references from the website that goes with this book or from any other source. The leader will start the session describing a clinical situation related to the topic chosen for that day. The special participant will then summarize the article or book he was assigned. This will be followed by discussion of the clinical scenario.

Please note that this is not a course on Humanism. In my view, humanism is an integral part of every clinician's skills. Humanism does not include specific skills in listening, observing, diagnosing and problem solving. Therefore, this course on Clinical Competency should be a separate course.

The following exercises can be used to teach specific clinical skills.

Exercises in Communication Skills

Assign the chapter on Communication Skills (Chapter 7) from this book to be read before the session.

- Divide the class into groups of 3 or 4.
- Give the following scenarios to the participants.
- Let them discuss and consider various options.

- Then let the class get back together.
- Let each group report its approach to the assigned problem.
- Let others comment and enhance the approach.

Suggested topics for group exercises: (You can make up your own)

1. Inform a parent about a child's death in an accident (Conveying bad news)
2. A parent refuses permission for spinal tap in a 1-year-old with fever (Convincing/negotiating)
3. Parent accuses you of failing to tell her about an important laboratory report (Defusing)
4. You have a loud and disruptive parent in the office (Calming)

Thinking and Problem Solving Skills

1. Assign Chapters on PMI, Alternatives and Lateral Thinking from de Bono's book on *Thinking Course* for students to read.
2. The course director may read the book on *Six Hat Thinking* by de Bono and explain the principles to the students.
3. This can be followed by the following exercises:

    a. You are treating a 4-year-old patient with severe rheumatoid arthritis. Given the current situation, you can go with methotrexate or try etanercept (Enbrel) or Infliximab (Remicade). Do some "white-hat" thinking on each option. Follow it up with "red hat" thinking.
    b. You have just retired. You do not have adequate space in your house to bring all your professional books from the office. Put on your "green hat" and come up with solutions.
    c. A 75-year-old woman from India is visiting her son in US and gets diagnosed with breast cancer during the visit. She is an orthodox Hindu coming from a village. Surgery is recommended. Do an "OPV" (Other People's View) on how she, her son, her husband, and other members of the family are likely to think.

(Reference source: Edward de Bono. *de Bono's Thinking Course*. 1985. Oxford, England; Facts on File Publications, 1985.)

Exercises in Observation Skills

In Chapter 4 of my book on Clinical Competency Skills, I have referred to four different techniques to improve one's observational skills. They are: Yo-Yo technique, Squinting, Pattern recognition and Visual logic. The "yo-yo" technique is the easiest to practice. Analysis of gait is ideal to practice this skill. Obtain a videoclip of normal and abnormal gaits. Have the participants look at the whole person from the front, side and the back. Then zoom in successively on the foot, the ankle, the knee, the hips, the spine, the shoulder and the neck. In between focus on one component, ask the participants to zoom out and see the whole person. Ask them to describe the whole gait and specific abnormality at each component site.

Use a slide of a patient with dysmorphic facial features (e.g. Down syndrome or Treacher-Collins or Fetal Alcohol syndrome). Ask the participants to zoom in and out on the whole face and each part. Have them describe the features.

To learn the squinting technique, use paintings by Monet who uses strokes that make the edges look fuzzy. These fuzzy edges will look more defined when one squints the eyes while looking. After this exercise, use a slide of a patient with thyroid swelling or diffuse swelling around a joint, particularly the knee. Practice squinting. Faint rashes may also be better visualized using this technique.

Pattern recognition and visual logic may be taught using dysmorphic facial features of children with various common syndromes.

Also, use Figs. 4.2 and 4.3 from this book to describe specific features of normality of facial structures.

The course director must read the following reference before this exercise.

Broadbent RT, Matthews VL. Artistic relationships in surface anatomy of the face: Applications to Reconstructive Surgery. *Plastic and Reconstructive Surgery* 1957; **20**:1–17.

Exercises in Listening Skills

1. Ask the participants to complete the following questionnaires and rate themselves. It is expected that most people will rate themselves better than they actually are. Therefore, ask them to write the estimated time as part of this exercise. Also, ask them to keep a log for a week afterwards and compare.

   a. How much time do you think you spend each day in the following activities? (estimated time)

      i. Speaking
      ii. Writing
      iii. Reading
      iv. Listening

   b. How much time do you spend each day listening to

      i. Your spouse
      ii. Your children
      iii. Your friends
      iv. Your supervisor
      v. Your colleagues
      vi. Yourself
      vii. Media

   c. How would the following people rate you as a listener? (good, bad or average)

      i. Your spouse
      ii. Your children
      iii. Your friends
      iv. Your supervisor
      v. Your colleagues
      vi. Yourself

   At this time, after they have completed the questionnaire, share with them the following facts and ideas.

   In one study conducted several years back, 68 adults in different occupations were found to spend 70% of the time in verbal communication. When broken down, 9% of the time was spent in writing, 11% in reading, 30% in talking and 45% in listening. Yet, we spend more time learning how to read, write and speak than how to listen.

Other's perception of how good a listener you are is more important than how good you think you are.

2. Divide the group into multiple pairs. In each pair, one will be labeled A and the other B. During the first section of this exercise, person A will be the "speaker" and B the "listener". The task is for the speaker to talk for about 2 minutes on some topic. The course director can suggest a few topics to get the group started. Some suggested topics are: The latest movie I saw; the latest book I read; my planned vacation this summer; my most recent vacation. During these 2 minutes, the task of person B, the listener is to stay distracted, or distract the speaker or not pay attention to the "speaker". Obviously, we do not want the distraction to be too noisy or disruptive to the whole group. At the end of 2 minutes, the course director rings a bell or calls the group to stop.

   Now, the participants change roles. Person B talks and person A listens — or supposed to listen, but distracts. This lasts for 2 minutes.

   At this point, the whole group gets back together. The course director asks the participants to *express their feelings*. The participants say how they felt when the other person was not listening. This list is then used to discuss how patients would feel when they go away with the impression that they were not listened to.

   Another important point to be made is: What is important is not how good a listener you feel you are, but what the perception of the patient is. If they do not match, you need to reflect on your listening habits.

   Follow this with a session exploring some barriers to good listening in a doctor's office, in an outpatient clinic and in an inpatient unit. (Look for participants recognizing barriers in the system, physical barriers and human barriers.)

3. Now repeat Step 2, but this time with a difference. When person A talks for 2 minutes, person B listens — truly listens. After 2 minutes,

they reverse roles, with B talking and A listening. At the end, the group gets back together.

4. Now, the participants are asked to *list the reasons why they think the other person was listening*. In other words, they list items of behavior that suggest true listening.

It is important to emphasize the items on this list with examples and participation by the attendees. Let the participants reflect on some of the characteristics they need to develop.

Additional resources for this session are:

Participants may be asked to read and discuss Tables 4.2 and 4.3 from Chapter 4 of this book. These emphasize good listening habits in general and good listening habits of great clinicians.

There are several exercises at the end of the book (a classic) on "Are you listening?" by Ralph G. Nichols and Leonard A. Stevens. 1957. McGraw-Hill.

www.listeningleaders.com has a number of resources including a weekly newsletter and reference to a book by Lyman K. Steil on *Listening Leaders: The Ten Golden Rules to Listen, Lead and Succeed.*

Another useful site is www.listen.org.

Yet another untested tool developed to measure Person Centered Attitude is called the Active Listening Attitude Scale. (The development of a questionnaire to assess the attitude of active listening by Mishima N, Kubota S and Nagata S. *J Occupational Health* 2000; **42**:111–118) Although this scale was developed for a different purpose, it has some interesting questions grouped under three headings: Listening Attitude, Listening Skills and Conversation Opportunity. The following are some of the questions used in the study with modifications. Answers to these questions may be helpful to reflect on one's listening habits.

Attitudes		
I tend to persist in my opinion	yes	no
I hurry the speaker	yes	no
I get irritated with some words	yes	no
I hear with a critical viewpoint	yes	no
I tend to deny other's opinion	yes	no
I tend to interrupt often	yes	no
I take offense easily	yes	no
I begin to talk before the speaker finishes	yes	no
Skills		
I pay attention to the speakers feelings	yes	no
I listen to others seriously	yes	no
I summarize in my mind what the speaker says	yes	no
I then give the speaker a summary	yes	no
I put myself in the speakers shoes	yes	no
When the speaker hesitates, I wait	yes	no
I am aware of my own feelings	yes	no
I tend to ask questions	yes	no

Additional Reading Lists

Chapter 1: Introduction

Aring CD. Gentility and professionalism. *JAMA* 1974; **227**:512.

Cousins N. Anatomy of an illness (as perceived by the patient). *N Engl J Med* 1976; **295**:1458–1463.

DeRosa GP. Professionalism — Where are all the heroes gone? *JBJS* (*Amer*) 1996; 78–A; 1295–1299.

Fishbein M. On Being a Good Doctor. *Medical World News*. January 18, 1974; p 68.

Lundberg GD. Medicine — A profession in trouble. *JAMA* 1985; **253**:2879–2880.

Meador CK. The last well person. *N Engl J Med* 1994; **330**:440–441.

Percy W. The Loss of the Creature, in *Message in the Bottle*. 1983. New York, US; Farrar, Straus and Giroux.

Southwick F. Who was caring for Mary? *Ann Int Med* 1993; **118**:146–148.

Stern DT, Papadakis M. The Developing Physician — Becoming a Professional. *N Engl J Med* 2006; **355**:1794–1799.

Tipler BM. Holding hands: The healing touch. *Diagnostic Imaging*. December 1993; p 76.

Tipler BM. Beware of invasion of vending machines. *Diagnostic Imaging*. February 1995; p 76.

Williams WC. Autobiography. In *The Physician in Literature*. Cousins N (Ed). 1982. WB Saunders Co. pp 249–261; pp 310–315.

Chapter 2: Clinical Competence and New Directions in Medical Education

Balint J, Shelton W. Regaining the initiative. Forging a new model of the patient–physician relationship. *JAMA* 1996; **275**:887–891.

Batavia AI. Accounting for the health-care bill. *Lancet* 2003; **362**:1495–1497.

Berwick DM. A user's manual for the IOM's "Quality Chasm" report. *Health Affairs* 2002; **21**:80–90.

Hurowitz JC. Towards a social policy for health. *N Engl J Med* 1993; **329**:130–133.

Johnson GT. Restoring trust between patient and doctor. *N Engl J Med* 1990; **322**:195–197.

King LS. Medicine — Trade or Profession? *Editorial. JAMA* 1985; **253**:2709–2710.

LaCombe M. What is Internal Medicine? *Ann Int Med* 1993; **118**:383–387.

Mechanic D, Schlesinger M. The impact of managed care on patient's trust in medical care and their physicians. *JAMA* 1996; **275**:1693–1697.

Medical Professionalism in the New Millenium: A Physician Charter. *Ann Int Med* 2002; **136**:243–246 (also *Lancet* 2002; **359**:520–522).

Reed R, Evans D. The deprofessionalization of medicine: Cause, effects and responses. *JAMA* 1987; **258**:3279–3282.

The Health of Nations. A Survey. *The Economist.* July 17, 2004.

Zuger A. Dissatisfaction with medical practice. *N Engl J Med* 2004; **350**:69–75.

Chapter 3: Getting to Know the Patient — Disease, Illness, and Illness Behavior

Caplan AL, Tristam Engelhardt Jr H, McCartney JJ. *Concepts of Health and Disease*: *Interdisciplinary Perspective*. 1981. Reading, MA; Addison-Wesley Publishing Co. (There is a newer, updated edition. It is the next one.)

Caplan A, McCartney JJ, Sisti DA. *Health, Disease and Illness: Concepts in Medicine*. 2004. Washington, DC; Georgetown University Press.

Chiong W. Diagnosing and defining disease. *JAMA* 2001; **285**:89–90.

Coggon DIW, Martyn CN. Time and chance: The stochastic nature of disease causation. *Lancet* 2005; **365**:1434–1437.

Cohen ML, Qunitener JL. Fibromyalgia syndrome, a problem of tautology. *Lancet* 1993; **342**:906–909.

Ferrari R, Kwan O, Russell AS, Pearce JMS, Schrader H. The best approach to the problem of whiplash? One way ticket to Lithuania, please. *Clin Exptl Rheumatol* 1999; **17**:321–326.

Hayakawa SI. *Language in Action*. 1941. New York, US; Harcourt, Brace & Co. pp 149–151.

Kirn W. I'm O.K. You're O.K. We're not O.K. *Time*. September 16, 2002.

Meador CK. *Symptoms of Unknown Origin: A Medical Odyssey*. 2005. Nashville, TN; Vanderbilt University Press.

Rang M. The Ulysses syndrome. *Can Med Assoc J* 1972; **106**:122–123.

Scadding JG. Essentialism and nominalism in medicine: Logic of diagnosis in disease terminology. *Lancet* 1996; **348**:594–596.

Temple KF, McLeod RS, Gallinger, Wright JG. Defining diseases in the genomic era. *Science* 2001; **293**:807–808.

Weiss E. Psychogenic rheumatism. *Amer J Med Sci* 1946; **26**:896–900.

Chapter 4: Listening Skills and Observational Skills

Bax M. Clinical analysis of the cry. *Develop Med Child Neurol* 1975; **17**:799–801.

Biorck G. The essence of the clinician's art. *Act Med Scand* 1977; **201**:145–147.

Boland BJ, Wollan PC, Silverstein MD. Review of systems, physical examination, and routine tests for case-finding in ambulatory patients. *Am J Med Sci* 1995; **309**:194–200.

Cohen H. The evolution of concept of disease. In *Concepts of Health and Disease*. Caplan AL, Tristam Engelhardt Jr H, McCartney JJ. 1981. Reading, MA, USA; Addison-Wesley Publishing Co. pp 209–219.

Cone Jr TE. Diagnosis and treatment: Some diseases, syndromes, and conditions associated with an unusual odor. *Pediatrics* 1968; **41**:993–995.

Conniff R. Reading faces. *Smithsonian*. January 2004; pp 44–50.

Dialogue: The core clinical skill. *Ann Intern Med* 1998; **128**:139–141.

Fitzgerald FT, Tierney LM. The Bedside Sherlock Holmes. *West J Med* 1982; **137**:169–175.

Fred HL. The numbers game. *Hospital Practice*. July 15, 2000; 11–16.

Green M, Sullivan P, Eichberg C. Avoid a "Swiss Cheese" history when psychosocial complaints are on the menu. *Contemporary Pediatrics* 2002; **19**:115–125.

Jauhar S. The demise of the physical exam. *N Engl J Med* 2006; **354**:548–551.

Linfors EW, Neelon FA. The case for bedside rounds. *N Engl J Med* 1980; **303**:1230–1233.

Mace JW, Goodman SI, Centerwall WR, Chinnock RF. The child with an unusual odor. *Clin Pediatr* 1976; **15**:57–62.

Markel H. The stethescope and the art of listening. *N Engl J Med* 2006; **354**:551–553.

Meador CK. The art and science of nondisease. *N Engl J Med* 1965; **272**:92–95.

Platt FW, McMath JC. Clinical hypocompetence: The interview. *Ann Int Med* 1979; **91**:898–902.

Reilly BM. Physical Examination in the care of medical inpatients: An observational study. *Lancet* 2003; **363**:1100–1105.

Schneiderman H. *Bedside Diagnosis — An Annotated Bibliography of Recent Literature on Interviewing and Physical Examination*. American College of Physicians. 1988.

Simons RJ, Baily RG, Zelis R, Zwillich CW. The physiological and psychological effects of the bedside presentation. *N Engl J Med* 1989; **321**:1273–1275.

Steele SJ, Morton DJB. The ward rounds. *Lancet* 1978; **1**:85–86.

Stickler GB. Clinical guidelines for the pediatrician. *Pediatrics* 1987; **80**:118–119.

Thibault GE. Bedside rounds revisited. *N Engl J Med* 1997; **336**:1174–1175.

Willis Hurst J. Osler as visiting professor: House pupils plus six skills. *Ann Int Med* 1984; **101**:546–549.

Chapter 5: Diagnostic Skills

Bowen JL. Educational strategies to promote clinical diagnostic reasoning. *N Engl J Med* 2006; **355**:2217–2225.

Campbell EJM. The diagnosing mind. *Lancet* 1987; **1**:849–851.

Goldberg M. Ten rules for the doctor–detective. *Postgraduate Med* 1997; **101**:3–24.

Hillard AA, Weinberger SE, Tierney Jr LM, Midthun DE, Saint S. Occam's Razor versus Saint's triad. *N Engl J Med* 2004; **350**:599–603.

Margolis CZ. Uses of clinical algorithms. *JAMA* 1983; **249**:627–632.

Szolovitz P, Pauker SG. Categorical and probabilistic reasoning in medical diagnosis. *Artificial Intelligence* 1978; **11**:115–144.

Tape TG, Mushlin AI. The utility of routine chest radiographs. *Ann Intern Med* 1986; **104**:663–670.

Chapter 6: Problem Solving Skills

Chase S. Six Methods for Solving Problems, in *Proper Study of Mankind*. 1948. New York, US; Harper & Brothers. pp 9–11.

Interview with Professor Stephen Brookfield. *Et Cetera*. Spring 1994. pp 4–17.

McNutt RA. Shared medical decision making. *JAMA* 2004; **292**:2516–2518.

Ross PE. The Expert Mind. *Scientific American*. August 2006; p 64071.

Chapter 7: Communication Skills

Froman R. How to say what you mean. *Et Cetera*. Winter 1986. pp 393–402.

Kon AA. Answering questions: "Doctor, if this were your child, what would you do?". *Pediatrics* 2006; **118**(1):393–397.

Lazare A. Apology in medical practice — An emerging clinical skill. *JAMA* 2006; **296**(11):1404.

Nierenberg GI. Negotiation by negation. *Et Cetera*. Spring 1983. pp 75–79.

Serwint JR, Rutherford L. Sharing bad news with parents. *Contemporary Pediatrics* 2000; **17**(3):45–66.

Chapter 8: Physician–Patient Relationship

Balint H, Shelton W. Regaining the initiative — Forging a new model of the patient–physician relationship. *JAMA* 1996; **275**:887–891.

Cousins N. How patients appraise physicians. *New Eng J Med* 1985; **313**:1422–1424.

Honigsbaum M. The art of medicine — The patient's view: John Donne and Katherine Anne Porter. *Lancet* 2009; **374**:194–195.

Katon W, Kleinman A. Doctor–Patient negotiation and other social science strategies in patient care. In *The Relevance of Social Science for Medicine*. Eisenberg and Kleinman A (Eds). 1980. Dordrecht, Holland; D. Reidel Publishing Co. pp 253–279.

Larson EB, Yao X. Clinical empathy as emotional labor in the patient–physician relationship. *JAMA* 2005; **293**:1100–1106.

Metzl JM, Riba M. Understanding the symbolic value of medications: A brief review. *Primary Psychiatry* 2003; **10**(7):45–48.

Soskis CW. Patient complaints about doctors: What you can learn. *Resident and Staff Physician*. June 1980; 83–85.

Steele SJ, Morton DJH. The ward round. *Lancet* 1978; **1**:85–86.

Chapter 9: Caring and Connection

Baggini J, Pym M. End-of-life: The Humanist view. *Lancet* 2005; **366**:1235–1237.

Bates MC. Into the Trees. In *Willing to Learn — Passages of Personal Discovery* 2004. Hanover, NH; Steerforth Press. pp 181–191 (On the death of her father).

Baulby JD. Chapter on "Voice Offstage". In *The Diving Bell and the Butterfly*. 1997. New York, US; Alfred A. Knopf.

Cassell EJ. Diagnosing suffering: A perspective. *Ann Intern Med* 1999; **131**:531–534.

Cutler SB. A survivor's tale. *The Pharos*. Spring 1996. pp 37–40.

Firth S. End-of-life: A Hindu view. *Lancet* 2005; **366**:682–686.

Fosarelli P. Medicine, spirituality and patient care. *JAMA* 2008; **300**(7):836–838.

Hart JT, Dieppe P. Caring effects. *Lancet* 1996; 3–8.

Kleinman A, Eisenberg L, Good B. Culture, illness and care: Clinical lessons from anthropological and cross-cultural research. *Ann Intern Med* 1978; **88**:251–258.

Sachedina A. End-of life: The Islamic view. *Lancet* 2005: **366**:774–779.

Tristram Engelhardt Jr H, Iltis AS. End-of-life: The traditional Christian view. *Lancet* 2005; **366**:1045–1049.

Index